ROCK KILLER

BY

S EVAN TOWNSEND

World Castle Publishing
http://www.worldcastlepublishing.com

World Castle Publishing
Pensacola, Florida

Copyright © by S. Evan Townsend 2012
ISBN: 9781937593452
First Edition World Castle Publishing March 1, 2012
http://www.worldcastlepublishing.com

Cover: Karen Fuller
Photos: Shutterstock
Editor: Maxine Bringenberg

DEDICATION

Dedicated to Robert Heinlein, Poul Anderson, and Larry Niven, with thanks.

CHAPTER ONE

"…someone in this room will be dead."

Charlene Jones sat in a high-sided bathtub, trying to calm down. She was angry: angry with Frank, angry at Space Resources Incorporated, and angry with herself for being angry. She'd planned for a special night with Frank, but he suddenly had to work late. She'd wasted her bath. About once a month, she could afford to take a bath instead of a quick shower; and she was wasting the luxury she'd normally allow to envelop her by being angry.

She sloshed around in the water, which, in the moon's gravity, moved like viscous oil but still managed to almost slop over the tub's tall sides. The way water moved on the Moon fascinated her and she spent some time doing amateur fluid dynamics experiments playing in the bath as she did as a child. She soaped up a washcloth and rubbed it over her dark skin; Frank called it chocolate-cheesecake colored. Charlie's maternal grandmother was as black as the lunar sky and Charlie had benefited from having such a grandmother in more ways than one. A soap bubble escaped from the washcloth, enjoying its freedom for a brief second before imploding. Charlie wondered what a bubble bath would be like. Maybe she'd have to bring some back from Earth next time. That amused her: bubbles on the Moon should last forever, taking six times as long to fall to the floor; or, actually, because of terminal velocity, longer even than that. *If I used some soap between my fingers and blew*, she thought, remembering how she'd made bubbles in the bath as a kid. She was watching a bubble's ponderous fall when the computer beeped obnoxiously, signaling it was receiving a communication. "On, no video," Charlie ordered, annoyed at having her fun interrupted. She had almost forgotten her anger.

The computer screen was behind her and she couldn't see the face that appeared. "This better be good," Charlie growled, not masking her annoyance. The answer didn't come for a few seconds, annoying her further.

"It is," an all too familiar voice said.

Charlie almost jumped out of the water. "Mitch?"

Two seconds later. "Yes."

Charlie turned in the tub to look at the computer screen. Space Resources Incorporated's Head of Security Mitchel's face stared back at her. "Oh, it's you, Mitch," she said, "Computer, video on."

If Mitchel responded to seeing Charlie in the tub, his face didn't show it. "Is Frank handy?" he asked after the light-speed delay. Charlie had forgotten how that almost two second light-speed delay grew interminably long during conversations with persons on Earth.

"No," Charlie answered. "He's working late. He's in the conference room giving the newbie briefing. A new batch arrived unexpectedly and you know he won't put off the initial briefing." She heard a little anger seep into her voice.

Two seconds later Mitch frowned. "Hmmmm. I can't interrupt that. I'll call in the morning–your morning."

"Is it important?" Charlie asked.

Mitch shrugged. "Somewhat, but I have to talk to him personally."

"Okay, I'll tell him you called."

"Thanks, Charlie," Mitch said. "And Charlie?"

"Yes?"

"Don't be too mad at him."

Charlie smiled. "I won't."

"Oh, by the way," he mentioned. "The next asteroid–" he looked off screen, "nineteen sixty-one– its tender will be leaving in a few weeks. Director Alex Chun—he's a good man—and Security Chief Bill Thorne. He could use a second. He's good, too."

"I know, Mitch. Frank's told me about both of them."

"You want to go? I could pull some strings. Thorne and Chun both owe me favors. It'd be a good career move."

Charlie frowned. "I don't know. I'd like to stay here with Frank."

"Charlie," Mitchel admonished, "you know there are people here that don't consider anything inside the orbit of the Moon to be 'space.' If you don't get some trans-lunar experience–"

"I know, Mitch," she cut him off. "But," she hesitated, biting her lower lip. "I don't know."

"Well, think about it, okay?"

"I will. Bye, Mitch."

"Good-bye, Charlie." The screen went blank.

Charlie shook her head. A computer call from Earth to the Moon was about the most expensive long-distance call possible— one of the few long-distance calls that cost anything—and Mitch had used time to berate her about her career. Although Mitchel was the number one security man in the company, it wasn't he that would be making decisions about her future. He'd already helped her by getting her away from guarding the warehouse at the Esmeraldas space facility in Ecuador.

Maybe she shouldn't be so mad, she decided. Frank was security chief for SRI's lunar facility, located in Nippon/European Space Agency Lunar Facility One. Frank had also helped her by giving her more responsibility than he normally would give someone with her few years in SRI, based on how well he knew her. And, when she needed it, he was ready with advice and help. Between Frank and Mitch, it seemed someone was always helping her. She didn't know whether to resent it or be thankful.

SRI didn't mind that Frank was living with one of his subordinates as long as there wasn't the faintest hint of favoritism, which meant Charlie got more than her share of shit assignments.

Small price to pay, though–Frank was medium height and had a strong build with dark curly hair, and the blackest eyes that had penetrated her to the soul when she first saw them.

And maybe, she wondered, I don't stay here because I want to stay with Frank. Maybe I stay here because I want to stay where I'm comfortable.

She settled back down into the tub and was working on another bubble when the claxon sounded. This time Charlie did jump out of the tub. The water stuck to her, flowing slowly down her lithe body. The claxon was reserved for dire emergencies: wall breaches, life support shutting down, incoming meteoroids. Charlie had never heard it before except in drills. "Warning," the computer droned as if announcing the weather, "intruders in access tunnel one."

***

While she was in the bathtub, Charlie's lover, Frank DeWite, was pacing at the front of the briefing room moving with practiced ease in the low gravity. He looked at the newbies, fresh from training at the SRI Low Earth Orbit Facility. Seven male and five female sets of wide eyes watched his every move. "Before six months are over, someone in this room will be dead," DeWite said. He waited while they almost unconsciously looked around. *Who will it be?* they were obviously thinking.

"It could be you," DeWite said. "And do you know what will kill him?" He looked at a female. "Or her?"

No one responded.

"Stupidity will kill them," DeWite said. "You don't have to die. 'Stay alert, stay alive.' They used to say that in war. We're not at war but we do have an enemy. The Moon will kill you if she can. Space will kill you. Don't let it. Don't hurry through your suit inspection, don't move too fast and rip your suit on a sharp rock or crack your faceplate. Remember, you may weigh one sixth less but you retain your mass and therefore momentum. It's very easy to get going too fast to stop."

Again he looked over the room. "Sure, you've all heard it a hundred times. But one of you will still get stupid, and he, or she,

8

will die and I'll have to write a letter. If you know you're stupid, let me know now and give me your next of kin's address. I'll get started on the letter.

"Oh," he continued, "one thing I always have to put in the letter is that there won't be an open casket funeral. Have you ever seen a body dead from vacuum exposure?"

Of course they hadn't.

"I remember my first time," DeWite said. "A young kid about your age named Joey Hernandez; died when he was murdered by someone who cut his suit open with a knife.

"And that brings me to our other enemy. We're SRI Security. We're the first line of defense between SRI and those who would steal from the company, both tangibles and information. We're the law off Earth where there is no law. Here on the Moon we're under the jurisdiction of the NESA Alliance." He pronounced it "nee-sa."

"But," he continued, "in the asteroid belt or Jupiter—" Claxons sounding interrupted DeWite. A computer-generated voice was heard: "Warning, intruders in access tunnel one." The computer droned the same message over and over and over.

***

The computer repeated the message as Charlie used her hands to scrape the water off herself.

"Computer, quiet."

The claxon and message stopped.

As she reached for a towel a muffled explosion vibrated the floor. She used the towel to do a superficial drying job then pulled on her red security uniform. The jumpsuit stuck indecently to her damp skin. Underwear would have helped but that luxury was for non-emergencies. She ran to the closet, pulled out her pressure suit and, throwing it over her shoulder (the helmet painfully smacked her in the back; she ignored it), ran to the door in the loping gait one used on the Moon. As she pulled it open, she thought about putting on the suit but decided against it. The SRI facility was so compartmentalized that unless the immediate area one was in depressurized, it was safe not to wear the suit. Also, wearing a

9

pressure suit in pressure was just a little less restrictive than a straitjacket in dealing with intruders that could be more dangerous that the possibility of decompression.

Other off-duty personnel were forming a confused cluster in the corridor.

"If you're not needed, go back in your room and close the emergency door," Charlie yelled. Most returned to their rooms, some left running toward the main facility. Charlie started running for the armory.

At the end of the corridor she started closing the emergency door.

"Hey, damnit, open up," a voice came from the other side.

"Smitty?"

"Yes, damnit."

Charlie pulled open the door. Smitty was standing there in a disheveled uniform. His hair was a tussled mess. He'd obviously been sleeping. He, too, had his pressure suit over his shoulder.

"That explosion," Smitty said tensely as he followed her running down the corridor toward the armory.

"The security door," Charlie growled, trying to keep the fear and anger from her voice.

"Must have been," Smitty agreed.

***

"Stay put and don't move," DeWite barked to the room and loped out the portal. On the other side he closed the emergency door that formed an airlock with the regular door that had room for maybe one person. He turned to find an experienced security man named Prince running toward him carrying two pump shotguns. He tossed one to DeWite who caught it after it sailed a seeming impossible distance in the low gravity.

"There's no word from Check Point Alpha," Prince spat. "We think they've gotten as far as the—"

An explosion rocked the floor and the air pressure dropped momentarily.

"They've breached the security door," Prince cried angrily.

DeWite pumped a shell into the chamber of his shotgun with almost unconscious, practiced movements.

"Great, they're inside and have access to everything. Who the hell are they?" he yelled, and bounded down the tunnel in the direction of the door.

"Hell if I know," Prince said, following.

DeWite started to smell acrid smoke. He stopped running. "Got a radio?"

Prince attached a radio disk to DeWite's cheek. A small plug went in one ear. The men resumed running.

"This is DeWite; I'm with Prince. We are moving toward the security door. What's happening?"

The voice that came back was high-pitched with excitement. The sounds of automatic weapons fire, punctuated with the boom of shotguns, were heard in the background. "They started a fire in the computer memory room. I think they have thermite grenades. They seem to be moving toward—" An explosion was followed by static.

"Toward what?" DeWite screamed in frustration. "Their radio went dead," he explained to Prince.

"Who was that?" Prince asked, taking a corner. The smoke got thicker.

"It sounded like Jimmy Nakamura. He was working in section two tonight," DeWite replied, trying to keep his voice level.

"The shipyard," Prince exclaimed.

"Damn," DeWite spat.

They passed the observation room. "Hold it," DeWite said.

***

The armory was a large cabinet expediently located near the quarters. Three other security personnel were already there; one was Assistant Chief of Security Rodriguez.

"What's happening, Rod?" Charlie asked, breathing hard from running.

"I don't know any more than you do," he replied as he put his ID card in a slot and punched a code onto the keypad. The armory opened. Rodriguez started passing out shotguns and bandoleers of shells. A few more security people ran up.

"I need two of you to stay here and guard the living quarters," he said. He pointed at two of the newer arrivals. "You and you—the rest are with me."

They started running toward the main SRI facility and passed a computer terminal.

"Computer, where are the intruders?" Rodriguez asked it.

The computer didn't answer. Charlie and Smitty exchanged a look.

***

DeWite moved into the observation room and Prince followed.

The room looked almost exactly like a bar since it was a VIP lounge for watching ships land and take off. A large window looked over the shipyard, where various types of spacecraft were resting on the lunar dust. The window, made of Crysteel, invented by SRI's orbital laboratories, began about half a meter from the floor and extended to the ceiling and was about five meters wide. Crysteel, made in a factory in Earth orbit one atom at a time, was almost as strong as aluminum. Its one weakness was a very high index of refraction due to tightly packed oxygen atoms. It made great lenses but was not good for use where a clear view was needed such as spaceship windows and pressure suit helmets. But the picture window in the lounge would have been impractical without the Crysteel.

Four pressure-suited figures were moving across the plain. The suits were not SRI issue and the figures were carrying submachine guns. DeWite recognized them as a South African made 9 millimeter caseless that were favored by criminals who bought them on the black market.

One, carrying a 40-millimeter recoilless rifle, knelt just a few meters from the window and aimed. Fire shot out of the rear of the weapon, dying almost immediately in the airless environment. A flame licked a small intra-lunar shuttle followed by an explosion. The ship's skin crumpled and it folded in on itself in a slow,

12

macabre death dance. Another explosion marked the rupture of the fuel tanks. Fire burned until the oxygen ran out.

***

Charlie followed Rodriguez down the corridor, stuffing shells into her weapon. They turned a corner and Rodriguez, moving too fast to stop his mass quickly, ran into a closed emergency door.

He moved to look at the tell-tales. "Damn. Vacuum," he said. "Jones, Smitty, you're my best vacuum people. Get your suits on. We need to get help to the inside."

Charlie and Smitty moved into an open area and began the task of putting on the pressure suits. Charlie pulled on her suit and tried not to worry about Frank. He can take care of himself, she thought. But she also knew his conscience would require him to take care of everyone else, and that worried her more.

***

"Goddamnit!" DeWite exploded. "We need to get to the airlock."

Just then one of the four figures outside noticed the two security guards. He tapped the others on their shoulders and pointed. The other three turned and again the recoilless rifle spat a fleeting flame. DeWite dove behind the bar—an easy task in the low gravity. The window exploded inward. Prince was thrown against the rear wall, his body shattered by the impact. Then the window exploded outward as the room decompressed. Prince's body was slammed against the bottom of the window and sucked out into the harsh sunlight.

***

Charlie, the more experienced, took the lead out the temporary airlock formed by the emergency and normal doors. The passage was dark as the lights had shattered in vacuum from their internal pressure. There was an intense, actinic white flickering from inside the computer room. *That might explain why the computer didn't work,* Charlie thought. The two moved quickly, weapons ready, to the room. One look inside showed it was empty except two bodies, and the computer had been destroyed by some kind of incendiary

13

device; a little of it was still burning. They moved on, Charlie wondering what could burn in hard vacuum.

The corridor came to an intersection but closed emergency doors blocked two routes. As they turned down the only open passage, Charlie saw suited people silhouetted in the beams of their own lights. They weren't more than ten meters away. She thumped Smitty on the chest and retreated around the corner before the intruders saw them. Smitty followed. They wouldn't have heard them: there's one advantage to working in vacuum. Charlie kneeled on the floor and carefully looked around the corner. She saw two people working on the airlock controls. One was rather fat. They were having trouble figuring out how to open the airlock that had gone into emergency mode. *Good, they're busy,* thought Charlie; less chance they'd notice her and Smitty. She pulled her head back.

"Okay," Charlie reported into her suit radio, "we've got two unknowns at airlock 4582."

"Armed?" Rodriguez asked.

"Yes, small weapons, look like submachine guns. We're taking them out, right Smitty?"

"Damn right."

"We can get help to you soon," Rodriguez said, sounding anxious.

"Negative," Charlie answered. "Hesitation kills. They'll get out that airlock and then who knows where. Ready, Smitty?"

"Ready." He pumped a shell into the shotgun and Charlie repeated the motion on her weapon. It was a strangely silent action in vacuum.

They went around the corner. The fat one was looking right at them. She (Charlie could see it was a woman) started firing wildly, the muzzle flashes strobe-lighting her grimacing face.

Charlie and Smitty jumped back around the corner as the bullets impacted silently on the walls and floors.

***

DeWite heard the emergency door slam shut, locking him in the room. He knew it would never open until the pressure in the room equalized with the pressure in the hall.

He stood, aimed his shotgun, braced his leg behind to compensate for the low gravity, and fired. He was surprised he heard it at all. *Must still be a little air in the room,* some part of him thought.

The figure with the recoilless rifle was thrown back and blood ejaculated from its torn body. It was freeze-dried before it hit the lunar plain. The remaining figures turned with their weapons firing. DeWite barely heard the bullets hitting the wall behind him. His ears felt as if they were going to explode. He screamed, not in fear, but to empty his lungs to prolong his already forfeit life a few more seconds.

Pump, FIRE, Pump, FIRE, Pump was DeWite's whole existence. Another figure crumpled, spouting blood. Then the bullets ripped into DeWite. Blood flowed like a fire hose. FIRE—DeWite could no longer stand, even in one-sixth gravity. He sank to the floor and died in a puddle of his blood that was boiling and freezing simultaneously.

***

"You okay?" Charlie asked, breathing hard with excitement, adrenaline pumping through her veins.

"Yeah, you?"

"Yes."

"What happened?" Rodriguez demanded, his tension coming through the radio.

"They saw us," Charlie said, watching the rounds hitting the metal structure of the corridor. Occasionally, she'd feel the vibration of the steel from the punishment it was taking.

When the bullets suddenly stopped, Charlie, again low, peeked around the edge. The airlock was closing with the intruders inside.

"Damn," she spat and ran after them. She fired and pumped another shell into the chamber. But the door was closed and the pellets just scarred the white paint then bounced back at her. Most lodged harmlessly in the fullerene armor of her suit. One chipped her faceplate.

Charlie tried to stop before hitting the door. In her anger and excitement she had allowed herself to get going too fast. Her momentum slammed her into the thick metal airlock door face first. She heard a loud snap. A rivulet of a crack cut across her faceplate. A shrill whistle indicated air was leaking out of the crack.

Smitty came up behind her.

"You okay?" he asked.

"No," she said, removing a shell from her bandoleer and shoving it into the magazine tube. Always have a full magazine, they'd taught her. "Rod, they went out. I can't pursue; I cracked my faceplate and I'm losing air."

"I could go," Smitty said.

"No," Rodriguez barked. "Get Charlie to safety."

"I'm okay," Charlie said. "It's a slow leak. I can get back by myself."

"No," Rodriguez replied. "Regulations —"

"Smitty," Charlie said cutting him off, "go and stop them."

"No," Rodriguez yelled, the radio distorting his voice.

Smitty started working with the airlock controls as Charlie walked quickly but carefully back to the provisional airlock.

Her faceplate shattered.

She started running and screamed, like they taught her, to empty her lungs. Holding your breath only increases internal injuries.

Her eyes and ears hurt unbelievably and her neck throbbed painfully. She began to weaken as she reached the emergency airlock and dropped her shotgun.

The controls seemed wrong; she couldn't figure them out. Her legs stopped supporting her and she slid to the floor.

The airlock opened and strong arms picked her up and threw her inside. The door closed behind her and warm, sweet air smacked her in the face as it was bled into the ersatz airlock. When the pressure was close to equalized, the emergency door was flung open and Rodriguez pulled her into the corridor. The emergency door closed again. Charlie took long, deep breaths. Her throat felt as if she'd been inhaling a gaseous acid. There was a strange pulsating sensation at her neck. She reached up to feel it but Rodriguez batted her hand away.

"Don't touch it, you've got a vein protruding," he said to her gently. Then he barked an order to the assembled personnel: "Get her to the medics."

Smitty came out of the airlock.

"Smitty," she croaked. "How?" It hurt like hell to talk.

"I heard the air rush out of your suit on the radio."

"Thank you," she whispered. It hardly seemed adequate.

***

Charlie and Smitty walked slowly across the lunar landscape toward the observation lounge, both in their pressure suits (Charlie using her spare), and both carried shotguns. Charlie had been cleared by the doctor and insisted on going on this trek. The lounge emergency door was closed and the sensors indicated the interior was in vacuum.

Charlie's stomach knotted as she moved. Two men were unaccounted for: Prince and DeWite. Frank DeWite, Security Chief and Charlie's lover: *Missing and presumed dead,* Charlie thought, swallowing hard on her impending grief.

Rounding a corner of the facility, they got a view of the shipyard. The intruders had left three ships, but some weapon had fired upon all three. One was a crumpled metal mass.

Two human shaped figures were prone in the dust. Charlie felt her heart try to move into her throat.

"We have two bodies in the shipyard," Smitty reported over his suit radio. Charlie hated him for the calm in his voice.

"Understood," came back Rodriguez's voice.

Then Charlie realized the pressure suits weren't SRI design.

Her heart settled into its usual niche. *Why did I volunteer for this?* she asked herself for the nth time.

They went to the bodies. There were black stains on the ground around them.

"These bodies are in bad shape," Smitty said. "There are shotgun wounds and automatic weapons wounds to the head area."

"Understood," Rodriguez repeated.

Charlie was looking at the grotesque tableau. Smitty looked toward the lounge.

"The lounge's window has been breached," Smitty said. "There's another body."

Smitty pointed. Charlie looked up. The body wore no pressure suit and was surrounded by debris sucked out of the lounge. Charlie's heart began its upward migration. She had never seen a man that died in vacuum; she didn't want her first to be Frank. They walked to the corpse. Smitty turned the body, which was literally frozen stiff. "It's Prince," he reported calmly. He and Charlie exchanged a look through faceplates. Grief and anger crossed the vacuum.

Charlie looked at the dead man. His face was calm, his eyes closed. He'd died before being thrown into the air-less shipyard. Blood was freeze-dried on his uniform and on the lunar dirt.

"Do you see DeWite?" Rodriguez asked. Charlie couldn't help resenting this man who was warm and safe inside the facility while they looked at a dead friend.

"Not yet," Smitty said, again, keeping his tone professional. "We're entering the lounge now."

"Roger."

"Watch that the shards of Crysteel don't rip your suit," Smitty warned as Charlie stepped through the window.

"I will," she replied, her voice still harsh and raspy from exposure to vacuum. For a moment, she wondered if this was another shit assignment to make sure she wasn't getting any favoritism from Frank.

The lounge was a disaster. Anything that wasn't nailed down had been thrown to the window or out of it. Liquor bottles had been smashed open and their contents vacuum-frozen.

The lights here, too, had shattered from internal pressure. Without air to refract the sunlight, anything in shadow was in pitch blackness. Charlie turned on her flashlight and passed its piercing beam around the room. It passed over a crumbled shape. At first Charlie thought it was a tablecloth or maybe a drape. But then the red color of the fabric made her realize it was an SRI Security uniform. She moved to it. Even from the back, she recognized Frank lying in a pool of black blood. He was still holding a shotgun. Three expended shells lay nearby. She bent down and gently turned him over. His face was a portrait of determination, frozen like that forever.

"We found the chief," Smitty reported over the radio, his voice catching on his grief.

Charlie's tears moved like a viscous oil.

S EVAN TOWNSEND

CHAPTER TWO

"...taking asteroids for your own, greedy purposes."

A few hours later, a space plane was crossing the Pacific Ocean, west to east, at about Mach 25. The plane had just reached the top of its parabolic trajectory. On board, Alexander Chun was glad these flights were short; it meant he spent very little time in free fall so he suffered only a short time with space sickness.

Alex watched the monitor in the back of the seat ahead of him. Working in space, he was usually too busy to pay attention to the news. This trip from Tokyo–where SRI Headquarters was located–to Denver–where his wife Kirsten lived–gave him plenty of time to catch up. The Tokyo to Seattle flight wasn't too long, but the Seattle to Denver flight would take much longer. The United States had a law against commercial supersonic flight over land dating back to the last century. The government was so lethargic that such an outdated law was still in effect.

Alex had instructed the plane's computer to load his configuration off the net—encryption kept everything private—so all he had to do was run a macro he had written that would search for and show major news stories for the past months while he was in space. He'd been the Assistant Director of SRI-1859. That was the 59th asteroid SRI had brought in from the asteroid belt, mining it during the two week trip, and put in Earth orbit at a Lagrange point to finish off the job, which took another four months.

Alex carefully followed the news when he could although it was usually depressing as hell. If somebody wasn't doing violence to someone else, someone was trying to start something stupid or stop something good. The Greens got three California and one Massachusetts seats in the House of Representatives in the last election. One, a California one, had been indicted in the sabotage by the Gaia Alliance of SRI's Mojave microwave power antenna field. A sympathetic judge threw out the indictment. The stupidity of the masses never ceased to amaze Alex.

Suddenly, a story was interrupted in mid-interview (Alex had it set up to break in with any stories containing keywords such as "SRI").

A reporter on the Moon was standing in a standard NESA-issue pressure suit in front of a security door that was being repaired. A small icon in the lower left corner of the screen indicated that this was a live report.

By the way the reporter's suit was crumpled, Alex could tell she was in a pressurized area and wearing the suit as a precaution. There were blackened walls as evidence of an explosion.

"Details are sketchy," she was saying over her suit radio, "but it appears the Space Resources Incorporated facility here on the Moon was attacked by unknown assailants." ("Damn," spat Alex.) "NESA and SRI Security personnel are inside the facility right now. Neither NESA nor SRI is saying if anyone was killed in the attack. However, there were two bodies found here. One was wearing an SRI uniform, the other a pressure suit, and there is no indication of who either is."

An unseen commentator said, "Susan, is there any indication of who carried out the attack?"

Susan said, "Yes. A radical environmental group, the Gaia Alliance, has claimed responsibility. In an anonymous email sent to NESA company offices here on the Moon the GA said, and I quote,—" she began to read from a tablet, "—'Space Resources Incorporated is the worst perpetrator of the pollution and desecration of both space and the Earth and will pay the price for their greed.'

22

"They also left this reminder." The camera panned to the wall. On the pristine white, in the blood of some unfortunate SRI employee, were the letters GA.

"God damn those bastards," Alex growled loudly. He violently hit the spot on the screen to close the news program and the monitor went to his default display of a map showing the plane's position. Only then did he notice that the other passengers were looking at him. He turned and looked out the tiny window at the peaceful looking planet below. Then he picked up the headset on the armrest and instructed the computer to call one of the people in his address book. There was no video available.

There was an unusually long delay before a woman's voice answered. "Mr. Mitchel's office," she said curtly. "Miss Oh speaking."

"Meyoung," Alex said. "This is Director Chun. Is Mitch there?"

"Yes, Director," she replied with a torrent of emotion her calm words belied. "Mr. Mitchel can talk to you."

"Thanks."

Waiting, Alex noticed the man seated next to him was pointedly trying not to listen.

A brusque "Mitchel," and Alex turned back to the computer.

"Mitch, Alex. What's happening? I just heard the news."

"The GA attacked our lunar facility. They killed everyone they met, which, luckily, wasn't many. Frank's dead, Alex."

"Oh, hell," Alex whispered softly. "How?"

"Not sure. They found his body in the VIP observation lounge. The window was blown out and he was shot. Prince's body was with him." Mitchel paused. "There were two bodies in the shipyard. They got two of 'em."

"Good," Alex barked angrily, not caring that he was happy about the death of two humans. "Did they do anything but kill people?"

"Yes, they sabotaged the file-server room with incendiary devices and destroyed all the ships on the ground. Except, one is missing–the *Rock Skipper*."

"Damn," Alex exclaimed. The *Rock Skipper* was the flagship of the newest, fastest interplanetary class of ships SRI had built. There were four altogether.

"It had just been provisioned and prepared to go to the belt," Mitchel added.

"Do you suppose that's a coincidence?" Alex conjectured.

"No. They were after that ship. But why?"

Yeah, Alex thought, *why?* The *Rock Skipper*-class was used primarily to scout asteroids. It carried ten "asteroid-probe missiles" that could be used as fairly effective weapons. *Boy,* Alex thought, *what a stink it would raise if the terrorists used the ship in some sort of an attack.*

While Alex thought, silence traveled electronically for a few seconds.

"This isn't a secure connection, Alex," Mitchel finally said. "I'd rather not talk about it anymore."

"I understand, Mitch," Alex replied. "Can you connect me with Nakata?"

"Sure, hang on." More expensive silence.

"Nakata."

"Sir," Alex reported, "this is Director Chun. Do you need me to come back?" he asked, hoping the answer was "No." He hadn't seen Kirsten in almost seven months. However, if he were needed, he would gladly do his duty.

"No," the Deputy Director of Space Operations for Asteroid Operations said. "Enjoy your vacation, Chun."

"Yes, sir," Alex breathed, relieved. He hung up the handset and again looked at the blue planet below him. It was hard to believe such a beautiful place could breed such ugliness as the GA and those that helped them.

***

Syria's president called him Faruq; everyone else called him *"aqid."* He had no official title in the government although he held rank in the Baath Party.

"News off," he said in English. He had tried to get a computer for himself that had the right software to understand Arabic–

money was no object. But when Baathist tanks rolled into Yemen and over the populace, most countries making computers or software had joined in the sanctions against the United Baath Arab States. The computer had to be purchased in Europe and smuggled in.

The Western environmentalists had succeeded, it would seem; they had started to hurt Space Resources Incorporated–and what hurt SRI hurt the West. The Party would be pleased even if the president would not; not that that mattered. Faruq had been pleasing the president since he was the governor of a small nawahi and the president was the minister of the interior. Now Faruq had other, more lofty goals. The president offered him a cabinet position regularly, and Faruq knew he could only beg off for so long. The president was not about to believe Faruq had lost all ambition, but a cabinet job would keep him too busy to pursue his aspirations–and Faruq had ambitions. The Alawite usurpers, Assad and his son Bashar, before his own Baathist Party rebelled (and the son died of lead poisoning, the nine millimeter type) had formulated the dream of Greater Syria: the return of lands that, by historical right, belonged to his country. Assad had succeeded in bringing Lebanon into the fold, but, since then, nothing. Faruq intended for his name to be whispered throughout history as the man that finished the dream of Greater Syria by bringing Palestine and Jordan inside Syria's borders. And, he would be the man who convinced Saudi Arabia–with the best convincer of all, a superior army–to join the United Baathist States. It did not strike Faruq as ironic that the UBS was based on the former Soviet Union, which had failed under the weight of its own system. He knew he could lead the UBS to glory. There would be no Gorbachevs to bring down the UBS.

But first, Faruq had to be president. His power base in the Party was almost large enough. The military was still a question but General Zuabi had privately, cautiously, expressed concerns about the president. The Baath Security Forces were his only worry. The secret police were, as always, loyal to the president–at least, most of them.

The pending *fait accompli,* about to be handed to him courtesy of the Gaia Alliance, could be the last step. He'd convinced many that the president had lost the temerity to face the threats of the West and the Zionist state.

He looked at the encrypted email from the embassy in the American capital of Washington. A delegation was to meet with this congresswoman that night, Columbia State time. There the final plans would be made. Another dispatch reported on the Frenchman's pending arrival. There were arrangements to be made. The Frenchman would want his payment to an SRI account. *The infidel also will require some "entertainment, "* Faruq thought with distaste. He'd have an underling arrange that.

Dealing with Westerners pained him, but the Arab Socialist revolution continued. Soon these Westerners would no longer be needed–and then they would be swept aside.

***

His name was Alan Griffin. He was a tall, skinny man in his mid-thirties. Brown hair fell straight to his shoulders and he always seemed about three days late for a shave. He moved from the galley to the adjacent bridge of the *Rock Skipper*, renamed the *Rock Killer* by those who stole her.

Griffin saw, standing and looking over the navigation computer, a shapely female form. Brunette hair, floating in the small gravity the ship's thrust provided, cascaded down a perfect back that tapered to a slim waist and an ass-leg combination that was rare in these days of leisure. Then the woman turned and, because he could see the hardness of her face, transformed into a fellow soldier whom he'd seen kill men with an almost erotic viciousness.

Griffin reminded himself that his thoughts were improper for guerrilla soldiers. The freedom fighters killed men and women guerrillas who had sex while fighting the oppressors of the people during the glorious years of the revolution in the middle of the twentieth century. That was before the Russians sold out to the capitalists, before even Cuba became a tourist resort for fat, American capitalists. Sometimes, Griffin thought he was born a

26

hundred years too late. He dreamed of being in the field with an AK-47, and fighting alongside Kim Il Sung, Che Guevara, Mao Tse-tung, the Mbundu, or Ho Chi Minh.

"Heard from Trent?" he asked between bites of a sandwich.

Trudeau was in his twenties and looked like he should be selling shoes at Penneys. He shook his head. "She must still be negotiating with the Syrians."

"They'd better come through or this will all be for nothing," Madalyn Cole growled. Cole was shaped like a pear with straight, stringy, greasy, graying hair. Griffin suspected she was gay by the way she reacted to Knecht. He didn't care what her sexual orientation was but he didn't want a sexual relationship, gay or otherwise, to interfere with the operation of the ship and the completion of the mission.

"Not for nothing," Knecht remarked with near glee. "Because they smuggled our weapons onto the Moon, we were able to hurt SRI." She smiled at the memory. "SRI is the most criminal of all criminal corporations. Only violence will stop them and their lust for profits."

Griffin nodded. "And there's more violence to come."

"If the Syrians come through with the rest of their promises," Trudeau reminded them.

***

Linda Trent was working late in the Sam Rayburn office building. She'd found something to go over and excused her staff for the evening. She did have to go over some bills for the Environment Committee. She was the only Green on the committee and she felt that was a great responsibility, though she thought the political process was a waste of time. The Greens were too conventional for her; but at least they could slow the damage until the revolution.

There was a knock on the outer door to the corridor. She'd left the door to her office open so she could hear anyone coming. She stood, walked to the door, and opened it. Two men in expensive business suits walked in.

Trent didn't like Middle-Easterners; their condescending attitudes toward women grated her. But they were a necessary evil right now, as their money and resources were needed for the revolution. And after the revolution, their oil would be worthless and they would be swept aside. She closed the door behind them.

"Congresswoman Trent?" one of the men asked in heavily accented English.

She held up her hand and moved to the window. She turned on a small radio and pointed it at the glass. She did the same for every pane in the office using about ten of the Rwandan-made radios.

Finally she spoke. "Congress*person*," Trent said emphatically. "Are you from Damascus?"

"Yes," he replied. "We are authorized to negotiate on behalf of the Baath-Arab states."

Trent smiled. "Good. We need to arrange a rendezvous. Do you have the missiles?"

"We have secured commitments for their delivery."

"Good," Trent said with a heartfelt smile.

***

Dr. Kirsten Hanna-Chun had quit the hospital she'd worked at for the first few years after school and started her own psychology practice in Denver. Although the hospital would always be special to her as the place she met Alex, with a private practice she could be free to see her husband for those brief times when he was on Earth. She was impatiently waiting for Alex, who was flying in from SRI headquarters. He was supposed to arrive two days ago but had been unexpectedly called to Tokyo.

Finally, he exited the airport's secure area. She looked over her husband. He was in his late thirties but could easily pass for younger. He was obviously an Oriental-Occidental mix. When she had met him, 17 years ago, Kirsten had been struck by his presence despite his small stature. His face, then and now, was a striking combination of his heritage that Kirsten found magnetically attractive.

He walked toward her with an ear-to-ear grin. She thought it seemed forced–she figured he'd heard the news about the Moon.

After the compulsory airport embrace–with her a full head taller than he–Kirsten asked him why he was so happy.

"I've just been promoted to director," he said happily.

Kirsten wrapped her arms around him in congratulations. If he didn't want to talk about the attack, she wouldn't push it. She knew from experience he would talk when he was ready, if ever, and not before.

"Shall we go out to celebrate?" Alex asked.

Kirsten took a deep breath. "I'm sorry," she breathed softly.

"What?"

"We have a dinner engagement at Dr. and Mrs. McConnell's in Englewood. I made the date before I knew you'd be late and this would be your first day here."

"Can't get out of it?"

Kirsten screwed up her face. "I could," she said low.

"But," Alex continued for her, "it wouldn't be good. Isn't he the head of the Denver Psychology Association or something?"

She nodded, bouncing her long, blonde hair.

Alex smiled. She was still as beautiful as she was when she first walked into his hospital room and they met. She towered above him at two hundred centimeters and still left her hair long down to her waist. "Well, I had to go to Tokyo. Mr. Nakata wanted to tell me of the promotion himself. Plus I saw Mitchel; oh, he says 'hi.' I'm sorry."

"I suppose we could leave early," Kirsten said coyly.

Dr. McConnell was about 65 and balding. His grizzled mustache moved in an undulating motion when he chewed. When he didn't have food in his mouth he puffed on a cigarette, oblivious to how his guests felt about the noxious fumes. Mrs. McConnell was a dumpy woman who needed to do something, anything, with her short, gray hair.

The meal was a vegetarian delight. Alex had just spent almost six months in space where meat was rehydrated, tasteless, and expensive as hell. Then he was in Tokyo for the past two days, and there, buying meat meant taking out a short-term loan. Alex was dying for a steak, pork chops, pulgogi, hot dogs, any flesh.

"So, Alex," McConnell said, bouncing his mustache around, "Kirsten says you work for Space Resources Incorporated."

Alex nodded. "Yes."

Kirsten, aware of McConnell's political leanings, was afraid of the direction the conversation could take. She tried to deflect it. "Alex was just promoted to director."

Dr. McConnell looked at Alex. "What does that mean?"

"I'll be in charge of asteroids as they come in from the asteroid belt."

Mrs. McConnell perked up. "Wouldn't that be the 'captain'?"

Alex shook his head. "No, traditionally it's 'director.' When SRI first went to the belt to bring back asteroids, the rocks weren't piloted; they were dropped. Chemical rockets were used to point the rock into the correct Hohmann orbit. Then the mass driver threw out ground up rock for about one thousandth of a gee—"

"Excuse me," Dr. McConnell interrupted, "a 'gee'?"

Alex smiled. He was always surprised to find people who didn't understand basic physics. "A gee is a unit of measure for acceleration, equal to the acceleration of gravity at the Earth's surface. It's about 9.8 meters per second per second or 32 feet per second per second."

McConnell just looked at him and Alex knew he hadn't understood; but he decided to just press on. "It took about six months to bring a rock in," he continued. "And once it was moving there was little that could be done. Turn around and orbit insertion was accomplished using solid chemical rockets, and they were hard to control. Remember about ten years ago, something went wrong and a rock missed Earth? Rescuing the personnel and the loss of ore and equipment really cost SRI."

Alex failed to notice the McConnells' eyes were glazing over with incomprehension. Kirsten forgave him, knowing this was his life and first love.

"But now," Alex continued, "we have a good, reliable constant acceleration drive, the Masuka drive, perfected. Masuka drives are placed to give yaw, pitch, and roll control—"

"Excuse me, what?" Mrs. McConnell asked.

"Yaw, pitch and roll." Alex repeated. He held out his hand, palm down, fingers extended. He then moved his hand as if he were waving goodbye. "Pitch: movement of the nose of the craft up and down or the angle, 'beta,' of rotation around the y axis. And roll," he twisted his hand at the elbow, "is rotation around the long axis, or x axis, measured by the angle 'gamma.' And yaw," he set an empty glass on the table and spun it slowly on its side. "Yaw, which is rotation around the vertical, or z axis, measured by the angle 'alpha.'"

Kirsten could tell he'd lost the McConnells again.

"Anyway," Alex continued, "Masuka drives were added to supplement the mass driver. Now we can accelerate the whole trip at about one-sixth gee, cutting travel time down to about two weeks, depending on the orbit of the asteroid and where it is in relationship to Earth. We still have a few ships that can't boost one sixth of a gee.

"Now the rock can be moved and navigated exactly as if it were a very large ship. That necessitated the addition of navigators, engineers, computers, gyros to maintain attitude, and everything a ship has. But they still call us directors."

It took a moment for their hosts to wake up.

"How very interesting," Mrs. McConnell finally said in a way that proved she was very uninterested.

Dr. McConnell took a long drag on his cigarette. "Do you support what SRI does, commercializing and polluting space?" he asked.

Alex frowned. "I don't know how we're polluting space. I'll agree SRI is commercializing space, but I don't see that as a problem."

"Well, you are ruining the pristine nature of space. You're taking asteroids for your own, greedy purposes."

Alex smiled. "I guess," he conceded. "But any asteroid we take, we discovered. We could take asteroids out of the belt for the next billion years at the rate we are now and there'd be no discernible effects."

"You're killing the only other life found in the universe," he attacked. "For profit."

"We're killing a bacterium that gets energy from the heat of Europa's rocky core. We have to in order to make the water we pump from that moon potable. The Denver water department does the same thing every day to make the water you drink safe. And we're killing a minute fraction of the bacteria that is in Europa's sea."

McConnell seemed to consider that for a moment while he crushed out his cigarette. Alex hoped he wouldn't light another but, in a practiced, almost unconscious series of moves, McConnell had another tube of tobacco in his mouth and it started glowing red at the tip as he sucked on it.

Then McConnell pounced: "How do you feel about the Los Angeles-New York tunnel project?"

Alex looked at Kirsten, who was embarrassedly studying her green meal. Then he turned to McConnell.

"I work for the Space Operations Division and before that the Security Division. The tunnel is being built by the Terrestrial Projects Division. I understand the basic technology and concepts, but other than that I don't know much about it. I assume Terrestrial Projects' engineers know what they are doing."

McConnell wasn't put off. "But it's all SRI, whether you're in space or in that private army they euphemistically call 'Security Division.' And don't you think this idea of drilling a tunnel straight through the Earth under the U.S. is dangerous?"

"I'm sure our people know what they're doing," Alex repeated, realizing he was running out of arguments.

"But it could destabilize the entire ecology of the continent. Plus, it would put thousands of airline, trucking, and train employees out of work. It's just another rape of nature by a criminal corporation. And is it any coincidence that they're doing it under the U.S? A Japanese corporation: Why don't they do it under Japan?"

Kirsten looked at Alex and saw his complexion grow darker.

She gave him a pleading look but it was too late.

Alex decided to ignore McConnell's subtle racism. "Because Japan isn't large enough to make it economically feasible," he started. "Look, the tunnel, as I understand it, will provide quick, cheap, and pollution-free transportation between Los Angeles and New York." Alex realized he was talking fast but anger was pushing his words out. "If it proves itself, SRI hopes to build tunnels between every major city in the world. Since gravity alone is used to move the trains, the only energy use will be parasitic. If the airlines are put out of business, that's the price of progress. People who use that argument are no different from the Luddites who opposed the Industrial Revolution because steam engines would replace human jobs. It didn't matter that those jobs were hellish, brute labor and the industrial revolution freed them to go do something better, like be psychologists, for example."

Alex stopped, having said more than he planned.

McConnell looked at Alex while pulling smoke into his lungs. It seemed that great, bushy mustache was pointing straight out. "Those are the same kind of arguments they used for fusion," he said softly. "That wasn't all they promised."

"That's because the paranoid, uneducated masses got it legislated to death with regulations. And they did the same thing to fission before that in the last century. We use fusion reactors on the asteroids and, while I'm deathly afraid of cosmic rays and solar radiation, I'll sleep on top of a tokamak. These environmentalists, like the damned GA, are unrealistic paranoiacs who want to return us all to the vile days before the nineteenth century."

McConnell noticed Alex's bitterness. "Is that how you feel about the Gaia Alliance? You don't think they do a lot of good?"

Alex snorted. "The GA is nothing more than punk terrorists, and the people who support them are as irresponsible and criminal as they are."

McConnell continued to drill Alex. "You said you were in SRI Security. Have you ever killed for SRI?"

Alex hesitated long enough to look away. An expression of pain and anger crossed his features before he faced McConnell again. "I have killed while on duty," he said flatly.

"Then what makes you different from the GA, other than you killed for profits and the GA kills to save the environment?"

Alex's face grew redder at he calmly spoke. "I killed in self-defense or in defense of another person."

"If you work for SRI, even if you've never killed anyone directly, you've killed for profit."

"If anything," Alex said barely containing his rage, "I killed for progress and technology that has made human existence better than could have been imagined just a few hundred years ago. That's what profits are: wealth to make everyone better off. The GA kills because they want the rest of the world to follow their beliefs and doctrines. They are no different from the Nazis or Communists that caused so much misery in the twentieth century."

McConnell stood slowly and dramatically removed his cigarette from between his lips. "I financially support the GA. If that's how you feel I think you should leave."

Alex stood to his full 172-centimeter height. "Gladly. Did you know two friends of mine were killed on the attack GA did on our lunar facility today? If you support the GA, you're culpable in their deaths." He turned to his wife. "Kirsten, we're leaving."

Kirsten looked up at him from her seat.

"Now," he barked.

Kirsten usually refused to react to Alex's occasional macho spells. But this time she decided it was better to accede to his demands and work it out later in private. She stood and looked apologetically at their hosts. Then she followed Alex out of the house and to her car.

McConnell watched them leave. "Fascist," he said.

His wife nodded.

In the car, Alex apologized.

"It's okay," Kirsten said with a sigh. "They're self-righteous snobs." She waited a few heartbeats. "Who was killed on the Moon?"

"Frank DeWite and someone you never met named Prince."

"I'm sorry."

CHAPTER THREE

"...that damn rope slipping through my fingers."

Bente Naguchi gazed out the window at the Earth. In the SRI Low Earth Orbit Facility at an altitude of about 400 kilometers, this was as close as she ever planned to get. Born on the Moon 25 years ago, she was sure she could live in one gee. She'd felt that and more on some ships she'd traveled in. But she knew she wouldn't like it one bit. Sometimes she wished she could visit the blue and green world of her parents.

She'd seen pictures, of course, but they couldn't convey the entire sensation of being outdoors with no pressure suit confining you. She'd heard there were places, in Europe mostly, where it was legal to go naked. She wondered what that would be like: to have nothing between you and everything. Maybe someday she'd visit; someday, for a very short period.

Bente was over 225 centimeters tall but massed about the same as a "normal" woman. She had long, black-brown hair and large, brown eyes with an exotic hint of an epicanthic fold. Her mother, a German, had given her skin a paler complexion than her Japanese father's. She knew that some considered her attractive. That was attested to by the number of men, and sometimes women, who approached her in this bar while she waited for transportation to the Moon. But she also told herself that "Moon Maidens" were considered a novelty, and relative attractiveness had little to do with the number of propositions she received.

"Shuttle to Lunar Facility One departing in ten minutes," a voice said over the public address. Bente put her SRI card in the slot, pressed her thumb to the plate, and pushed herself out of the bar. She didn't notice the numerous pairs of eyes following her.

On the shuttle, Bente didn't need a window seat–she gave hers up to a tourist. At turn-around, during the few minutes of free-fall, Bente made sure she was far, far away from the tourists and others on their first space excursion. Frankly, watching others with space sickness made her sick. She watched the descent to the Moon on a monitor. She could see the original NESA site: a metal dome less than 100 meters in diameter. From this, like a spreading plant, the facility grew. It was a hodgepodge of domes, tunnels, and corridors.

Occasional windowed boxes that were a few stories tall marked NESA hotels and resorts made to resemble their terrestrial counterparts. The farther the facilities were from the original dome, the newer the construction. A lot of the facility was under the surface, and the parts that weren't were partially covered with black slag from SRI asteroids. The slag provided extra protection from radiation but still, during solar flares, everyone huddled in shelters under meters of lunar rock.

NESA Facility Two was a framework about a kilometer away. Occasionally she'd see the sharp sparkle of a welder. Bente caught a glimpse of the SRI area and the shipyard, and saw workers crawling over the carcasses of the destroyed ships. She had a passing acquaintance with some of the dead people. *Murdered people,* she reminded herself.

The shuttle landed and the enclosed ramp extended and mated to the ship. Bente let the tourists, giddy with excitement–the space sickness only an acrid memory–de-shuttle first. Then Bente threw her bag over her shoulder and entered the shuttleport. As a resident she skipped lightly through customs and went to the subway. A few minutes later she was in the residential area. She found her parents' new apartment with little trouble. Since both she and her brother had moved out, they had moved into a smaller domicile.

When Bente entered her parent's home, Mozart's Requiem was playing on the stereo system. *How fitting*, she thought as the mournful basses droned out the dirge that only the son of Leopold could make that beautiful. This might be her swan song with her family if she and her father couldn't work out their differences.

Bente's mother loved Mozart, Beethoven, Bach. Once someone asked her how she felt about Rimsky-Korsakov–her mother almost spat. "Russians," she said. "The Russians have been conquered by everybody including the Communists. Conquered people can't write powerful music." That the listener was a scientist from the University of Moscow didn't make her any more reticent in expressing her low opinion of Russian composers. Bente had been raised on a combination of classical music and the stuff kids listened to all over the world and even in space. Now, if she happened to hear popular music, she had to wonder if it had gotten worse or her tastes had gotten better.

She suspected the former.

"Mother," she called out, closing the door behind her.

Bente's mother came into the foyer of their apartment. Her mother seemed to have gained a few kilos in the months Bente had been gone, and her hair's blonde color seemed to have faded to a dull shade bordering on gray. Her round face, though, probably would never develop wrinkles.

"Bente, welcome home!" her mother exclaimed, wrapping her arms around her daughter. Bente could literally look down on her head.

Releasing Bente, her mother asked, "How are you?"

"Fine, Mother. Is Father home?"

Mrs. Naguchi shook her head. "Not yet. He's still at the lab working late. He didn't know you'd be coming."

"I should have called from the Low Earth Orbit Facility."

"SRI pays you enough to afford trans-lunar connections?"

Yes, she thought. She shrugged. "You're right."

"I've got good news," her mother beamed. "Akio's home."

Bente didn't groan like she wanted to. She didn't even roll her eyes.

Dinner at the Naguchi residence was always an unusual combination of Japanese and German tainted by the lack of meat and by the abundance of vegetables available from the NESA farms. Akio deftly put the sauerkraut into his mouth with chopsticks. Mr. Naguchi had developed a taste for the putrid vegetable, but it seemed to him his wife thought it was a staple.

"Is the development of the lunar-equatorial accelerator going well?" he asked Akio.

"Yes," Bente's younger brother replied. "We hope to start digging the tunnel by next year. I hope I'm alive to see its completion."

"Are you still having financial problems?" Mr. Naguchi asked.

"It's getting better. Even the American government is putting in money–almost as much as the Russian Federation."

"What energies do you hope to obtain?" Mr. Naguchi asked as if reading from a script.

"Near primordial energies: About ten to the minus one hundred seconds after the big-bang," he said proudly.

"And, Bente," Mr. Naguchi chided. "What do you do? You go off to make money. You mine asteroids."

"I'm a navigator, Father," Bente said patiently. "And I don't do it for money."

"Then why would you throw your education away on SRI? You could be working with your brother on the accelerator, or on some other research project."

"Father, research is fine," Bente replied. "But it takes money. Akio? How much was SRI's contribution to the accelerator?"

"About five billion euro," Akio admitted reluctantly.

"You see," Bente said. "The reason I joined SRI is that they're doing something other than sitting around theorizing. They have a manned outpost on Europa, for heaven's sake. They've gone farther into space than any government. They're moving man into the frontier. Sure it's for profit, but in history that's why all the new lands were explored. It was only in the twentieth century that 'profit' became a dirty word."

"Yes," Mr. Naguchi retorted. "But SRI was started by NESA; a multi-government research agency."

"And then NESA sold SRI to the stockholders and made enough to afford to bring more research scientists to the Moon. Like you and Mother."

Mr. Naguchi looked at his daughter. "Do they teach you disrespect at SRI?" he asked quietly.

"No, Father."

"Then where did you learn it?"

"I'm sorry, Father. I meant no disrespect."

The rest of the meal was unusually quiet.

***

Griffin woke from a light sleep and exited the closet-sized captain's quarters. He climbed the ladder that put him on the deck with the galley and bridge. Knecht was sitting in front of her computer. The ship was small and most of it was devoted to equipment, not living space.

"How's it going?" he asked.

Knecht literally jumped a foot off the chair in the low gravity. She turned and a short yet lethal-looking knife was in her hand. She didn't relax until she saw Griffin, and that he was a good, long ways away.

"What do you want?" she asked, more than just a little suspicious.

Griffin spread his hands in supplication. "I couldn't sleep. I thought I'd check on how things are going."

"You need to sleep," Knecht stated flatly. "As shorthanded as we are."

Griffin nodded. He hadn't anticipated losing three on the Moon; that damn security man. But Knecht took care of him.

"I know," he said. "How's the navigation?"

Knecht started to relax. She enjoyed computers and the challenges of navigation. *One uses computers, they don't use you,* she thought. And they didn't hurt you, at least not maliciously. Everything a computer did was logical, even if their programmers were not.

"Fine," she said. "If the Syrians get here soon and if the information we got out of the computer on the Moon is correct, we should reach the belt way ahead of time; even with this delay. Matching orbits shouldn't be a problem. We can accelerate nine times as much as they can." She smiled at that thought.

Griffin also smiled. *God*, he thought, *she is beautiful when she's not trying to prove what a cold bitch she is.* "That's good," he said. Silence hung thick in the room.

"You should get some sleep," Knecht stated. She almost sounded caring. Griffin moved closer; he could reach out and touch her. His hand hesitated, then moved for her shoulder. But she caught the action and flinched away. The knife was less relaxed in her hand.

"Go to sleep, Griffin," she ordered.

He nodded and turned to the opening in the floor. As he descended the ladder he watched her watch him leave.

***

Security Chief Mitchel looked at the faces on the screen that covered one wall of his office in the SRI Headquarters building.

"NESA is very embarrassed," Rodriguez said on the Moon. "They are willing to help any way they can in the investigation within the confines of their privacy laws. But they don't think we'll ever know how the weapons got on the Moon."

"Did you," Mitchel asked, "tell them about the Syrians?"

Two seconds later Rodriguez nodded. "Yes. But they can't really investigate in the UBS area any more than they can investigate in our area."

"Okay," Mitchel said. "What about Trent?"

Another man on the screen spoke from Washington. "Our people watching her say she met with Syrians last night. We put an ultrasound beam on the windows but all we got was a local radio station."

"Damn," Mitchel grumbled. They may be radicals but they weren't stupid. "What about Damascus?"

Elisa Morgan was the boss at SRI's Middle Eastern terrestrial information gathering office in Tel Aviv. "Our agents in Damascus have trouble," she reported. "Syria's too much a police state. But, we've connected with an underling in the Baath party. He's getting some information to us. A French arms seller, Philippe Thorez, will be visiting Damascus soon. He specializes in space-borne weapons. This isn't his first visit."

"Find out why he's there," Mitchel ordered crisply. "It may be important."

Morgan nodded. "I will."

"Anything else?" Mitchel asked. No one said anything.

"Okay. Let's get on this. We need to find out what the GA is up to. Rodriguez, stay on. Everyone else, thank you and good-bye."

The screen cleared and showed the SRI logo. Mitchel turned to the smaller screen on his desk. "Rod," he said, "I'll be arriving on the next shuttle. How's Charlie?"

"Really well, considering," Rodriguez replied two seconds later, a shade of sadness in his voice. "Anything else?"

"No, not now. I'll see you tomorrow."

***

Alex held Kirsten's hand across the table. He'd been home a few days and they finally found time to drive to Denver to his favorite Korean restaurant, the Sai Han Sheik Dong. It was in the lower downtown district near Union Station. Denver had closed its city center to private vehicles so they parked Kirsten's car in a huge underground parking lot at the edge of town and took a light-rail into the city. The train stopped at Union Station and from there it was a short, albeit cold, walk to the restaurant.

Mr. Pak, the proprietor, and his employees knew Kirsten and Alex well and, after delivering their food, left them alone unless called.

Alex looked at the device on his wrist that was being grossly underutilized by only displaying the time. The security memorial service on the Moon was about to start. It was for the three security people killed: DeWite, Prince, and a kid named Nakamura whom Alex didn't know. The services for the others killed were being held by their divisions. He'd debated taking time to go. Kirsten would have understood, but would have resented it after making arrangements to spend all her time with him. At least, that's what Alex decided. That, and he preferred to honor the memory of his friends his way and in private.

Out of one of the multitude of small dishes on the table, Alex used chopsticks to select a slice of kimchee and put it in his mouth. He followed the pickled cabbage with a gob of rice.

"I suppose," Kirsten chided playfully, "you expect to sleep in the same bed as me after eating that."

Alex nodded and swallowed. "All you have to do is eat some and we'll cancel each other out."

Kirsten made a face. "No thanks, Mr. Chun." She used a fork to eat a piece of duk-gogi.

"It's real embarrassing," Alex teased, "to have a wife that can't eat with chopsticks."

"Sorry," she replied. "I don't eat Oriental food very much. My friends like Middle Eastern food. About a month ago, Alysia and her husband and I went to this new place in Boulder, on a Monday night, and the place was packed. We almost left but everyone was there. The McConnells, the Kims–you remember Jason Quinn from Aspen?–he was there. We pushed all our tables together and talked and laughed until the owner threw us out–it was two in the morning. I almost fell asleep during a session with one patient the next day. But it was so much fun."

"Oh," Alex said simply.

"I'm sorry, Alex," she said quietly. "But you don't expect me to pace the widow's walk the whole time you're gone?"

Alex shook his head. "No, of course not. It just seems sometimes I'm only a footnote in your life."

"Well, Alex, you're only here about six weeks a year. I love you, but I have to have a life. And while you're here I put everything off. I even send my patients to other therapists; because I want to be with you."

"I know," Alex intoned. "And I appreciate that."

"You could quit SRI," Kirsten speculated. "Join my life full time. You've met most of my friends and get along with most of them. You have enough money in your SRI account we could both retire."

Alex shook his head. "I can't. I mean, I can, but I won't. I owe SRI. They took me and educated me and gave me a job–and kept educating me. Because they require employees to continue their education in order to get promoted, I have the equivalent of a B.S., at least. I'd never have gotten that if I'd stayed in L.A. My parents couldn't afford to send me to college, and you know how it was then. The government was broke and there were no grants or students loans. I'd have worked in my father's store on Olympic Boulevard forever; if the gangs didn't get me, too."

The last sentence was stated with a mixture of anger and pain.

"And," he continued after a few moments, "I'd have never met you."

"Joey probably would still be alive if you two hadn't gone into SRI," Kirsten noted. "You still call out his name in your sleep."

"I know," Alex replied softly. "I usually wake up right afterward. I still dream about that damn rope slipping through my fingers–if only I'd caught it. But Joey would probably be dead if he'd stayed in L.A. I never told you, or, hell, anyone this, but one reason we joined SRI was that there was a gang out to kill him."

"Why?"

"He refused to join. The courts were so lenient with criminals that the gangs were the *defacto* government in many parts of L.A. They didn't have to worry about getting caught. You could do two years for murder. If only..."

"If only..." Kirsten repeated. "Let's stop playing 'if only' games. Let's make the most of the two weeks you have at home. Have you decided whether to go to Frank's memorial service?"

"Yes," Alex said with conviction. "I'm not going. It would take four days. I really haven't seen Frank in years. Besides, it's starting in about ten minutes."

"Oh, Alex," she cried. "You should have gone if you wanted."

"I didn't want to."

"You sure?" Kirsten asked. "I wouldn't have minded."

"Yes," Alex replied curtly. He picked up a round slice of kimbop. "Want some?"

Kirsten wrinkled up her nose, scrunching together the sparse population of freckles residing there. "No, thanks. Reminds me too much of sushi."

***

Mitchel didn't wear his full uniform very often anymore. At SRI headquarters, he wore a suit and if he needed a security uniform, he used one that had its red space-qualified color as its only pretension.

But, standing in front of the briefing room, the same one Frank had lectured in just before he was killed, Mitchel wore the red jumpsuit with the SRI patch on his left shoulder, the SRI Security patch on his other shoulder, and his Head of Security insignia over his heart. A cluster of yellow stars under the security patch represented each trip to the asteroid belt and back. Each silver bar in a row on the right sleeve represented one year in space. The NESA emblem on his right breast showed he worked for SRI back when it was a division of the multi-government agency.

He had eulogized Frank DeWite, speaking of his work and their long friendship. He concluded, "It's been seven years since Theresa Gold was murdered. Until Frank DeWite, Jimmy Nakamura, and Roger Prince, she was the last member of SRI Security to die because of violence," he said to the group. He saw Charlie Jones, in the back, staring blankly toward him. "When one of us dies we all feel the pain. When one of us is murdered we all feel the anger."

Mitchel left the podium. The chaplain gave a generic prayer (just about every religion was represented) and the crowd filed out slowly and solemnly. Mitchel meant to catch Charlie but too many others stopped to talk to him.

***

When Charlie was a young, pre-teenaged girl, just starting to clumsily discover her own sexuality, her maternal grandmother invited her to visit her for a weekend. That wasn't unusual; Charlie felt close to her grandmother and she often spent weekends in her apartment and they would talk about Africa and her grandmother's childhood in the Congo. The country was going through one of those occasional spasms of violence that seemed the baptism of many emerging nations. Grandma never talked about the horror she must surely have witnessed.

But that weekend was different. Instead of the plateaus and rain forests of the Congo, Grandma started out by asking about boys.

Charlie flushed. She'd noticed boys and had some idea the big, goofy creatures might have some use after all.

Grandma smiled at Charlie's perception of the males around her. Then she talked about boys she knew as a young girl. The conversation went on late into the night and continued for almost all waking hours of the weekend.

When Charlie returned to her parents, she'd changed subtly.

And while other girls in her school were having abortions, or worse, babies, Charlie, with a healthy social life, made it to graduation without any biological mishaps: a major accomplishment in her neighborhood.

What Grandma had taught her in that one extraordinary weekend was respect for and responsibility to herself.

Grandma died while Charlie was still in high school. Charlie thought she'd never feel pain like that again. She'd learned that "heartache" is an actual physical discomfort in the chest.

Now, for the second time in her life, she felt heartache.

They'd sent Frank's body to the NESA farm where it would be broken down into its constituent elements and would give life to the next generation. To Charlie that was much better than a concrete box in the ground like they did to her grandmother.

Rodriguez insisted she not work for her safety and others'. Charlie wondered if he thought she'd be ineffectual without Frank to guide her.

Let's see, she thought, *I've denied it; I've been angry–now it's time for depression. Or is it bargaining? It sure as hell isn't acceptance.*

The door to her (and Frank's) quarters gave its annoying buzz, interrupting Charlie's self-pitying.

"What is it?" she asked, not really caring.

"It's Mitchel."

"Come in; it's open."

Mitchel had changed uniforms to a simple red jumpsuit with a security patch. "Hi, Charlie, how are you doing?" As the door closed behind him he held out his arms.

Charlie stood and walked to him. "I'm okay," she said simply, slipping into his embrace. They held each other a moment.

"Yeah, right," Mitchel said gently, disengaging himself and holding her at arm's length. He looked at her. "That scar..."

He fingered her long neck.

"A vein in my neck protruded after the explosive decompression of my suit. The doctors fixed it. As soon as it heals it'll be barely noticeable."

Mitchel nodded. "Good. Listen, Charlie, when you feel up to it, come to Tokyo."

Charlie made a face. "Is this about the asteroid? I don't want to go."

"No, it's something else. Please?" the Head of Security for SRI asked.

"Okay," Charlie replied noncommittally.

"I've got to catch the shuttle; it's leaving soon. Come on the next one; call Meyoung when you get to headquarters and set up a meeting."

"Okay, I will."

"Thanks, Charlie."

***

"Come in, Mr. Rodriguez," Helga Moeller said, standing.

Moeller was a middle manager in NESA's security office.

Rodriguez shook her offered hand and sat in the indicated chair. Moeller was an archetypical blonde, blue-eyed Aryan with a rubenesque build that Rodriguez found attractive despite himself.

"It was a nice service," Moeller commented.

"Yes, it was," Rodriguez replied.

46

"We've just about completed our investigation," she said, sitting behind her desk, indicating it was time to get down to business. "We're helped by the fact that there are so few people on the Moon."

"What did you learn?"

"There are five persons unaccounted for in both NESA Facility One and Two. All are from Earth."

"Do you have names?"

She tapped keys on her desk and a paper-thin screen in front of Rodriguez lit up. It had five passport pictures with data next to each.

"You can see they are all Americans," Moeller said. "They arrived over a period of a week. Only one, Alan Griffin, had been here before. All their visas were secured with cash deposits at the Japanese embassy in Washington, Columbia."

"Can I have this?" Rodriguez asked.

"Yes." She tapped more keys and the device on Rodriguez's wrist chimed indicating it had received the file. SRI's main computer was still down and everyone was relying on their personal computers.

"Did you have any luck with the bodies?"

"Yes. The body at your Check Point Alpha was William Fetterly. That was a relatively easy identification. The other two bodies were both male. The bodies were damaged by shotgun wounds, exposure to vacuum, and automatic weapon's fire to the face."

"To slow identification?" Rodriguez speculated.

"Yes. But we have fingerprints. The bodies were Hector Balgos and Frank Green. The last may be an alias."

Rodriguez nodded. "Thank you."

"If there's anything else we can do," Moeller said perfunctorily.

"Thank you," Rodriguez repeated and stood to leave.

***

The Frenchman, Philippe Thorez, was a large man. His clothes were tailor made out of expensive, natural fibers. It's amazing the money to be made by selling death.

Thorez greeted the Baathist leader. *"Mah'hun ah'sah'hun."*

Faruq smiled and ignored the man's mangling of his language.

"The missiles?" he asked. English was the common denominator.

"Because of the sanctions," Philippe began, "It is very difficult."

"Yes, I know," Faruq acknowledged. *So the negotiations begin,* he thought with glee. He actually enjoyed this part of his job.

"But," the arms dealer went on, "there is a shipment of 'humanitarian items' for the poor, suffering children of Oman from the generous people of the EU. The ship will leave Marseille in a few days. If my SRI account has grown substantially, a container full of powdered milk also will contain a crate of ten missiles."

"How substantially?" the Arab asked.

"That is the question, *mon ami.*"

CHAPTER FOUR

"Marin County, wouldn't ya know."

The Frenchman snored like a pig. That was a good metaphor, Karen, the American that had majored in English, thought. He had sex like a pig, also. At least he had the decency to turn over and go to sleep immediately afterward.

What I'll do for money, she thought ruefully. But after graduating from Columbia with a student loan obligation just under the national debt, and the government throwing defaulters in jail, and the old rich man who gave her money for her company because she was pretty and willing...well, she just fell into it.

She slipped out of the Western-style bed. Philippe had made the mistake of keeping his luggage in this room and a short search produced his thin, paperback book-sized computer. She went to the bathroom, stopping for her one bag.

The Baathist enclave was really like a fortified hotel in some respects. That morning, she'd flown out of Tel Aviv to Athens and from there to Damascus. She was greeted at the airport by a greasy little man who threw her into the back of an old Mercedes (it burned gas!) and drove her to the enclave. She traveled the road to Damascus laying on the dirty back seat and climbing into a black *abaya.*

What I'll do for money, she thought again.

In the bathroom she looked at herself in the mirror. Her makeup was smeared by the pig's brutal kisses. Her negligee was soiled and even torn. Karen gave herself a dirty look. What she did for money was unpleasant, and had a few inherent dangers such as disease or freaks. Still, what she was about to do could get her killed. But SRI's money was too damn good. When that Morgan woman approached her, told her she was going to be called to Damascus, and offered enough money that Karen could vacation for a few years, she'd jumped at the offer.

She put the toilet seat down–the pig had left it up–sat on the lid and pulled her bag onto her lap. From her bag she removed a makeup kit. Turning it over, she pried off the back with her long thumbnail. The assortment of chips was impressive; four were labeled "HACK" and about ten were standard data chips.

She chose one of the hack chips at random, slipped it into the appropriate slot, and turned on the computer.

Nothing happened.

She tried another chip, as Morgan had instructed.

Again the computer refused to boot.

"Damn," she sighed softly. If none of the hack chips worked, she'd have to steal the computer to get her money, and that was very risky.

But when she tried the third hack chip, the computer immediately came on, its screen lit up and it let out a frightfully loud beep.

The screen displayed "WAIT" then "INSERT DATA CHIP #1", and when she did the data chip light glowed a cheerful yellow.

"PLEASE REMOVE DATA CHIP #1 AND INSERT DATA CHIP #2," the screen read and Karen complied. This continued for six chips and the screen displayed "DOWNLOAD COMPLETE."

Karen turned off the device and put all the chips back in the hidden compartment in her makeup kit. She flushed the toilet and washed her hands and face. Back in the room she replaced the computer where she'd found it and slid back into the bed, staying as far from the man as possible. She knew he would expect her to be in his bed in the morning.

***

Charlie didn't like Tokyo and Mitchel's request for her to come see him had her perplexed. She thought about it while trying to catch a subway from Haneda Airport. Tokyo was too damn crowded. She'd forgotten how bad the subways were, and missed her stop because she was packed in too tightly. She finally got off the train two stops late and walked back. The mega-crowds were bad but not as bad as being a human sardine in a subterranean can.

She was wearing civilian, casual clothes, comfortable for traveling, instead of her security uniform. The first person she met at the entrance to the SRI building was a security guard who stopped her with a raised hand.

"Excuse me," he demanded arrogantly. "May I ask what your business is here?"

Charlie regarded the dirt-side security man. Like any person in any kind of position of power, he was implicitly demanding her respect. Silently she showed him her SRI identification. It was red: red for space qualified.

"Thank you," he said sheepishly, his whole power base eroded.

"You're welcome," Charlie said offhandedly and strolled by. She passed through three detectors: metal, explosives, biological and chemical. She went to the receptionist and flashed her ID again. No power games here.

"Yes?" the pretty, young Japanese girl asked in very good English. "What can I do for you, Ms. Jones?"

"I'm here to see Security Head Mitchel. Would you inform his secretary I'm here? Also, I need a room. I just came in from the Moon."

"Fine," the woman replied, working her computer. "Here or the Arcology?"

Charlie was surprised. "Is the Arcology that much completed?"

"Yes," the woman answered. "The SRI hospital has been moved there, making more room for offices here."

"How long does it take to get there?"

The girl looked sympathetic, or she was hoping Charlie wouldn't ask that. "The direct subway isn't finished, yet. A helicopter trip takes about half an hour. But the rooms are much bigger."

"Too long. I'll take a room here."

"Fine," the girl said, as if it really was. "ID, please?"

Charlie handed it over and the girl put it in the computer.

"Room 2356-A," she recited, looking at her computer. "Twenty-third floor." She held out Charlie's ID.

"Thank you," Charlie said sincerely. She went to the bank of elevators, found the hostel express (floor 20 through 25), and took it to the prescribed level. Her ID card opened the room.

She'd seen closets bigger than the room, but she'd stayed here before and knew what to expect. First she used her computer—the room had an interface—to access the SRI company store. She looked over the dresses; her attire was a little too casual to be seen on the executive floors. Something appropriate but not necessarily business-like was what she wanted.

All the dresses had long, flowing skirts; apparently the current fashion. She picked one with a color she thought would look good on her—and was very close to SRI Security red—and arranged to have it delivered with corresponding shoes and foundation. Charlie enjoyed dressing in nice clothes but hardly ever got a chance in space. That, and Mitch was an old bachelor and friend. He'd appreciate the extra effort.

***

Charlie remembered when she met Mitchel what seemed ages ago, but was in reality only about five years. It was in Boulder; Charlie was in the SRI school. She'd been there long enough that her weekends were free and a group of girls had talked her into going out with them. Near the University of Colorado was the usual series of bars aimed toward collegiate clientele, and the SRI security trainees were going to try to pass themselves off as co-eds. But Charlie grew tired of the drinking and the behavior of the college boys. Even though she was the same age, they seemed so frivolous and self-possessed. Her friends didn't want to leave so Charlie walked to the light rail terminal by herself.

There was an older man waiting for the train with a suitcase and a briefcase, marking him in her mind as a traveling businessman. Charlie assumed his destination was the expensive neighborhoods in the foothills of the Rockies. He was big and muscular with wide shoulders and a narrow waist. *Only advanced age is ever going to widen his girth,* she mused. He had a large head and was bald except a circle of graying, reddish hair. His deep, intelligent blue eyes twinkled when he looked at Charlie. Charlie had dressed in the tightest pair of jeans she owned and a low cut sweater. But he looked her right in the eye, at least when she was looking at him.

"Hi," Charlie said.

"Hello," he replied.

"Late to be just getting in," she offered.

"Yes, it was a long trip."

"I hate to travel," she said. "It's arriving that's fun."

He laughed. When the train came they were still talking.

Instead of boarding they left the platform and went to a cafe. They ignored the stares and talked, so much that their food was cold before they began consuming it.   Charlie was amazed that this older man–he called himself Eugene–was so interesting. He also seemed genuinely interested in what she had to say. When the time came to pay the bill, Eugene used his computer to transfer the funds. As it sat idling on his wrist, Charlie noticed it displayed a familiar logo.

"Do you work for SRI?" she asked. The subject of employment had never come up in their conversation.

"Yes," he said, somewhat apprehensive. "I didn't tell you because some of the locals think SRI is a Japanese plot to buy up all the land."

"I know," Charlie bemoaned. "I get that all the time."

"You work for SRI?" he asked more nervously.

She smiled. "Yes."

"What do you do?"

"I'm a trainee at the school."

Eugene's eyes rolled up. "Wonderful. I thought…"

"You thought I was a student at CU?"

He nodded mutely.

"I was trying to look like one. Like you said, the locals sometimes don't give SRI employees the warmest of receptions."

He just looked at her.

"What do you do?" she asked innocently.

He hesitated.

"Are you in security?" she prodded. The SRI school specialized in security.

He nodded. "Yes, I'm in security."

"So, what do you do for Mitchel?"

He hesitated, then smiled wryly. "I am Mitchel," he said.

Charlie's eyes grew wide. "You're Chief Mitchel?"

"Yes," he replied matter-of-factly.

"Oh, my," she whispered. "I heard you'd be here Monday. I didn't think…"

"I came early. I was going to visit a friend's wife and get settled." He paused. "This is a problem," he said.

"Why?"

"Because, this isn't…"

"Isn't what?" Charlie asked. "Don't worry. I won't say anything to anyone."

"It's not that simple," he protested.

"Yes it is," she stated. "Just because you happen to be my superior—really my superior—doesn't cause me any concern. I don't think it should concern anyone else, either. Were you thinking I was going to try to use this to my advantage?"

"Well," he said in such a way that she knew he was thinking she would.

"Well, I wasn't. I don't do things that way. I want to succeed for better reasons than, 'I know the boss.'"

He looked at her for a few moments. "Trainee Jones, your career should be successful as hell."

"Friends then?"

He nodded. "Sure. And my friends call me Mitch."

"Okay, Mitch."

"Although," he said with a smile, "You'd better call me 'Chief' or 'Mr. Mitchel' around the school."

***

Whether either of them meant for it to be, Mitch and Charlie's friendship did help her career. When Mitchel found Charlie working as dirt-side security when she was space qualified he quickly got her an assignment on the Moon. When Takada, the Director of the Lunar Facility, protested that Charlie shouldn't be living with Frank, Mitchel stepped in and made it possible for Charlie to stay at the lunar facility.

Charlie showered in the minuscule bathroom. She wondered if Mitchel was going to intervene in her career again and if so, how? If it weren't for his help she wouldn't have had the position she had on the Moon. Then he tried to get her a job on an asteroid. Charlie wasn't sure if she'd turned it down because she resented the help or because she was afraid she couldn't do the job.

The dress arrived by robotic courier a few minutes later. A message on her computer indicated her appointment with Mitch was in an hour. Charlie dressed, fixed her hair, and put on makeup, enjoying the luxury of feminine things again.

She left the room and took the elevator to the hundred and thirtieth floor. There were two men on the elevator. She noticed they were strangely quiet.

She had to wait a few minutes in Mitch's outer office but that gave her a chance to chat with Meyoung before she showed Charlie in.

The office was expansive. One wall was a window with a view of Tokyo and the bay to drive any acrophobic batty. Another wall was a computer screen. The other two were almost bare except for a few mementos of Mitchel's SRI career.

Mitchel smiled when he saw Charlie. His eyes started with her feet and moved up. Mitchel was a big man and looked as uncomfortable in a business suit as he looked out of place.

"Charlie," he said coming around the desk and giving her a friendly hug. "You're looking good. Damn good. How are you?"

"I'm fine," Charlie said with a chuckle that may have been a bit forced.

He inspected her neck. "Your scar looks better–barely noticeable. I hear you almost didn't make it back to the airlock."

"Yes. Smitty saved me." She said it as a flat statement.

"You shouldn't have gone back alone. If Smitty hadn't heard your suit blow on the radio

"He didn't detail the results.

"I know," Charlie replied. "Rodriguez gave me the same lecture."

Mitchel smiled. "Okay, enough of that." He returned to behind his desk and Charlie took a chair. When she crossed her legs her skirt fell open, exposing an almost indecent amount of her strong, tawny limbs. Charlie suspected it was designed that way.

Mitchel said, "I'm sorry about Frank's death. I know it's locking the door after the horse has escaped, but I think this will finally convince Kijoto to let us use auto-loaders. I told him the time spent pumping his weapon may have cost Frank his life and SRI the *Rock Skipper*. I know he was trying to minimize the violence, but our security people need that option. I'm looking into an HK twelve gauge that has select-fire: pump or auto-load." He shook his head. "I'm sorry, I'm babbling. How are you doing, really?"

"Okay, really," Charlie said softly. "I loved Frank; we were going to marry."

"I know."

"But life in space is dangerous. We all accept that," she added with conviction.

"But space didn't kill Frank."

Mitchel could see Charlie's chocolate skin redden. "I know," she growled, barely containing her anger.

"I feel somewhat responsible," Mitchel said with a frown.

Charlie looked at him, surprised.

"When I called that night, we had information that the Syrians were up to something. I wanted to warn Frank. But I put off calling until something was confirmed. I should have called earlier. Frank would have been prepared."

"What did you have?"

"Elisa Morgan had information out of Damascus that the Baathists were smuggling arms onto the Moon for some terrorist group. We had some agents in Mirbat–where the Syrians launch their ship–look into it. They didn't find anything, so I didn't give it priority. I should have called earlier, anyway."

"You couldn't know," Charlie said. "You can't know what idiots such as the Gaia Alliance will do."

They were quiet for a moment, each tangling with their respective ghosts.

"Look at this," Mitchel finally said, touching his computer. A picture appeared on the far wall, a composite of six photographs that looked like mug shots. "Rodriguez sent that from the Moon. Those are the passport photos of who NESA thinks attacked us. You're the only one to see one of the terrorists and live. Any of those look familiar?"

Charlie pointed. "That's the fat bitch."

"Cole," Mitchel noted. "I've got the San Francisco office looking into her background."

Charlie nodded and looked at the face on the wall. She wondered what motivated a person like that.

"Would you like to help nail them?" Mitchel asked, interrupting her reflections.

Charlie didn't hesitate. "How?"

"The Gaia Alliance is based in the U.S. Since they've committed no crimes there, the U.S. won't do anything; at least in this case. But since the attack took place at the Nippon/European Space Agency Facility, both the EU and the Japanese governments say they will prosecute. But the U.S. won't extradite without evidence."

"Okay, how do I get it?" Charlie asked.

Mitchel smiled. "Computer, display 'Freeman picture.'" A handsome black man's face appeared in place of the passport photos. "That's my friend, Special Agent Gordon Freeman of the FBI. He wants someone."

"Who?"

"Congresswoman Linda Trent of California's forty-sixth district–Marin County, wouldn't ya know? She's a Green but also in the GA. We think she got the Syrians to smuggle the weapons used in the attack to the Moon. Freeman needs someone to infiltrate the GA organization. I think you're perfect."

"Why me? I'm Extraterrestrial Security, not Intelligence Gathering."

"I know, but you're unknown. All our people, or the FBI's, risk exposure. Trent can look into any FBI file she wishes, including the ones on our people in the States."

"Isn't that illegal?" Charlie asked.

"That and a million other things governments do. So we have to be careful. You're literally from out of the blue. You make friends with Trent, get into the organization, and get the evidence we need."

"Like what?"

"First, anything linking Trent to the Syrians; but that's not enough. Then, if you get into the organization, anything linking it to the attack. Computer, show 'L.A. Times archive photo.'" The picture on the screen was replaced by a group of angry people protesting something. "This is a few years ago at the San Joaquin Fusion site. Computer, GA-overlay." Three heads were circled. "This is the GA leadership as far as we know. Computer, print that." A paper slid out of a slot on Mitchel's desk. He handed it to Charlie. "The man on the left is Harris Beatty. He has a few convictions for violent crimes. We think he's the leader of the GA's underground activities."

Charlie looked at the paper. Beatty looked like a blue eyed, blond denizen of a California muscle beach. "Doesn't look like an environmental terrorist," she commented.

"Beatty's more of a mercenary," Mitchel said. "Doesn't care what the cause is as long as it's violent.

"The other man is Alan Griffin. He seems to be some kind of sub-leader in the GA. The FBI thinks he's responsible for the bombing of the Mojave antenna field. The woman is Trent. She was arrested in the Mojave bombing, but some crucial evidence was thrown out by a judge."

"Why?" Charlie asked.

"Who knows? Maybe the arresting officer looked at her cross-eyed."

Charlie looked at the three. Beatty was a big man, Griffin smaller and rather hirsute. Trent was a generally unattractive woman.

Charlie shook her head. "Okay, what do I look for?"

"The suits on the two dead terrorists," Mitchel continued, "were Russian made, sold on the open market. According to the serial numbers, they were sold to Yemen. They could have sold them to the Syrians or directly to the GA. I have someone looking into that end of the deal. The bullets taken out of—uhm—the wall—"

"And Frank's body."

"Yes, the bullets were nine millimeter caseless. Computer, display 'Lunar Facility surveillance still.' This was taken by the computer on the Moon before the terrorist burned it with thermite. The only reason it survived is somebody downloaded it to a tablet before the computer was destroyed. It was the only picture of them to survive, and you can see some data was lost."

Charlie looked at the fuzzy picture. Although large pieces were missing she could see it was a person holding a sub machinegun of some sort.

"As near as we can tell," Mitchel said, "That's a conversion of a South African made nine millimeter caseless automatic weapon called the KS-900. Here's a picture of one." He tapped the computer again and the screen split with the surveillance picture sharing the screen with a full color picture of a black weapon. "If you can link the GA to the purchase and conversion of those weapons, to the purchase of those suits, Freeman says we can get an extradition."

"That's all, Mitch?" she asked sarcastically.

"That's all."

"I don't know. I'd like to but I don't think I'm qualified."

"You hate the GA as much as I do?"

"Probably more."

"You're qualified," Mitchel pronounced.

Charlie smiled but wished she shared his confidence in her.

Perhaps he sensed her diffidence as he asked, "You feel up to it?"

She held up her left wrist. "Download that information into my computer," she said, effectively changing the subject.

Mitchel worked with the computer a few moments and then the device on Charlie's wrist beeped, indicating it had received the data.

"The worst part's going to be living on this dirt ball again," she grumbled. "How do you stand it, Mitch?"

Mitchel shrugged his shoulders. "As soon as the Arcology is finished I'll be living on the three hundredth floor. That's quite a ways up."

***

The President of Syria, the Secretary General of the United Baath Arab States, and the Chairman of the Arab Socialist Baath Party sat behind his bullet-proof desk and surveyed his office as he oft surveyed his lands from a helicopter.

Two guards of the Baath Security Forces were at the door. They were so still one easily forgot they were there. Sitting in massive leather chairs were General Zuabi, from his headquarters in Tyre, and General Sa'ud, who as Commander in Chief of the United *Baath Revolutionary* Army was Zuabi's only superior.

Faruq, the president's old friend was, as usual, present. Lately Faruq seemed preoccupied. The president wondered if he should just make his friend minister of the interior. No, that would give him control over the security forces–perhaps the Ministry of Economic Development. Men had gone into that job young and full of vigor and emerged weak and wizened. That was the place for Faruq and his ambitions.

"The accuracy of the new Chinese missiles is astounding," Sa'ud was saying. "We could target the Knesset; although with nuclear warheads that seems somewhat unnecessary."

The president chuckled politely. "And our intelligence?"

"The Zionist state is only 20,000 square kilometers," Zuabi reported. "We know the location of their Jericho missiles thanks to our Palestinian brothers who can traverse the territory with impunity. Even the Shin Bet dares not touch them lest American public opinion turns against the occupiers of Palestine and with it stops the flow of foreign aid." He had sneered sarcastically when speaking of the Palestinians. No one in this room thought Baathist anti-Zionism was based on concern for the Palestinians rather than the quest for power.

The "peace process" in the '20s died when the new Palestinian state attacked Israel with the help of Syria and Iran. The occupiers of Palestine reacted in their usually overwhelming manner and destroyed the Palestinian state and took back the Golan Heights, the West Bank, and the Gaza Strip. It would be a long time before they were tempted to make the strategic error of trading land for peace again. So, once again, the Palestinians were refugees without a homeland. A homeland that Syria was not going to provide them for they were not going to give up their land to those repellent peasants; plus, having them as victims of Israel served a useful purpose. The United States would decry every aggression by Israel, reported faithfully by their media, while the persecution of Syria's Alawite minority was virtually ignored.

"The Mossad," he continued, "cannot know the location of our silos. The Chinese have supplied us with accurate and powerful nuclear weapons. If we strike first we can destroy their missiles in their bunkers before they can retaliate. With the destruction of the Zionist leadership we will be able to walk in unopposed."

"Unless," the president added, "the Americans come to their aid."

"The Americans," Zuabi said, "cannot threaten the United Baath Arab States. They are a degenerate country. If they were going to stop us they would have long ago."

"I don't know if the Americans would stand for a nuclear attack on Tel Aviv," Sa'ud said. "We have reports the Americans have assured the Zionists that they will retaliate in kind for a first strike against them."

"Where do these reports come from?" Zuabi asked.

"I cannot reveal their source."

"Without knowing the source," Faruq said speaking for the first time, "it is hard to give them credence."

"Nevertheless," Sa'ud retorted, "they are accurate. The United States' limited space-based anti-ballistic missile screen only protects their territory. They'd have no alternative other than to use nuclear force against us."

"Or do nothing," Faruq said.

"We will wait," the president concluded. "We are making progress diplomatically and our client revolutionary groups continue to hurt the Zionists and the West." As if that reminded him, the president asked, "Faruq, how are your dealings with this Gaia Alliance?"

Faruq was surprised. The president had hardly acknowledged Faruq's activities before.

"Fine," he said quickly. "They have already struck a blow and will soon strike another."

"The expenses," the president retorted almost angrily, "have been very high: the space-to-space missiles, diverting the *Ath-Thawra Baathiya.*"

"And so will be the rewards," Faruq assured the president.

"*In sha'allah,*" the president said almost automatically–if God is willing.

CHAPTER FIVE

"Do you have the missiles, *aqid?*"

Karen never thought she'd be so glad to see Tel Aviv. When, working in New York, it was suggested she go to Israel, she thought the idea was crazy. But she made more money here than ever back in the States. And now, SRI was going to pay her a handsome sum.

For some reason the Syrians insisted she not fly back. She suspected that her presence in the Arab Baathist Republic would embarrass somebody and they were afraid she'd be picked up at the airport.

So, she was loaded in an army truck and driven to the Mediterranean coast at Tyre. It was hard for her to believe that the little, dirty town, full of defeated Lebanese doomed to live under Syrian occupation, had spawned the city of Carthage 30 centuries ago.

In Tyre she boarded a small, black rubber boat. They'd shoved her pink bag down into the bottom of the craft. She heard water sloshing and hoped her things weren't getting wet, especially the data chips.

The electrically powered boat moved with eerie quiet down the coast. An Israeli patrol boat passed near enough they could make it out on the horizon and hear the engines. But the Syrian craft went unnoticed, being barely higher than the waves.

During the trip Karen changed into a swimming suit, ignoring the leers from the Syrians.

The boat pulled close to shore and Karen climbed out into waist deep water. They handed her bag to her and moved silently away.

Karen walked toward the beach. She could hear music somewhere. If a patrol found her now it wouldn't be totally incongruous. They might wonder why she took her bag swimming, though. They wouldn't if they found the thousands of euros in amongst her delicates.

The next morning she took a cab to Tel Aviv. Soon after arriving in her apartment there was a message from building security that someone was there to see her.

Elisa Morgan came into her room and almost wordlessly checked the chips for data with a hand computer. She smiled as the data scrolled across the screen.

"Any problems?" she asked.

"No. He didn't suspect a thing."

"Good," Morgan said. She turned a debit card from the SRI bank over to Karen. Karen went to her computer and checked the balance—it was to her liking.

Morgan left and Karen went back to her computer. She wondered what the south of France was like this time of year.

And how many rich men she could find.

***

Democracy had swept through the Middle East like some unstoppable jihad early in the twenty-first century, starting with what was called the "Second Arab Spring" (after the first, in most cases, simply replaced one bastard with a worse bastard). Many countries made their royalty figureheads after the British model, some had a spate of violence as the labor pains of the birth of freedom. Some flirted with radical Islam, but those states soon found their people rising up against them—except those countries where the Baath party held the population in control with tactics developed over 80 years of brutal rule in the now-defunct Soviet Union.

Unwilling or unable to resist, the West allowed the Baathists to march into country after country, aborting fledgling democracies by preying on their inherent weaknesses. The vacuum left when the United States pulled out of the region needed to be filled, and the Baathists were brutal enough to do it.

Oil, replaced by hydrogen as the fuel of choice in the wealthy Occident, was still used for internal combustion in the third world, including the Russian Federation. Russia was often called a third-world country with a first-world space program.

Oil was also used everywhere in the manufacture of plastics, lubricants, and fertilizers. In the West, environmental concerns guaranteed their oil reserves would remain in the ground; the Russians still couldn't get enough of their petroleum to the surface to even take care of their own needs. So the Baath Party controlled almost all the world's accessible oil. With that money they bought arms they hoped to eventually use against the Zionist state and the wealthy, greedy West. They also built a space facility with Russian help.

When their tanks rolled into Muscat, Oman, the Baathists claimed they were invited in by a popular, rebel government that had taken control in a bloody coup. Why the people would overthrow a government they had elected, the Baathists didn't explain.

When the rulers in Damascus decided the United Baath Arab States needed space capabilities, it built a space facility at Mirbat in southern Oman. Once it was built, educated men (not women) were needed to operate it. But schools and science were not Baath priorities. Educated men, like many commodities the Baaths couldn't seem to produce domestically, had to be imported.

And, like all things imported from the West, these, too, carried unseen dangers.

Jackson didn't listen when his friends told him he was making a big mistake. They asked if he noticed the Baaths weren't hiring women. They asked if he was willing to help the Butchers of Damascus. But he shrugged off their protests. How else could a recent graduate, with less than sterling grades, work on space systems? So Jackson left the U.S. for Oman.

In Frankfurt he had a long layover. Flights into the United Baath Arab States had to be on their airline and its schedule was sporadic at best.

He was approached in an airport lounge by an attractive, Asian woman. She said he could make even more money than the Baaths were offering.

The danger didn't put him off but rather excited him. He took the job suspecting his new employer was either the Japanese government or Space Resources Incorporated. He was to report on everything he saw and make special reports of anything unusual.

A few weeks after arriving, he received from his contact, a taxi driver, a coin-sized camera. He'd shoot its 100-frame memory full and exchange it for another.

One morning the same taxi drove him to work. He'd missed the bus from the dormitories to the facility again.

"I saw something unusual yesterday," Jackson said after turning over the camera.

"What?" the driver asked handing back the new camera. He wondered to himself if this was going to be anything. Given a specific task a few weeks ago this engineer found nothing. It seemed unlikely he'd just stumble on something.

"They brought something in. It was in large trucks," Jackson reported. "They were in crates, big crates. They put them in a warehouse and put a guard on them."

"Can you get into that warehouse?"

"Maybe."

"Get a picture if you can. We need it today so turn it over to your secondary contact."

"I will."

The taxi stopped in front of the facility. Jackson left the cab, paid the driver in view of the guard and walked to the gate.

"Miss the bus again?" the guard asked.

"Yeah," Jackson said. "Overslept." They went through the drill of ID checking and finally Jackson was in the massive compound.

***

William Thorne stared out the window of his apartment over the Saigon River. Hanoi's capitalist reforms even extended to giving the city back its old name. The view was of row after row of expensive apartment buildings. The area was, before it was decided it had better uses by the free market, pure industrial property. Now it was where the new, rich capitalists lived.

The glass was actually warm to the touch as the sopping late summer heat broiled those residents unfortunate to be without air conditioning. But those were few as the country's wealth grew quickly after the liberalization of the economy. Add to that the longest period of continuous peace the land had seen since World War II and Vietnam was quickly catching South Korea as an "Asian Tiger" economy.

Thorne turned from the window to face Thi, who was staring at him with her fierce, black eyes.

"You heard me," she barked. "Don't come back."

Thorne looked at her. She was small, almost frail looking, in a way that suggested prepubescence. But her face was enough to dispel that notion as she glared at him in smoldering anger.

"Fine," Thorne said simply. In three months the lease would be up. She could have the apartment until then. After that he didn't give a damn what she did. She had a good job working at the Toyota plant outside the city.

She watched as he packed his bags and called the doorman to get a taxi. While waiting for his ride he thought he'd done pretty well. At almost two years, this was his longest relationship, yet.

"Good-bye, Thi," he said, walking out the door. She slammed it shut behind him.

He had the taxi take him to the airport. There, he stood in the lobby, his bags piled around him, wondering what to do. He didn't really know where he'd go. He had a few days left before he had to return to space. SRI had sent the information about his next trip.

67

He'd be chief of security for the next asteroid under Director Chun. Chun was a good friend and he was looking forward to the trip. In the meantime, he was stuck. He was alone with no place to go.

He found a public terminal and punched in an address that he couldn't forget if he wanted to. He wondered if it was still the same. The screen was blank for a long time with "Please Wait" displayed in Vietnamese, English, Chinese, and for recent immigrants, Tagalog.

The woman that answered had tight, short hair surrounding her hard face. Anachronistically, she wore glasses that were plain, black, horn rims.

"Yes?" she said automatically. Then her face lost all its color. "Bill?"

"Hi, Ma. Can I come home?"

***

"So Griffin's still alive," Mitchel asked in his office.

"Apparently he's on the *Rock Skipper*," Rodriguez said on the Moon.

"Okay, what do you know about these people?"

In San Francisco a man named Joe Murda looked off screen. "Our data on the GA identifies all but the Cole woman."

"From their visas," Rodriguez said, "Cole lives in a town called Gilroy. Knecht lives in L.A."

"I have more bad news," Murda added. "Knecht was trained in space navigation. She's undoubtedly operating the *Rock Skipper*."

"Who trained her, where?" Mitchel demanded.

Murda hesitated. "We did. She's an ex-employee/trainee."

"Damn," Mitchel spat. "And she was living in L.A.?"

"According to her visa. L.A. is where the GA operates a safe house," Murda said. "Gilroy's a suburb of San Jose and not too far from here. Let me try something."

"Computer, directory, Gilroy. Cole, C-O-L-E. List all Cole, M." He looked at the computer display just visible to Mitchel. "I've got a Madalyn Cole in Gilroy. Computer, call Madalyn Cole. To my screen only." A short wait.

"Hello?" a female voice queried. The new screen read NO VIDEO.

"Hi," Murda said in friendly tones. "Is Madalyn there?"

"No," the voice replied. Everyone heard her suspicious tone. "She quit her job and moved out a few weeks ago. I'm her roommate; or I was."

"She quit her job?" Murda exclaimed with mock shock. "I thought she liked that job."

"Are you kidding?" the girl said as if she considered Murda an idiot. "She hated it, but it paid good. Who is this anyway?"

"A friend from school," Murda said. "Do you know where she went?"

"No," the voice replied. "She just left. I came home from work and she was gone." Bitterness in that statement.

"Did you work where she worked?"

"No. I tried but they wouldn't hire me. Not enough school."

"Yeah, I know what that's like," Murda tried.

This is going nowhere, Mitchel thought.

"Yeah," the girl bemoaned. "They're really jerks at WCMS."

"WCMS?" Murda asked.

"Yeah, you know. West Coast Missile Systems."

Oh, damn, Mitchel thought. West Coast was the subcontractor for the missile systems on the *Rock Skipper*-class ships.

"Well, I got to go," Murda said and tapped a button on his computer disconnecting the call.

"Get over to West Coast and find out what she did," Mitchel ordered.

"I sure will."

Meyoung broke in just then. "Mr. Mitchel," she said. "I've got a call from Ms. Morgan, Tel Aviv."

"Put it in the conference," Mitchel barked, still unhappy about the news he'd just received.

Elisa Morgan's pretty face appeared. "Mitch—oh hi, Rod, Murda. Mitch, the Syrians bought space-to-space missiles from the Frenchman, Philippe Thorez."

"How do you know?"

"One of our contacts in Mirbat sent us some interesting photos. We think they're Puma space-to-space; the quality was pretty poor. I'm trying to get information from the French but you know how tight lipped they are.

"But," she continued, "Thorez, the French arms dealer I told you about, visited Damascus two days ago. We have his computer records. The Syrians are paying him 20million euros to an SRI account. You want the number?"

"Send it in your report."

"Okay. Three months ago he paid eleven and a half million to the Chinese."

"And the Chinese," Mitchel finished for her, "buy Pumas from the French."

"Yes," Morgan said. "He even noted the expenditure as 'Inventory, space-to-space missiles.'"

"Good work, Elisa," Mitchel said with more enthusiasm than he felt. This was adding up in ways he didn't like.

***

Cole was in the bottom of the *Rock Killer*, née *Rock Skipper*.

Griffin was glad. When Cole was around, she and Knecht heterodyned on each other and Griffin and Trudeau were left watching the escalating pitch of their conversations.

Griffin walked up behind Knecht as she peered out the large bridge window. He was so close to her shapely back, another few inches and they'd be touching. Because they were conserving water he could smell her: a not altogether unpleasant sensation.

Either she didn't notice how close he was or didn't care.

"Where are they, Knecht?" he asked her.

She didn't move. "I don't know."

"They're late," he growled, stating the obvious. "Any radio contact?"

Trudeau shook his head. Knecht moved toward the window.

Griffin sensed he was pushing his luck with her and moved away, passing back and forth. He looked at the black sky out the bridge dome window. He'd lost three people stealing this ship and if those camel-jockeys didn't come through it would be for nothing.

"You did a good job on the Moon," Griffin said to Knecht.

She looked at him and stated, simply, "Thank you."

"I've got them on radar," Trudeau reported. "At least I hope it's them."

"Figure the odds of someone else being here," Griffin replied.

He hit the intercom button. "Cole, prepare the airlock to dock."

"Okay," she answered.

Griffin again hit the intercom button. "Prepare for free-fall, Cole." He turned to Knecht. "Match that ship up with the *Janes* program."

Knecht worked efficiently with the computer. "*Janes* says it's a modified, Russian Federation *Tsiolkovshy*-class, lunar shuttle, versions of which were sold to, among others, Syria, who renamed it the *Athwara Bathy* or something like that."

"*Ath-Thawra Baathiya*," Griffin corrected. "It means '*Baath Revolution*.' Real imaginative, huh?"

"So, is it them?" Knecht asked with some impatience. "It's the right kind of ship, but," and she looked out her window. There was a flashing as if someone was pointing a flashlight out a window—low tech but effective.

"There's the light," Knecht said. "It's them all right."

"Great. Cut the engines," Griffin ordered. "Let's see how long it takes them to match velocity."

It took a great while. The Russian equipment wasn't up to SRI standards, but Knecht's training wasn't enough to allow her to use the *Rock Skipper*'s ability to its full extent. But eventually the two ships were mated. A swarthy fellow pushed over through the airlock.

Griffin greeted the man. "*Marhaban sadiqi*," he said. Greetings, friend.

The visitor smiled sardonically. "*Marhabtain*." Two greetings to you.

Griffin smiled also, although he felt the need to scrape the Arab's sarcasm off his face. "Do you have the missiles, *aqid?*" Sir. He didn't understand the other's need to humiliate him.

"Yes, *habibi.*" My love. The Arab's continued sarcasm was floating thickly in the air.

"And are they fully capable?"

"Of course. How do you plan to mount them?"

"This ship," Griffin said, "is used to survey asteroids. In order to determine the composition of the asteroid, it fires a missile very much like these. It releases a projectile, like a sabot round, and they do a spectroscopic analysis on the explosion of the impact." His voice revealed his low opinion of the method. "These missiles should fit in those tubes with very little modification."

"Can you do it?"

"Of course. We have plenty of time to get to the asteroid belt. We are in no hurry. And we have an ace in the hole."

The Arab looked as if he didn't understand the idiom. But he ignored it. "I will send the missiles over. *Ma'salamah.*" God be with you.

"*Ma'salamah,*" Griffin echoed. "We will inform you of our victory."

"*In sha'allah.*" If God is willing.

***

Charlie Jones took a spaceplane from Tokyo to Washington over the North Polar Region. Most of the trip her intestine seemed to be trying to tie itself into a bowline. This job Mitchel had sent her on, into the fiery furnace of the Gaia Alliance, could get her killed. And she'd be all alone, without Frank, Mitchel, or even Grandma to call on for help.

The spaceplanes didn't land at National so she had to take a cab from Dulles. She thought about renting a car but it had been ages since she'd driven and she didn't really have a use for one. Plus her license had probably expired.

With her bag over her shoulder she climbed in one of the taxis lined up outside the front of the terminal.

"FBI building," she said closing the door.

The driver turned in his seat to look at her. He hesitated long enough to rake his eyes over her. "Do you know where that is?" he asked when he was through leering.

"No," Charlie replied. "Can't you punch it up on your computer?"

"No," the driver said turning around and starting the car.

Must be broken, Charlie thought.

He pulled away from the curb and thumbed a button on his steering wheel. He had an earphone in one ear and a mic tube extended to near his mouth. "Hey, I got a fare here who wants to go to the FBI Building," he said. "Do you know where that is...? I don't know."

The car picked up speed and they approached the freeway entrance. "Okay, yeah, I got it."

"Where?" Charlie asked.

"Between the White House and the Capital on Pennsylvania," he said.

"Good," Charlie said.

The drive was long at the maximum speed of the taxi.

Charlie had to convert the speedometer reading she could see over the driver's shoulder to kilometers to realize just how slow 55 was.

It was getting dark when Charlie started recognizing landmarks from pictures. They crossed a bridge and Charlie knew this was the Mall with the Capital at one end and the Washington Monument extending skyward in the middle like some poor, Earthbound, square rocket. Although Charlie considered herself a citizen of space before the U.S.A., she still felt a stirring of pride, if not for what her native land had become, then for what it was before.

The street signs said they were on Constitution Avenue. She was surprised there weren't more people. *Tourists,* she thought, *should be crowding the mall although it is getting late.*

Then she saw why there were so few people. Military vehicles were patrolling the streets. They were stopping anyone walking, apparently checking identification and directing them away from the mall. Huge concrete barriers blocked off the streets.

"We're too close to the White House," the driver said. "You don't want to be around here after curfew."

Charlie remembered from high school civics that Pennsylvania Avenue ran from the White House to the Capital. It should be on their left. She was about to say something as the taxi passed behind some Smithsonian museums. She saw a cross-street sign for Pennsylvania Avenue, which cut across Constitution at an oblique angle. The driver kept going, seemingly oblivious to their location.

"Hey," Charlie said, "That was Pennsylvania."

The driver looked around. "It was?"

"Didn't you see the sign?"

"I can't read."

"Excuse me?" Charlie exclaimed, noting Pennsylvania was getting farther behind as the discussion proceeded.

"I can't read," the driver repeated

"Then what in God's name are you doing driving a taxi?" Charlie exploded. My *God,* she thought, *what if he missed an important safety sign?* Maybe the computer wasn't broken, he just couldn't use it.

"Just because I'm illiterate don't mean you can deny me a job. It's the law."

"It's a stupid law," Charlie said. "Stop the damn car and let me out. I'll walk."

"The streets ain't a good place to be," the driver advised, pulling the car to the curb. "If you get within the security zone after dark they'll arrest you."

"I'll take my chances," Charlie growled.

She used her computer to pay the fare. She rolled her eyes when the display indicated the tip had been automatically added.

She climbed out of the cab and angrily threw her bag over her shoulder. The taxi moved away and Charlie could smell the ozone from its hydrogen-burning engine.

She started back down Constitution toward Pennsylvania. She had to divert a few blocks towards the capital to get around the security zone, well-marked by armored vehicles and concrete barriers.

Back on Pennsylvania, with the FBI building's gray slab sides in view, a young man—*a boy really*, Charlie thought—stepped in front of her. He was holding a knife.

"Okay, bitch, give me the bag," he said in the most menacing voice Charlie ever heard come from someone so young.

"Do you realize you're about 20 meters from the FBI building?"

"Shut up and give me the bag," he spat as if he didn't understand her.

Charlie took the bag from her shoulder and held it out for him. He reached for it. Once he had his hand around the strap, she pulled back hard. The boy was pulled off balance and Charlie grabbed the wrist of his knife-wielding hand and twisted hard.

She was rewarded with a dull, moist pop as she broke the joint.

He howled in pain and dropped the knife. Charlie pushed him away with her other hand.

He turned and ran.

Charlie talked to her computer on her wrist "911."

There was a short wait.

"You have reached 9-1-1," another computer said, "all our operators are busy. If you'll please hold, your call will be answered in the order it was received."

Charlie was beginning to wonder if this was a mistake.

"Nine-one-one," a bored human said a few minutes later.

"I was just mugged," Charlie said.

"If your loss was less than 1,000 dollars I can give you a report number for your insurance."

"Insurance?" Charlie asked.

"You do have insurance that covers mugging, don't you?" the emergency operator droned. "To cover your loss."

"I didn't have a loss. I fended him off."

There was a pause. "You attacked the alleged perpetrator?" the voice asked incredulously.

"I defended myself, yes."

"Wait there," the voice said. "What is your name?" The computer automatically sent the operator Charlie's GPS-determined location to the square meter.

Charlie was still giving vital statistics to the operator when a siren howled behind her. She turned to see a police car pull up to the curb and two officers jumped out with their guns drawn.

Charlie smiled. Late help was better than no help.

Then one ordered loudly, "Get on your knees and put your hands behind your head."

Bewildered, Charlie complied.

They loaded her into the back of the police car and drove to the police station. She was treated with less consideration than a bag of sheep dung. They took a mug shot, fingerprinted her, took a dental mold and scraped for DNA samples on her palm.

They pointed her to a pay computer terminal and gave her a dollar. She gave the dollar back and called Mitchel collect. A bored officer questioned her in a white, acoustical tile-lined cubical with a single table and two chairs. Charlie related the details of the attack while he wrote on a tablet. She was informed she would be charged with an "unlawful self-defense."

Then they left her in the room alone.

"Who the hell are you?" Charlie barked at the handsome, black man that came into the interrogation room four hours later.

Charlie was in a foul mood. It was late at night and she had been left waiting impatiently in the locked room. She couldn't even go down the hall to the bathroom without permission from the female turnkey. There were even hints she'd be charged with a "bias crime" because, as far as Charlie could surmise, she had told police the "victim" was black and Charlie wasn't black enough.

"I'm Special Agent Freeman," the man said, sitting. He was wearing a good but inexpensive suit. "You're Charlene Jones?"

Charlie looked him over and finally recognized him from the picture Mitchel had shown her. He'd aged since it was taken.

"Yes," she said.

"It was a good idea to call Mitchel," Freeman continued. "He called me and told me what happened."

"Thanks for coming." Charlie was genuinely grateful.

Freeman shook his head. "It's against the law to attack a person. You know that, don't you?"

Charlie stared at the man. "He threatened me with a knife," she exclaimed. "Is it against the law to defend oneself?"

"Yes," Freeman retorted, "in the United States, it is."

"It's a stupid law," Charlie said for the second time that day. She had a feeling that as long as she stayed in this country she'd be saying that a lot.

"I agree," Freeman said.

"Excuse me?"

"I agree," he repeated. "Listen," he leaned forward and lowered his voice. "Unfortunately, it's the law. An act of Congress, signed by the president, and tested before the Supreme Court. Doesn't make it right; it does make it the law. I talked to the DDA and—"

"Excuse me," Charlie interrupted, "the what?"

"DDA: Deputy District Attorney for the County and State of Columbia."

"Wonderful," Charlie said sardonically.

"Anyway, I talked to the DDA and convinced her you weren't racially motivated, so they're dropping the 'bias crime' charges. Also, she's agreed to let you ask for just a fine and probation because this is a first offense and there were extenuating circumstances."

"Extenuating circumstances? What was I supposed to do? Stand there and let him stab me? I want to press assault charges against him."

"Okay," Freeman said leaning back in the old, wooden chair. "You may if he comes forward."

Charlie had to think for a second. "He hasn't come forward to press charges against me?"

Freeman shook his head. "In 'unlawful self-defense' cases only a witness is necessary. It was felt the victim may be afraid to

77

come forward. And since you confessed to the 911 operator, and the police, that is all that's necessary."

"Wait a minute. Isn't that a Constitutional guarantee, to face your accuser?"

"Well," Freeman breathed, spreading his hands, "the Sixth Amendment means less today than it used to. Hell, the Second almost means nothing. The property rights provisions of the Fifth and the Fourteenth are violated daily in the name of environmental protection and growth management. And 'equal protection under the law,' as stipulated in the Fourteenth, is ignored by bias crime laws and affirmative action. But, all of those laws have been held up by the Supreme Court. The Constitution, unfortunately, means exactly what the current court says it means."

"Can I still file a complaint?"

"Yes," Freeman replied. "But they'll probably never find him."

"You mean they'll never look."

"Yes."

"Well, what does probation mean?"

"It means that if you commit another crime during the probation period, you will definitely get a harsh sentence."

"Am I free to go? I live on the Moon, you know."

"Yes, you can come and go as you wish." He stood. "Come on. Let's go talk to the DDA."

"Boy," Charlie commented dryly while standing, "things have sure changed since I was last dirt-side." Either that or she was no longer used to it.

***

Alex held his wife as she slept in the large, four-poster bed that dominated the master bedroom in their Boulder home. The next day he would return to space and leave her again. He felt unbelievably lucky that she married him almost 17 years ago. He kissed her china-delicate white shoulder and she stirred and opened her eyes.

"Hi," she said groggily and turned in the bed to face him.

"Hello," Alex whispered.

"Can't sleep?"

"No."

"Wha'cha thinking about."

"Oh, nothing."

"Yeah, right," she retorted, turning on her side to face him.

She wrapped her arms around his back. "I know you. You're worried about something."

"I was thinking about McConnell. I really screwed it up for you, didn't I?"

"Don't worry about it. It'll be okay. But that's not all of it."

Alex smiled. "Why did I ever marry a psychologist?"

"You didn't. A psychologist married you."

He pulled her to him and kissed her gently but persistently.

That stopped her questions about things he didn't want to talk about. And it got his mind off Frank, and the *Rock Skipper*, and the Gaia Alliance.

Later he asked playfully, "Why did I marry you, anyway?"

"Must have been my bedside manner," she whispered dreamily. She fell asleep with her head on his shoulder.

He looked at the room's computer display. The green numbers unsympathetically indicated that his plane left in less than twelve hours.

CHAPTER SIX

"...no compromise when it comes to protecting Mother Earth"

The deputy district attorney was a harried looking woman. She met Charlie and Freeman in her cubical-like office. Also present was the public defender, a snide young man who regarded Charlie as if she were something he'd stepped in. Freeman explained to Charlie that a court ruling had determined everyone got a public defender, not just the indigent. If she wanted to pay for a better lawyer, she could, but that would delay the proceedings.

Charlie stuck with the public defender. She wanted this ordeal over.

Freeman then explained to her lawyer that Charlie planned to plea bargain. Charlie's stomach turned at the phrase. She'd always thought plea-bargaining was something criminals did to get out of the punishment they deserved; she never thought she'd be doing it herself.

At one point, as the DDA and Charlie's defender conferred, Charlie said, "I feel like I'm being railroaded here."

The two lawyers looked at her.

"I mean," she added, "what are my options?"

"You may," the public defender explained, "plead not-guilty, be held over for trial, which will take about nine months, most likely be found guilty, and probably be sentenced to time in jail."

"Oh," Charlie breathed. *Doesn't leave me much choice,* she thought ruefully.

Her lawyer and the government prosecutor talked about the deal, the details were established, and Charlie was told to wait to see the judge.

A few hours later, a bailiff escorted Charlie into the courtroom. The judge was a middle-aged woman with fading blonde hair. The public defender stood next to Charlie and the DDA read the charges. Freeman sat in the gallery.

All the while, the judge peered down on Charlie. "Ms. Jones," she said in a New England nasal tone, "it has been decided not to charge you with a bias crime, because it cannot be determined that you were motivated by bigotry. However, you are charged with unlawful self-defense."

"He assaulted me," Charlie explained in vain. "I was protecting myself and my property."

"It is the job of the police to protect the citizen. We cannot tolerate citizens taking the law into their own hands. You acted unilaterally to punish the alleged perpetrator without due process. This is intolerable in a lawful society."

"How many police officers are there in Washington?" Charlie asked.

"I don't know," the judge replied. "What does that matter?"

"Because there aren't enough to protect everyone," Charlie answered. "You take away a person's right to defend themselves and they are automatic victims of anyone willing to break the law. First, you disarmed the law-abiding with gun control laws. And now you've made it illegal for them to fight off an assault with their bare hands."

Charlie remembered the fire in her grandmother's eyes when she showed Charlie her illicit handgun. She said she didn't care what any idiotic law stated; she would kill anyone who tried to violate her home. She'd rather spend time in jail alive than be permanently dead.

The judge glared at her and the public defender said, "Ms. Jones has decided to plead guilty in exchange for the government's recommendation for a fine and a suspended sentence with probation."

The judge looked at Charlie. She was debating if that was acceptable.

"We have a rather full docket," the government's attorney stated flatly.

That decided the judge. "Okay, Ms. Jones," she proclaimed, "sixty days suspended and one year probation, plus a thousand dollar fine, court costs, and police department reimbursement. You can pay the clerk when you leave."

Charlie was about to stand to leave when the judge said, "However, Ms. Jones," and proceeded to lecture Charlie on a) not taking the law into her own hands, b) no property is worth protecting with violence, and c) she was in the U.S. now, not in space, and subject to the laws of the United States and not, what the judge implied, were the low moral values of Space Resources Incorporated.

Charlie waited with infinite patience during the diatribe. When the judge was finished Charlie stood silently and walked out of the office. Freeman followed, hurrying to catch Charlie, who was almost running.

"God damn it!" Charlie growled at him in the corridor.

"I'll take you to a hotel to rest," Freeman said calmly. "We'll meet tomorrow. I'll pick you up so you won't have any trouble."

"Damn that woman," Charlie spat, refusing to calm down.

"Come on," Freeman said, reaching for her arm. "You'll feel better after some rest."

Charlie let him hold her arm and pull her toward the elevator. They paid the clerk, who accepted Charlie's payment from her computer's SRI account. Charlie was sure Mitchel would approve the expense.

Then the clerk asked, "Residence?"

"Huh?" Charlie blurted.

"We have to sign you up on probation," the clerk explained. "Residence?"

Charlie looked at Freeman.

"Tell him what he needs to know," Freeman instructed her.

"Space Resources Incorporated Facility, Room 210, Nippon/European Space Agency Facility One, the Moon, in care of Space Resources Incorporated, Tokyo, Japan."

The clerk looked at her. "Don't you have a more, uhm, local address?"

"No," Charlie said, again growing angry.

The clerk sighed and typed on his computer. "Employer?"

"Space Resources Incorporated, Tokyo, Japan."

"Do they have a more local office?"

Charlie knew there was a United States Liaison Office in Washington but she didn't know anything about it other than part of its function was to house security's Eastern United States Terrestrial Information Gathering Office. "Yes," she said. "But I don't know the address or number."

"Fine," the clerk mumbled. "Name and address of a person who would always know how to locate you?"

Charlie rolled her eyes and wondered when the humiliation would stop. "Eugene Mitchel, Head of Security, Space Resources..."

***

Griffin watched Knecht work the computer. She was plotting their course to the asteroid belt.

"Where'd you learn this stuff?" he asked.

"Stuff?" Knecht asked without looking up.

"Yeah: navigation, computers, ship piloting."

"The Space Resources Incorporated School in Boulder, Colorado."

"You worked for SRI?" he asked incredulously.

She nodded. Griffin liked the way her hair moved in zero-gee when she did that.

"I wanted to get out of the United States. I saw SRI as the way out."

"Didn't you know what they're doing to the environment and to space?"

Knecht shrugged. "Not really. I didn't get involved in the GA until later."

84

"How?"

She turned and looked at him. For the first time he noticed the blaze of her sea-green eyes.

"SRI recruited me in Los Angeles. After graduating the SRI school, I had no place to go for the customary vacation, so I went to L.A. You know, Disneyland-California, the beach, the whole thing. That was where I met Linda."

"Trent?"

"Yeah. She taught me about SRI and its degradation of the environment. She taught me there can be no compromise when it comes to protecting Mother Earth and her solar system. I honestly didn't know the danger of taking asteroids out of the asteroid belt. She got me into the Gaia Alliance. Then I went to the safe house in Los Angeles and Beatty taught me about the revolution."

"Beatty," Griffin snorted, "is slime; right now, a useful slime."

"He's all right. Besides, the world's full of slimy people," Knecht stated flatly.

"What do you mean?"

"Nothing."

Griffin could tell from her voice that it wasn't "nothing."

If I could get her to open up, talk about what makes her so angry, he thought. "Okay," he said. "I understand."

"I doubt that," she snorted, almost mockingly.

"I've had my problems," he said. "I know what it's like."

"No," she grumbled, "not like me."

"What do you mean?"

Momentarily her eyes flashed in anger. Then they softened and he could see deep, searing sorrow. "When I was fourteen," she said softly, "I ran away from home. My stepfather liked me too much. I was just a thing to him to get what he couldn't get or didn't want from my mother. It was typical–I've read up on this kind of thing. When I told my mother, she said she didn't believe me and called me a slut. I went to her for help and she rejected me, I think because she did believe me and was jealous; I'd taken her husband away. I sure as hell didn't want him."

"Oh, God," Griffin whispered. "I'm sorry." This confession was not what he had expected.

Knecht shrugged her shoulders. She knew his sympathy would do nothing about what she felt. "I ran away," she said, "to Seattle. I met a man in a bus station. At first he said he loved me. Then he beat me and was worse than my stepfather. To him I was just a thing to make money."

"You mean...?" Griffin asked.

"Yes, I prostituted for him. At first he was all sweetness and love. Do you know what that will do to a love-starved fourteen-year old? It was like a drug. I'd do anything for it. And I did, even after the 'love' was gone. I blamed myself when he beat me, thinking I'd failed him and deserved it. And he beat me almost daily for not making enough money, for not pleasing some john just right. All a man had to do was look at him funny and he'd think I hadn't done a good job. He almost killed me a couple of times."

"Oh, God," Griffin said softly.

"I finally got away. He said he'd kill me. That's why I joined SRI. I figured he couldn't find me off Earth. But I was just a thing to them to make a profit: although the prostitution wasn't as personal.

"Then I met Linda Trent in L.A. She convinced me I could find what I was looking for in the Gaia Alliance. But even to her I was just a thing to advance the revolution." She shook her head. "I've known since I was eleven and a half what sex is. I still don't know what love is."

Griffin looked at her. Like this, open and trusting, she was a lovely woman, not a guerrilla soldier. He took a chance.

"Is that why you hate so?"

"I don't hate, except my stepfather, my pimp, and SRI. I just can't trust. I put up a barrier between myself and others that I never let down."

She looked at him and for a moment their eyes locked.

Then she looked away. When she looked back, Griffin could tell her armor was back in place, protecting her from any possible hurt another may cause her. "Anyway," she said, "Trent told me about the real danger of taking asteroids out of the belt. That's why I agreed to help with this attack."

"You mean," Griffin asked, "the GRT? That taking asteroids upsets the gravitational balance and having asteroids' orbits decay so that they could hit Earth?"

"Yes," Knecht acknowledged. "I resigned from SRI and joined the GA. How about you?"

Griffin shrugged. "My parents were Earth Firsters. They taught me what you said about no compromise. But their methods were ineffective. Hell, Earth Firsters have been around a hundred years.

"When I heard about the GA, I joined. I agree that chaining yourself to trees isn't enough. Nothing is ever going to change without violence. Revolution is the only way to change society."

Knecht nodded in agreement. Griffin smiled and she smiled back. They'd found a common, albeit bloody, ground.

***

"I'm sorry about your reception," Freeman said, driving Charlie to the FBI building in his nondescript, late-model Fiat the next morning.

"I'm sorry I yelled at you," Charlie growled, shaking her head. "I was just so damn mad. Now I know why I got the hell out of the United States."

"Yeah," Freeman said. "Like rats leaving a sinking ship."

"Huh?" Charlie asked angrily, not sure if she'd just been attacked verbally again.

"It's just that some of the best Americans are going into SRI, or NESA. Some are even going to the Russian Federation. I know the U.S. has problems, lots of problems, but I'm not going to abandon it."

Charlie looked at Freeman differently. He was a patriot and a man who took duty and loyalty seriously. Charlie admired that even if she felt the U.S. was a long lost cause.

"Okay," she said conciliatorily. "How can I help you?"

"I need your help to nail Linda Trent."

"I understand. Mitch said she could look into FBI files."

"That's not totally true. But she has a friend, Congresswoman Polasky, on the Congressional FBI Oversight Committee, who can. So I can't move against her without her knowing it. Then she can put pressure on the administration and my boss, the director, is part of that administration."

"Why does she have so much power with the administration?" Charlie asked. "She's not in its party."

"No," Freeman said. "But that party is bending over backwards to cater to the Greens. They see part of their power being eroded by small, one issue parties like the Greens, the National Party for Womyn, the Economic Justice and Peace Party. The majority coalition in Congress would fall apart without support from the minor parties.

"Also, the president was partially elected on an environmental platform. They say they're going to clean up the environment."

"Are they kidding?" Charlie asked. "The environment is the cleanest it's been for centuries. Don't they remember when cities had smog because of gasoline and diesel burning cars? There's hardly a hydrocarbon burned in the U.S. except for plant-based ones. The water's clean. Per person, man pollutes less now than since we first crawled out of the slime."

Freeman held a hand up. "I know, I know. I'm on your side. Anyway, under the last administration, the FBI investigated environmental groups to determine if they were possible terrorist threats. But we were a bit overzealous and newspaper reports that we were investigating little old ladies that contributed to the Sierra Club were not too much of an exaggeration. Now the FBI Oversight Committee frowns on any action against environmentalists."

"But the GA blew up SRI's antenna field in the Mojave," Charlie protested.

Freeman nodded. "I know. But according to the GA, that was an individual act of a member, Trent, and not sanctioned by the group. The indictment was thrown out after it was shown that

Trent's car had been illegally searched so the fuses and explosives couldn't be admitted as evidence."

"Right," Charlie said sarcastically.

"Fourth Amendment protection," Freeman intoned.

"Don't talk to me about Constitutional protection," Charlie grumbled. "I learned about that last night."

"I know, I'm sorry." Freeman added, "I'm in a tenuous position because I don't have the 'proper sensitivity' to the environment, minorities, the homeless, the differently abled, etcetera."

Charlie shook her head. "Okay, what do I do?"

"First, get close to Trent."

"How?"

Freeman looked at Charlie. "That shouldn't be too hard."

***

Bente Naguchi didn't enter the lab but, from the door, watched her father work. He moved purposely and exactingly from instrument to instrument. She knew he was working on low-pressure superconductors. High temperature superconductors were common but all were pressure sensitive and became resistant to electrons as the atmospheric pressure decreased. None worked in vacuum. A low-pressure superconductor would be a great help to all space work. The Moon was the perfect place for her father's work. On Earth a vacuum is an expensive and tenuous thing to create. On the Moon, vacuum was free and on the other side of every exterior wall.

Mr. Naguchi finally noticed his daughter's long form filling the doorway. "Come in, Bente," he said. "I've just about got this machine programmed."

She watched him work silently for a few minutes. She realized just how much she loved this cranky old man. Finished with his machine, he walked over to her and looked up at her face. She sat in a chair to be polite, almost bringing them face to face.

"Father," she said, "I'm leaving today. I'm going to the asteroid belt."

He nodded. "Be careful, Bente."

"I will, Father. But there is really very little danger."

"Yes, of course. Have you said your farewells to your mother and brother?"

"Yes, Father."

"Good."

There was heavy silence.

A chromatograph beeped anxiously.

"Now what is wrong?" Mr. Naguchi exclaimed. He walked to the petulant instrument and looked at the display. "This will take a while, Bente."

"It's okay," she whispered. "I've got to go."

"Fine," he replied, waving over his shoulder but already enmeshed in working the instrument.

She watched him work, already in total concentration. His work was always so important to him. She guessed that was true of any dedicated scientist, or anyone committed to their work.

She loved him for it, but wished he'd find time for her.

"Good-bye, Father," she said.

"Good-bye," he replied perfunctorily.

***

It was the first truly spring morning of the year in Boulder. The sky was a dome of lapis lazuli etched with high, white cirrus clouds. The wall of the Rocky Mountains, which ran right up to the city's western edge, was dressed in frosty white and cool green. The morning sun was like a warm klieg light highlighting their best features. From the kitchen window in their house, Alex could imagine they grew right out of the backyard.

Alex, while washing his breakfast dishes, thought it was just his luck. The first nice day and he was leaving. His southern California childhood and the shirtsleeve, temperature controlled environment of space had given him an unusually large aversion to cold weather.

He heard Kirsten walk up behind him. She enveloped him in her long arms and kissed his neck. She smelled of soap and the clean towel she was wrapped in. Alex turned in her arms and found her mouth ready for a quick kiss.

"'Morning," she breathed a moment later. "You're up early."

He nodded. "Couldn't sleep."

"Anxious about going back into space?" she asked, sitting at the small breakfast table in a sunny atrium just off the kitchen.

Her towel almost fell off but she caught it and adjusted its tension.

He shrugged. "I guess." He dried his hands on a dishtowel and joined her at the table. *She's damn sexy like this,* he thought. He wondered briefly if she was doing this on purpose.

"You want some breakfast?" he asked casually.

"I'll just have a grapefruit," she replied.

Alex made a sour face but went to the 'fridge after securing a knife.

"Is it because you're the director you're nervous about going back?" she called after him.

"No," he said with his head in the refrigerator, "it's that you look too good to leave behind."

"Thanks," she purred. Then she took on a more serious tone: "But really, Alex, is it that you're the director now?"

He returned with a spoon and half the pink citrus on a small plate.

"Maybe," he mumbled, setting the fruit down in front of her. "It's kind of intimidating."

Sitting down, he noticed the room's computer monitor was displaying "ORDERING MORE GRAPEFRUIT" with a choice to cancel or modify inventory. He saw that the half he gave her had the chip embedded in the skin that the refrigerator used to count grapefruit. Since only Kirsten ate the, in Alex's opinion, disagreeable fruit, she wouldn't have to adjust the computer's inventory records since he was leaving.

"How's that?" she asked, ignoring her food.

"Well," he said, "there's about 130 people on a typical asteroid. I'm responsible for all of them. People get killed out there, Kirsten. Accidents happen and now this damn Gaia Alliance. I don't know what I'd do if I screwed up and someone died."

Kirsten looked at him intently. "You're good at your job, aren't you?"

"Yes. But am I good enough?"

"I don't know, Alex. You'll have to decide that."

Alex looked at her askance. "I hate when you do that."

"Do what?"

"Psychoanalyze me."

"I'm sorry," she said. "I was just trying to help."

"I know. And I guess I'll just have to do my best and hope it's good enough."

"I'm sure it will be," she said. She looked at her bare wrist. "What time is it?"

Alex looked at the computer (now noting, "GRAPEFRUIT WILL ARRIVE NEXT DELIVERY"). "Ten after ten."

"Damn, I really slept in. I'd better get dressed if I'm going to drive you to the airport." She stood up and kissed him. "I won't be long."

The separation at the airport was, as usual, painful.

"I love you," Alex said. Two weeks had gone too fast. Kirsten held him tight. He had to turn his head or be smothered in her shoulder. "I love you, too," she replied. "Be careful."

Alex nodded. "Aren't I always?"

"I know, but this GA thing–it scares me. Nobody knows what happened to that ship and what they're going to do with it."

Alex pulled away so he could look at his wife. "Yeah, it scares me, too. You can predict the dangers of space but these fanatics are unpredictable." He'd thought hard about it. The *Rock Skipper* accelerated at one and a half gees; it could build up velocity, and therefore kinetic energy, very quickly. If the terrorists were on a suicide mission, just ramming the ship into something like an asteroid at a high difference of velocity could be devastating.

The P.A. system announced, "Last call for United flight 102 with non-stop service to Los Angeles at gate seven." In L.A. Alex was going to connect with a spaceplane for the flight to

Esmeraldas on the Ecuadorian coast, where SRI's space facility was located.

"I've got to go," Alex said quickly.

"I know."

"Love ya."

"You, too."

Kirsten watched him wave his wrist-mounted computer over the sensor at the gate, which opened to let him pass. He walked into the secure area, getting ready for inspection, and out of her sight.

They never did talk about Frank's death, she realized. She mentally kicked herself and returned to her car.

***

The red Ford pickup maneuvered along the road. It was old and dirty with enough dents and bends in its sheet metal to look like a refugee from a demolition derby. But William Thorne knew that, to his father, a vehicle was a tool and, if it could do its job, its appearance did not matter.

"This road is terrible," the younger Thorne observed as the truck was jostled over the crumbling asphalt.

"Every year it gets worse," his father said. "Winters are hard on the roads around here; gets harder to get the harvest to market. They keep raising taxes but we don't seem to see the benefits."

Bill looked around. The fields were barren now, as the last of the snow had disappeared. The mountains bordering the arid Snake River Valley were still snowy-white, but the irrigated potato farms around the river were quagmires of mud. The interstate highway followed the general course of the Snake River south where, in a Nile effect, the only towns of any consequence lined up along its shores.

"You've been living in Saigon?" his father asked perfunctorily.

"Yes."

"Alone?"

"No. I lived with a local woman."

"Why?"

"I dunno," Bill said. What could he say to his father that the old man would understand? That she was the best damn thing in

93

bed he'd ever known? That it ended as all his affairs did: with a painful rupture that left Bill, at least, hemorrhaging emotionally. He assumed the women felt the same, but didn't know. Could he tell his father he wanted to fall in love and make it last? No, his father would want to know—

"Bill," Mr. Thorne said, cutting off his son's thoughts, "when are you going to settle down and have a family?"

"My job, Pa..."

"No one working for SRI has a family?"

Thorne thought briefly about Alex Chun and his wife. "Some do."

"Then, why not you?"

"I dunno." What was it about being with his parents that turned him into a child?

"You should have stayed here," his father continued. "You could raise a family here."

"I know, but..." But what? How could he tell his father what it was like having your feet in Idaho mud while your head was full of stars? Those damn stars that, in the pitch-blackness of the night sky over the family farm, called to Bill as he finished his chores late at night? No, his father never looked up–always down at the dirt, not able to see beyond next season's planting and harvest.

So he'd stayed away from his family and rejected their simple values. Everything was black and white to them, good or evil. He wished his life was that simple but it never could be again. How you going to keep them down on the farm when they've seen the stars from space?

"Thanks," he said, "for driving me to the airport, Pa."

"You're welcome, son. And thank you for visiting. It meant a lot to your mother. You should come more often."

"Pa, I haven't been here in ten years, at least."

"I know, son."

The pickup bounced down Interstate 15.

*** *** ***

"Hello," the very tall girl said. "You must be Director Chun."

94

Alex looked at her. She was obviously a native of the Moon and, like himself, Oriental-Occidental mix. On her it was a combination that made her a rare beauty.

Alex was waiting in an employee lounge for the shuttle from the Low Earth Orbit Facility to the *Kyushu* that would take them to the belt. He was, as usual, not feeling well in free-fall.

It wasn't any surprise she recognized him. Like her, he was wearing the blue, standard jumpsuit/uniform with the SRI patch on the left shoulder. The director insignia over his heart and the security patch on his right shoulder identified him as the only director to come out of Security Division. Under his director insignia was a crescent Jupiter with a gray, mottled Europa he'd earned as part of the first expedition to that moon. The row of bars on his sleeve testified to his years of space experience. His constellation of stars was smaller than Mitchel's, but Chun had three red stars for trips as Assistant Director. On this trip he'd earn his first blue star.

"Yes," he answered her, "I'm Chun. I'd guess you are Bente Naguchi. I hear you're a very good navigator."

She smiled self-consciously. "I just do my best."

"Well, I hear your best is pretty good," Alex said.

"Thank you," she replied. She had only two stars and one bar.

"Director Chun?" a deep, resonant voice said. Alex turned to see the biggest and blackest man he'd ever faced. He was tall, taller than Chun's wife, probably almost 200 centimeters. With him was a pale woman with a long, angular face who Alex recognized as Lorraine Taylor.

"Yes?" Alex asked the massive man.

"I'm Philip Banda; your Assistant Director."

Alex nodded, looking up at the man's black face. "I'm glad to meet you, finally. I've heard a lot of good things about you. I thought you'd be taller," he joked. Banda just stared at him but Naguchi smiled.

"Hello, Director Chun," Taylor said.

"Hi, Lorraine," Alex replied. "It'll be good to have you on life support."

95

"Thank you," she said, smiling.

Alex looked at the bunch and thought they were typical of SRI: a Korean-American man, a white American woman, a Japanese-European woman born on the Moon, and an African black man all working together.

"Alex, you son of a—" a familiar voice called out. Alex turned his head to see his old friend William Thorne move up to the group. Thorne was looking at Bente. He turned back to Alex.

"How ya doing, Alex?"

"Fine," Alex said extending a hand. Thorne took it and they clasped hands without shaking. "How are you?"

"Pretty good, Alex. Thanks for requesting me for your security chief."

Alex frowned. "Bill, I didn't."

Thorne shrugged. "I just assumed when I heard you were the director."

"I guess we just got lucky," Alex said with a chuckle. "It'll be good to have at least one old friend to pick me up when I step on it."

"You should have never left security, Alex."

Alex looked at the people he was to lead and they were only a few of the hundred and thirty or so.

"Sometimes, Bill, I think you're right."

CHAPTER SEVEN

"...asked to sacrifice your life to the Earth and Her solar system."

Mr. Kijoto was a hard man to see. As CEO of SRI, in his hands were virtual strings that ran to hundreds of divisions, contractors and sub-contractors all around the Earth and as far away as Jupiter. Some said that, other than national leaders, he was the most powerful man in the world. Others said even some national leaders didn't hold the power cradled in the old, Japanese man.

But he made time when his Chief of Security Mitchel said he had news concerning the *Rock Skipper*.

One might think that the graying, wrinkled man, as he sat quiescent in his massive chair with his eyes closed and his fingertips touching, was a doting old man. But his questions always proved his mind to be as keen as an edge filed down to mono-atomic thickness.

Mitchel had just related all he knew about the *Rock Skipper*, the missiles, Cole, former employee Knecht, the Syrians, and the Gaia Alliance.

"Why," Kijoto asked, "was this Cole woman allowed to work on a sensitive project?"

Mitchel sighed. "Joe Murda, from the San Francisco office, talked to a manager at West Coast Missile systems. According to her, a California law prohibits job discrimination on the basis of political affiliations or sympathies. Cole was denied the security clearance necessary to work on the missiles, a better paying job, because of her GA sympathies. She complained to the state. It threatened to sue West Coast Missile Systems. So they put her to work on the missiles to avoid a long and expensive court battle."

Kijoto thought for a moment. Then: "Did you question anyone from the Syrian ship?"

"Yes," Mitchel said. "The Syrians rarely let the crew out of their compound, just the officers. Rodriguez found a junior officer who was willing to talk if we kept him well lubricated with alcohol and offered him some euros. He said the Syrian ship did indeed rendezvous with another ship somewhere between Earth and the Moon. We showed him a picture of the *Rock Skipper* and he thinks that's the ship. But he knows the missiles were transferred to the other ship."

"Could the space-to-space missiles be installed on the *Rock Skipper*?"

"I talked to engineers at West Coast Missile Systems and sent the specs Elisa Morgan got from the French on the Pumas. They think it could easily be done. And Cole probably could do it."

"What is the possibility the missiles are nuclear tipped?"

"Slim," Mitchel said. "The Puma is a modified anti-ship missile. It carries about a five hundred kilo warhead. According to information the Mossad gave Morgan in Tel Aviv, the Syrians can't make nukes that small. That's why they use the Chinese Long March: they need the lifting power. Also, I don't think they'd give away a nuclear weapon, and even the GA couldn't afford to buy one."

Kijoto considered that a moment. "Do you have any idea for what they intend to use the missiles and the ship?"

Mitchel shook his head. "No idea; obviously an attack on something. It might not even be us."

"Yes," Kijoto said, "but it would be our ship. That makes us responsible. You have done good work. You will bring me the information on the target as soon as you can."

Mitchel knew when he was excused. He stood and walked out the door.

Kijoto waited until Mitchel had made his way out of the expansive office. Then he turned to his computer and called up an address.

"Review all contracts we have with companies located in California. We may need to cancel them...yes, all of them."

***

Charlie left her SRI ID with Freeman. She also gave him her watch/cellular phone/pager/computer terminal in exchange for a generic, cheap one.

Her face was devoid of makeup and she had let her hair go its own frazzled way. She wore corduroy pants and a flannel shirt. She hoped she wasn't overdoing it. At least her Nikes weren't replaced with hiking boots.

She waited on the east side of the Capitol. It was pretty safe with the Capitol police watching for threats against the Congress. They eyed her suspiciously but didn't harass her and probably wouldn't, at least until curfew.

Some workmen were cleaning black graffiti off the white marble. They also eyed her.

Charlie recognized Trent when she came out of the building. She was about 40 and dumpy with short, brown hair. She wore hiking boots.

"Congresswoman Trent," Charlie called out.

The police watched carefully as Charlie walked toward Trent.

"Yes," Trent confirmed.

"Hi," Charlie said coming closer. She kept her hands in sight as some of the police closed in.

Trent looked Charlie over. Charlie had seen that look before but usually from men.

"What can I do for you?" Trent asked. She made some signal and the police backed away, but still watched carefully.

"My name," Charlie said, "is Shari Johnson. I'm from Maine. I came here to meet you, Ms. Trent."

"Why?" Trent asked, starting to walk toward the south.

Charlie followed. "I read about you, how you are involved in the Gaia Alliance and how you're fighting for the Earth. I admire that. I admire that a lot."

"Thank you."

"And," Charlie said, "I was wondering if I could help in some way."

Trent stopped walking and looked her over. From the way she looked at her, Charlie half expected her to lick her chops.

"I think you might. Where are you staying?"

"At a homeless shelter on Massachusetts."

Trent nodded. "You'll be there about nine tonight?"

Charlie shrugged her shoulders. "I can be."

"Good," Trent said. "What's the address?"

"Two-fourteen Massachusetts Avenue Northeast."

"Someone will meet you there."

"Great," Charlie said, trying to sound enthusiastic.

Trent walked away.

Charlie didn't like the homeless shelter at all. These people may be homeless but they weren't weaponless. While she could defend herself, she didn't want to be accused of any more "unlawful self-defenses." And, as she waited, every hour her tension grew exponentially. If she screwed up with the GA, not Mitchel or Freeman or anyone else could save her–she was on her own.

Charlie had arrived about six and eaten the free meal. She wanted to keep up appearances in case she was watched. Freeman warned her not to underestimate the resources of the GA. Hell, Shari Johnson was a real person that Freeman had convinced to disappear for a while. He didn't elaborate how he accomplished that.

About nine, Charlie saw a woman walk in and look around. She was tall and thin, almost to the point of emaciation. She had a hard, chiseled face. She spotted Charlie and walked over to her.

"Shari Johnson?" she asked.

"Yes," Charlie replied.

"I'm a friend of Linda Trent's. Come with me." The woman turned and walked away. Charlie grabbed her bag and followed. They left the shelter and walked down the street a few blocks in silence. The woman didn't seem to even acknowledge Charlie's presence.

They took an escalator down to the Metro. Stepping over the prone bodies of the homeless and ignoring the almost overpowering smell of human waste, they bought tickets and went to the platform. When the next train came the woman got on a car and Charlie followed. After a few seconds there was a low dinging to warn that the doors were about to close.

"Come on," the woman barked and jumped out of the car.

Charlie hesitated a second before complying. Hesitation kills, she thought, as the doors just about closed on her.

Wordlessly the woman climbed back to street level (the up escalator was inoperative). About a block away she unlocked a battered, old electric car. They drove a circuitous path around town while the woman checked her mirrors frequently. Finally, they passed the Pentagon and crossed into Alexandria.

The woman pulled the car into the driveway of an old house in a wooded residential neighborhood. They pulled under a carport by a side door to the house. The woman got out of the car and Charlie again had to follow. Charlie wondered why all the cloak-and-dagger if their base of operations was a house in a suburb. One wouldn't have to follow them, just stake out the house.

The woman used a key to open the door and they entered the kitchen. Charlie looked around and noticed that the kitchen's technology was circa late twentieth century. Linda Trent came into the simple but clean room. She was wearing a plaid robe over her cottage-cheese like skin.

"Thank you, Vera," Trent said. "Hello, Shari."

Charlie nodded politely. "Hello, Congresswoman Trent."

Trent moved closer to her. "Linda, please."

Charlie smiled. "Linda."

Trent reached out for Charlie's arm. "Come here, Shari. Tell me about yourself."

***

Mitchel studied the picture on his computer screen. The woman was pretty, he noted, with thick brunette hair. She didn't look like a terrorist. He berated himself for judging her by her appearance; he didn't do that to men nearly as often as he did to women.

He looked at her school record. She'd been what was internally referred to as a political trainee. Most Americans that applied to SRI were products of the degenerate education system in the U.S. and ended up in security simply because it was the least technical job in SRI. But every new employee was scrutinized for intelligence with a simple logic test that required no knowledge. Those that tested well were trained in technical jobs no matter what their education level. This meant the Boulder school, which started as a rock climbing school for SRI security and miners, taught everything from basic math and algebra to advanced space navigation. This was an attempt to get Americans into better jobs than security and dissuade the popularly held belief, in the U.S. at least, that the Japanese-owned Space Resource Incorporated discriminated against Americans. That perception had actually prompted some American politicians to call for economic sanctions against SRI. SRI did enough business in America to warrant action to counter that threat.

The need, the political need, for such a double standard bothered Mitchel. SRI would train in the space-skills that no terrestrial university had yet bothered to add to their curriculum. But, anyone, other than an American, coming into SRI had better know their math and science first.

Knecht had done well and learned fast. Her navigation instructor indicated she did so well on her training cruise to the Moon and back she should be assigned to a trans-lunar shuttle as a third navigator.

Knecht took some vacation time and failed to return. Only a terse computer call resigning, long after she was due back, indicated she was still alive–until she showed up on the Moon with the GA.

That's strange, Mitchel thought. Why she would give up a promising career in SRI for the Gaia Alliance was a complete mystery.

The computer beeped, suspending Mitchel's ruminations.

"Yes?"

"Mr. Mitchel," Meyoung said over the terminal in voice mode only, "I have a call from Mr. Lloyd of the liaison office in Moscow."

"Russia?" Mitchel asked. "Put him through." The SRI logo on the desktop monitor was replaced by an unfamiliar face.

"Yes?" Mitchel asked.

"Mr. Mitchel, this is David Lloyd," the caller said. He was wearing a business suit but was using an SRI Security code.

"Yes?" Mitchel repeated.

"I am," Lloyd stated, "the SRI liaison officer to the Russian Federation."

"Nice to meet you, Mr. Lloyd," Mitchel said. "What can I do for you?"

"The Russian Space Command informed me that their ship, the *Peter the Great,* found ten missiles two days ago." A blue box appeared in the lower left-hand corner of the screen. It was covered with groups of ten alphanumeric characters. "Those are," Lloyd continued, "the serial numbers from the missiles."

"Just a moment," Mitchel said. He had his computer call up the data on the *Rock Skippers'* last load-out of probe missiles. Another box appeared in the lower right-hand corner of the screen with those numbers. The screen was getting too complicated so Mitchel transferred the numbers to the wall screen where they lined up next to each other. He had the computer sort both sets alphanumerically.

They matched.

"Mr. Lloyd," Mitchel asked, "did the Russians say where these were found?"

"They were in Earth orbit at an altitude of about 150 thousand kilometers."

Mitchel wondered briefly what the Russians were doing out there.

"The Russians," Lloyd added, "will return the missiles for standard rescue fees."

"I can't authorize that," Mitchel said.

"Then who can?"

"Nakata or Yamada; I can connect you."

"Thank you, that would be fine."

Mitchel used the computer. "Meyoung, transfer this call to the Director of Space Operations and if he's busy, to Nakata."

"Yes, Mr. Mitchel."

Mitchel sat back and thought. They'd need to jettison the missiles on the *Rock Skipper*. It was just dumb luck the Russians found them. Or was it? No, if he thought that way he'd be chasing shadows. But this confirmed that the Syrian ship, *Baath Revolution*, rendezvoused with the *Rock Skipper*. It was only a matter of time before the GA used those Puma missiles somewhere.

***

The next morning Charlie took a long shower; she had to.

The water came out of the showerhead at about the rate a baby drools and around the same temperature at its hottest.

Charlie got out of the shower and was drying when Trent walked in. She kissed Charlie on the mouth.

"You shouldn't take such long showers," she said. "Wastes water and energy."

"I'm sorry," Charlie said, wondering how these people got clean.

"Don't be," Trent said. "You're still learning. Breakfast is soon." She dropped her robe and climbed into the shower. She was out before Charlie thought she had time to get wet.

Breakfast was fruit and homemade cereal. Some fruit was going bad and Charlie was about to throw it out when she noticed her hosts were actually consuming it.

Charlie forced herself to eat it but wondered why the fruit was going bad when there were so many ways to keep it fresh.

During the meal Vera didn't meet Charlie's eyes and Trent noticed.

"This is wonderful," Trent said joyfully.

"How's that?" Vera asked sullenly.

"Us three women," Trent explained, "united for Mother Earth."

"Oh," Vera mumbled.

"You know, Shari," Trent continued, "as women we have a special bond to the Earth and a special responsibility. We are the givers of life and the nurturers, just as the Earth nurtures us and gives us life. Men, on the other hand, exploit the Earth just like they exploit women, and abuse the Earth just like they abuse women. Women must band together to protect the Earth, and each other, from the violations of men."

Charlie nodded as if she understood, but knew that Trent's libel of all men was as invalid as every other racist or sexist stereotyping she had ever heard.

"Shari," Trent said, "I want you to stay here while Vera and I go into Washington to work. Don't leave this house, don't answer the phone—understand?"

Charlie nodded, thinking, "Phone"? Since the early part of the century the phone, television, and computer had all been pretty much integrated into one instrument usually called the computer; although some people were starting to call them "'puters" for short and even "putes." She wondered if this meant Trent had an actual voice only, antique and obsolete-as-hell telephone. She would have to have some kind of converter to convert digital fiber optic signals to analog copper wire, but why bother? The house was old but most older houses had been retrofitted with central computer systems. Charlie hadn't noticed until then that this one didn't. She later found the "phone" and it was just a simple computer with a handset.

Later Vera and Trent left. Charlie could hear them arguing outside before they got in the car.

"I don't want her here," Vera growled angrily.

Charlie couldn't understand Trent's reply that came just before she heard the car doors slam shut and the car scrape against the pavement as it pulled into the street.

Charlie searched the small house looking for... anything.

It was an arduous task. Judging by the clutter, Trent and Vera were a couple of pack rats. Every room was filled with clutter composed mainly of books, magazines, and articles. The house was clean, but messy. She was amazed at the amount of paper in the house. Apparently Trent and Vera didn't use tablets to read like most everyone else. She was surprised to find some magazines still printed on paper that had to be hand delivered. *How inefficient is that?* she thought to herself.

Not uncovering anything Freeman or Mitchel would find interesting, she looked for a way to pass time. She finally found a computer but it was a portable model with password protection. Charlie had taken the information security class at Boulder but that was more on how to protect data than extract it. She tried a few obvious passwords but nothing worked. Without a computer, downloading any entertainment off the net was impossible. Also, there might be something useful on the computer. It frustrated her that she couldn't get in it.

There were the books, though–actual paper books. She looked at the authors: Commoner, Mills, Carson, Li, Chomsky, and Foremand. She didn't recognize any of the names but the titles told her what they were all about. Most were environmental; some were just straight politics and always, it seemed, the discredited ideas that wreaked so much havoc in the twentieth century. She skimmed some shorter, environmental ones thinking that if anyone quizzed her on her environmental commitment she'd have a few things to say.

About three in the afternoon the phone/computer beeped loudly. This surprised Charlie; she half expected carrier pigeons in keeping with the low-tech motif.

"Shari, pick up the handset," she heard Vera say.

Charlie complied. "Hello?" There was no video on this small computer, apparently.

106

"Shari," Vera said, "Congresswoman Trent wants to see you in her office. It's in the Rayburn building. You need to hurry so take a cab instead of the bus."

"I don't have any money," Charlie said.

"I'll meet you out front to pay the fare, okay?"

"Okay."

"And don't dawdle."

"Right."

Charlie got a literate cab driver this time. He even knew where the Sam Rayburn building was located. In fact, he said he had a degree in civil engineering.

"They why are you driving a cab?" Charlie inquired.

"No work," he said. "Either our government doesn't have the will or the money to expand or even repair the country's infrastructure. That's why it's crumbling and insufficient for our needs." He said it as if making a speech.

"Spending too much on health care?" Charlie asked.

"No," the driver said. "It's not making the rich and the criminal corporations pay their fair share."

Charlie wondered why "criminal" and "corporation" seemed inexorably linked in the minds of some. Also, last she heard, the U.S. corporate income tax was right around 90 percent, and the rate for those making over a million a year, like herself, was 95 percent. That was yet another reason she'd stopped calling herself an American and paid taxes in Japan.

"Why don't you," she offered, "apply to Space Resources. They use civil engineers, especially with this tunnel project they're working on."

"Are you kidding?" the driver said angrily. "A Japanese company? The Japanese are responsible for the loss of millions of American jobs. I wouldn't work for them for anything."

Charlie wondered why the Japanese (and the Koreans and the Thai and the Filipinos and the Rwandans and everyone else) were blamed for America's economic problems and not the policies of the government that drove business away. She didn't feel like arguing with this victim of common misconceptions. He raged on about "unfair competition" until he stopped his car in front of the old, ugly Rayburn building. Vera was there and she paid the fare from her computer. She lectured Charlie that she should have asked for an electric cab. Hydrogen burners produce nitrous oxides and ozone, Vera intoned. And, she continued, the burning of hydrogen fuels added water vapor to the atmosphere, increased cloud cover, and was responsible for global cooling.

Charlie apologized and followed Vera to Trent's office.

They passed the secretary–he hardly even looked up–and entered Trent's inner office. Trent was sitting behind her desk talking to another woman. Trent looked up.

"Oh, hi, Shari," she said smiling. "Come in; sit down."

Charlie sat in one of the simple chairs that dotted the room. Vera stood behind her.

"Shari," Trent said, "this is Congresswoman Polasky. Janice, this is Shari Johnson."

Charlie smiled at the woman. She was older, about 60 Charlie decided. Unlike Trent's lumberjack basic wardrobe, Polasky was dressed in a stylish red business suit and her silver hair was tastefully done up, and she wore just the right amount of makeup for a woman her age. Charlie wondered what these two had in common except possibly ideology.

Polasky studied Charlie. "No, I don't recognize her. But I'll look into it. Shari," she said, "do you mind?" She held a small camera in her hand.

"No," Charlie said.

Polasky snapped the photo, looked at the camera's display to see if she liked it, and, apparently deciding she did, put the camera in her purse.

"Thanks, Janice," Trent said.

"I'll see myself out." Polasky commented simply. She walked out the door.

"Shari," Trent said after the door closed. "I'm sending you to Los Angeles."

"Los Angeles?"

"Yes. That's where the headquarters of the Gaia Alliance are. You'll be trained and educated. How does that sound?"

"I don't want to go to Los Angeles," she protested weakly. That was exactly what she wanted. There didn't seem to be anything to learn here, living with Trent. She wasn't sure how long she could put off the woman's advances without angering her.

"Don't worry," Trent cooed soothingly. "You'll be in good hands. And you have to stop thinking about yourself and learn to think globally. You may be asked to sacrifice your life to the Earth and Her solar system," Trent preached. "Although that's unlikely," she added quickly.

"Now," she continued, "There's a flight leaving for Los Angeles tonight. What's your computer's address? The GA has limited resources, so don't spend any more than you need, okay?"

Charlie told her the address of the computer on her wrist. Trent punched that into her computer and Charlie's beeped.

"That's a ticket and some money."

"Thank you," Charlie said, not sure what else to say.

"This isn't a game," Trent said in a low voice. "It's a revolution."

"I understand," Charlie confirmed, trying to sound confident.

"I don't think you do," Trent said. "But you will."

Trent stood up and came around her desk and gave Charlie a hug. Then Vera put her hand on Charlie's shoulder in an almost camaraderie-like gesture and smiled. It was the first time she'd smiled in Charlie's experience.

***

The *Kyushu* was an old ship. It was roughly bullet shaped, a hundred meters in diameter and 200 meters long. About seven years before, she'd been one of the first ships with the constant acceleration drives. The power source was a tokamak fusion reactor, cooled by vaporizing lithium. The lithium plasma was used by an MHD generator to produce electricity that the Masuka drives turned into thrust. Before the diminutive Dr. Masuka invented his drive, ships had to get around the solar system via painfully slow Hohmann "low energy" orbits. These took many months. Constant acceleration provided by the Masuka drive shortened the trips from months to weeks. The *Kyushu* left the Lagrange point and accelerated outward. Dragging the kilometer long mass driver behind and burdened with the other equipment to be installed on the asteroid, it barely made 0.07 gees. The trip would take about 18 days. That was slow by modern standards and the *Kyushu* was overdue for a new, more powerful Masuka Drive and the structural reinforcement more thrust would require.

Alex was spending time with each department. He watched drive techs practice installing an emergency door, a skill that every department was supposed to train. All but the tech chief were in pressure suits that were more than usually cumbersome since they weren't in vacuum.

"Okay," the chief said over a hand held radio. "This is simulated vacuum and simulated no acceleration. You've got three minutes. Don't forget to secure your tools." She looked at Alex. "We give 'em some extra time because of the suits."

"I know," Alex said.

The foreman talked into the radio. "Go!"

The three technicians started setting up a metal ring inside a pipe two meters in diameter. The pipe simulated a tunnel cut in the rock of an asteroid.

"So, how are you, Alex?" the chief asked while they watched the exercise. Her name was Diane O'Rourke.

"Fine."

"And Kirsten?"

"She's fine."

"How long's it been since we worked together?"

"Two—"

"Zalesky, you can't do that in free fall," O'Rourke yelled into the radio. "Sorry. You were saying?"

"Two years," Alex said. "The 1752. I was AD and you were the second drive crew foreman."

"Yeah," Diane confirmed. "That's right." Occasionally, Alex noted, he met a person with whom he immediately seemed to have a rapport. This usually developed into a good, strong friendship, and Alex cherished these relationships. Once, when he developed such a relationship with a woman, it metamorphosed into an affair. Now Alex was amazed he'd ever risked his marriage. But Theresa Gold was dead; he'd watched her die but couldn't save her, and he'd killed the man who killed her. It didn't make him feel better like he thought it should, and that was one of two major sources of pain in his life.

When Diane and Alex first worked together they developed such a friendship, although Alex was ten years older. Alex sometimes wondered if she wanted something more. He didn't even let himself think about it.

They watched the work in silence. Once the ring was constructed, a cutting device, much like a circular saw, was mounted to it and started. It circled the frame cutting the pipe, instead of the rock for which it was intended. After circumnavigating the ring the cutter was removed and the ring dismantled. The emergency doorframe was unfolded into the cut slot, the door installed in the frame, and one of the techs simulated sealing the whole thing with damage control foam.

"Okay," O'Rourke said, "Two fifty-four: close. Okay, get out of those suits."

The technicians stripped. They were all sweating heavily and only wore tee shirts and shorts. One was a tall, athletic woman with curly strawberry hair. The sweat made her clothes cling to her skin, accentuating her attractive form. Alex tried not to stare.

"Alex," Thorne's voice drifted through the corridors of the ship. He came into the room. He didn't fail to notice the two attractive women, especially the one with long legs. "Alex," he repeated, "I'm done for the day. How 'bout a drink?"

"Sure," Alex replied. He turned to O'Rourke. "Want to come?"

"Great," she said with a smile, then spoke to her subordinates. "Okay, let's get this gear stowed and call it a day."

The techs moved briskly to secure the training equipment.

When Alex turned to talk to Thorne, he found him enmeshed in conversation with the other woman.

"Bill," Alex called.

"We'll be right there," Thorne replied, waving Alex and Diane away.

***

Faruq drank coffee with General Zuabi. Faruq found it interesting that once, almost five centuries ago, Islamic law prohibited coffee drinking, imposing typically draconian penalties. Now the drink was heavily associated with Muslims that abstained from alcohol. Was it a Westerner that said the only permanent thing was change? Less than 50 years ago, Syria's women dressed in Western garb, including swimwear and high heels. Alcohol was as available as in any Western nation. The ouster of the Alawite usurper's son, Bashar, and the Great Conclave of 2023 changed all that. The meeting, to unite the Syrian and Iraqi arms of the Baathist party, formed a loose confederation of the two nations. United, they conquered the small states on the coast of the Arabian Peninsula, prudently avoiding Saudi Arabia. Once the threat of the occupiers of Palestine was eliminated, Saudi Arabia could be brought into the fold of the United Baath Arab States. Then the president of Syria, Faruq, would be the most powerful man in the Middle East since the Prophet.

However, the unification of the Arab states under the Shia Muslims returned fundamental Islamic law, or *shariah*, to Damascus. When the Americans left Iraq, the out-lawed Baathist party took over. The Iraqi Baathist party, under pressure of a popular revolt supported by Iran, had in less than a twenty-four hour period replaced the American puppet leader, adopted the *shariah*, and made final peace with Iran.

When Iraq and Syria settled their differences at the Conclave, Syria embraced Islamic law. Sunni Muslims had to be oppressed almost as badly as during the days of the Alawite usurper. But, almost overnight *abaya* and *burqa* clad women were the norm, and alcohol couldn't be found. Today, there were villages in Syria almost indistinguishable from the sixteenth century Ottoman province. The more things change, some other Westerner said, the more they remain the same.

"The president," Zuabi said, interrupting Faruq's thoughts, "has lost his revolutionary zeal. He does not move against the Zionist state for fear of the Americans." Since the meeting with Sa'ud and the president, Faruq had noticed Zuabi seemed disheartened. In charge of the Southern Lebanon Occupation Zone, Zuabi had to deal with the Zionist daily.

"Do you really believe," Faruq probed, "a first strike against the Zionist state can succeed?"

"Yes," Zuabi said. "If I were the CinC of the Revolutionary Army, I could make such an attack a triumph for the *Baath Revolution*. But, we need," Zuabi continued, "a leader that can act decisively when the opportunity presents."

Faruq nodded.

The general took a sip of the black brew. "The military would support such a man."

Faruq didn't smile. But he knew the general would support him when the time came. The general commanded Syria's contingent of the United *Baath Revolution*ary Army. And where the Syria contingent led, the army followed. And when Faruq had the presidency, Zuabi would be commander of the United *Baath Revolution*ary Army. Then the final, nuclear solution of the cancer of the Zionist state would be realized.

S EVAN TOWNSEND

CHAPTER EIGHT

"...only in violence there is revolution."

"Then Milhano asked Joey," Alex related with a smile, "'What did Mitchel say?' And Joey says, 'Kill him.'" Alex stopped to laugh with Thorne. "And then Frank DeWite says, 'Great. I haven't seen blood for ages.'" Alex looked around the table. The women were staring at him.

"He was kidding," Alex clarified after he stopped laughing.

Thorne was chortling. "That was what, your second trip to the belt?"

"My third," Alex said. "God, we were young and dumb and full of—" Alex stopped and smiled sheepishly at the women.

"Anyway, Frank had the greatest sense of humor."

"I guess," Diane O'Rourke said incredulously.

The other woman–her name was Diana coincidentally, Diana Vuilard–shook her head. In the low acceleration her long hair continued to move for some time after her head stopped.

"And Milhano was killed about ten years ago," Thorne said somberly. "Three years before Theresa Gold."

The table was quiet. Alex played with his drink in the Erlenmeyer flask-shaped glass.

The *Kyushu*'s saloon was filling with asteroid crew and some off-duty personnel from the ship. Many were already paired up, or something. The long trip gave the asteroid crew much free time.

115

While a great deal of time was spent training, a lot was expended the old fashioned way.

Alex watched these trips with a mixture of fascination, humor, and horror as shipboard romances between the asteroid crew flourished brightly and often withered painfully. The life of an asteroid crew was hard on relationships and creativity in their love lives kept the emotional wear and tear to a minimum.

Some relationships seemed to be continuations of old affairs. The relationship would continue even if years had passed since the two (and sometimes three and four) had been together. Some crew seemed to have extended marriages with a group of people that, wherever two or three gathered together, the nuptial bliss was renewed. Then there were those that moved from one brief relationship to another. From a distance, they seemed to be having a lot of fun. But scratch the surface, and Alex was sure one would find sorrow and loneliness. Thorne had been one of those. Alex had hoped Thi would settle him down but in space, Thorne had acted as if she didn't exist. Now, he had told Alex, that affair was over. And he was moving in on Diana.

Alex, strictly monogamous, was thankful he'd found a wife that didn't mind, even seemed to like, having him gone most of the time. He stayed out of romantic relationships but enjoyed making new friends.

Life Support Chief Taylor passed by arm in arm with a woman from security. She greeted Alex and her friend acknowledged Thorne with a nod. Some music started. It was older stuff, late thirties.

"Wanna dance?" Thorne asked Diana.

She looked at the low gravity gyrations on the small dance floor. "I don't know."

"Come on," Thorne said, pulling her out of her chair and almost losing her because he misjudged her momentum. They went into the crowd and Alex soon lost track of them.

"What do you think the Gaia Alliance's going to do with the *Rock Skipper*?" O'Rourke asked.

Alex looked at her. "What brought that on?"

116

"All your friends that have died–I'm wondering if any more will have to."

Alex looked at his friend. "I hope not," he said softly.

***

Charlie's flight over the continent was hours long. She could almost have saved time flying by spaceplane to Moscow and then to LA. Actual airtime would have been shorter but there was a long layover in Russia. Charlie suspected the Russians planned that for reasons she couldn't discern. And of course, she didn't have SRI resources to pay for such an extravagance anymore. The GA seemed to be a low-budget affair.

Charlie's plane landed at the over-used, too crowded, old, and downright dangerous Los Angeles International. But, there was no place to build a new, better airport or expand LAX. In the city, no one wanted an airport in their backyard. And outside the city, environmentalists bemoaned the damage or loss of habitat or something a new airport would cause. The plane waited on the ground an hour and a half for a gate. This was part of the scheduled duration of the trip. The additional hour of delay wasn't, while they waited in the plane that was slowly roasting in the California sun. The air conditioning was shut off when the engines were shut down, by law, to save fuel and lessen pollution.

In the terminal there was a two-hour wait for the luggage, the stewardess announced. Charlie was glad she only had her one, carry-on bag.

Trent had told her to make a call to a certain address when she arrived. There was no video (yet another "phone"? Charlie wondered). A woman's voice instructed her to wait in front of the baggage claim area and a car would be by.

It was about an hour before an old electric stopped and a man got out. She recognized Harris Beatty: the man Mitchel said had violent crimes in his resume. He was bigger than his picture had led her to believe. She guessed he was over 200 centimeters and a hundred kilos of muscle. He had wavy blond hair and pale blue eyes. His features were melting pot American WASP. If his face wasn't so hard, Charlie would have found him attractive.

117

He looked around, spotted Charlie, and walked over.

"Shari Johnson?" he asked in a way that demanded an immediate response.

"Yes," Charlie said, trying not to sound too nervous.

Perhaps he'd dismiss nervousness as natural for the situation.

"Get in the car," Beatty ordered and walked back to the vehicle. Charlie followed and climbed in. The car moved silently away.

"It's really great to be here," Charlie said lightly.

Beatty just snorted.

"What's your name?" she asked.

"Beatty," he replied simply.

"Where we going?"

"Covina."

"Where's that?"

"East."

Tired of the monosyllabic answers, Charlie relaxed and watched the traffic. That was easy–it moved about ten miles an hour. When they stopped to pay a toll on the freeway, Charlie noticed that the machine punched a card that Beatty carried.

"What's that card?" Charlie asked Beatty.

"Road use ration card," he said.

"Couldn't they automate that?" Charlie wondered out loud. She knew automatic tolling had been around since the 1990s.

Beatty shrugged, making it obvious he didn't care.

The rest of the trip neither spoke. They pulled off the freeway and, after paying another toll and getting the card punched, drove through a housing suburb to a subdivision.

Charlie decided, based on the architecture, that it was built circa 2010. The houses were pretty dilapidated.

Beatty pulled the car into the driveway of one of the houses. It was a larger house but seemed more run down than the rest of the neighborhood.

He got out of the car, plugged it in, and led Charlie inside the house.

***

"The asteroid tender is slow," Knecht explained. She shut down the drive on the *Rock Killer* after getting it into an orbit around the sun. To any radar beam that might happen to wander across it, the ship would appear a very small asteroid. "It'll take two weeks, about, for the tender to get here."

"When was it supposed to leave?" Cole asked.

"A few days ago," Knecht explained, "if they didn't change their plans."

"That's why we burned their computer," Griffin said. "So there's no chance they'd know what we accessed."

"How long after the tender arrives at the asteroid before it's moved?" Cole asked.

"Another two weeks, about," Griffin said.

"So we have nothing to do for a month?" Cole asked, exasperated.

"We'll have to rendezvous with that miner," Griffin said. "Until then, you can get those missiles working."

Cole flushed. She'd had some problems she hadn't anticipated and was having to jury-rig some components.

"Shoulda brought more books," Trudeau grumbled sourly. And he meant books; heavy, bulky paper things that all could have been easily transported on a tablet weighing less than a half a kilo.

"This ship was ready to go. We had to take it then."

Griffin explained. "While we're stuck here I want every component of this ship checked. Knecht, do what you can with the engines."

"There's schematics in the computer," Knecht said. "I can do a lot."

"Good. Trudeau, see about communications and make sure the secure gear's working. If the GA calls I want to be sure we get it. Okay?"

"Right," Trudeau replied, a little less enthusiastically than Griffin would have liked.

"I'm going to get some rest, right now," Knecht said. "I'm beat." She'd been navigating the *Rock Killer* to the asteroid belt without relief. She was able to sleep some, but had been bent over her computer all her waking hours.

"Okay," Griffin said.

Knecht pulled herself down the ladder to the deck below the bridge. Griffin had set up residence in the captain's quarters, leaving the crew's berth for the other three. Knecht went in and undressed. She zippered herself into the shower, her head stuck out the top, and cleaned herself.

She stepped out of the shower and was drying when she heard a noise behind her. She turned to see Cole hovering by the door.

Knecht wasn't startled; casual nudity was the norm in both this ship and the GA safe house in Los Angeles.

"Maddie," Knecht said simply in greeting.

"Hi, Barb," Cole replied. She watched as Knecht completed drying.

"We haven't had time to get to know each other, Barb," Cole said.

Knecht wondered what Cole wanted. "Yes," she replied. She pulled out fresh clothes from the small pack she'd brought on board with her and started dressing which, in free fall, was harder than it looked.

"Linda said that she recruited you into the Alliance?"

"Yes."

"Were you and Linda close?"

Knecht looked at Cole. *So, that's what this is about,* she thought. "No, not really." Linda Trent tended to bring her lovers into the GA.

"We were," Cole mentioned, trying to sound casual.

"Oh," Knecht said, also trying to sound indifferent.

"Why did you join the GA?" Cole asked.

"Trent told me about the dangers to the environment. I've always heard about it on the news, but didn't realize it was as bad as it is."

"Oh," Cole tossed out casually.

Knecht could tell the fat woman was disappointed. She'd hoped that Knecht had joined because of Linda. She was sure that was why Cole joined.

"I really believe in the work of the GA," Knecht continued. "Once in the house in Los Angeles, I learned to hate SRI, and the capitalists like them that are destroying the planet. We have to stop SRI at all costs." Knecht hadn't planned to make a speech. She really did hate Space Resources Incorporated, but Cole should know that already.

"I know," Cole said.

"I will stop SRI no matter what it takes."

"Me, too," Cole droned.

The women looked at each other. Knecht wasn't sure, but she thought Cole looked disappointed. But Knecht had learned that love meant allowing someone to hurt you, no matter the gender of the lover. Even if she liked Cole, which she didn't, she wasn't about to make that mistake again.

"Listen, Maddie, I need to get some rest. And you need to work on the missiles."

"You're right," Cole said. "Sleep well." She turned clumsily in free fall, and moved out of the room.

***

Alex spent a large portion of his days on administration duties. Sometimes he wondered if SRI wasn't going to suffocate in a morass of paperwork. Of course, there was very little actual paper involved, but time spent at his computer was time away from his people.

Alex was working in his quarters when the door chime rang softly. He was one of the few on the ship with a private room.

"Come in," Alex called, actually relieved to have an excuse to stop talking to the computer.

Diana Vuilard walked in. She was in her gray technician uniform and her long hair was under control with a few strategically placed fasteners. "Sorry for the interruption, Director," she said. "May we talk?"

"Sure," Alex replied. "Close the door; sit down."

121

She did, with grace: not easy in the low gravity.

"Director," she started. Alex found it interesting that the other night in the bar he was "Alex" and now, both in uniform, he was "Director."

"How well," she continued, "do you know Bill?"

"Thorne? Pretty well," Alex said, wondering what this was about. "We've worked together a lot."

"He seems kinda old to still be only security chief."

"I don't know," Alex said lightly, although she was right. "But there's nothing wrong with security chief."

"No–but you're younger than him and you're a director."

"Yes?" Alex prodded.

"Well, Director," she said quietly. "I've heard rumors."

"About what?"

"About trouble he got into years ago. They say you were involved."

Alex hesitated. Diana's questions were bringing up old, painful memories. "Why do you ask? That was a long time ago." *Almost 18 years,* Alex thought. And it still hurt, damn it.

"We've grown close the past couple of days," she answered.

Shipboard romance, Alex thought. He hoped this kid was mature enough to handle it.

"But then some others told me stories," she went on. "I don't care if they're true or not, but I'd like to know."

"I don't know what you've heard," Alex said. "Bill made some mistakes when he was younger and they hurt his career. But he's older and a lot smarter now."

"They said," Diana said softly, "something about a murder."

Again Alex had to wait until his emotions boiled down to normal.

"You tell no one this," he ordered.

She nodded her concurrence.

"Eighteen years ago, Thorne and I were in security on an asteroid, just security men." He didn't add that Mitchel was the security chief on that rock. "Thorne had an affair with the director's wife who worked in life support. Either he was a bad husband or she was a bad wife; it doesn't matter. The director tried to kill Thorne. His first attempt he killed my friend, Joey Hernandez, by accident." Alex watched Diana's expression go from surprise to shock to pity.

"The second attempt," Alex continued, "I tried to stop him and accidentally amputated the director's arm. The whole messy incident promoted my career and slowed Thorne's. And for years I blamed him for Joey's death. But after we worked together a few times, I discovered he's a good man who made a dumb mistake. But haven't we all?" This last brought memories of Theresa Gold bubbling up again. *Damn,* Alex thought, *you'd think I'd get through a day without feeling guilty about that.*

While Alex contemplated his past, Diana thought for a moment or two.

"Thanks," she murmured thoughtfully. "I really like Bill. I didn't want to have doubts."

"I hope I've helped," Alex said.

"You have, Director. I have to go back to work. Diane will be wondering what I'm doing."

"What does she have you doing?"

"Emergency procedures drills," she said, rolling her eyes. "She says at turn-around we're going to have an emergency shutdown drill in actual free fall."

"That's a good idea," Alex said cheerfully. "Anything else I can do for you?"

"No," she answered, standing carefully so as not to have her feet leave the floor. "Thanks, Director."

"No problem, Diana."

***

Mitchel talked to his computer. "Projecting normal use for four persons, when will the *Rock Skipper* need to resupply?"

The computer displayed "MAR 14-17." It was the tenth.

"Computer, transcribe message."

A small icon appeared in the corner.

"To: Head of Security McKenna, Ceres station. Sue, the *Rock Skipper* will need provisions in the next week. Independent miners

123

are the logical source. Investigate using any means you can to get information on the *Rock Skipper*. Mr. Kijoto authorized unlimited funds for this investigation.

"Stop transcribing." Mitchel looked at the text on the screen. Light speed delay made conversations impractical and sending text rather than voice would save bandwidth. Satisfied with his message he told the computer to send it. The computer displayed an acknowledgement.

"Maybe we'll get lucky," Mitchel told himself.

***

The problem with these trips, Thorne thought, *is the same problem of peacetime armies.* The only thing to do was drill in the skills one assumed one needed in case of war; or on the asteroid, in security's case. But the repetitious training was demoralizing and it was Thorne's job to make sure the security personnel took it seriously. It made him less than popular with his own subordinates. Once they got on the asteroid and started working the animosity would evaporate, to be replaced by a mutually respectful and amicable working relationship. For that reason, he socialized outside security. Diana Vuilard had been a godsend. After spending the day with his recalcitrant security people, the genuine affection he had felt from the tall, attractive blonde improved his disposition considerably.

But in the last couple of days she'd turned off the relationship like a bad entertainment program. So he was re-reading Niven in the quarters he shared with the asteroid's doctor.

There was a knock on the door.

"Come in," he said, expecting a subordinate with a problem.

Diana walked in. She had replaced her technician uniform with a clinging dress. In the low gravity the skirt was trying its best to indecently expose her.

"Diana," he said, surprised.

She closed the door and locked it. Then she flowed, like mercury, into his arms.

A few minutes later Thorne asked, breathlessly, "What about my roommate?"

"Don't worry," she breathed, and kissed him again.

In the *Kyushu*'s saloon, Alex looked at Dr. Jubair. "Ibrahhim, what would you like to drink?"

"Nothing, thank you," the doctor replied in his soft voice.

Alex looked at Diane. She shrugged. Diana had asked them to keep Jubair busy for at least an hour. But the reticent physician was a challenge to keep entertained.

"Your records show," Alex said, "that you're from the Trucial Coast, Ibrahhim."

"Yes," he replied. "But we don't recognize that name. The Baathist changed it when they conquered the United Arab Emirates."

"How did you get out?" Diane asked. "I thought the Baathists didn't allow educated people to leave."

"My father anticipated the attack and we all left for Europe just weeks before the tanks of the Baathist army rolled across the border."

The doctor spent the next hour describing the rape of his homeland by the Baathists. He stopped the stories of horror only after a very happy looking Thorne and Diana joined the group.

* * *

Charlie spent the next few days at the house doing menial tasks. The interior of the house was old but clean. The walls needed painting and the posters that had been tacked up weren't sufficient to hide the problem. The old carpet, though, seemed to be half dirt and half fiber. The furniture was sparse and old. One corner of the small living room was piled high with books and magazines. The dates on the magazines were all from early in the century, before most everything went electronic online. Charlie counted 15 permanent residents in the house including herself and Beatty. Six were women. There was always cleaning up after the crowd packed into the small domicile, and a garden that needed manual weeding. Charlie didn't wonder why they didn't use genetically engineered bacteria and viruses that attacked only weeds. She found these people had an antipathy for technology.

The house, like Trent's, didn't even have a computer. She wondered why they used electricity.

Charlie helped clean the house using vinegar and baking soda and lemon juice. Her grandmother did the same thing years ago because it was cheaper.

The communal meals of organically grown vegetables were spent in indoctrination. Charlie was learning that organically grown meant pest-infested. There were round table discussions that Beatty or someone else would lead. Charlie wanted to counter their arguments with a few of her own but her "Shari" persona agreed with these nuts. They lectured her on the dangers of industrialism, capitalism, and individualism. It was assumed that totalitarian government was the only solution. She heard about the problems of overpopulation and why drastic measures had to be taken to control the production of babies. The Chinese model was often praised. Charlie had heard about that, and the mandatory sterilization and the post-natal abortions of second children.

When Beatty said there'd have to be a large reduction in human population, she noted all present seemed to assume they weren't the ones that would be sacrificed on the altar of radical environmentalism. Charlie wasn't old enough to know the arguments hadn't changed in almost 100 years.

She was told the joy of living in unity with Gaia. It was almost a religion with these people, she noted. The Earth was almost always anthropomorphically referred to as "Mother" or "Gaia." In fact, almost everything but humans were humanized, so killing off large amounts of people as necessary to save Mother Earth was somehow acceptable, but chopping down a tree became murder. They talked of an invisible spirit world, of magic and special powers of everything from Native American symbols to chunks of quartz. Many in the house wore jewelry with crystals of quartz, hematite, even obsidian. Charlie wondered, since every non-organic solid is a crystal, why doesn't a tin can have the kind of special properties they ascribe to the pretty crystals?

In the Gaia Alliance value system, the superstitions of ancient peoples were preferred to the knowledge of modern science, which was dismissed as non-holistic empiricism, cold and unfriendly, and the creation of dead, European, heterosexual men. This "materialistic science", it was argued, was developed by these men solely to suppress competing world-views that would erode their power over non-Europeans, women, and deviants; that is, unless it backed up their positions on the dangers of global cooling and what SRI was supposedly doing to the asteroid belt.

According to what Charlie was being told, the scientific method of requiring reproducible evidence was a conspiracy to derogate metaphysics and was sexist, racist, and homophobic. To Charlie's thinking, the GA's platform consisted of the wholesale destruction of thousands of years of human struggle to improve life. She continued to look for clues that could lead her to the evidence she sought. But the communal lifestyle—she shared a tiny room with six others—made it almost impossible.

A week after she arrived, Beatty, Charlie, and three others piled into the electric car and drove out of Los Angeles heading east. They stopped in Barstow to buy some electricity. Hours later they continued into the Mojave Desert. They left the interstate and traveled a series of worsening roads. Finally they came to a dusty stop and stiffly got out.

There was a corrugated metal shack, standing forlornly in the desolate landscape covered with low brush and an occasional lava outcropping. Charlie wondered how far they were from the SRI antenna field that fed Los Angeles electricity from one of SRI's solar power satellites—the field the GA had planted a bomb in. Beatty had related with zeal the circumstances during the drive from Barstow.

The Greens in the California State Assembly were trying to make receiving microwave energy from space illegal. Beatty hinted that it wasn't coincidence that just as their bill died, the sabotage happened. Los Angeles needed state money to repair the field and Sacramento didn't provide it. What they couldn't obtain legally, the radical environmentalists obtained through violence. The Greens, of course, claimed always that they didn't have any connection with the GA, didn't condone their actions, and were shocked–*shocked*–that the GA resorted to violence.

Beatty's face grew red as he explained that SRI loaned the funds needed to the city and let them pay it back through slightly higher cost of the energy. He didn't mention if the GA had further designs against the antenna field. Apparently they'd moved on to bigger and more violent things.

Beatty unlocked a large padlock on the shack's door and went in. Charlie was glad it was winter, since it was only about 25 degrees out. Beatty came out of the shack with an honest-to-god M16; it had to be 70 years old but was in good shape, although the plastic parts looked a bit ragged.

Beatty lectured for interminable minutes on the use of the weapon. He showed them how to load and charge it. Then he talked about how to fire it effectively. Charlie tried to look attentive and didn't correct his mistakes.

Then, in turn, each of them fired the weapon. One, a young girl Charlie guessed was barely 18, was so frightened she could barely stand the touch of the plastic hand guards. Charlie went last. She aimed the weapon at the paper target and jerked the trigger back, missing high and to the right. She didn't want to hit it the first time, after all.

Beatty lectured her on trigger squeeze. She tried it again and did better but still missed. Finally, she hit the target dead on. She repeated the feat.

"Have you fired a gun before?" Beatty asked.

"Of course not," Charlie said. Guns were completely banned in the U.S. and only criminals and governments used them.

"Beginner's luck, I guess," Beatty said.

They broke for dinner using the hood of the car as a table to eat a packed meal. As it grew dark, Beatty again lectured them. "The problem with democracy," he said, "is compromise. There will always be those that oppose what is correct. In a democracy you have to compromise with those fools. And there can be no compromise in the protection of the Earth. We're talking about mankind's survival. Only in revolution there is no compromise and only in violence there is revolution. That is why we must learn to use weapons."

Charlie walked away from the group.

"Where are you going?" Beatty demanded.

"To piss," Charlie snapped back.

"Okay," Beatty said, and turned back to continue his monologue.

Charlie went behind the shack for privacy. When finished she walked the long way around the building. Looking around the far corner of the structure, everyone had their back to her, still listening to Beatty. She slipped into the hut.

It was very dark inside and it took Charlie's eyes a long time to adjust. The first shape she saw was a wooden crate, square on the end and about a meter and a half long. The lid was loose and she pulled it up.

There were three weapons, of a type Charlie didn't recognize, under the lid. Charlie guessed there were three layers of three weapons for a total of nine. She looked around more and found some cases of ammunition both 7.62 millimeter for the strange weapons and a case of 5.56mm for the M16. There was nothing indicating the presence of the South African made KS-900 used in the attack on the Moon.

"What are you doing in here?" Beatty yelled from the door.

He reached in and grabbed her arm, roughly pulling her out of the shack.

"I was looking for some toilet paper," Charlie explained.

"There's none in there," Beatty growled loudly.

"Okay," Charlie said. "I'm sorry."

"You don't go anywhere until I say so, okay?"

"Okay," Charlie repeated softly.

"Don't let it happen again."

"I won't."

Beatty walked away and only then did Charlie let out the breath she'd been holding even while speaking.

***

The border between Syria and Israel had seen an unsteady peace for almost half a century. There were incidents, of course, but most of these were covered up. Deaths were explained as training accidents, destruction as wear and tear.

The border resembled the demarcation lines that had been synonymous with the cold war of the last century. There was a kilometer of "no man's land" mined and covered by robotic weapons. On each side there were both silicon and human eyes searching out for intruders from the enemy's side. Tall fences bordered the tortured strip of land. There were breaks in the fences on the Syrian side known to their border guards.

Through such a break, four men moved silently in the black of a moonless night. They had a map of the mines and robot weapons' killing fields on both sides. Traversing the one kilometer to the Zionist state was the most dangerous part of the mission–it took hours. The sky was lightening behind them as they cut through the barbed wire. They knew that would set off alarms. They were counting on it.

The Israeli border guards drove to the break in their Korean-made four-wheel-drive vehicles. The invaders used Chinese-made rocket launchers to destroy the little trucks. The orange balls of flame boiled against the purple sky. The invaders moved inward. Israel is a small, crowded nation. It didn't take long for them to find innocents.

A day later the Israelis responded. Their American-made jets bombed Syrian army positions in the rugged southern end of the Al-Biqa' Valley.

There were protests in the U.N. and tape on CNN of dead civilians on both sides. Then the rest of the world forgot perhaps out of a callousness that comes of seeing violence used too much for political gain.

But General Zuabi remembered, and Faruq knew he would expect to be rewarded for arranging the incident. The command of the United *Baath Revolutionary* Army would be open as soon as Faruq became president and eliminated its leader, who was loyal to the current president.

CHAPTER NINE

"...we'll decide whether to blow you out of space."

The rear Masuka drive had failed and the drive techs didn't know when it'd be up again. Bente ordered the mass driver to full power, which wasn't much more than it normally gave.

The rock was going to miss Earth orbit if she didn't act quickly and correctly.

She yawed the rock, which moved too slowly, and accelerated toward the Earth. This gave her some breathing space. She used the computer to project a braking maneuver using the Earth's gravity. She'd have to avoid too low of an orbit as the odds she'd plow the asteroid into a satellite or a shuttle grew the closer to Earth her path went. And she had to avoid geosynchronous orbit where satellites were orbited in a crowded swarm. She hoped there was nothing else in her new, unplanned course.

The computer showed the velocity she needed. They were going much too fast. She yawed the asteroid more to put the mass driver in front. The numbers were changing too slowly. It was only a matter of time and the asteroid would fly by the Earth to probably orbit the sun. She could calculate whether it had enough velocity to escape the solar system, but why bother?

"Damn," Bente said. But the simulation had been the hardest she could think up. The Masuka drive failure just as she was inserting the asteroid into Earth orbit was very improbable.

She took a deep breath and wiped the sweat from her forehead.

She'd try it again after a break. The computer beeped and Bente hit the answer button.

"Navigator Bente Naguchi?" a voice asked.

"Yes."

"This is the communications room. You have an emergency visual message from Akio Naguchi on the Moon. We can send it to your computer."

"Okay," Bente said, wondering. It must be pretty important to spend the money on visual.

Her brother's face appeared in a new window on the screen. He looked tired. "Bente, Father had a heart attack today. He's in the NESA hospital. The doctors don't know if he'll live much longer. I know you can't come back, but I thought it important you know.

"Good-bye, Bente." The screen returned to the navigation simulator.

Bente didn't know if Akio meant to make her feel guilty for being away, for working for SRI, for not following their father's wishes. But she did.

"Computer," she said, "Record visual message."

"Recording," the computer said.

"Father," Bente began, "I'm sorry I can't be there. I know you'll be fine." She stopped. "Stop recording; erase message. Record."

"Recording."

"Father, I'm sorry I can't be there. But I want to tell you that I love you and respect you. I'm sorry my decision to work for SRI came between us. But you were always my inspiration, and I wanted you to be proud of me. As proud as I am of you."

She stopped again. "Stop recording, erase, record."

"Recording."

"Father, I'm sorry I can't be there. I wish you the best. Get well soon. Stop recording. Send to Naguchi, Katsuya, NESA hospital, NESA Lunar Facility One, the Moon. Charge my SRI account." There was no plate for her thumb so she gave her alphanumeric personal identification code: "NAVNABESH8168745."

"Sending," the computer said.

***

"I'd like to run a test," Cole said. "But I think it's ready."

Griffin shook his head. "I understand, but we have only ten missiles. I don't want to waste any. We'll save them for the attack."

Knecht walked over from her computer to where Cole had rigged up a fire control panel using both the ship's original equipment and that obtained from the Syrians.

"I think we should do a test," she said. "We don't want to be all ready to go and find the missiles won't fire."

Griffin saw Cole and Knecht exchange a supportive look.

"Cole," Griffin asked, "don't you think you could install this correctly?"

Cole stared at him. "Of course I can."

"Then we can trust your abilities and don't have to do a test."

Cole just looked at him. "Can I at least try the missile lock radar to see if it works?"

Griffin thought. "Sure. When we rendezvous with the *Ginney Mae* I want you to get missile lock on it, okay?"

"Okay," Cole said flatly.

Griffin walked away and Knecht followed.

"Are you sure?" she asked.

Griffin stopped and looked at her. "What if we fire nine missiles and still haven't done enough damage? Then we'll want that tenth missile."

"I guess you're right," she conceded.

"Thanks," Griffin said sincerely. He wanted this woman's approval, although he didn't want to want it. Knecht returned to her computer. She was trying to find that miner's ship.

Three weeks to go, Griffin thought. In that time he might want to kill that complaining bitch, Cole. She didn't understand revolution and the sacrifices necessary.

"I've got the *Ginney Mae* on radar," Trudeau reported.

Cole was suddenly busy trying to acquire the other ship with her acquisition radar. The test proved fortunate. The French missiles were having trouble communicating with the SRI equipment. Cole started trying to find the problem.

Later, Cole was sweating as she ran from the bridge to the missile compartment and back again. Griffin had Trudeau helping her and Knecht was continually at her computer. The ship was accelerating at a few tenths of a gee while they made fly-bys of the miner's ship. The miner was probably wondering what the hell they were doing.

"Stand by for free fall," Knecht ordered. Griffin, who was looking over her shoulder, grabbed the back of her chair. The thrust stopped and Knecht yawed the ship so it would accelerate back toward the other vessel. She put on the thrust again. Griffin was pleased with himself that he maintained his balance when some weight returned.

Cole came up the ladder. "I think that'll do it." She padded to the rigged-up fire control panel and worked at it a few seconds. She got a green light.

"Okay!" she cried out. "I have missile lock and the missiles are seeking the ship. I wish I could launch."

"Don't worry," Griffin said. "You will. Knecht, rendezvous with that ship."

"Okay. I suggest everyone strap down. I'll be changing acceleration a lot."

Griffin patted her on the shoulder. She didn't flinch. He walked to a chair and pulled the seat belt across his lap.

***

The miner was fat from years of low acceleration living. He let the GA people do all the work carting the provisions from his ship to theirs. As Knecht and Cole passed by, carrying cases of packaged food, he smiled lecherously as he had four previous times. He knew this would be the attractive brunette's last trip onto his ship.

"Why don't you let that go," he sneered, "and let me show you around my ship?" He reached out and grabbed Knecht's arm.

Knecht looked to Cole but the other woman moved along, trying not to notice what was happening.

Knecht let the package go with a shove and it continued on with its momentum. She turned like a cat in mid-fall and in one motion ripped herself free of his grasp and had her knife against the man's throat. Her other hand held his fat neck to the blade.

"I'll cut your balls off and feed them to you," she whispered in his ear. She pressed the blade until it drew blood, a red globe clinging to his slack skin. Then she pushed him away. "Don't ever touch me."

Cole entered the *Rock Killer*.

"Where's Knecht?" Griffin asked as he packed food in the galley.

"On the other ship," Cole said.

"Why?"

Cole shrugged.

Griffin left the galley and crossed through the airlock to the man's ship. Knecht and the man were just past the airlock. Griffin summed up the situation with one look. "You all right?" he said to Knecht.

She nodded.

Griffin looked at the man. "Well, we were going to pay you for this. But I think not."

"We had a deal," the man pleaded.

Griffin smiled. "You blew it."

"You can't do this."

Knecht moved back to Griffin with her knife ready. "Try to stop us," she hissed.

"And then," Griffin growled, "we'll decide whether to blow you out of space."

They backed out of his ship, sealed the airlock, undocked, and accelerated away.

Cole walked up to Knecht. "Are you all right?" she asked.

Knecht looked at the other woman. "I'm fine," she said tersely and walked to her computer. Automatically, she began entering instructions to move the *Rock Killer* away from the other ship. She was rewarded by acceleration. She double-checked the program, then lifted her eyes from the screen to look at the stars outside the bridge window.

The fat miner reminded her of Waltham, the fat leader in the Gaia Alliance. Waltham had tried a similar trick one night at the LA safe house. But Knecht had learned a few tricks on the streets of Seattle, from SRI when she was originally going to be in security, and from Beatty's tutelage. She suspected Waltham would be making less nocturnal visits to the women of the GA.

She wondered how an asshole like Waltham got into the GA. Perhaps, like Beatty, he was useful–probably had money or political connections. Trent wouldn't tolerate him, otherwise.

Beatty, on the other hand, was one of the few men she'd ever met that didn't immediately react to her looks. She liked him for that. They'd formed a friendship of sorts, as close as a man like him was capable of. Beatty taught her many interesting things about how to kill people with various weapons, and unarmed. They talked, both privately and with the group at the house, about the environment, both Earth's and space's, and how SRI was about to destroy both. She loved to hear him talk, and easily came to share his hatred of SRI specifically, and the material-based society of America generally.

Linda Trent had already begun that instruction before Trent introduced Knecht to Beatty. At this point in her life, Knecht could hardly imagine anyone wanting to work for SRI except out of pure greed motivation.

Knecht had met Linda Trent in LA, when she had gone there for her vacation after graduating from the SRI navigation school. A vacation was tradition, and Knecht's instructors insisted she take time off before going into space.

She briefly considered returning home, for about a second. She was sure she could handle her stepfather; she just didn't want to have to.

So she went to L.A. to see Disneyland-California, visit the earthquake memorial, and generally play tourist for a while.

She was outside Mitsubishi's Chinese Theater looking at the actors' names in the cement, some lovingly recreated from photographs after being destroyed in the '14 earthquake. A woman about her age approached, holding a hand computer.

"Hi," the woman said almost too cheerfully. "Would you like to help save the Earth?"

Knecht looked at her. "Save the Earth" and "Save the Planet" were near mantras in American culture. Every child was taught almost before they could walk what they could do to help "Save the Earth." So, Knecht naturally answered, "Of course, how?"

"By donating to the Green Party of California and signing our petition to stop the importation of space derived resources."

That grabbed Knecht's attention. "Why?"

"The exploitation of space is ruining the pristine nature of the universe. Man's greed has screwed up Earth enough; we can't let robber corporations rape outer space for profits."

Knecht didn't know what to say. The other woman must have taken this as a sign to keep talking.

"We're having a meeting, the Green Party, that is. You're welcome to come. Congressperson Trent will be speaking on the dangers of space exploitation."

"Who?"

"Linda Trent, one of the Green Party members in Congress. You really ought to come. Let me write down the address for you—" not transfer to from her computer to Knecht's as would be the norm—"You can get there by bus."

Out of boredom and curiosity, Knecht went.

Linda Trent was a pudgy woman who spoke with a harsh, grating cadence. She explained the Gravitational Resonance Theory and the danger Space Resources Incorporated's practice of removing asteroids from space presented. Knecht knew enough physics to know about gravity and resonance, but she'd never heard anyone mention this at SRI. She decided to check it out. After the official meeting ended, she sought out Trent.

"Ms. Trent," she said after introducing herself, "I don't understand completely. I work for SRI and—"

Trent cut her off. "You work for them? Do you think they are going to tell you about this? They only worry about their all-important bottom line."

"But Jupiter—"

"Jupiter has nothing to do with it. What do you do for SRI?"

"I'm a navigator."

Trent was silent for a moment. Then she smiled broadly.

"Would you—what is your name, anyway?—like to learn more?"

"Yes, because I don't understand. And it's Barbara. Barbara Knecht."

"We could go someplace and have coffee and talk. Would you like to do that, Barbara?"

"Yes, I would." She left with Trent that night. She knew Trent was interested in her both for her inside knowledge of SRI and also sexually. She succumbed to Trent's advances slowly, thinking perhaps this was the love she'd never known.

It wasn't, and neither was the friendship with Beatty. As a greenish-blue dot passed into her view, just before the sun's blaze activated the automatic darkening window, Knecht wondered if the Earth Mother, Gaia, would love her for what she was about to do to SRI.

She hoped so.

***

Kirsten Hanna-Chun went to the dinner party alone. She was almost surprised she had received an invitation after Alex's fight with McConnell. An associate, Dr. Breton, was the hostess and Kirsten always thought Breton seemed a little too anxious to please McConnell.

Kirsten parked her car in the street and walked to the door.

The house was large both inside and out. The interior was decorated with original art that Kirsten frankly found ugly. She was greeted by Dr. Breton.

"Welcome, Kirsten," Breton said, holding out her arms for Kirsten's coat. "I'm glad you could make it."

"Thank you, Alysia," Kirsten said, handing over her wrap.

Alysia took her burden and Kirsten headed into the crowd.

"Alone?" Dr. Plotnik asked, stepping in her path.

Kirsten turned to him. "Yes, as usual; Alex is in space. Have you seen Dr. McConnell?"

"Yes," Plotnik said. "He's here somewhere."

"Thanks," Kirsten said, moving on with relief. She found Plotnik to be singularly unattractive.

The shiny dome of McConnell's head was like a beacon over the guests. The smoke from his oral retentive habit curled up away from his mouth. Kirsten made her way to him. He was talking to a young, new psychologist. Kirsten touched McConnell's shoulder.

He turned to her. "Kirsten," he said simply.

"Can we talk?" Kirsten asked, trying not to sound desperate.

McConnell paused, thinking. "Sure," he said to her and "Excuse us, please," to the young man.

They walked a short distance away.

"What can I do for you, Doctor?" McConnell asked condescendingly. He held his cigarette so the smoke curled around her head.

"I'd like to apologize," Kirsten said through the cloud, "for what happened at your house last month."

"I think your husband is the one who needs to apologize."

"I know. But he's not on Earth. I'd like to apologize for him."

"Where is Mr. Chun?" McConnell asked, sucking on the cigarette and blowing the smoke her direction.

"He's going to the belt."

"He'll be bringing back an asteroid?"

"Yes," Kirsten acknowledged.

McConnell got a funny look of satisfaction on his face.

Then he looked at Kirsten and smiled under that bushy mustache.

"Apology accepted, Kirsten."

"Thank you, Doctor," Kirsten breathed with relief.

"I'll be going out of town for a few days," he said. "But when I get back let's get together and talk, okay?"

"Sure," Kirsten said.

"Call my secretary," he finished and patted her upper arm and walked away.

Kirsten thought he gave in awfully easily. But, still, she was sure her burps would taste like crow for a few months.

***

Charlie and the others spent the night in the desert. The temperature dropped dramatically and Charlie froze in the inadequate sleeping bag that had been provided. Beatty took a portable hydrogen-burning generator out of the trunk of the car, hooked up some hydrogen storage cells, and charged the car until the cells were empty. They took turns guarding, with a loaded M16, during the night. Charlie strongly suspected it was to get them used to the weapon more than to protect against–what? Police, scorpions?

The next morning they watched a magnificent sunrise as the sky went from black through every shade of purple and orange to deep, deep azure.

They ate another meal on the hood of the car and then practiced firing the other weapon that had been in the shed. It was a small assault rifle. Arabic writing was stamped into the side of the upper receiver. Beatty didn't offer much information about it except how to use it.

Charlie sent a few rounds at the paper target missing a good deal.

"What happened, Shari?" Beatty asked. "Yesterday you were doing a lot better."

"Beginner's luck, like you said," Charlie offered.

"Guess so," Beatty said.

"Are these the kinds of weapons we'll always use?" Charlie asked as innocently as she could.

"No, we have others," Beatty replied simply. "Next," he called.

Charlie knew she was dismissed.

The return trip was almost unbearably hot. They didn't use the acoustic air conditioner. Charlie was starting to believe these people didn't believe in doing anything that made them more comfortable, even if the impact on the environment was none or negligible.

They arrived at the house late at night. Charlie immediately found her room and crawled into the sleeping bag, dead tired. She knew they'd be up early doing more chores and listening to more lectures.

***

Alex watched the miners practice reacting to a breach in the outer asteroid shell. Damage control foam flew like food in a toddler feeding. But the simulated hole was plugged efficiently and effectively. Alex congratulated Tsuji, the miner chief, a muscular, Japanese woman who told Alex not to worry about her people; the implication being he should butt out.

Alex left the training area for the saloon. Thorne and Diana probably would be there if they weren't in Thorne's quarters, and in that case, Ibrahhim would be there. The doctor had, after some initial coolness, come into the circle of Alex's friends. He'd seemed surprised that others thought he wanted to be left alone. Apparently, Dr. Jubair was just plain shy.

And Bill and Diana, Alex mused, seemed to be falling in love. Alex had never seen him happier. He hoped it lasted.

Alex passed his chief navigator in a corridor. "Hello, Naguchi," he said, still wrapped in his thoughts.

"Hello, Director," she said softly and continued walking.

"Bente," Alex called after her.

She stopped. Alex was impressed how well she handled herself in low gravity. "Yes?" she asked.

"I was just headed for the saloon to meet some people," Alex said. "Would you like to join us?"

"No, thanks, Director," she said.

Alex debated insisting but changed his mind. "Fine. We'll probably be there a few hours. Drop by if you want."

"I will," she said and turned to leave.

Alex watched her go. She was very attractive but seemed laconic to the point of almost being rude. Oh, well, he decided, he had other problems and didn't need to worry about his navigator as long as she could do her job.

***

The next morning there was a change in tone at the GA house. Beatty was more demanding and everyone seemed on edge. Late in the afternoon a cab pulled up and a man got out. He was balding and fat and had a grizzled mustache. As soon as he exited the car he lit up a cigarette.

"Who's that?" Charlie whispered to the girl standing next to her.

"Whaltham," she answered.

Beatty and the newcomer spent hours in private. The rest went about their chores but in a more quiet, subdued manner. Charlie worked in the backyard of the house. She tried to find an excuse to be under the window of the room Beatty and Whaltham were in. But, even then, she couldn't hear anything other than muffled voices.

Charlie pulled weeds from the garden, amazed at how fast they grew. A blonde girl was working beside her. Usually the girl, named Annie, was hard to shut up. Today she was even quiet.

"What's going on?" Charlie asked softly.

"Last time Whaltham came, Maddie and Barb left with Griffin," the girl answered back. "He only comes when something's about to happen."

Charlie nodded and continued working quietly. She hoped something would happen soon. She was going nuts in the organically grown, communal atmosphere.

***

The United States' "Federal Comprehensive Bias Crime Act of 2021" stipulated that police departments around the nation report to the Justice Department any crime that was investigated originally as a bias crime but charges were reduced or dismissed and the reasons why. When the officer that had interrogated

Charlie in Washington, County and State of Columbia had tapped the "bias crime" icon on his computer pad, noting that it may be a bias crime, it had made an indelible mark on the computer record. When Freeman talked the judge out of pursuing the bias crime aspect of Charlie's offense, she had noted in her computer the reasons she decided the unlawful self-defense wasn't also a bias crime.

Because of the limitations of the computer filing system, it was necessary for Washington police officers to spend hours, when they could be protecting under-protected civilians, at their computers sorting through the files with the bias crime marker looking for ones where the bias crime was not charged. These were copied onto data files and transferred electronically to the Justice Department, where they sat until over-worked clerks sorted through them on their computers to determine if the reason was good enough and, if not, how the law had to be changed to close that loophole.

A clerk named Brian Hocking eventually came upon Charlie Jones' file. The first thing he noticed was the mug shot. If the woman looks that good in a mug shot then she must be outstanding, he imagined. He read the excuse, given by the judge, for not pressing the bias crime angle of the offense.

Hocking frowned. An FBI agent had convinced the DDA that the woman's motives weren't racial. He wondered if this was an overstepping of the bounds by those fascists in the Hoover building. He knew someone on the FBI oversight committee from their work together on political issues, so he downloaded a copy of the file to his personal computer and called Congresswoman Polasky's office for an appointment.

***

Director Chun made a courtesy call on Captain Takashara as the *Kyushu* maneuvered to rendezvous with the asteroid. The trip was almost over.

The captain, in her small quarters, greeted Alex enthusiastically. The two had a passing acquaintance.

"The asteroid is in a relatively fast tumble," she reported. "Your people should be able to stabilize it okay, though. The *Elara* arrived on site yesterday with the water and oxygen from Europa."

"Great," Alex said. "It's been a long time doing nothing."

"I understand," Takashara said with a chuckle. "I took two months off last year to visit my family in Hiroshima and about went crazy." She smiled bitterly. "My ship is due for an engine upgrade after this trip. I'll have to spend almost a year on the Moon. I'm not looking forward to it. If I wasn't the captain I could transfer to another ship, but I have to supervise the overhaul."

Alex nodded in sympathy. He was probably the only person on the ship she dared reveal her feelings to. "The Moon's a nice place," he said consolingly.

"Yes," she agreed. "Better than Earth."

"Yes," he said. If it weren't for Kirsten, Alex wondered if he'd ever bother returning to that planet.

"I understand," Takashara said softly, "you were friends with some of those killed on the Moon. My sympathies."

"Thank you."

"I don't understand these Gaia Alliance people," Takashara growled angrily. "And those that support them."

"I know," Alex agreed. "I met a couple on Earth that supports the GA. What idiots."

"Who were they?"

"A psychologist in Denver and his wife."

"I don't understand," Takashara started, "how an educated person can support terrorism."

"You have to understand, Captain, his education was different from ours. I'm thankful I didn't learn a damn thing from the American education system. Instead SRI taught me just about everything I know. The American schools didn't have a chance to screw up my thinking."

"I suppose," she said, shaking her head and making her long, midnight hair wave about. "I guess that's the main problem."

***

Faruq never, ever said anything bad about the president. He let others do that.

The Baath Party Headquarters' central meeting room was full of delegates from all the United Baath Arab States. But Faruq met in a smaller, more private room with those that actually wielded the power in the portions of the Middle East controlled from Damascus.

"The Zionist State continues to be a thorn in our side," a member said. "What has the president done other than support ineffectual terrorists that only serve to harden the resolve of the Zionists and the Americans?"

There was general agreement.

"What needs to be done," another man added, "is something that will cut at the heart of the West that supports the Zionists."

Faruq smiled inwardly. These friends were doing their parts well. They would be rewarded with power and wealth when Faruq became president–but not too much. What made the president vulnerable was the trust he placed in his friends.

Faruq only had to wait. The asteroid would soon leave the belt and the attack would take place shortly after. Once he revealed his connection to this event, the party would be behind him completely. And then, it was only a matter of time.

CHAPTER TEN

"And then, we'll kill a rock."

Whaltham stayed at the house for almost a week, spreading the gospel of radical, revolutionary environmentalism along with a lot of fumes from his ubiquitous cigarettes. The tension eased after a few days but the place never returned to the joyful revolutionary spirit it had had. Whaltham repeated the same, old, tired arguments Charlie had heard from Beatty and the others. But he seemed more dedicated to violence than even Beatty.

At the communal table one night, Whaltham said, "For most of the twentieth century the Soviet Union contained the spread of capitalism and the ability of criminal corporations to steal natural resources." He stopped to take a drag. "But," he continued, "when the CIA was able to subvert the Soviet Union, there was no deterrent to unfettered capitalism and the exploitation that goes hand in hand with free markets. So we have to use violence to stop the expansion of capitalism. SRI couldn't have existed in the twentieth century. Today it's free to steal resources even from space, even though it could mean the end of life on Earth."

"How?" Charlie couldn't help but ask.

Whaltham regarded her with a yellow grin. "I'm glad you asked, Shari. The Gravitational Resonance Theory. According to the theory, accepted by almost all scientists, the asteroid belt is in a delicate, resonant equilibrium. Taking asteroids out of the belt disrupts the resonance. Eventually, the asteroid belt will fall apart and asteroids will move toward the sun. And what's between the sun and the asteroid belt?"

"The Earth," someone said.

"Right," Whaltham agreed.

Charlie had heard of the GRT. It came up in the papers about every three years. A few "scientists" (usually the concerned type) were quoted. It was the current, popular disaster. And the villain was SRI. That was better than the Greenhouse or the Ice Age or the Swarm of Locust because the villain in those scenarios was "our industrialized society." SRI was a lot more tangible, and had offices where one could protest.

Unfortunately for the advocates of the GRT, Jupiter affected the asteroids all the time and exponentially more than the small asteroids SRI took.

Whaltham had continued, "But we can stop them with blood. I'll give you an example. A month ago we attacked Space Rape Incorporated's base on the Moon. We killed five employees, including three security people. Since then, SRI has been unable to recruit people into their private little army they call 'security'. They don't want to get killed. So not only did we hurt SRI in the short term, we hurt it in the long run. And we'll hurt it more soon. Very soon."

"How?" the young girl who was afraid of the weapons asked innocently.

Charlie was glad someone else asked because she didn't want to draw attention to herself. Also she was so angry she was afraid she'd reveal her feelings for this fat pig.

Whaltham glared at the poor girl. "If you needed to know, you would."

The girl withered like a flower in her chair.

The dinner finished in silence and the dishes were washed. Then they sat around the living room of the house on the floor and Whaltham preached. Dissenting opinions were not encouraged so these "discussions" turned into confirmation sessions. Someone would say something like, "We're fighting for the survival of mankind but more importantly, Mother Earth," and everyone would agree. Charlie wondered why these people put mankind after nature in their priorities. She wondered just who had lied to them.

Eventually some of the Gaia Alliance members would wander off from listening to Whaltham. Most headed for the bedrooms. Charlie was genuinely tired. And tired of the tripe she was listening to and confirming and occasionally, just to fit in, parroting. So, she went to the room she shared with six others. They all slept on the dirty carpet in sleeping bags.

She was wakened in the night by someone unzipping her bag. She reached up, grabbed his head and twisted. The big man fell to the floor with an unceremonious plop and yelled in pain and anger.

"God damn it!" Whaltham spat. He slapped Charlie as she sat up. The force strained her neck as it tried to keep her head connected to her shoulders. "Don't ever do that again," he added.

Charlie heard someone rustle in their bag but stay uncannily quiet.

Charlie rubbed her cheek where his blow had connected. It felt hot. "Sorry, I grew up in a rough neighborhood. I didn't know it was you."

"Well, God damn it," Whaltham repeated.

"What do you want?" Charlie asked, dreading the answer.

Whaltham looked at her by the illumination provided by a streetlight outside that came through the dirty window. Then he roughly grabbed her around the neck and pulled her to him. He kissed her harshly and that mustache brutalized her face. She could taste cigarette residue in his mouth. She almost gagged. She pushed him away and he slapped her again, harder, and again groped for her and pulled her against his rotund body. Without thinking, she kneed him in the crotch. He howled and rolled away, but remarkably, came back toward her. His eyes were bulging and his mouth was clenched like a fist ready for the blow. He seized her around the neck and, using strength Charlie wouldn't have thought the fat man had, pulled her face to his.

"God damn," he repeated, "I'll kill you if you do that again."

I'd like to see you try, she thought.

149

"You don't act like a kid from Maine. That's where you said you were from, Shari?"

"Yes," she mumbled softly. *If I fight him, I'll blow this whole deal,* she realized. All this effort would be for nothing and Frank's killers will never see justice.

As he again attacked her mouth, Charlie pushed herself way down inside herself. She didn't resist and passively let him have her.

At one point he said, "What's this scar?" His lips were on her throat near the scar from her decompression.

"Nothing," she said quickly, not wanting to come to the surface for long. "An accident."

That seemed to satisfy his curiosity.

When he was otherwise satisfied, he left and Charlie went to the bathroom to clean up. She looked in the mirror. *What I'll do for SRI,* she said to herself bitterly. *I should have killed him and raised humanity's average IQ a few points,* she decided.

She wished Frank were there to comfort her. But Frank would never be there again.

If anyone noticed her crying they didn't mention it.

The next morning Whaltham was gone.

***

Griffin awoke in a good mood. It was almost time. According to Knecht, the asteroid would be leaving the belt in a couple of days, depending on what problems they had getting it ready.

He left the captain's quarters and pulled himself up the ladder to the bridge. Knecht was still working on the computer.

"Morning," Griffin said.

Knecht turned to look at him. "Hi, Alan."

"Cole and Trudeau sleeping?"

Knecht nodded. Griffin loved the way her hair moved.

"Let 'em," Griffin said. "The next few days are going to be busy. What's our status?"

"The asteroid tender should rendezvous with the asteroid today. It's a week to ten days to get the asteroid ready to go. That's a three-day window in which they could go. Look," she said,

150

pointing to the computer, "I've been working on this. I've projected their routes for making Earth orbit depending on when they leave." She pressed a key and the holographic display showed a curved area superimposed on a diagram of the solar system. It was wider near Earth. "Since the asteroid is orbiting the sun and so is the Earth, this is the area they must be in."

"That's not too bad," Griffin said.

"You're not taking into account the scale," Knecht said. "That asteroid is traveling about seven kilometers a second. In three days that's over two million kilometers for this arc segment. Earth travels about 300 kilometers a second so this end is an arc about 80 million kilometers. The total area is—"

"Never mind, I get the picture," Griffin interjected. "What are our chances of finding them?"

"Slim unless we get more information."

"You know where the asteroid is now. We got that information from their computer on the Moon."

"Sure," she acknowledged. "But I don't know when it will start accelerating. I explained this to you and Whaltham back in L.A., but you were so hot to go kill some SRI personnel you didn't listen."

"So now what?"

"If Trudeau can intercept their transmissions," Knecht explained, "they should give a good indication of their departure."

"What about picking up the asteroid tender's telemetry?"

She shook her head. "Again, I explained this on Earth. The beam is too narrow, for one thing. Also, they scramble it. Let's hope Trudeau can pick up their transmissions." Knecht looked up at him. "If he can't, we'll never be able to do this, unless we get unbelievably lucky."

"He should," Griffin said. "Maybe I'll wake him up."

Griffin turned in the air (he was getting better at zero gee maneuvers). Knecht grabbed his arm and pulled him around.

"Griffin," she said softly.

"Yes?"

"Before you go, I want to talk to you."

151

"Yes?"

"On the miner's ship. You helped me."

"I don't know. I think you were doing okay."

"Yes, but I appreciate the attempt."

"No problem, Barb," Griffin said.

She smiled at him and let him go.

***

Charlie found the door two days after Whaltham left. She happened upon it while cleaning in the kitchen. It was behind a false wall. She kept cleaning as if nothing happened.

On some days, the comrades had time to read the books and magazines in the house. After cleaning, Charlie sat on the floor next to Annie reading a book. It was about over population and predicted in ten years over population was going to doom humanity and the environment. It was written a hundred years ago.

"Annie," she said. "I'm going outside for some fresh air."

"Okay," the girl replied. Charlie stood and stretched, then went to the back door. She walked out into the lawn were there was a small patch of brown grass. She sat cross-legged on the dying lawn and faced the sun. It was above the house and she studied the foundation of the structure while warming her face with the sun's heat.

The cement rose about half a meter off the ground. Now that Charlie thought about it, that seemed awfully high. There were two spaces where the cement was a different shade from the rest of the foundation. They would just about be right if someone had covered up a window. The house had a basement!

***

The *Kyushu* matched orbits with the tumbling asteroid. The *Elara* was a few kilometers off, holding position relative to SRI-1961, as the crew of the SRI ship that had found it had dubbed the rock.

Tsuji, the head miner, looked out a port with Alex.

"This one will be difficult," she said. "It's tumbling a little faster than I like."

Alex nodded. He'd seen this procedure a dozen times and it still made his stomach queasy. He looked out the port. The asteroid was roughly a kilometer long and half a kilometer in diameter at its widest. It was an unusually dark M-type nickel-iron asteroid. SRI preferred the M-types; they were rich in metals, and poor in less valuable silicates. It looked like a lumpy potato and was spinning on all three axes.

"I'll go first," Tsuji said.

"Right," Alex concurred. "I'll keep everybody out of your way."

"Thanks, Director," she said perfunctorily and pushed herself toward the equipment storage area.

A few hours later, Tsuji, in a maneuvering pressure suit, stood in the airlock. On her back were ropes, hammers and pitons, and a hefty device that looked like a very large caliber shotgun. Over that was a Masuka drive package that gave her the same maneuvering abilities of a ship: yaw and roll and a good deal of thrust. There was a large, powerful battery to provide energy for the drive. Her four best miners were with her. Every member of the team carried ten chemical rockets, each about the size of a baseball bat.

The *Kyushu* had maneuvered within a few hundred meters of the asteroid. Tsuji used the small drive to accelerate into space. She then was simply another object orbiting the sun.

She used the yaw drive to twist her body so she was facing the opposite direction to the one she, the asteroid, and the two ships were traveling. She did an old-fashioned retro burn with her Masuka drive, putting her into an orbit closer to the asteroid but also moving faster.

Tsuji was a two meter-long spaceship. She used orbital mechanics to get within 50 meters. The face of the asteroid was moving so fast below her she didn't dare look. Her brain would assume she was moving and panic would set in despite her knowledge of her true situation.

She pulled the "shotgun" off her back. It had a roll of monofilament line above the stock. Not much more than a spider web strand in thickness, the fiber, made at the Low Earth Orbit

Facility one atom at a time, had more strength than a steel cable as thick as the wrist.

She used a snap link to connect her suit to two O-rings on the butt of the instrument. Satisfied she was secured, she aimed at the limb of the asteroid that was spinning toward her and fired. Missing would mean taking time to retract the line but, more importantly, would ruin her record. She was six for six.

A diamond tipped projectile jabbed into the rock. The light coating of dust on the asteroid near the impact fled the site in a growing cone. Line began playing out of the roll but automatically was slowing. As it slowed Tsuji was drawn toward the asteroid. Now it was the stars she couldn't look at as they spun crazily around her. She kept her eyes on the surface of the asteroid that was moving slower and slower relative to her.

Soon she was stationary relative to the surface. Alex watched from a *Kyushu* port as his miner chief was swung around at the end of the line like a rock in a slingshot.

Tsuji hit a switch on the gun and was reeled in to the surface. The fishing analogy always struck Alex although it was like a mosquito trying to land a whale.

Tsuji hit the asteroid slowly as the last of monofilament line was reeled in. She immediately brushed aside the thin layer of dust and drove in a piton, then another and then a third. She roped herself to the surface. If she was flung off, she might hit the ship like some large projectile or, much more likely, be flung into space making for an expensive and time-consuming rescue.

Now the hard part: she turned on her helmet light, so the other miners could see her, and waited while the other miners took their shot at the asteroid. Another line of monofilament connected to the rock and a miner descended to the surface and secured him or herself with pitons and rope. Eventually, all four were on the exterior of the rock with her. Each had lashed himself to their quarry as soon as they had touched the surface.

The data link to the *Kyushu*'s computer was busy as the miners consulted it for the locations to place the rockets. Each headed across the asteroid's skin, making sure he or she was always firmly tied to at least two pitons driven securely into the rock. They planted their rockets in the proper places and correct orientations as called for by the computer.

The rockets were connected by ignition wires. The process took six long, nervous hours from the time Tsuji was swinging around the asteroid at the end of her filament until they were ready to fire the rockets. The five miners were again tied down and the rockets fired.

The asteroid's tumble slowed considerably and the dust coating swirled as each grain continued tangentially as the asteroid's spin was retarded beneath it. Another miner came over from the tender with more rockets and the process was repeated. Once the asteroid was stable and all the miners had returned to the *Kyushu*, the ship was maneuvered behind the asteroid. Alex admired the skill of the navigator under Takashara's command as he worked with his computer to use the complexities of orbital mechanics to put the asteroid right where it needed to be.

Using the *Kyushu*'s tokomak's copious energy, a laser beam as thick as an arm drilled a hole down the center of the rock. Then ropes were strung between the ship and asteroid. The miners, like stone carving pirates, swooped down on the captured rock and attacked the hole, widening it and preparing the asteroid for the installation of the mass driver, tokomak, MHD, Masuka Drives, and all the other sundry equipment that turned an artifact of the formation from the solar system into a ship.

***

Charlie waited until everyone was asleep. The couple in the corner had finished for the evening and one was snoring loudly. She guessed it was about one in the morning.

She got up and went to the kitchen; midnight snack if anyone saw her. She thought about throwing on a robe but the other women had displayed a definite lack of modesty and to fit in, Charlie had gotten used to tramping around in just her panties.

The false panel slid aside easily. She turned the doorknob. It was locked.

She replaced the panel and went to bed. There was nothing to do. Beatty would have the key. The problem was how to get it from him without his knowledge. That would have to wait until later.

Charlie kept an eye on Beatty the next few days. She hadn't noticed before how he patrolled the house like a watchdog. He tried to sneak up on people, catch them doing something he didn't approve of. If he ever went into the basement she didn't see it.

As she cleaned she looked in every place she could think of to hide keys. She found nothing. She wondered how she could get that key. She wondered if he could be susceptible to her charms. She wondered if she dared try.

When he was alone once, Charlie walked up to Beatty.

"Yes, Shari?" he asked.

"I know I'm new around here," she said. "But I've been pulling weeds and cleaning and pulling more weeds and cooking and pulling weeds some more for three weeks."

"Yes?" Beatty prompted.

"I feel like you don't trust me. I don't know anything about what's going on. Like when Whaltham was here—"

Beatty cut her off viciously. "Listen. You don't know because it's for your protection. The less you know the better off you are. We'll decide what you need to know. Understand?"

Charlie nodded silently, acting subdued by Beatty's rebuke.

She wanted to physically attack him, but she went back to the garden. She couldn't believe how fast those damn weeds grew. They just got through with one end of the vegetable rows and the other end needed weeding again.

She needed a different tack. She decided to break in somehow.

***

Trudeau was bent over his radio computer. He scanned the spectrum up and down with the RF gain on maximum. He'd heard some Russian (Mars? he wondered), a lot of static, but nothing that sounded like SRI transmissions. He wasn't too worried. He had a week, at least. It was just that Griffin was breathing down his neck to find the asteroid's transmissions.

He scanned down the spectrum watching the signal analyzer's display. There was a small peak, just barely distinguishable from the background noise. It disappeared and reappeared. Trudeau set the radio frequency to that of the peak.

"*Kyushu*, this is *Elara*," he heard.

"Go ahead, *Elara*."

"We have completed transfer of the water and oh-two to the rock. We will be unhooking the umbilical and maneuvering away."

"Understood, *Elara*. Have a good trip back."

"Roger that, *Kyushu*. Give our regards to Director Chun and his crew and our hopes for a safe trip home."

"Will do."

"*Elara*, out."

Trudeau smiled and stored the frequency into the computer.

"Griffin," he called.

"Yeah?" he replied, pushing over.

"I've got them."

Griffin slapped him on the back so hard Griffin sailed halfway across the room. "Good job," he said, laughing while he tried to stop his flight.

He collided with Knecht. He turned to apologize but she wrapped her arms around him in celebration.

"Now we'll show SRI they can't fuck with the sanctity of space," she said.

"Damn right," Griffin said. They held each other for a second then clumsily let go.

Cole watched and then pushed herself into the galley.

***

Alex pulled himself over to the asteroid by one of the many ropes between it and the *Kyushu*. Captain Takashara had maneuvered the combination so that the long axis of the ship and asteroid was pointed toward the sun and perpendicular to the vector of velocity of the asteroid's orbit. Tidal forces were just enough to keep the ship and asteroid apart, bound by a network of taut cables. But the effect was too small to be noticed by Alex as he climbed toward the asteroid.

As he reached the stone surface, he turned back to look at the *Kyushu*. The roughly bullet-shaped vessel filled most of his vision but was dwarfed by the mass driver still attached to the ship's exterior. The driver looked like a kilometer-long radio tower laid on its side. Attaching the base of the mass driver to the asteroid was the last operation that would be performed before the rock was a fully functioning ship.

He cycled through the huge temporary airlock in the opening for the mass driver's mass feeder. Through this airlock the internal equipment was transferred.

Tsuji met him there, hanging onto a handle. Alex pulled off his helmet and grabbed his own handhold. She handed him a dust mask. Everyone wore them as the asteroid was being carved open to accept the equipment. Dust from the carving, with no gravity to settle it, floated freely throughout the interior of the rock. The air was passed through electrostatic precipitators but they couldn't keep up with the volume of dust particles. Before the conversion was finished, every interior surface would have to be wiped down to eliminate the dust. Since water was more precious than gold, rags were treated with an electrostatic attractant.

Alex and Tsuji were in a large cavern carved from the asteroid. Once, a long time ago, Alex had joined Kirsten in an expedition to a cave in the Rocky Mountains. The damp smells and dripping water surprised Alex. He had expected it to be like the bone-dry interior of an asteroid. The man-made chamber's walls were varying shades of gray and black. *The monotony could drive one crazy,* Alex thought as he looked around.

In this room, the interior components of the mass driver would be installed. This was with equipment that ground the tailings to a powder so fine it almost moved like a liquid. The dust was ionized as the conduit passed between two massive, charged plates and then fed outside to the tower that would trail behind the asteroid. The tower accelerated the mass to just a little slower than the average photon. The grinding machines were already working on what the miners had dug out. *This part is always so wasteful,* Alex thought. None of the valuable metals were separated at this stage;

it would take too much time and the lost ore cost less than the time to separate it.

"Greetings Director," Tsuji said, her voice muffled by her dust mask.

"Hello, Chief," Alex replied. "How's it going over here?"

"Great. We've had no problems."

Alex pulled along a rope heading deeper into the rock. "How long before equipment can start coming in?"

"Tomorrow we'll start bringing in the big items for the far end and work our way back," Tsuji said, following on another rope.

"So about three days until the mass driver's installed?" Alex asked from experience.

"Yes, barring unforeseen circumstances," Tsuji said as they reached the far end of the chamber and started climbing up the two-meter wide tunnel the miners had dug from the pilot hole drilled by the laser. A small tube ran the length of the pipe-like passage carrying rock to the grinders.

They passed a room with three miners cutting rock and shoving it into a branch of the tube.

"The tokamak room?" Alex asked.

"Yes," Tsuji said. "It'll be finished in time."

Alex looked at Tsuji. He realized that she thought this was an inspection. "I'm sure it will, Chief. You're doing a good job. I just want a look around."

Tsuji seemed to relax, Alex thought. "Fine," she said. "Do you need me?"

"No," Alex said. "Go do what you need to do."

"Okay, Director. If you need me—"

"I won't. I'll just look around."

"Okay," she said and pulled herself up the rope.

Alex watched the miners work. It was hard, dusty work, not without its element of danger. One saw Alex but acted as if he hadn't. Miners were a clique and few, not even the director, were worthy of their notice.

Alex moved on. In a large room he assumed would be life support in a few days, miners were installing bracing for when the rock would be accelerating.

He found a side passage and followed it. There was a small room and outside the opening where the door would go was a passage just wide enough for a man. A ladder would be installed so he could climb the tube when the rock was under acceleration.

Alex knew the small room would be his quarters and office. He moved up the tube to the control room. On a ship it would be called the bridge, but control room was another misnomer left over from the days when the asteroids couldn't maneuver without chemical rockets.

Already conduits were protruding from the rock surfaces and some had fiber optics and wires spilling out. Alex marveled at the work being done. His, or rather Chief Tsuji's miners, and technicians from the *Kyushu* were working around the clock to turn asteroid SRI-1961 into ship SRI-1961. When finished, the center of the asteroid would be a three dimensional maze of corridors and rooms. The chambers would have walls of virgin rock. Conduits would bring power for lights and equipment would snake along the rock surfaces. It looked primitive but it worked. The luxury of metal walls was too expensive for the asteroid's temporary status as a ship. Once the asteroid reached Earth orbit, it would be stripped of all useful material and then merely be an oversized ore ingot.

The work to convert the asteroid had to be done quickly; keeping the *Kyushu* in space cost SRI one to two million dollars a day. And having the billions of dollars worth of equipment that comprised the mass drive, Masuka drives, tokomak and MHD–and all the other equipment for the asteroid–idle probably cost another couple million a day. Then the billions of dollars of ore in the asteroid weren't making any money out here. The demand for the iron, nickel, gold and platinum on Earth was growing almost as fast as the population. And SRI, NESA, and the Russian Federation's ambitious space programs required huge amounts of the metals. Mining asteroids meant less mining on Earth was necessary and less damage was done to the environment. And the demand was still met for the raw materials that supported the standard of living almost everyone but those in the poorest nations enjoyed. Manufacture in orbit, also made economically feasible by asteroid mining, threw pollution to space on the solar wind. To Alex, SRI and NESA were the real environmentalists while the GA simply used the environment as an excuse to grab power for themselves.

And that reminded him of the *Rock Skipper*. He felt his stomach knot and bile seeped into his mouth. Was he nervous, or space sick? he wondered.

***

The *Rock Killer* accelerated to a stop.

"Okay," Knecht reported, "We're about a hundred kilometers closer to the asteroid."

"Good," Trudeau said. He called up the frequency on the computer that controlled the radio.

The spike on the signals analyzer was larger.

"*Kyushu*, this is 1961."

"Go ahead, sixty-one."

Trudeau transferred the broadcast to the ship's intercom so all could hear.

"We are powered up and self-sufficient. We will commence acceleration within 15 minutes."

"Roger, 61. We're heading home. Safe trip, sixty-one."

"Safe trip, *Kyushu*."

Trudeau looked at Griffin, who was smiling.

"We've got them," Griffin cried happily. "Knecht, it's your show."

She replied, "Okay," and bent over her computer. "Trudeau, stay on them. They'll announce to the asteroid tender when they start acceleration. Then I can plot an intercept course."

"And then," Griffin said, "we'll kill a rock."

CHAPTER ELEVEN

"Tell the miners it's time to earn their pay."

To the rest of the solar system it was SRI-1961. But to Director Alexander Chun it, or she, was the USS *Enterprise,* the *Long Shot,* the *Skylark,* and "*Gay Deceiver*" all rolled into one.

And although those ships had capabilities that were still, and may always be, science fiction, Chun wouldn't trade SRI-1961, his rock, his command, for the lot of them. *Well,* he thought, strapped down in his chair in the control room, *I wouldn't mind the "Star Trek" artificial gravity.*

"Reactor on line," the voice of the reactor chief came over the intercom.

"Roger," Chun barked. He tasted acid in the back of his throat. Fifteen years making a living in space and he still got sick in free fall as his guts desperately searched for "up."

"Mass driver powered up," Diane reported over the intercom.

"Roger," Chun repeated. *Soon,* he thought. "Masuka drives?"

"On line, sir," Diane replied. "Ready for acceleration."

Chun looked at Navigator Naguchi. She was curled up in front of her computer console, her long legs bent up so her shoulders were resting on her knees.

"Ready, Bente?" Chun asked her.

"Anytime, Director," she replied. "Computer reads positive control of yaw, pitch, and roll."

Chun looked at his beautiful navigator and wondered briefly why she was so reticent and seemed so lonely. If he wasn't married, he'd have been on her like self-righteousness on an eco-politician.

Chun hit the intercom button. "Everyone prepare for acceleration in one minute. Report by section to the AD."

"Mass driver and Masuka drive section ready," Diane informed Assistant Director Banda.

"Reactor ready."

"Miners ready," Tsuji said.

"Life support ready," Taylor reported.

"Security ready," Thorne said.

"Navigation ready," Naguchi said.

"Communications ready," said Hikiru Manna, Communications Chief for the asteroid.

"All ready," Assistant Director Banda reported in his resonant voice.

Chun smiled. "Roger. Acceleration, now. Communications, inform the *Kyushu*."

"Yes, sir," Manna replied.

A few hundred meters away, six Masuka drives started to release a steady stream of ions. In conjunction, the kilometer long mass driver started throwing rock, ground so finely it ran like a liquid, out behind the asteroid at velocities just under that of light. Acceleration slowly built up to 0.16G. The asteroid shrugged off the last of the minuscule layer of dust that was left behind like a cloud of confused gnats.

Chun unstrapped himself and stood. He took in a deep breath of the air, composed of oxygen from Europa and nitrogen bought from the Russians on Mars–for their price but still cheaper than lifting it from Earth. His stomach stopped protesting as up and down became realities again.

"Ah, that feels better. Bente, how's the course?"

Nuguchi studied her computer and then turned to Chun with a broad smile. "Right down the pipe, Director."

"Good work. AD?"

"Yes, Alex?"

"I'll be in my office. Tell the miners it's time to earn their pay."

"Yes, sir."

***

Ceres, if it was in orbit about a planet, would be a respectable moon. At 1,000 kilometers in diameter, and somewhat centrally located in the asteroid belt, this smallest of minor planets (some still insisted on calling it the largest asteroid) was the logical place for SRI's asteroid facility. Made more of ice and carbonates and clay, the SRI facility was built on the surface using technology developed building the company's facility on Europa.

The mass of the asteroid provided about one fiftieth of a gee gravity so that everything eventually floated to the floor.

Independent miners came to Ceres for supplies, to sample the "entertainment," and to sell their finds. A person could make a few million euros in the span of half a decade, if they didn't get themselves killed. Some returned to Earth or the Moon. Most stayed in the belt, too damn independent for even NESA's lose control.

At the public spaceport, Caroline Zalesky waited at the airlock leading to the independent mining ship, the *Ginney Mae.*

Zalesky waited patiently, knowing the owner would eventually return. She thought about her husband, David, who was right then on the asteroid SRI-1961. They'd met and fallen in love on the Moon last year. But he was a mass driver tech and she had committed herself to working on Ceres. She hoped to get an asteroid assignment soon so they could work together.

Since Head of Security Mitchel had sent his order to her boss, Sue McKenna, about checking on independent miners, Zalesky had checked the computer records on every miner that returned to the asteroid.

From the interior of the facility, a fat man floated into the staging area. Zalesky mused to herself that he should have "Goodyear" painted on his side. She noticed a bandage on his neck.

"Mr. Mouret?" she said before he could pass by.

It took him a long time to stop his considerable mass.

"Yes?" he asked, eying her security uniform.

"Are you the owner-operator of the *Ginney Mae*?"

"Yes."

"Would you mind answering a few questions?"

Mouret looked at her. On Ceres, when an SRI Security person asked politely, it usually paid to be cooperative lest they become impolite. SRI had a monopoly on independent miner support. No one dared risk raising the ire of Space Resources.

"No problem," he said.

"You were here just a little over a month ago. Records show you bought large quantities of supplies, enough for six or so months, and paid cash."

"Yes."

"And, yesterday you bought more supplies for about four months in space and had to use credit."

"Does SRI doubt I can pay my bill?" Mouret asked.

"No," Zalesky replied. "But it is curious that you should return so soon and with nothing to sell."

Mouret's eyes shifted as if he were looking for an escape.

"I sold my supplies. Or actually, I was ripped off."

"By whom?"

"I don't know who they were," he said almost whining.

Zalesky didn't know if he was lying or not–and didn't care.

"Would you come with me, please?"

He nodded. "Fine," he said noncommittally.

***

Faruq heard a scuffle outside the thick oak door of his office. He pulled open the middle drawer and removed a Makarov nine-millimeter pistol.

The door flew open and General Sa'ud bounded into the room. Faruq could see through the door where two armed soldiers held Faruq's private bodyguard.

Faruq let the general see his weapon. "Marhaban *sadiqi*," he said calmly as if nothing were out of the ordinary.

Sa'ud stood erect and straightened his uniform in a slow, dignified ritual. Finally he spoke with a deliberate casual air. "Someone is trying to erode the support for the president in the Party."

"I don't think so, aquid."

"But delegates are openly speaking seditiously against the president. Some say you, Faruq, would be a good replacement," Sa'ud said, as if retelling a little joke.

Faruq took his cue from his adversary. "Surely you are mocking me, *habibi*. I am the president's most loyal and humble servant. I have no ambition but to serve him."

Sa'ud sneered. "You speak well. Perhaps it is that talent that moved support in the Party to you."

"Or, more likely, it is disappointment with the actions of the president in dealing with the Zionist state. I, too, have heard these voices of dissent and I assure you, General, I am as concerned as you for the future of the president."

The large man released a loud, snorting laugh. "I have no time for your deceptions, Faruq. But remember, I will see you dead before I see you president."

"Perhaps it won't be me that dies," Faruq said with a hint of menace in his voice.

"*In sha'allah*," Sa'ud growled back. He executed an about-face and strode out of the room, the clack of his boots on the tile a perfect, rhythmic cadence. The soldiers released Faruq's man and followed their leader.

"Forgive me, aquid," the guard said sheepishly.

Faruq replaced his pistol in his desk. "It is already forgotten. Now, back in the hall; I have work to do."

Faruq saw the admiration in the man's eyes. You can't force that kind of loyalty from a man with weapons; you have to earn it. If Faruq had one skill it was gaining the loyalty of those around him. He'd need it in the next few days.

***

Congresswoman Polasky had long ago checked FBI files against the photo of the woman named Shari Johnson. She even did a face recognition search through federal government archives of digital photos that matched the face in the digital photo she took of the woman. Nothing turned up and she basically forgot the whole thing.

She went to her office late in the afternoon after spending time on the floor voting on this and that amendment to this or that bill. She entered the outer office and her secretary told her that she had an appointment with a clerk at the Justice Department named Brian Hocking. Polasky said she knew him and went into her office.

"Hello, Brian," she said, doffing her wet raincoat. It was a rainy, early spring in the state of Columbia.

"Good afternoon, Congresswoman," Hocking replied respectfully.

Polasky sat behind her desk. "When was the last time I saw you, Brian?"

"The rally for the complete shut-down of NASA."

Polasky nodded. She remembered. She'd voted for the bill that stipulated eliminating the useless, wasteful National Aeronautics and Space Administration and spending the money on low-income housing. The United States didn't need a space program. Weather and communications satellites could be rented from the Japanese or Russians. In the U.S., only the military was involved in space, maintaining the exorbitantly expensive and needless "Star Wars" system. Repeated attempts to shut it down were blocked by the military-industrial complex and their radical, right-wing dupes. But the war machine was so entrenched in American society it would literally take a revolution to dismantle it. Polasky was just one of the many working toward that revolution.

"Yes," Polasky said, "I remember that. What can I do for you today?"

Brian took a computer from his briefcase. "This is strictly confidential," he said almost officiously. "But I feel I must bring this to your attention."

"Yes?" Polasky prodded.

Brian explained his job at the Justice Department. "I found this file. It seems an FBI agent interfered in a bias crime case." He held up the computer.

"May I see?" Polasky asked.

He handed the computer to her.

Polasky looked at the picture. "Brian," she asked "does this file have 'Employer' on it anywhere?"

"It's towards the bottom, under her registration for probation for the unlawful self-defense offense."

"Oh, yes, here it is." Polasky studied the screen for a few long minutes.

"Brian," she said casually, "this is interesting. May I have a copy of this file?"

"Yes. But, I would appreciate if you would not reveal your source."

"Of course." She handed the computer back to him, told him the proper code, and it downloaded to her computer.

Of course she wouldn't reveal her source; she wasn't going to leak this to the press, as is the usual practice in Columbia. She shooed Brian out of her office and turned on the computer. But before she could tell it whom to call, her secretary interrupted.

"Congresswoman, there's a Mr. Fowler of the Green Party here to see you."

Polasky vented a sigh and switched and said, "Show him in, please."

It took Polasky until almost nine to get Fowler out of her office. She didn't want to evict him out on some pretense. She always tried to help the Greens whenever she could. The Greens had endorsed her in her district since there was no one from their party running. If she didn't take Fowler seriously, it could jeopardize her career.

As soon as Fowler left, Polasky called Trent's office. A computer answered, reporting that the office was closed for the evening.

She then called Trent's residence. Vera answered; there was no video since Trent insisted on using a simple computer with no video.

***

Beatty seemed to be watching Charlie more. She didn't know if it was because he found her suddenly attractive or suddenly suspicious. She knew she was being paranoid. But was she being paranoid enough? In any case she didn't want any attention, amorous or not, from that man.

As she went to bed that night she decided to break into the basement. She hoped she would find something, anything for Freeman and then get the hell out of this house.

About midnight, the couple in the corner finally was quiet. Charlie, dressed only in panties again, padded barefoot to the kitchen. She didn't like being so naked but, then again, a bare chest might give her a needed distraction.

She slid the panel back and studied the door. It didn't look incredibly sturdy. She got a chef's knife out of a drawer and, keeping her ears open, began prying the doorjamb off. Charlie used the tip of the now much-abused knife to push back the bolt. Before she could push the door open the bolt sprung back into place.

She tried again and this time the door opened easily. A dark set of stairs descended into black velvet darkness. She found a light switch and bathed the stairwell in light. Charlie carefully went down the wooden stairs, closing the door behind her.

***

The *Rock Killer* had been chasing the asteroid for just over a day. Knecht smiled and turned to Griffin. "I've got it visually."

"What do you need to plot intercept course?"

"Range, velocity, bearing, course."

"Can we get that without using radar?"

Knecht shook her head. "This ship doesn't have laser range finders. I can only estimate range visually based on an estimate of the rock's size. Velocity and course I would have to estimate on stellar occlusion, subtracting the component of our velocity in their course. It's pretty tricky."

"I want only passive observations. No telling what kind of equipment they have on that thing. How long before we can get radar lock on for the missiles?"

Knecht shrugged her shoulders. "About an hour."

Griffin smiled. "At this distance, how long for a message to reach Earth?"

Trudeau spoke. "About 22 minutes."

"Knecht," Griffin said, "let me know 20 minutes before we can launch missiles. We can send the message then and it'll get to Earth just after the attack begins."

"Okay," she said. Then she smiled at him.

Griffin climbed down the ladder to the level below the bridge. He went into the captain's quarters and sat at the desk. His stomach was knotted with anticipation and he stared at the blank wall. Griffin didn't believe in the Judeo-Christian God of his grandparents, but he did presume some superior force existed in the universe that would approve of Griffin's actions on behalf of Its environment. To that idea, he prayed for success.

Suddenly, he felt himself get heavier. The *Rock Killer* was accelerating at one full gee for the first time since leaving the Belt. His watch said only 15 minutes of the hour until launch had passed when he heard someone descend the ladder. Knecht came into the room.

"Is it time, already?" he asked her.

She shook her head. "No, about 25 minutes until you want to send the message. I wanted to talk to you alone."

"Have a seat," Griffin said.

She shook her head. "No, this won't take long. I just wanted to say I appreciate..." her voice trailed off.

"What?" Griffin asked.

"I appreciate," she tried again, "how you..."

"Yes?" he prompted.

"How you don't–or rather, how you accept me for what I can do, not how I look."

Griffin shrugged. If she wanted to believe he didn't consider her looks that was fine with him. "I know you're good at your job," he said.

"It's the first time anyone, any man, has accepted me as a person and not a..."

"A what?"

"A thing," she spat with disgust.

"What do you mean?"

"Remember," she said," when I told you about my step-father and all that?"

"Yes," Griffin breathed. The implicit horror of her story had haunted him since.

"Well," she continued, "I just want to tell you that you're the first person I've trusted for a long time. It's so nice to be able to confide in a person."

"You do keep up quite a barrier," Griffin observed.

"I know," she agreed. "Force of habit. Last person I confided in, Trent, didn't care about me. She only wanted me to advance the revolution and for her own gratification."

"What about now?" Griffin asked.

"I guess," she whispered, "I trust you."

Griffin stood and moved toward her. She didn't move away. As he touched her, she stiffened momentarily. She put her arms tentatively around him and slowly met his mouth with hers. Then all reluctance disappeared. Hands reached expectantly for zippers and Velcro as the bodies moved to the bunk.

He wondered briefly why she was suddenly lissome—perhaps the tension of the impending attack. But he soon stopped wondering and continued acting on instinct. She lay beneath him and he supported his weight on his knees and one hand while the other investigated her strong yet silky body. She strained to kiss him while they finished undressing one another.

He moved his hands across her skin and finally touched her between the thighs. She gave a startled yelp, then relaxed and her face showed her contentment.

"No one ever did that before," she said softly before pulling him down until they fused.

***

Charlie held a KS-900 nine-millimeter submachine gun, like the one that had killed Frank, in her hand. It was shaped like a pound of butter with a short barrel and long magazine and a pistol grip. She smiled. This weapon could get Beatty and Whaltham extradited to Japan or Europe to pay for Frank's death.

She continued to search the basement. There were more weapons, some explosives, and enough ammunition for the revolution that Beatty and Whaltham kept hoping for. She didn't find any space suits, though. In one corner on a desk she found a very modern, very expensive IBM superconducting portable mini-mainframe. She turned it on and discovered the operating system was the current standard. But the files were encrypted. But the encryption system was in the memory. She almost laughed when she found it.

Upon opening the first file, Charlie's eyes grew wide. The computer documented GA finances for the past twelve years: where the money came from and where it went. The money came mostly from small donations from individuals, the occasional large donation from some persons with more money than brains, and some charitable foundations. There was one such foundation listed that SRI had contributed funds to in the past.

The money went to the mortgage on the house, various vehicles, and incidental expenses. What Charlie was really interested in was the weapons, ammunition, and supplies bought on the black market, including the purchase of Russian pressure suits from Yemen. The purchase of the South African KS-900 was well documented. Someone in the GA organization was a fastidious record keeper. *They'll regret that,* Charlie thought.

She found a data chip in a drawer and began copying the files.

***

It was early evening in Tokyo when the message from Ceres arrived. Mitchel had just sent Meyoung home and ordered up some dinner from the restaurant on the top floor of the building when his computer beeped and an email message popped up in a box. Mitchel expanded the box to fill the screen and read it:

27 APR 0802Z

TO: SEC HEAD MITCHEL, SRI HQ, TOKYO

FROM: CHIEF OF SEC MC KENNA, SEC DEPT, SRI ASTEROID FACILITY, CERES ASTEROID

SUBJECT: *"ROCK SKIPPER"* PROVISIONS INDEPENDENT SHIP, THE "GINNEY-MAE" RETURNED CERES YESTERDAY. OWNER, JEAN-CLAUDE MOURET, COMPLAINED OF ASSAULT BY GAIA ALLIANCE MEMBERS. SAID HE RENDEZVOUSED WITH *"ROCK SKIPPER"* AT COORDINATES: 297,406,500 KM RHO, 087 DEGREES THETA, 95 DEGREES PHI, FOUR DAYS AGO. HE HAD NO IDEA WHAT THEIR PLANS WERE. NOTE: MOURET SAID THE GA MEMBERS REFERRED TO *"ROCK SKIPPER"* AS *"ROCK KILLER."*

"Damn," Mitchel whispered. He worked on his computer a few minutes. Soon it displayed all SRI assets within four days travel at 1.5 gees from 297 million kilometers from the sun, 87 degrees from Earth's position on January first and 5 degrees above the plane of the elliptic. It was a sphere with the radius of almost three astronomical units, or just over Ceres' mean distance from the sun. That meant they could be almost anywhere in half the solar system. *Rock Killer*, he thought. *Damn*. While Ceres was sometimes called an asteroid, it wasn't referred to as "rock" like an asteroid moving to the inner solar system. Even the media referred to SRI's mobile asteroids as "rocks."

Currently, there were three such asteroids in space. SRI-1859 was pretty much in pieces at Lagrange point five and attacking it would be redundant. SRI-1960, at L-4, was vulnerable but could be evacuated easily. Also, why would they go all the way to the asteroid belt, just to return to attack a target in Earth orbit? Rendezvous with the miner? No, the Syrians could have supplied them close to Earth. SRI-1961, just leaving the belt, had to be their target.

"Computer, record outgoing message."

174

The display showed "RECORDING."

"Message as follows: To: Director Chun, SRI-1961; from: Security Head Mitchel, SRI HQ, Tokyo. Subject: Possible attack on SRI-1961 by *Rock Skipper*. Text: *Rock Skipper*, armed with space-to-space missiles, may attack SRI-1961. SRI-1961 seems the most likely target of SRI-1960, SRI-1961, and Ceres. Time of possible attack is unknown. Alex, I don't know what you can do but be prepared. End Message. Send, top priority."

A cute little icon of a piece of paper with wings fluttered off the screen in a display that always struck Mitchel as silly and at this moment downright ludicrous.

He requested data on SRI-1961's distance from Earth. It was over 360 million kilometers. At 300,000 kilometers a second, the light speed delay was about 20 minutes.

"Damn," Mitchel said. "Computer, send a copy of that message to Ceres appended to the attention of the Director of Ceres, Kuffer."

Another winged icon took flight.

"Computer, call Nakata."

The Deputy Director of Space Operations for Asteroid Operations probably would want to order the evacuation of SRI-1960 as a precaution.

Nakata was in his office, despite the late hour. Mitchel didn't know anyone on the executive floors who didn't regularly work 60 to 70 hours a week.

"Yes, Mitchel?" Nakata said on the screen.

Mitchel was always at a loss about what to call the DDSOAO. Technically, they were peers. But Mitchel was younger and had been a section chief fewer years than Nakata. Also, the other man had an ambiance around him that made it impossible for Mitchel to call him anything other than, "Mr. Nakata. I have reason to believe the Gaia Alliance will attack either SRI-1961 or 1960. I have already sent a warning to Director Chun. I wondered if you would want to evacuate 1960?"

Nakata thought for a moment, then said, "Do you think an attack is imminent?"

"Yes, I do. However, I believe 1961 is the most likely target. I still thought you might want to evacuate as a precaution."

"Yes," Nakata said. "That would be prudent. I will have all personnel evacuated to the support ship and the ship return to the Low Earth Orbit Facility. It shouldn't take long."

"Thank you, Mr. Nakata." The screen went black and Mitchel sat back in his chair. He looked over the metropolis below. He'd done all he humanly could do. He was afraid it wasn't enough.

***

Trent picked up the phone/computer and punched in a remembered address. "Whaltham," she said, "Do you know who this is?"

"Yes. It's the middle of the God damn night. This better be good."

"It is. I sent a woman to Beatty two months ago. Shari Johnson."

"Yes, I know. I met her."

"She works for Space Resources Incorporated."

"Shit!" he yelled into the computer's handset.

"I just found out," Trent defended herself.

"God damn it. Okay, I'll take care of it."

"Okay," Trent said, not knowing what else to say.

"It'll be taken care of," he repeated before disconnecting.

"What is it?" his wife asked.

"Nothing, go to sleep. I have to make a call. I'll do it from the terminal in my den."

"A patient?"

"Yes."

***

Griffin and Knecht emerged from the lower depths onto the bridge. Trudeau and Cole watched them climb up. Cole's face registered her disgust.

Knecht walked to her computer. "We can launch in 15 minutes." She turned to Griffin. "Sorry, Alan."

"No problem, Barb. Trudeau, send the message."

The plan was that, since they were about 20 light-minutes from Earth, the announcement of the attack should be timed to be received just as the attack was happening. That meant the message had to be sent before the actual strike.

Trudeau tuned the radio to a frequency that was monitored by the press and most governments. He sent the prerecorded message on that frequency. He turned on the bridge speakers so his companions could hear it, too.

"This is the *Rock Killer* of the Gaia Alliance to all the people of Earth and space."

***

SRI-1961 bristled with antennas like a pincushion. A computer scanned all frequencies used by man in space using technology and software developed for the SETI project late in the last century. The computer was programmed to key in on certain words and phrases and then notify the operator using algorithms developed by intelligence agencies in the nineteen hundreds.

One of those phrases was "Gaia Alliance" or "GA," recently programmed in.

The operator on shift was using the computer's spare memory to read a book since the screen was displaying nothing. He was in the middle of a sentence when the screen cleared the novel and the computer started beeping almost frantically.

The screen displayed: GAIA ALLIANCE. Out of a speaker came the voice message the computer had locked the receiver on. At the same time the computer started recording the incoming message.

"...to all the people of Earth and space," the male voice, obviously reading a text, said. "Space Resources Incorporated will not learn the price of greed. SRI was served a blow in the Mojave Desert after their desecration of that fragile environment with their cancer causing microwave antenna field. But still they did not learn. A month ago, they were dealt a blow on the Moon after their continued desecrations there. And still they did not learn. SRI is continuing to treat the asteroid belt, specifically, and space in general, as if it were their private property and they can do as they wish with it. Even now they are stealing yet another asteroid and taking it back to Earth for their own greedy purposes.

"So, the Gaia Alliance," the message continued, "has destroyed that asteroid to prevent SRI from using it. We regret the loss of life, but we are fighting a war for the survival of the human race."

"Oh, shit," the operator almost yelled. He hit an intercom button connecting him with communications chief Manna's office/quarters.

"Boss, you've got to hear this."

***

"What the hell are you doing?" a voice growled loudly.

Charlie looked up from the computer to the base of the stairs. Beatty was standing there, dressed in shorts and a tee shirt.

"I said what are you doing down here?" he repeated, moving menacingly toward her.

Charlie looked around. There were no other exits. She hoped there might be an emergency escape tunnel. This was definitely an emergency.

"I'm sorry," she said as innocently as she could. She stood and displayed herself to him. "I couldn't sleep. I wandered down here and found this computer. I thought it might have some games on it." She walked toward him slowly. His shorts didn't hide that he was noticing her state of undress.

"There are no games on that," he said firmly. "Besides, you had to break in to get down here."

She moved closer to him and reached out to touch his shirt. "I was curious. Locked doors do that to me. I'm sorry."

She moved so close that their bodies were almost touching. "I'm not in trouble, am I?"

"Yes," he said, but not too firmly.

"Please," she pleaded with her sea green eyes wide open.

Inwardly, she convulsed as she wrapped one arm around his thick neck and guided his lips to hers. "Please," she whispered as their mouths touched.

He grabbed her and kissed her.

***

Griffin could see the asteroid through the dome ceiling window of the *Rock Killer*'s bridge. Because of its low albedo, SRI-1961 was more visible because it occulted stars rather than reflected sunlight. The mass driver was a thin, bright line extending behind the rock. The combination looked like a thick wire embedded in an ellipsoid-shaped lump of coal. The *Rock Killer* was approaching from behind and on angle of about 30 degrees from the asteroid's velocity vector.

"How soon?" Griffin asked.

"A few minutes," Knecht said.

"Are you ready, Cole?"

Cole was bending over her fire-control panel. "I'm ready," she said. "But acquisition radar would help."

Griffin shook his head. "No radar until just before launch."

He looked at the asteroid. *Good-bye,* he thought to himself.

CHAPTER TWELVE

"...we're all going to be trying to suck down vacuum."

Charlie had all of her weight on her left leg and was slowly bringing her right knee back. Beatty had relaxed as she kissed him and his legs were just far enough apart.

The computer in the kitchen, just like the simple one in Trent's house, beeped.

Beatty released her and looked up the stairs. *Damn, saved by the bell,* Charlie thought. Another moment and he would have been rolling on the floor in pain.

"I've got to get that," he said. "Don't go anywhere," he ordered.

"I won't," Charlie breathed as demurely as possible.

Beatty bounded up the stairs.

Charlie grabbed the chip out of the computer, hoping she'd downloaded enough data. She scooped up one of the South African made weapons and a box of ammunition. She didn't bother reading the label.

She heard Beatty pick up the handset and say, "Hello?"

Charlie climbed the stairs three at a time. The back door of the house was not two meters away, but Beatty was between her and the exit and the back yard was bounded by high fences.

"Hey, stop," Beatty yelled, dropping the handset and rushing her.

She stepped out of his way at the last moment and tripped him. He fell hard but she didn't wait to see him hit the floor. She ran for the front door.

The midnight streets were abandoned. Charlie sprinted in bare feet across the dry grass of the lawn to the house next door. It was small and well cared for. The windows were covered with iron bars. Charlie pounded on the door and screamed at the top of her lungs. Beatty exploded out of the GA house and ran toward Charlie.

The porch light came on and the door opened, stopped by a thick chain. An elderly woman looked out at Charlie with wide eyes.

"Help me," Charlie said simply, trying to hide the gun and ammo box behind her leg.

"*Pour Dios*," the woman said and closed the door. But Charlie could hear her working the chain off. Beatty was almost to the porch when the door opened again.

Charlie slipped in and the woman started to shut it. Beatty's hand grabbed the side of the door and started to push it open. The old woman resisted but she hadn't the strength or the mass to prevail.

Charlie rushed the door and hit it with her shoulder. It slammed shut, closing on Beatty's hand. He howled in pain and rage but pulled his hand away. Charlie shut the door, locked the dead bolt and replaced the chain. Beatty pounded on the door, yelling more obscenities than Charlie knew existed. He ran to a window and tried to pull off the bars.

The old woman was talking frantically to her computer in Spanish. She finished about the time Beatty gave up and went away. Charlie was sure he'd be back soon and with weapons.

"The police," the woman said, "are coming. I get you clothes now."

And Charlie was suddenly aware she was only in panties.

***

Alexander Chun was doing administration work on a computer in his office/quarters. He could feel the vibration of the miners' tools as they dug out corridors through the rock. They could get a lot done in the two weeks the trip took. They had to be careful not to change the center of mass of the asteroid too much. Small changes Naguchi's navigation computer could compensate for by varying the thrust of the rear Masuka drives. Too large a change in the center of mass and the rock would tumble.

The intercom system beeped. Alex tapped the button and returned his hands to the keyboard.

"Chun here," he said.

"Director," a voice said tensely, "this is Manna, communications. We've intercepted a broadcast from the GA I think you need to hear."

Alex turned, giving intercom his full attention. "Send it."

***

Beatty returned to the house. He planned to get some reinforcements and some explosives and weapons from the basement. He didn't know what Shari was up to, but he was going to stop it.

"What's happening?" one man asked as Beatty came through the front door. There was a cluster of GA membership in the living room in various states of undress.

"And the computer has a call on it," a woman said.

"Shit," Beatty spat. "It's Whaltham." He went into the kitchen and picked up the handset that was still dangling on its cord. "Sorry about that," he said to Whaltham.

"What happened?"

"I caught Shari Johnson messing with the mainframe. She just ran away. I went after her but she got into a neighbor's house."

"She's an SRI plant," Whaltham said. "Kill her."

"I can't go in after her. Trent said poor people are off limits. When the revolution comes, she said, it is the oppressed poor that would rise up to support the GA."

"To hell with Trent's stupid political ideals," Whaltham barked. "Poor people get hurt in revolutions, too! And prepare to get out of that house. Get everything and everyone to the secondary house and burn that sucker down. But first, kill that bitch!"

"My pleasure," Beatty growled and hung up the handset. He returned to the living room and barked orders to start packing.

The GA had an electric van parked in a garage a few miles away. He sent two people for it. The rest he started packing up the equipment in the basement. Then he pulled three men aside.

"Come with me," he said and then went into the basement, not to pack but to get the weapons.

***

"We should be close enough," Knecht reported.

Griffin nodded. "Cole, you may now use radar."

"Right," she said. A few moments later she exclaimed, "Damn, we can't get lock yet. We're out of range for the Pumas."

Knecht looked at Griffin. "I'm sorry. It must be smaller than I thought."

***

The communications room operator had just settled back in his seat. He was developing his own theories of what the intercepted message meant and didn't like the answers he was getting. Then he jumped when, again, the computer beeped wildly. The screen displayed:

RADAR SOURCE X:154.3, Y:094.7, D:???.?
CORRELATING FREQUENCY, MODULATION, AND POLARIZATION WITH USES. PLEASE WAIT ONE MOMENT....
AN/XPS-119(V) U.S. LANDING CONTROL RADAR

The operator down loaded the information to Chun's computer. He wasn't supposed to do that without consulting Communications Chief Manna, but this was too important considering the intercepted message.

Chun had just finished listening to the Gaia Alliance statement when his computer displayed the radar data:

AN/TPG-209 (it continued) U.S. FIRE CONTROL RADAR FRENCH "PUMA" RADAR GUIDED SPACE-TO-SPACE MISSILE ACQUISITION RADAR.
RUSSIAN –

Chun stopped reading. He again hit the intercom button. "Control room, we could be attacked by space-to-space missiles at any time. I'm on my way. Close all emergency doors and evacuate the outer areas."

AD Banda's voice came back. "Understood. We don't have very many emergency doors installed yet."

"I know," Chun growled in frustration. *And no way to fight back.* he realized angrily. SRI-1961, like all space facilities and ships, was on Coordinated Universal Time, or Zulu time. So it was "morning" and the "day" watch was on. Chun was thankful for that. It meant all his best people were on shift and rested.

This was the best time to have an emergency, he realized as he left his office for the passage to the control room.

***

Cole smiled, wrinkling her piggy face. "I've got missile lock."

"Fire a missile," Griffin said. "Let's see what she does."

Cole punched a button on her console and the ship shuddered.

Out the bridge window, they saw the flame of the missile's exhaust as it slung itself at the rock.

"Travel time is about two minutes," Cole said. "Should impact about center of the radar aspect."

***

The computer in the communications room displayed:

RADAR SOURCE #2: X:154.4, Y:094.6, D:???.?
CORRELATING FREQUENCY, MODULATION, AND POLARIZATION WITH USES. PLEASE WAIT ONE MOMENT...

Hikiru Manna waited impatiently while the computer searched its database. He remembered wondering why they bothered putting such a sophisticated computer on an asteroid. Now he was thankful for the foresight of the SRI executives that decided the computer was worth the expense.

The display eventually read:

AIM-10A U.S. "COBRA" RADAR GUIDED AIR-TO-AIR MISSILE GUIDANCE RADAR

SA-29 REPUBLIC OF RUSSIA RADAR GUIDED SURFACE-TO-AIR MISSILE GUIDANCE RADAR

SRI/XPQ-009 SPACE RESOURCES INC. DOCKING GUIDANCE RADAR

FRENCH "PUMA" RADAR GUIDED SPACE-TO-SPACE MISSILE GUIDANCE RADAR.

Manna looked at the screen over the operator's shoulder and released a few Japanese expletives. "I want the computer to only warn us when it picks up a new source of that. The acquisition radar would be on the ship. We need to know where that is. And continuously download this to the control room."

"Yes, sir," the operator said, his fingers pounding on the keyboard.

***

Chun was climbing a ladder through the passage to the control room. Suddenly his world literally moved. The ladder moved up to violently kiss him in the face. His hands and feet transmitted a massive vibration as if the rock had been hit by a hammer. Then he felt a change in "up." No longer was the ladder and tube parallel to up and down but at an angle. He found himself hanging from the rungs as if he were climbing the underside of a ladder resting against a building. If he'd been in full one gee he might not have made it up the ladder. But he was able to climb to the control room. The floor had a definite tilt. Navigator Naguchi was quickly but calmly working at her computer. "We've picked up a spin and we're tumbling," she said. "I can correct it."

"The center of mass?"

"It changed, but I can still compensate for it."

It was a good thing they weren't very far off the center of the asteroid, Chun realized. Farther out and the centrifugal force might have plastered them to the outside wall instead of just giving a perceived tilt to the floor.

Chun turned to Banda. "Do you know where it hit?"

Banda shrugged his huge shoulders. "In the rear. We were lucky. It hit nothing but rock. Nothing breached."

"Thank God," Chun said, then realized he had to wipe blood from his lip where the ladder had hit him. The floor became magically level. "Good job, Bente."

***

The bridge of the *Rock Killer* echoed with cheers. The asteroid had grown a cone of flame and rock dust, then began spinning and tumbling. Griffin looked at Knecht and she smiled broadly.

When the flame died, Griffin looked over the asteroid through the telescope. As he watched, the spin slowed to a stop and the tumble ended with the asteroid in the same attitude it had before the attack.

"Damn! Fire again, Cole."

***

"Control room, this is communications. We're picking up guidance radar again. They've launched another."

Chun watched the numbers on the screen from communications.

RADAR SOURCE: X:159.8, Y:173.3, D:???.?

He looked around the bridge. Everyone was braced for impact.

"Control room, this is Thorne. All outer areas except the mass driver are evacuated. The techs figured we'd need the thrust."

"Negative," Chun replied to the intercom. "The mass driver can't make that much difference."

"Roger."

Chun looked at the display.

RADAR SOURCE: X:160.3, Y:172.7, D:???.? it read. The ship was almost directly behind. Alex had seen a man, Theresa Gold's murderer, fall into the exhaust of a mass driver. He, his suit, and his weapon had been atomized.

"Thorne!"

"Yes, Alex?"

"Never mind. We'll need the mass driver crew."

After a slight pause Thorne said, "Okay."

"Mass Driver, shut down and stand by. I want full thrust on my call."

"This is Zalesky," a man's voice said. "Chief O'Rourke said that she understands."

Oh, hell, Alex thought. Diane O'Rourke and Diana Vuillard were in the drive section. The knot in his stomach grew worse at the possibility of losing friends. Then he forced it out of his mind. He had more people to worry about.

"Bente," he said.

"Yes?"

"I want you to make that 'X' number one—"

The room moved and vibrations rattled Chun so hard he thought his insides would be mush. Again the floor took on a tilt, smaller than last time.

"Correct that spin," Chun began again, "and make both 'X' and 'Y' equal one-eighty. That's one eight zero. Let me know when you have it."

"Yes, sir." She bent over her thruster controls.

"Diane, still with us?"

"Yes," she said, her voice taut with tension. "But that one hit close."

***

"They're turning," Knecht reported anxiously. "Away from us."

"Don't worry, they can't get away," Griffin commented casually. "It looks like we've damaged the mass driver. Fire again, Cole."

***

Naguchi worked her computer and turned to look at the slaved screen occasionally. She ignored the warning of a new launch. The rock agonizingly slowly changed pitch and the numbers changed digit by slow digit. Normally she'd have the computer calculate a combination of pitch, yaw, and roll, called the Euler Angle, to bring the asteroid to the attitude needed. But since she was trying to line it up with a moving target (which she assumed to be the stolen *Rock Skipper*), she had to do it manually. She was helped by the fact the *Rock Skipper* had yet to change heading. Another missile hit and again the control room vibrated and the floor tilted. A fine touch on the controls and she had the rock stabilized. She now had to change yaw. She gave the port yaw Masuka drive full power. Then, with a practiced hand, she used the starboard drive to start slowing the rock's swing.

"Another launch," she heard Manna say.

The ship's yaw was slowing. She stopped it when the 'X' number was 179.7 and 'Y' read 180.1. Close enough.

"Got it, Alex."

Chun smiled grimly. "Mass driver, full thrust now!"

***

"We're directly behind them," Knecht barked as a warning.

"Launch again," Griffin ordered. "It should go right up their ass."

The ship shuddered for the fourth time.

"Do you want to change heading?" Knecht asked urgently.

"What for?"

"The mass driver," she said emphatically.

"What about it?"

"If they—" Knecht started, then noticed Griffin was enthralled by watching the missile and not listening. She turned to her controls. The ship pitched 90 degrees. She slammed on the drive.

"What the hell?" Griffin yelled as the asteroid swung from above his head to in front of him. He turned to Knecht but the full 1.5 gee acceleration of the ship grabbed at him.

Unprepared, he was slapped to the floor. He stood and looked at Knecht.

"What the hell?" he screamed at her.

"The mass driver," she yelled back. Griffin turned to look out the window in time to see the mass driver start up. But, just behind the photons that brought that information, the dust-like reaction mass smote the ship with the powerful kinetic punch its incredible speed gave it.

***

The missile the *Rock Killer* had just launched was just outside the angle the mass driver threw its exhaust and therefore escaped its fury. It was locked on the center of the profile its radar eye saw. Gyros changed its heading so that it headed straight for the profile's center. That happened to be where the base of the mass driver was connected to the asteroid.

***

"Control room, this is Manna. The acquisition radar is gone. There's still guidance radar."

"Damn," Chun said. "We got the ship but the missile is still coming. It's coming almost right up our tail pipe."

"Why doesn't the mass driver—"

The gravity momentarily grew greater. Then the air pressure and the gravity started dropping alarmingly fast.

"Mass driver," Chun said. There was no answer. Chun felt himself start to float. "Diane?" he yelled at the intercom.

Again nothing. "Bente, give us some thrust."

Naguchi worked her computer. "I've no response from the rear Masuka drive or the mass driver."

"Chun, this is Thorne," came over the intercom. His voice seemed subdued.

"Go ahead."

"The missile took out the mass driver. We're losing air. I don't know how soon we can patch it up. It blew out the emergency door. If they hit us there again..." He didn't need to finish the sentence.

Chun bowed his head. There were five people in the mass driver section, including his friends and Thorne's lover.

"Alex?" Thorne's voice came.

"I'm sorry," Alex whispered.

"If they hit us again," Thorne repeated.

"The ship is gone," Chun said with voice void of any emotion.

"How do you know?"

"Its radar is gone."

"They may have just turned it off, Alex."

Alex shook his head berating himself. "Damn, you're right." *I must be getting stupid,* he thought. Again he was letting his personal feelings interfere with what his duty demanded. He noticed Thorne had remained professional. The asteroid didn't have any rear-facing radar so there was no way to use machinery to check on the fate of the *Rock Skipper*. Alex could only think of one solution: "Send someone out to eyeball it and let me know."

"Understood."

"Director, this is Manna in communications."

"Go ahead."

"We just got a message from Security Head Mitchel."

"Send it to my computer."

"Roger."

***

"Damn it!" Charlie swore. She'd grabbed the wrong ammunition. The KS-900 used nine millimeter caseless. In her haste she'd picked up a box of 9x19mm parabellum rounds used in older pistols and submachine guns. With no ammo, the weapon was about as useful as a rock.

"What is happening?" the woman asked handing her a housecoat.

"Long story," Charlie answered putting on the paisley thing. It was too short yet too big, but it covered the essentials.

Sirens cut off the woman before she could ask another question. Soon there was a pounding on the door. Charlie opened it with the chain on. Two LAPD officers, one male, one female, stood on the porch in their flack uniforms. Charlie let them in.

"What's the problem?" the woman asked. The male spotted the weapon and bullets Charlie had left on the woman's couch.

"What the hell's that?" he said pointing and his hand went to his pistol.

"Listen," Charlie said, keeping her hands in sight, "my name is Charlene Jones. If you'll contact special agent Gordon Freeman of the FBI in Washington he'll explain everything. That weapon and this chip," she held it up, "are evidence in the murder of Space Resources personnel on the Moon."

The two cops looked at each other. The female looked at the old woman and asked her a question in Spanish. This brought forth a rapid stream of the lady's native language. The police officer occasionally asked short questions. Eventually she turned to her partner. "The lady, Mrs. Cortez, says that this woman came to her door almost naked and carrying that weapon. She said a man from the house next door tried to come into the house after her. She said she thinks the house next door is a smash house or something."

"Maybe we'd better check it out," the male said.

Charlie shook her head. "That house is national headquarters of the Gaia Alliance, the terrorist group. You'd better get some help."

The cops looked at her in disbelief. "Damn," the female whispered. "Okay," she said. "You're coming with us."

"With pleasure," Charlie said. She turned to the lady.

"Thank you, *Gracias*."

Mrs. Cortez smiled and nodded. Charlie made a mental note to see that SRI thanked her more substantially.

The male cop talked into the radio attached to his cheek. "This is delta five-three, requesting back-up and a sergeant at—"

The explosion blew the front door apart in a shower of splinters. The male cop's fractured body careened into his partner.

The spitting sound of automatic weapons fire crackled through the night. The doorframe was burning and through the smoke and flames Charlie saw the muzzle flash from a weapon being held at hip level. She pulled the old lady to the floor.

The female cop pushed the gory mess off of her and returned fire with her service pistol while yelling into her radio, "Officer needs assistance, officer down."

Charlie crawled over to the dead cop and took his pistol from its holster. The female stopped firing to see what Charlie was doing and a burst of fire made mincemeat of her face.

Charlie fired twice at the door. She saw the profile of a man falling.

The carpet was on fire and the flames were rolling against the dead bodies of the cops. Charlie took the female cop's weapon and emptied its magazine toward the door and yelled at Mrs. Cortez. "Out the back door, now!"

***

"We're losing a hell of a lot of air, sir," Security Man Perez said, pushing himself up the corridor from the remains of the emergency door that led to the mass driver. The door had been blown off its hinges.

Thorne nodded, then, remembering they were both in pressure suits, said, "I know."

"The DC foam," Perez continued, "is being sucked out the cracks before it hardens. If we don't get a new door in here we're all going to be trying to suck down vacuum." Damage control foam was designed for little breaches cause by micro-meteors or accidents, not battle damage.

"The miners are working on it," Thorne said turning to see where, behind him, miners were installing a new emergency door. It was a race to see who would finish first. Thorne didn't care, but Perez was right. Their life was being sucked out the hole where the door had been.

"I'm going in," Thorne said.

"By yourself?" Perez queried.

"Yes, I don't want to risk more than one man."

"Yes, sir."

And, thought Thorne, *if I cry, no one will see me.*

***

Mitchel sat in his office overlooking Tokyo. As the evening progressed the lights became more garish and glaring, even from this height.

Mitchel knew that in sections of Tokyo and Yokohama there were places one could purchase almost whatever one wanted. Right now he wanted a message from Alexander Chun worse than anything else. The broadcast from the *Rock Killer* had made the news a while ago and still not one bit had been broadcast from SRI-1961.

The computer beeped.

"Yes?" Mitchel yelled at the machine.

"Incoming message" the computer said in its soothing voice.

Mitchel smiled broadly. "Display."

Two icons appeared on the screen indicating the message was encoded and high priority.

Elisa Morgan's face appeared. She looked worried.

Mitchel felt his emotions sag like a sapling under a heavy snow.

"Yes, Elisa?" Mitchel asked.

"Mitch," she said, apparently not noticing Mitchel's disappointment. "I'm with Mr. Zvi Patai of the Mossad. He has come to me with a concern." The view widened to show a middle-aged man. Mitchel could tell he was a disciplined, serious person just from the determination in his tanned face.

"Mr. Mitchel," Patai said, "we have a concern."

"Yes?" Mitchel asked. He knew this would lead to something important. Elisa wouldn't waste his time during a crisis. "We have reports out of the Baathist States that there is the possibility of a *coup d'etat* soon. One man, an advisor to the president of Syria that we know only as 'Faruq,' has support from the Party and elements of the military."

"This is very interesting but what," Mitchel said, "does it have to do with SRI?"

"Mitch," Elisa said, "Mr. Patai came to me just after the announcement of the attack on the asteroid. We shared information. We knew of the Syrian support for the Gaia Alliance, the Mossad knew of the planned coup. It seems the usurper Mr. Patai is concerned about is the same Faruq we've been investigating; the one that authorized the purchase of the Pumas for the GA."

"It seems," Patai continued, "that this man plans to use this attack to his political advantage."

"Are you saying this Faruq acted without authorization?"

"No," Patai replied. "He may have over-stepped his bounds, though. But what's important is that this man must not reach power."

"Why?"

"We believe he would use Syria's nuclear missiles for a preemptive strike on Israel. Of course, we will retaliate as best we can. But still, Mr. Mitchel, millions of lives will be lost."

"Also," Elisa said, "This man is almost solely responsible for the GA having the resources to attack SRI-1961."

Mitchel looked at the faces on the screen. Patai displayed no emotion but Morgan was so untypically distraught it visibly showed.

"This man must be stopped," Patai stated firmly.

"What about your people?"

Patai's fortitude seemed to falter. "We have political considerations," he said sardonically. "The ruling party has placed many restrictions on the activities of the Mossad. It is hoped that SRI could do something."

"Such as?" Mitchel asked.

"I do not know," Patai admitted. "But something, anything."

Wonderful, Mitchel thought, *nuclear war in the Middle East. Now, not only do we have to save our own people from terrorists, but stop Armageddon.*

CHAPTER THIRTEEN

"We can save them."

The cops' bodies were making an effective firebreak, halting the advance of the flames across the rug. The front of the house was an inferno and the smoke and heat were a mixed blessing. No one was shooting at Charlie or trying to come into the house, but Charlie knew she couldn't stay put much longer.

She checked the stamp on the slide of the cop's weapon; it was a .40 caliber Smith & Wesson. Again, her box of 9mm was useless. She thought that between herself and the female cop the other gun emptied in eleven or twelve rounds. That meant she had nine or ten to go in the male cop's gun.

She waited until she thought the old lady had enough time to escape the house. Then she ran in a low crouch to avoid the smoke, putting her back to the flames.

As she got away from the roar of the fire, she could hear bullets impacting the exterior of the house. Glass shattered behind Charlie as she slipped into the backyard. From the fire or the bullets, she didn't know.

The old woman was stooped on the lawn, praying in Spanish. Charlie grabbed her arm and pulled her with her. *"¡Vamanos!"* Charlie yelled hoping that meant what she thought it did.

She half led, half dragged the poor lady across the meticulously cared-for grass. They came to a waist-high chain link fence just as someone ran around the far corner of the burning house. Charlie literally threw the woman over the barrier then turned and fired at the man. He was looking in the wrong direction and never saw what hit him. Nine rounds left.

Charlie jumped the fence as Beatty appeared from behind the house where the body of the man Charlie had just killed lay. The old woman was trotting amazingly fast for her age toward the back door of the house next door.

Beatty yelled and fired a long burst. *Stupid,* Charlie thought. He didn't control the weapon and missed her completely.

Charlie turned and squeezed off two rounds and Beatty ducked behind the corner. Seven rounds left, or maybe six.

The woman was pounding on the back door and yelling in Spanish. Charlie was going to be real surprised if anyone was foolish or brave enough to open it.

Charlie heard sirens as she saw Beatty look around the house corner and fire wildly. The flames were reaching the back of the house and Charlie suspected Beatty was starting to panic as he faced burning or risked getting shot by Charlie. She fired, driving Beatty around the corner again, closer to the inferno.

Six rounds left. She walked backwards, watching both corners of the old lady's house. Flames were showing in the back windows and the entire scene was lit with the macabre orange light that cast dancing shadows. A movement near the street caught her eye and she turned to see a GA member, the man in the duo whose coupling had kept Charlie awake, bring up a weapon. Charlie fired two rounds at him and he took cover behind a parked car. Four rounds. Beatty discharged a fusillade at Charlie, still missing. She shot back at him. Three. The man behind the car rose and Charlie fired at him, shattering a windshield. Two, or maybe one round left.

Beatty released another burst and Charlie shot at him. The slide locked back; the magazine was empty. Charlie turned and ran. She heard both Beatty's and the other man's weapons split the air as each fired a long volley at her. The bullets hit her from behind and threw her forward, face down. She could smell dirt and grass and felt wet warmth cover her back.

Sirens screamed at her and stopped suddenly. She heard almost incessant gunfire: both bursts and single shots. A helicopter was overhead. She could feel heat from the conflagration that was the woman's house; she smelled smoke and cordite. The reports from weapons slowed and finally stopped.

Someone touched her and said, "Ohmigod," as Charlie lost consciousness.

***

In his pressure suit, Thorne moved through the mass driver section, pulling himself along handholds and equipment. Some machinery was damaged and some was, incongruously, still running.

He shut off what he could.

The lights were off and he used his helmet light to survey the damage. The beam passed through a cloud of silvery snow.

The equipment and rock walls were coated in frozen water. A water pipe had burst and the water flash froze as it boiled out.

It looked to Thorne as if a lot had been lost before life support shut off the water supply.

He found one body wedged in a supporting framework. It was Diana. Under a sheath of bubble-laced ice, black blood matted her long hair and her face was a swollen horror.

Thorne clamped his throat shut. Vomiting in a pressure suit in free fall was not only messy but potentially lethal. He moved away, toward the hole in the base of the rock where the missile hit.

He used a rope to secure himself to a handhold and then swung into the jagged hole. The sky was like black felt someone had spilled sugar on. Thorne looked at the base of the mass driver. It was still secured to the rock. To the limit of his vision its lactic-like structure was undamaged. But the missile had hit some of the Masuka drives.

Lastly, Thorne surveyed the sky. He would look at a point watching for any "star" that moved. He repeated this for all the space he could see. He didn't find anything to indicate the *Rock Skipper* was still out there.

He pulled himself back into the relative security of the asteroid.

***

The control room crew was donning emergency pressure suits. The air was breathably thick but slightly cooler, about like being on a high mountain; but safety demanded that precaution.

Naguchi was having trouble fitting her lean frame into the one-size-fits-none suit. Banda pulled his suit on and helped Chun. It allowed them to talk.

"What was the message from Mitchel?" he asked.

Chun waited to seal his suit and flicked on the radio control on his arm. "A warning we may be attacked."

Banda smiled and shook his head in the bubble helmet. "We need to tell them."

"It takes about 20 minutes," Chun said. "I think we should radio Ceres first for help. They're closer."

Banda shrugged his shoulders. "I don't know what they can do for us. They have trouble keeping enough air themselves."

"I know, but it's worth a shot. How about Mars?"

"Farther than Earth now."

"Well, I didn't want to pay the Russians' price anyway."

Both smiled grimly. "Get on those messages," Chun ordered. "I'm going to life support. Find out how bad it really is."

The director of life support, Taylor, shook her head. "It's really bad. We have some reserve air but I won't release that until the second emergency door is in place." Standard procedure was to place two emergency doors between the inside and any irreparable breech.

"Then what?"

"Eight hours at most."

Alex stared in disbelief. "What about the air recycler?"

Taylor shook her head again. "Look," she said pointing.

Alex saw a group of people working on the device, which took up one wall in the cavern.

"The second missile hit blew it off its supports," Taylor said. "The third bounced it around. I don't know if we can fix it. It wasn't designed for combat."

"I know," Alex said. He looked at the device. They didn't carry a spare. The added weight and expense was deemed superfluous. It was triple redundant inside. The odds of all three of its systems, any one of which could keep the crew alive, failing simultaneously were considered as remote as, well, someone lobbing missiles at them.

"I was thinking," Taylor said, "what if we found some ice?"

"That would help. But M-type asteroids don't have much, if any, water. Our chances of finding ice in this rock are slim. And the exertion of mining will use our air faster."

"I meant, maybe there's a carbonaceous chondrite nearby. They have a high percentage of water."

Alex shook his head. "Even if there were, we couldn't maneuver to it."

"I understand," Taylor said as if she didn't want to. Understanding meant knowing how desperate their situation was.

"What are our options?" Alex asked.

"Stop all activity that's not absolutely necessary and try to rendezvous with a ship that can supply us with air or pull us off."

"That's my plan. I just don't think there's anyone that can get to us in eight hours." He'd have to ask Bente. The nearest ship was probably the *Kyushu*. He doubted it could get to them in eight hours. Alex involuntarily thought of Kirsten. *No,* he thought, *I have to keep my mind here.*

Thorne's voice over Chun's suit radio shook him out of his thoughts. "We've got the leak stopped. The miners say they broke the record for emergency door installation. In three minutes they'll have a second, back-up door installed."

"Thanks," Chun said.

"And," Thorne continued, "I went out. I didn't see anything but that doesn't mean much."

"Understood. We need to find out if we can repair the mass driver and the Masuka drive."

"I already looked. I don't know about the mass driver. It looks repairable to me. A tech could tell you better."

Damn, Alex thought. *The off duty techs should be down there looking at it right now. Why hadn't I thought of that?* "Okay, I'll send some down. What about the Masuka drive?"

"Useless. Four of the six drives are gone. The two left are right next to each other, off the center of mass. If we used them, we'd tumble."

And moving them would take much longer than eight hours. "Understood. Good job."

"Thanks," Thorne said.

"And, Taylor."

"Yes, sir?"

"Eight hours is unacceptable. Think of something, anything."

***

Charlie opened her eyes to see green. Green, like her eyes. *I thought I was supposed to see a tunnel first,* she thought.

Then she heard talking, and something beeping. Something stabbed her arm just above the wrist.

"Okay, the IV's in," a woman's voice said.

Charlie smiled. She was alive and lying prostrate with her head turned to the side. A nurse's uniform had been blocking her vision. She looked around without moving her head to see more green-suited figures orbiting her prone figure. Her vision looked like her father's attempt to use a manual camera: out of focus.

"Where am I?" she asked. Her voice was thick. Drugs, she decided. She should be in extreme pain.

"You're okay," a man said and Charlie realized it was the nurse. "You're at a hospital. Now be still and rest."

"Call the FBI," Charlie breathed. "My life is in danger."

A swatch of blue came into her vision. "It's okay. I'm a police officer."

"Call the FBI."

"Excuse me?"

Charlie felt herself going to sleep. She fought it; damned drugs. "FBI, Freeman, Washington, please." Consciousness slipped away like a wet bar of soap on the shower floor.

***

Noon prayers were over and Faruq walked with the president as they headed back to their offices. The president's loyal guards followed at a discrete distance behind.

"There are those," the president said, "that say we are not doing enough against the occupiers of Palestine and the West that supports them."

"I have heard that," Faruq answered.

"There are those," the president went on, "that say if one man showed leadership against the West he could take my place."

"I don't think that is possible, Mr. President."

"You don't?"

"No, aquid."

"Good," the president said. "Because your dealings with that eco-terrorist group could be construed as leadership against the West, and word of it is spreading in the party."

"Everything I've done has been in your name and for the *Baath Revolution*."

"Did you catch," the president said, "before going to pray, that the environmentalists you supported had attacked an asteroid."

"No," Faruq lied. The president was fishing. Did he see his support failing? Did he know Faruq had labored hard to erode it?

"Hum," the president huffed. "Do you think it is right to be involved in this adventure?"

"What hurts SRI hurts the West," Faruq said.

"Yes," the president intoned, "you've said that." The president stopped walking and faced Faruq. "But who else could it hurt?"

Faruq tried to look confused. Inwardly he smiled. If the president was making threats he must feel threatened. Faruq's plans were coming to fruition.

"*Habibi*," Faruq said, "there is no one who can threaten you. No one."

203

The president walked away and his guards followed. "I wish I could believe you, Faruq," he called back.

***

Alex looked at his computer on his wrist, then, realizing it was under his pressure suit, looked at the nearest computer screen. *Nakata should have gotten our message by now,* he thought. He doubted the asteroid chief could help them. It seemed they were on their own like no persons had ever been, millions of kilometers from the nearest other humans.

"Director?" Taylor's voice came over the intercom, interrupting Alex's thoughts.

"Yes?"

"I've got a solution. Can you come down here?"

"On my way."

"I've got some good news and some bad news," she said when Alex arrived.

"Good news can wait. What's the bad news?"

"A pipe burst in the drive section. We didn't realize it because we were all rattled by the attack. By the time we cut off the water supply we were down to about a hundred and ten liters in the main tank."

Normally, Alex would have been livid about the loss. Down to a hundred and ten liters, or about 27 gallons, would have been an inconceivable loss. But it seemed trivial, now.

Alex shrugged. "So what. That'll last us eight hours. What's the good news?"

"Water," Taylor replied. "My ice question made me realize that we could split our water into hydrogen and oxygen. The amount you get out in any period is proportional to the voltage applied. I've talked to the reactor section. They said we have plenty of power since the main drive is out."

Alex considered. "Is excess CO_2 a problem?"

"No," Taylor said. "We have emergency scrubbers."

"Good. How are you going to do it?"

"We'll drill into the top of the main water tank and put in the electrodes. Then the oxygen will just bubble out. We can feed the main tank from the rest of the water system if we need more water."

"How long will that last us?"

"That's the problem. Normally we'd have more than enough water. But that damn leak. We can feed the main tank from the rest of the water system and run the sewage recycler at maximum and that should give us around 130 liters, total, of water. Too bad we can recycle it so well. We'd have to carry more and what we lost wouldn't be so significant."

"So, how long?"

Taylor drew in a long breath. "Let me see," she said, "a person breaths about 20 grams oh-two per hour. A liter of water holds, uhm," Taylor looked at the rock ceiling, "about 880 grams oxygen. Times a hundred and thirty liters of water is—" she pushed to her desk and started punching on a calculator. "Is 114,400 grams oxygen. Divided by 20 grams an hour per person is 5,720 person-hours. Divide that by the 130 on board—"

"Hundred and twenty-five," Alex corrected. "Five were killed in the drive section."

"Oh," Taylor said, shaking her head. "Well, that leaves us about 45 and three quarters hours. Plus the seven we have left of the reserves is 53 hours, about."

"That might be enough," Alex said. "Navigator Naguchi told me that, unless one of the *Rock Skipper*-class ships is close and ready to go, the closest ship is the *Kyushu*. It can reach us in about fifty-two hours."

"I would guess I could be ten percent off in either direction," Taylor added. "If we don't do much, we could extend that time. If we're too active we'll shorten it. Also, I'm not positive how much water we have all together.

"Plus, I need to keep the partial pressure of oxygen above a tenth of an atmosphere. I could go as low as 0.07 atmospheres for survival mode but you can't expect people to do much physical or mental exertion. I can use voltage to control how much oh-two I put out, but the less space I have to fill, the better."

Okay," Alex said, "we'll keep everyone strapped down and move everyone close to life support and shut off all other areas with emergency doors. Good enough?"

Taylor nodded.

"One thing though," Alex continued, "aren't bubbles floating to the surface a function of gravity? Without some acceleration you'd just get a bubble around each electrode and then it'd shut down."

Taylor shook her head. "I didn't think of that. Do we have any acceleration?"

Alex shook his head, hitting the inside of his plastic helmet. "No, none at all."

"Then it's not going to work," Taylor said dejectedly.

"Could you put the electrodes on the surface of the water?"

"Maybe, but we have no way to contain it. If it does produce a gas, in free fall the escaping gas will push the water away from the electrodes."

"Can't you contain it somehow?"

"If I had a small enough container–but then the gas couldn't escape without water escaping."

Alex could feel a knot forming in his stomach. This electrolysis scheme seemed to be falling apart on him, and taking his crew's lives with it.

"If only we had some gravity," Taylor sighed.

Gravity! Alex realized. They didn't need acceleration, they needed gravity. And, outside of neutron star material, there's one sure way to produce artificial gravity in space. "Spin."

"Excuse me, sir?"

"We'll spin the asteroid. We'll spin it fast enough to give you enough gravity at the water tank to confine the water and make the bubbles float out. The asteroid has roll controls. I'll have Naguchi roll the ship until we have the gravity we need."

Taylor looked at him for a second, then smiled. "That'll work." She suddenly frowned. "But..."

"But what?"

"Everything on the asteroid is supported for acceleration along the axis. If we spin the asteroid, everything will be accelerated outward."

"True," Alex said. "The tokomak, the water tank, anything massive and off the center line very far. We'll contact dirt-side engineering for help on how to do it with minimal materials and effort. It'll work, Taylor. It'll work."

She still looked skeptical. "I'm gonna need some help in here."

"Whatever you need," Alex assured her. "What are you going to do about the hydrogen?"

Taylor looked blank for a moment. Then said, "Oh, yeah, we'll have to vent that."

"Get on it," Chun ordered.

***

The computer beeped. Freeman sat up and looked at the screen. It displayed "INCOMING CALL." Since he'd put the no-video switch on when he went to bed, he said, "Yes?"

A female police officer appeared on the screen. "Is this Special Agent Gordon Freeman?" she asked.

"Yes," he said reaching over and turning on his video.

"This is Sergeant Amy Knight of the Los Angeles Police Department," the woman said, visibly reacting to seeing Freeman sitting bare-chested in bed. "I got your home number from the FBI. We have a Jane Doe in the hospital who asked us to call you."

"Is she black with long brown-black hair and green eyes?"

"Yes," Knight said. "Do you know her?"

"Yes, what happened?" Freeman asked urgently.

"She was assaulted by men with automatic weapons. We captured all but one. She's in police protection but we'd like to know what this is all about. You should have seen what we found in that house."

"I'll bet," Freeman said. "Listen, she is very important to an ongoing investigation, Sergeant. Her name is Charlene Jones. I'm flying out as soon as I can. Keep her safe. What hospital is she in?"

The sergeant told him.

"Good, thanks," he said and closed the connection. He called his boss.

***

The conference room at SRI headquarters was full at 1:30 in the morning. The members of SRI executive board had come from their homes in response to the crisis. Each wore suits despite the hour and aides had also come in and were hovering around. The water pitchers had been filled and the coffee was brewing. If the city below hadn't been a tapestry of lights, one wouldn't have known it was the middle of the night.

Mitchel, the first, and still only, Occidental to sit on this board, looked around at the executives encircling the large, mahogany table. Everyone was agitated. Nakata was working over calculations on his computer, perhaps hoping he'd made a mistake and the inevitable wasn't going to happen.

Mr. Kijoto seemed visibly shaken. His features paled as the message from Director Chun was read by the Director of Space Operations, Mr. Yamada, to the assembled department heads of SRI.

When Yamada had finished Kijoto spoke. "Eight hours?"

"Yes, sir. And that report is just about an hour old."

"What can we get to 1961 in that time?"

"Nothing."

"Nothing?"

"Yes, sir."

Mitchel turned to Yamada. "What about the other *Rock Skipper*-class ships?"

Yamada shook his head. "We have been very unfortunate. The *Star Hopper* just arrived on the Moon; turnaround time is three days. The *Comet Chaser* is in the belt but on the other side of the solar system scouting asteroids; it would take about five days to reach the asteroid. The *Cloud Skimmer* developed a problem with its gyros and is being worked on at Ceres. Estimated repair time is at least a week as the *Star Hopper* will have to take repair parts to it when it's ready to leave the Moon."

Kijoto leaned forward onto the table. "What is the nearest ship of any type?"

Nakata looked up from his computer and sighed. "The asteroid tender *Kyushu*'s about 2.9 million kilometers behind. She only has one-tenth of a gee boost but is the only ship that can reach them in a reasonable amount of time. Nineteen sixty-one is traveling at about 150 kps relative to solar system. It would take the *Kyushu* 52 hours to match velocities and position.

"According to Director Chun's message," Nakata continued, "the main Masuka drive is destroyed but the mass driver may be repairable. That would give them one tenth of a gee acceleration. If, starting now, Chun accelerates antiparallel to the *Kyushu*'s acceleration vector, effectively adding his acceleration to the asteroid tender's relative acceleration, it would shorten the time to rendezvous considerably, to 31 hours. That is, however, still much more than the seven hours they now have left."

"Damn," Mitchel spat, ignoring the protocol of the conference room. No one seemed to mind.

Then the printer in the table ejected a paper like a rude tongue. Mitchel took it. He smiled as he read it.

"What is it?" Kijoto asked.

"It's from Director Chun. 'Life support reports that power normally used for destroyed Masuka drive can be used to split water reserves into hydrogen and oxygen. Will spin asteroid at a rate of four one-hundredths of a revolution per second to produce one tenth of a gee at the water tank. Calculations indicate that will give oxygen for 46 to 53 hours. Our navigator reports the *Kyushu* can rendezvous in 52 hours. Currently attempting to repair mass driver but doesn't look hopeful. Need engineering to calculate minimum support needed on heavy equipment that will be accelerated outward by spin.' There follows data for engineering." Mitchel handed the paper to Kijoto.

The old man looked it over. "We can save them." As if trying to get used to the new territory, a smile slowly settled on his face.

***

"Captain," a communications tech said over the intercom.

"Yes?" Takashara asked after reaching to punch the appropriate button on her computer. She was in her quarters doing paperwork.

"We just received a message from Yamada."

Takashara frowned. When the Director of Space Operations calls, it's rarely good news. "What is it?"

"Messages is as follows: 'Asteroid SRI-1961 has been attacked by *Rock Skipper*. It was able to stop the attack but is heavily damaged and in short supply of oxygen. You are to rendezvous with 1961 as soon as possible. 1961 has no acceleration capabilities and is currently moving at 147 kps relative.' Ma'am, there's a lot of technical information on the asteroid's position and velocity vector. Do you want to hear it?"

"No, send it to navigation."

"Yes, ma'am. Then it goes on to say, 'Evacuate personnel from 1961 and return to lunar orbit.'"

"Okay," Takashara said, stalling while she thought. "Confirm message, then establish link with 1961." She thought a second. "Does the message say about how far 1961 is away from us?"

"Yes, ma'am. Uhm, about three million klicks."

"Okay, fine," Takashara said. At three million kilometers the light-speed delay would only be ten seconds. "Establish a voice link with the asteroid," she continued, "and tell the bridge I'm on my way."

She left her quarters and climbed to the bridge, one deck above. "Navigator," she said, walking through the hatch, "calculate an intercept course for the asteroid."

"Already have. Take about 52 hours unless the asteroid can accelerate."

"I wouldn't count on that. XO."

"Ma'am?" he first officer said.

"Get the damage control teams and drill them on their jobs. DC is number one priority."

"Yes, ma'am."

Just in case, Takashara told herself. The rumors of the *Rock Skipper*'s demise may have been exaggerated.

***

Alex watched the miners glue pipe together and arc welding supports on the "outside" wall of the water tank. He tried to remember his chemistry: did hardening glue use oxygen? Everyone had removed their pressure suit helmets but Alex required them to wear the suit and carry the helmet–just in case. It was God-awful uncomfortable. As the new supports weren't in place yet, the asteroid still wasn't spinning and working in free fall made every simple task that much harder. The miners had no problem with it but everyone else found themselves grabbing anything they could to stay in one place. Plus, as usual, Alex's stomach was strongly protesting the lack of acceleration.

Taylor was in a corner of the life support section with a woman in an armored security pressure suit. Alex recognized her as Taylor's companion on the trip to the belt. The women were talking softly among themselves with their hands resting lightly on each other's upper arms in a proto-hug. Alex looked away as they embraced briefly and separated. Taylor moved toward Alex. She showed him a pressure valve. "We'll install this at the end of the H-2 pipe. When the hydrogen gets enough pressure in the pipe, just under the interior air pressure, it'll vent it to space. The valve will keep any water from being sucked out."

"Good," Alex said. "Any problems?"

Taylor took a breath. "Not really. I cannibalized some platinum from the damaged Masuka drives for the electrodes and got some sulfuric acid from the assayer. I used all she had. I hope it's enough."

"Enough?" Alex asked. "For what?"

"To aid ionization of the water–helps the electrolysis process."

"Wouldn't salt work?" Alex suggested. "SRI has taught me a little chemistry. Table salt is a strong electrolyte and dissociates completely in water. The galley's probably got kilos."

Again Taylor shook her head. "Since chlorine oxidizes almost as easily as oxygen, if I got the concentration too high we'd get poisonous chlorine gas instead of oh-two. I don't want to take that chance."

Alex shook his head. "Never mind. I'll shut up and let you do your job."

Taylor smiled. "Okay, boss."

"It's looking good, Taylor," Alex said. "You're doing a good job."

"Thanks, Director."

Alex turned away from her. "Thorne?"

The security man, who had been watching the procedures, pushed himself up to Alex, dragging his hand on the wall to slow. "Yes?"

"Listen," Alex said, "we need to keep activity to a minimum. The only activity I want is life support and repair of the mass driver. Your people will enforce, keeping everyone still. I don't want anyone to move for anything. And nobody drinks water. If they get thirsty have them drink whatever's in the galley."

"Alcohol?"

"No, that will just make them more thirsty." He turned to Taylor. "I know solid wastes are dried and stored to sell to NESA but what about urine? Will it be a problem if people use the usual system?"

"No," Taylor said. "The water recycler can handle their wastes and it'll be added to the stuff we're splitting. So let 'em piss all they want."

"Will the plumbing hold up under spin?" Thorne asked.

Taylor looked as if she were going to be sick. "I don't know," she said rubbing her brow. "It all works with pumps so I think so, as long as the massive sections are supported."

"Good," Alex said with a smile. "We just might make it."

***

Beatty ran and ran and ran. He knew everyone else was either arrested or had been killed by the storm troopers. He'd seen the cops attack the house. There must have been a hundred of them. He'd also seen them put that bitch in an ambulance. The only point now was revenge. That was enough.

He found a couple necking in a car. With his submachine gun he easily got them out of it. He'd start at the nearest hospital.

212

CHAPTER FOURTEEN

"You and your damned ecologist consciousness probably just killed my husband."

The KS-900 was small enough to fit under the shirttails of Beatty's untucked, plaid shirt. This time of night, the only open entrance to the hospital was the emergency room. Beatty entered, trying to look worried. When he saw the female cop, he didn't have to try anymore.

A nurse was in a booth by the door. Beatty could tell the thick glass was bulletproof. There was an intercom for communication.

"Can I help you?" the nurse droned, obviously bored.

"My girlfriend was brought in," Beatty replied.

"What's her name?" the nurse asked, turning to his computer.

"She didn't have any ID. They probably didn't know who she was. I came home from work and the neighbor told me about it. My neighbor said she was wearing a short robe or something with a print pattern."

"A housecoat?" the nurse asked.

"Yes!" Beatty said excitedly.

"We have a brown haired, green eyed, African-American Jane Doe. Age about 25, five-ten, around a hundred and thirty pounds: gunshot wounds."

"That's her," Beatty exclaimed.

The nurse looked at the cop and she walked over.

"Sergeant Knight, this man claims to know your gunshot victim," the nurse said.

Knight regarded Beatty.

"I'm her boyfriend," Beatty pleaded.

"Okay," the Knight said. "Come with me." She wasn't going to take him to the victim but she did want to ask him some questions.

As they approached the metal detector, Beatty reached under his shirt.

***

Charlie heard Beatty fire. She knew it was him: the sound had the cadence and tone of the South African submachine gun and the burst length was extra-long. Beatty liked long bursts.

She also heard screams. There was a single report of a pistol. Adrenalin began pumping into her blood in earnest. She looked around her. She was still in the ER in the trauma room where they had operated on her. She was on her stomach on a high bed or a gurney. An IV ran down to her left arm. A screen near the bed displayed her vitals. The name "Jane Doe" was glowing at the top. She also noticed her blood pressure was really low.

One wall of the room was all light blue cupboards and drawers. She rolled off the bed and landed on the floor with a loud, painful smack. Wires ripped from her body as she tried to move toward the drawers. She felt the same way she did the first time she tried to move in three gees; maybe worse. Her IV tore out of the heparin lock and her blood and lactated ringers splattered onto the tile. Charlie ignored that and got herself to her knees. She was leaving a trail of blood wherever she moved. There were more screams; the sound was getting closer. If she didn't figure out a way to save herself, she'd die, if she didn't bleed to death first.

She pulled open the first drawer she found–bandages. She jerked the next open. Yes! Surgery tools. But the scalpel had an extremely short power cord and it would only cut through a few millimeters of skin and not through clothes at all. It was pretty much useless as a weapon but might have a psychological effect.

Damn, she thought. Then she opened the next drawer and found assorted scissors. She scooped up the biggest pair. They were blunted on the end but if she opened them and held them at the crux she could use them to slash. She moved to her bed, still more crawling than walking, and found the scalpel power source. She plugged the tool into the idiot-proof socket and flicked it on. The laser beam was invisible but the unit buzzed when she pressed the button labeled "CUT."

By the bed was a light switch. Charlie tried it and the room became dark except for the glow from the video read-outs by the bed. She hid behind the monitor, the scalpel in her hand.

The door slammed open and Beatty stood in the frame, back-lit by the light in the hall. He walked in the room slowly. Charlie held her breath and fought to stay on her feet.

He walked close to the gurney and into the puddle formed by her still-dripping IV bag. He studied the floor and the plastic tubing for a moment, then looked at the read-out. He was about three feet away from Charlie and she hoped the brightness of the screen would make her hard to see behind it. She could feel and hear the blood dripping off the end of her finger onto the floor.

"Jane Doe," he growled angrily. "This has got to be it."

Charlie aimed the scalpel at his eyes.

He must have seen the movement because Beatty looked right at her. He started to raise the weapon when Charlie pressed the "CUT" button on the laser. She smelled burning flesh and hair as she moved it back and forth with small flicks of her wrist.

Beatty screamed in pain and grabbed at his eyes. The dropped gun skittered across the tile like some scared animal. He slipped in the liquid and was slapped to the floor.

Charlie grimaced as she nearly fell onto the bed, letting go of the scalpel but still clutching the scissors.

Beatty was trying to stand while holding one hand over his eyes. Charlie turned on the lights. He didn't even respond; he was apparently blinded.

215

Charlie struggled to the end of the bed, using it as a prop, then let herself plop to the floor. She crawled after Beatty's weapon. All she had to do was hold him until help arrived.

A hand clamped onto her ankle. She twisted to see Beatty pawing blindly for her like a crazed animal with his free hand.

She could see where the laser had cut into his eyes, the skin around them, and the bridge of his nose. She kicked his face with her free foot but he only grunted and grabbed at it. She tried to pull her ankle loose but it was if her leg and his hand were welded together. In fact, he was pulling her toward him.

His flailing hand ripped off her heparin lock, opening the vein on her arm before connecting with her side. He latched onto the fabric of her hospital gown like it was a rope thrown to him as he drowned. He continued to pull her toward him. There was no doubt in her mind that he was capable of killing her.

She opened the scissors and grasped them at the middle, ignoring how they cut into her hand. She swung them at his face. They cut across his cheek, opening a bleeding gash from his ear to his jaw. He screamed in pain and anger and let go of her gown to try to grab her hand.

She swung again, this time slashing his arm. Her wrist slipped through his fingers and he almost caught her hand.

As he probed the air for her weapon, she waited until his arm was swung aside and he was vulnerable. She swung again with all the strength she had left. If this didn't work, she knew she was dead.

Hot blood spilled over her fist as his jugular opened. She ripped with the cutting edge, splitting the vein wide. He let go of her and she crawled slowly away. He reached up and grabbed his neck but the blood flowed unabated. Slowly he slipped down to lay on the floor.

Charlie's adrenal gland stopped propping her up. She, too lay on the floor, breathing heavily. She tried to stop the blood spilling out of her arm but was unsuccessful. Cold darkness enfolded her as she lost consciousness.

***

Freeman's supervisor wasn't pleased with being rousted out of bed in the middle of the night. She listened patiently as Freeman explained the situation.

"I called back the LAPD," he said, "to find out what happened at the house. When the other police officers arrived there was a major gun battle. They killed four GA members and captured the rest. They say at least one escaped. They found two bodies near the burning house that Ms. Jones apparently shot in self-defense. In the safe house they found weapons, explosives, ammunition, and a computer in the basement. They're going to get a court order to see what's in it. And they found a data chip on Ms. Jones. They say it's hers and they're keeping it safe for her."

Special Agent Chaikin shook her head on Freeman's computer's screen. "We'll talk about this unauthorized investigation later. Personally, and unofficially, I'm glad to see you go after the GA. But the FBI oversight committee will draw and quarter us for this. I can't believe we have to answer to that group of politicians," she finished, saying "politicians" as if it were a vulgarity.

"I know," Freeman said. "But I thought it was necessary. The GA is, or was at least, on its way to becoming a major terrorist threat."

"I agree," Chaikin said. "You going to LA?"

"Yes, and I'm going to get all the evidence I can on Trent and the GA."

"Fine. I don't have to report to the committee for three days. That gives you that time to work up a case even they can't argue with. Up until then, the FBI is officially uninvolved."

"Thank you."

"Don't thank me. Now say good-bye so I can go back to sleep. When this hits the news it's going to be a long day."

"Good-bye," Freeman said.

***

Faruq watched the news report on his computer. The scene was a house in Los Angeles. The sun was just coming up and

Faruq could see police were crawling all over the building. The neighboring house was a smoking pile of black cinders.

"Los Angeles Police Department," the reporter was saying, "reports that this house was the scene of a major shoot-out between police and a suspected terrorist organization. Three police officers were killed and six suspects. This neighboring house was burned to the ground. No motive was given for that burning. Police are being tight-lipped about what terrorist group was using the house but we have this tape." The scene changed to the same street but it was night. Medics were loading bodies in ambulances and police were putting people in a van.

Some were young, pretty girls dressed, or rather not dressed, in ways that offended Faruq's Islamic sensibilities.

Suddenly there were tire squeals. The scene was a blur as the camera panned to a civilian van, a modified antique Volkswagen, that was turning in the street. A police car moved to cut it off. Two men jumped out and were quickly overpowered by the police. They were struggling as they, too, were taken to the paddy wagon. One looked at the camera. "The revolution is coming!" he said. "The Gaia Alliance will prevail and all the greedy..." The man was shoved harshly into the police van.

The scene cut back to the reporter on the dawn-lighted street. "Police won't confirm that this house was a Gaia Alliance safe house. Neighbors say they thought it was a smash house. This is Linda Chavez reporting from Los Angeles."

"News, off," Faruq growled in English. *This was unexpected but is it a problem?* he thought. It could be beneficial since the GA was no longer around to pester him. The report on the asteroid on the news had caused a rumble through the presidential mansion and in the Party. Faruq decided he would test the waters before proceeding, and proceed carefully when he did. The president still had enough power to eliminate Faruq if he perceived him to be a threat.

***

Dr. Kirsten Hanna-Chun had an early morning meeting with Dr. McConnell. Although he'd accepted her apology, it never hurt

218

to keep him happy. He could help her or hurt her as he wished. More than one young psychologist had failed to impress McConnell and found themselves professionally isolated. No one would give them referrals and risk McConnell's wrath. She did, however, have to deal with the lingering pain that came with trading pride for professional gain.

But, as she pulled her car into the parking garage of the multi-storied professional building with McConnell's office, the car's computer turned off the music she was listening to and a news bulletin came on, since she'd instructed it to immediately play any news about SRI. Kirsten listened intently. At the end of the announcement she stopped the car and went to the elevator. A few minutes later she was facing McConnell's receptionist. McConnell could afford a human secretary. A woman, apparently a patient, was seated in the waiting room.

"Dr. Hanna-Chun here to see you," the secretary said to an intercom speaker.

"Thank you," McConnell's voice answered back. Kirsten grated at the sound of his voice. Another psychologist, one of McConnell's partners, stepped up to the receptionist and began speaking with her.

The door to McConnell's office opened and the rotund form of McConnell moved into the waiting room. He had a cigarette in his maw and the foul order preceded him. Kirsten briefly wondered how he got away with that since smoking was banned in all public buildings.

Kirsten moved to him, clenching her right fist.

"Kirsten," he said removing the cigarette, "good to—"

Kirsten's fist connected with his jaw with force that came from regular exercise and irregularly great rage. McConnell was floored by the blow and looked up at her with great, hurt puppy eyes. The patient, the receptionist, and the other doctor all stared with wide eyes at the scene.

"You pious son-of-a-bitch," Kirsten threw her words at him. "You're damn lucky I have high regard for life, even yours, or I'd kill you now. You and your damned ecologist consciousness probably just killed my husband."

She turned and walked out of the office toward the elevator. Her arms were quivering with anger. The elevator was blessedly empty. She leaned against the wall and began crying.

She walked to her car and drove home, almost driving automatically, as if the car knew the way.

When Kirsten opened the front door of her and Alex's house, the computer was beeping and displaying "INCOMING CALL."

"Computer, answer that, no video," she said, walking in. She didn't want anyone to see her like this.

"Hello?" she answered. She got the icon that the other person was also sending no video.

"Ms. Hanna-Chun?" an unfamiliar voice asked.

"Yes."

"This is Judy Rice of Fox-CNN news."

"I'm sorry," Kirsten cut her off. "You'll have to contact SRI's public relations department, Tokyo." She tapped the hang-up button and instructed the computer to contact another address. A few minutes later she was talking to Mitchel, the only man in Tokyo she personally knew.

"Yes," he said after she explained the situation, "we can provide you with security from our Boulder facility. Worried about the press?"

"Thank you, yes," Kirsten exclaimed. "Mitch, tell me. Will they make it?"

"There's a good chance," he said and explained the planned rendezvous.

"That's good, Mitch," she said, her voice full of relief.

She actually had thought Alex was as good as dead. Now, there was a chance. "Thank you." She then had the computer call her secretary computer. It would call all her patients with appointments for the next few days and cancel them after she used the house computer to instruct it. Even while doing that she had four incoming calls. She instructed the computer to only allow calls from SRI through. The ringing stopped.

"Computer: Fox-CNN on the big screen."

One wall of the living room changed from a scene of Pike's Peak to a computer generated news anchor. "We now take you, live, to a news conference at SRI's headquarters in Tokyo," it said.

A PR man for SRI was in mid-sentence. "...a very good chance the asteroid tender *Kyushu* will get there in time and we will be able to save all the survivors."

"How many have been killed?"

"Five. We are, of course, withholding information pending notification of kin."

"If you," a voice asked, "take the crew off the asteroid won't it be out of control and isn't there a chance it could hit the Earth?"

The PR man is good, Kirsten thought. He didn't even crack a smile at the ludicrous question.

"No," he said. "We've plotted the course. It will not hit the Earth."

"What happened to the terrorists and their ship?"

Who the hell cares, Kirsten thought, *as long as they died horribly in the vacuum of space like the five people they killed?*

"As far as we know," the PR man said, "the ship they stole is destroyed and they are dead."

Kirsten watched as the news conference droned on. Security men arrived about 40 minutes later, just in time to stop the news crews from a frontal assault on her home.

***

Charlie heard voices. They were quick and efficient voices talking in steady tones.

"Get another unit of PFD with leukocytes started," one said. "Damn, she's lost a lot of blood."

"And she didn't have much to lose," someone else said.

Charlie relaxed. She was still alive and they were pumping perfluorodecalin into her veins to substitute for the blood she'd lost.

Beatty was either dead or incapacitated. It angered her that someone may be trying to save his life. But she decided that could wait for later. She wanted to sleep.

Damn, her feet were cold.

***

The *Rock Killer* was tumbling in space like a lifeless hulk. She almost was. Knecht ignored the pain from multiple bruises to work the controls in an attempt to give the ship a stable attitude. Griffin was bending over Trudeau. Blood and brains from Trudeau's smashed head were painting the walls as the tumble carried it to the outside. When the mass from the asteroid hit, the ship had moved so violently they had been bounced around like beads in a baby's rattle. Trudeau's head had connected with the communications panel and both had been damaged beyond repair.

"He's dead," Griffin said. He was ignoring the unnatural bend and searing pain in his arm.

"What about Cole?" Knecht asked.

"I'm fine," she replied, then vomited, forming a liquid mass that moved to mingle with the gore on the walls. "Can't you do something about this god-damned spin?"

"I'm working on it," Knecht screamed. *The spin shouldn't make Cole dizzy,* Knecht said to herself. She couldn't take the gore. "We're damn lucky the mass only grazed us. It only breached the hull in the power room. Unfortunately, we have only battery power now."

The ship stopped spinning but the blood and vomit began entering the air in a sickening dance of thick globs.

"Now I can get some work done," Knecht said.

"Can you fix it?" Griffin asked?"

"Maybe."

"Where's the asteroid?"

"We got about 50 kps of delta vee from the collision. If I can fix the main power fast enough we can catch up. I just hope we can find it again."

"Cole, the missiles?"

"Just a second, damn it." She made her way to the fire-control panel, ducking the foul mixture floating around the bridge. The panel had somehow escaped damage. All lights were green. "Get me to that rock and I'll kill it."

***

Dr. McConnell canceled his morning appointments and called his lawyer. He made an appointment to see him that afternoon. Driving home, rubbing his jaw, he thought about the lawsuit. With pain and suffering, public humiliation, and loss of professional reputation he should be able to put quite a dent in the late Mr. Chun's estate.

McConnell smiled. He'd send a good chunk of that money to the GA. Ironic, having SRI money financing the Gaia Alliance.

Once home, he looked for his wife but she was off spending time with her volunteer projects. He had the computer turn on the news to catch what there was about the attack. He lit a cigarette and waited for the story.

He swore heavily when he heard it wasn't a complete success.

Mr. Chun, it seemed, was alive and well. *Oh well,* thought McConnell, *we'll hurt Space Rape Incorporated and the suit will make a dent in Chun's SRI income.*

Then another anchor introduced a story about a large gun battle in Los Angeles between police and suspected terrorists in Los Angeles. McConnell recognized the house. He switched to C-SPAN. Someone was making a speech.

"Chamber view," he said. He could see the whole House. It was about half full, as usual. He knew where the three Greens sat. Two were there; Trent was not.

"Damn. Is the environmental committee meeting?"

The word YES flashed at the bottom of the screen.

"Is it available for viewing?"

NO.

"Shit," he said putting his cigarette in his mouth and picking up the handset on the computer. He punched in an address from memory. He didn't want to store it in the computer's directory. Trent's secretary said she was indeed at the committee meeting.

McConnell didn't dare leave a message–not the message he had.

He called another number. There was no video with the simple computer Trent used. At least it had a message-taking function.

223

"This is Whaltham. The police have the records. I'm going to the emergency location. I suggest you do, too. It's over for now." He hung up and went upstairs to the bedroom to pack. With luck he'd be gone before his wife got home.

***

Freeman arrived in Los Angeles in the late morning. Chaiken approved a government jet for him. He was met by an agent from the local office who drove him to the hospital. She tried to quiz him but he was as silent as many perceived space to be.

Freeman had to use his FBI identification to get past all the police. They were jumpy and Freeman knew something had happened. He asked for Sergeant Knight and a body bag was pointed out. Finally he found a captain who would talk to him. The man, obviously agitated, explained what happened while Freeman was in the air.

Eventually Freeman was shown into a room in the Intensive Care Unit. There were two police officers with riot gear and submachine guns guarding the room. They, too, wanted to see Freeman's ID.

In the room he saw Charlie on her stomach. She had the usual assortment of biosensors and probes on and in her body. Freeman looked at the readout. He walked near her head. Her eyes were closed.

"Charlie?" he said softly.

She opened her eyes, blinked a few times, and then looked at him. She smiled a little. "Hi, Freeman," she said slowly.

"Hi," he said. "You've been busy."

She made a small, shoulder shrugging motion, then immediately regretted it. "The GA, what happened?"

Freeman explained about the gun battle and the arrests.

"They found the guns and the computer in the basement. The captain told me they got a court order and they'll have all the data analyzed soon."

"My chip?"

"The police have that also. But it may be inadmissible because it could be ruled an illegal search."

224

"Why? I'm a private citizen. Hell, I'm a member of the GA."

"Yes," Freeman said, "but if they can prove you were acting as my agent then it is an illegal search."

"That's stupid."

"It's the Fourth Amendment."

"What about my right to face my accuser. They threw that out for my 'unlawful self-defense.'"

"I know; like I said in Washington, the Constitution means exactly what the current Court says it means."

"So–what about the evidence against the GA?" Charlie asked.

"The LAPD has it all. As soon as we get the evidence we can get Trent–and maybe Whaltham."

"I saw him," Charlie said.

"Could you identify him?"

"Damn right."

"Good. We may find out who he is."

"Beatty? Is he alive?"

"No," Freeman said. "He bled to death. You got the jugular. You're one tough girl, Charlie." He reached out and squeezed her hand.

Funny, she thought, *I don't feel so tough.*
***

Alex spent most of his time in his office/quarters. It was just off the centerline of the asteroid, so he felt almost no outward acceleration because of the spin. Bente calculated that at the surface of the rock there was almost 13 gees of pseudo-gravity. Fortunately, there was very little equipment far from the middle of the asteroid. There were four tunnels, perpendicular to the long axis of the asteroid, with airlocks on the surface. Spinning the asteroid turned them into half-kilometer long pits. Alex had them sealed up before the spin was applied and was doubly glad he did when the airlocks ripped out under the force of the air pressure they were designed to hold and those 13 gees they were never expected to endure. Alex wondered what other surprises were in store from them, and if they'd continue to be lucky.

Taylor reported the electrolysis was going as planned.

"Under the low gravity, the bubbles look like they're rising in oil," she reported.

"As long as we get it out eventually," he said over the intercom.

"No problems so far," Taylor said. "We had to adjust the voltage. Too much voltage and the bubbles couldn't rise fast enough and I'd get that bubble on each electrode you talked about. I had somebody from the reactor section install a voltage regulator and I can adjust the voltage."

"Good," Alex said. "Is the H-2 going out okay?"

"Yes," Taylor replied. "That's going great."

"What about the partial pressure?"

"Point zero nine-eight."

"Good," Alex repeated. Taylor signed off.

Alex had needed to make a decision. Almost everyone on the asteroid wanted to send a message home, but that would tie up the communication gear. That wasn't a major problem because the computer had "look through" transmission capability and would shut down an out-going transmission if something came in.

But he had everyone packed like sardines in the galley, and there was only one computer in there. Everyone moving to the computer to send their message was a bigger problem. Moving was surprisingly difficult because of the unexpected direction of acceleration, and that would burn much precious oxygen.

Alex decided everyone could write down a message on a handheld computer and one person would take the computer and send them.

Alex's computer in his office/quarters could interface directly with the communications computer. He sent his message to Kirsten from his office; rank has its privileges. He kept it down to a short: "I'm fine. I love you. Everything will be all right. I'll be home soon."

***

The bridge was clear of blood and vomit. Cole had at first balked at cleaning up the mess, but Knecht and Griffin sternly insisted. She helped grudgingly and Griffin, with his bad arm, wasn't much help. It seemed Knecht was going to have to do everything.

She was pulling on one of the emergency pressure suits SRI had been kind enough to provide in the *Rock Killer*, but she was having trouble with it.

Griffin pushed over to help but he got going too fast. He grabbed her arm with his good appendage to try to stop. She jerked her arm out of his hand and he hit the bulkhead hard with his broken arm.

"Ow, God damn it!" he yelled. "I just wanted to help."

"I don't need your help," she said angrily.

Griffin swallowed his anger. "Hey," he said softly. "What's wrong?"

She stopped struggling with the suit and looked him over with her blazing green eyes. "Just leave me alone, okay?"

Griffin was silently surprised.

Knecht pulled the bubble helmet over her head, effectively cutting off conversation. Griffin passively watched her finish putting on the suit, checking it, and move to the airlock. She ignored him the entire time.

Once the airlock swallowed her form, he shrugged, which caused him more pain, and moved to the first aid station.

"Cole," he ordered. "Come here."

The other woman glared at him.

"I broke my God-damned arm. I need your help."

Cole pushed over. "What do I do?" she said reluctantly.

"There should be some splints in there. We need to immobilize it."

"Okay," Cole said with a heavy sigh of annoyance.

S EVAN TOWNSEND

228

CHAPTER FIFTEEN

"There's two men from the FBI here."

McConnell took a taxi to the airport. There he used the electronic ticket agent to buy a ticket to Seattle in his name with his computer. He then moved to another airline and bought a ticket to Los Angeles using a computer in Whaltham's name.

Finally, at a third airline, he bought a ticket to New York, JFK, using a computer with the name of Roger Oaks. He dropped the other two computers in a trash can. Nice thing about electronic ticket agents was they couldn't remember a face. Their cameras only operated if someone tried to cheat or damage them.

He endured the flight without smoking and in New York he bought a ticket on the spaceplane to French Guiana. At least that would be a shorter flight. Normally he wouldn't take a spaceplane because of the damage he believed they did to the ozone layer. But this was an emergency–it would have flown anyway, and if he could save himself he could do more good in the future than the spaceplane did harm. At least that was how he rationalized it.

The spaceplane landed in Cayenne and McConnell took a taxi to the NESA facility near Kourou, about 60 kilometers through sweltering jungle. He'd read somewhere that the road had been built by Devil's Island inmates. *Little better than slavery,* he thought. The West always built their "progress" on the backs of the oppressed.

There was never a line at the NESA public spaceport. Space travel was still too expensive for most people. McConnell walked up to the girl behind the counter labeled "English." She was pretty and had a slight French accent when she spoke. The use of humans indicated the level of luxury.

"May I help you?" she asked cheerfully with her plastic smile.

"Yes," McConnell said. "I need a ticket to the Moon on the next shuttle."

"Do you have a reservation?"

"No. Is that a problem?"

She worked the computer. "No, we usually have a seat available. Do you have a visa?"

McConnell showed her the plastic card, much like what credit cards were like. She raised an eyebrow.

"Been planning to visit the Moon for a long time, Mr. Oaks?" she asked.

"Yes."

She put the visa in a slot on the computer and asked him to step on the scale. She typed on the computer then indicated he could step off. "Okay, Mr. Oaks, you have a seat on the next shuttle. It's leaving in about eight hours. Please be in the terminal at least an hour before. In low Earth orbit you'll transfer to the intra-Lunar shuttle. In the meantime, there's the NESA hotel. Shall I get you a room? You can rest up before your trip." She handed back the visa.

"Thank you, yes," McConnell said.

"Also," she said, "do you need reservations at a NESA hotel on the Moon? You'll be arriving in two days. You never know if they'll be full. You may end up in a dorm."

"Yes, I do."

"And which hotel, Mr. Oaks?"

"The best one," McConnell said, as if it were obvious.

"Yes, sir. That would be the Selene. And how would you like to pay for that today?"

"Credit." He held up his wrist with the Roger Oaks computer on it.

"Fine. You realize there will be a reweighing at check-in and any significant weight gain will be charged against your credit account."

"I understand," McConnell replied.

***

"Hi," the woman entering Charlie's hospital room said. "I'm Cathy Williams. I'm with the SRI West Coast Terrestrial Information Gathering Office in San Francisco. Joe Murda sent me down at Mitchel's behest." As she spoke, she glanced about the room, surveying it.

"Hi," Charlie said to the petite, black woman. At first glance she didn't look as if she could harm a fly. But Charlie noticed Williams was aware of every aspect of the room. She seemed like a chemical mixture that just needed the right activation energy to give a violent exothermic reaction. A sizable bulge under her leather jacket was either a congenital defect or a very large weapon. She wondered how she got it past the locals. "You here to protect me?"

Williams nodded. "Yes, and Mitchel wants you back in Tokyo as soon as you can travel. The local constabulary already failed once to keep you safe. The corporate spaceplane can be at Orange County Airport within a few hours, waiting for you, when you're able to leave." She had moved to the window, looked out, and closed the shades.

Charlie's eyes grew wide. "How did I rate that?"

"Apparently," Williams said, "Mr. K. liked what you did."

"Excuse me," Freeman said, coming in the door.

Williams spun, placed her body between Charlie and the door and had her hand in her jacket. She relaxed, but not too much.

"Oh, it's you," Williams said.

"You know each other?" Charlie asked.

"Agent Freeman," Williams explained, "got me in here, past the LAPD."

"It's great," Freeman said. "We got Trent's activities to obtain support for the GA by a foreign nation. That violates the Anti-Terrorist Act of 2024. We've got her ass," Freeman said with glee.

"Whaltham?"

"You won't believe it. The computer had records of his financial dealings with the GA. He's a damned psychologist in Denver named James Whaltham McConnell. The Denver office will pick him up.

"Charlie, what you did effectively has shut down the GA. Beatty and Griffin are dead and Trent and McConnell will be arrested soon. Without them the GA is just a bunch of overzealous idealists. I'm flying back to D.C. right now to personally arrest Trent. I'm looking forward to it."

"That's great," Charlie said.

"I forgot to give these to you earlier." Freeman reached into his briefcase. He handed Charlie her SRI ID and her wrist computer.

"Thanks," Charlie said. She looked at her ID as if it were a holy totem.

"Freeman?" she asked.

"Yes?"

"Why haven't I been charged with unlawful self-defense?"

Freeman put his finger to his lips. "Shhhhh!"

Charlie looked at him quizzically.

"Listen," Freeman said softly, "this isn't the state of Columbia. Yes, technically, you are guilty of unlawful self-defense. But no one is going to file charges. The only person they can prove you killed is Beatty, and he killed three cops to get to you. You're a hero; even the media is treating you as such. The local authorities know that, politically, they can't touch you."

"I didn't mention it," Williams said, "but that's another reason Mitchel wants you out of the U.S. Once the hubbub dies down, you may be liable for indictment. But NESA won't extradite you from the Moon."

"Well, I've got to go," Freeman said, stepping toward the door.

"Okay, bye," Charlie said.

Freeman stopped short of pulling the door open. "You did a great job."

Charlie smiled. "Thanks. You too."

"I didn't do anything."

Charlie laughed. It hurt a little. "You're right."

"Well, bye."

"Good-bye, Gordon."

He smiled and walked out of the room. The door slowly closed.

"He's cute," Williams said. "Yours?"

Charlie laughed again. "No."

There was soft knock on the door. A thin, tall man with longish auburn hair and beard walked in. He was wearing a lab coat and a stethoscope was draped around his neck.

"Excuse me," he began, "I need—"

Williams was on him immediately. She pushed him against the wall and, while holding him with one arm, frisked his lab coat with her free hand.

"Who are you?" she demanded.

"He's my doctor," Charlie explained.

"Oh, sorry," Williams said, releasing him.

***

The environmental committee meeting went late. Late for Washington that is: about six.

Trent went to her office. Most of her staff had gone home and she scooted her secretary out the door. Trent had some work to do and there was no need for the fellow to be there.

Vera picked her up about nine and they drove to the house in Alexandria. Neither noticed the gray Fiat parked across the street. They parked in the carport, plugged the car in since its batteries were about drained, and went in through a side door into the kitchen. They started working on a light dinner together.

"I'd better check the computer messages," Vera said.

"Okay," Trent said, slicing some vegetables.

Vera walked into the living room. The light on the old computer was blinking. Vera walked toward the machine but the front doorbell (another obsolete technology Trent and Vera preferred) rang.

That's strange, Vera thought. *Who'd be ringing the doorbell at this late hour?* She went to the door and looked through the peephole. It was two men in business suits. Vera didn't have much use for men starting with, and especially, her father. She picked up the baseball bat kept near the door.

"What is it?" she yelled through the door.

"FBI," one said. "We're looking for Congresswoman Trent."

Vera chained the door and opened it, holding the bat behind her. "Congressperson Trent is busy," she said through the crack. "May I see some ID?"

One of the men held up a wallet with a badge and ID card.

It looked official but Vera wouldn't know an FBI badge from one found in a Cracker Jack box. "Okay, hang on." She closed the door and locked it. The men could wait outside; it was starting to get chilly.

Vera moved to the rear of the house where the kitchen was. She walked slowly, wasting as much of the men's time as possible. And, of course, there was no energy wasting central computer system in this house to transfer messages.

"Linda," Vera said.

"Yes, Vera?"

"There's two men from the FBI here." *Men* and *FBI* were spat out like obscene words. "They want to speak with you."

Trent let out a long sigh. "Damn. Can't they come to my office tomorrow?"

"I'll ask," Vera said, leaving the room to hike back to the front door. She smiled slightly. This would mean more time the men would have to spend in the chill outside. She again walked slowly back to the entry, unlocked it, leaving the chain attached, and opened it. "Can you come to her office tomorrow?"

"No," one, the African-American, replied rather forcefully. "We need to see her now."

Vera swallowed hard on her anger at this impetuous man.

"Fine," she said simply and closed the door again and walked back to the kitchen again taking her time.

Trent was listening to the computer messages.

"We've got to get out of here," Trent cried anxiously.

"What?" Vera asked.

"We got a message from Whaltham. The police know everything. Those FBI men must be here to arrest me."

"What can we do?" Vera asked.

"The car?"

"It's charging but it's pretty low."

"We'll have to try it," Trent decided. It might just get them far enough away. "Out the side door."

Outside the front door, Freeman pulled his coat around him. Why that woman wouldn't let them in was beyond him. He looked at the other agent, named Palmer. Palmer pulled the radio pinned to his lapel closer to his mouth. "Report."

"Nothing here," the woman watching the back door replied.

"Nothing, yet," the man watching the side door reported.

"I give them 30 seconds and then we break down the door," Freeman mumbled.

Palmer nodded. "Everyone, prepare to go in," he said into the radio.

Trent and Vera ran out the side door. Another man was there, walking up to the door.

"Ha—" he started before Vera tried to knock his head over the centerfield wall with her baseball bat. The man crumpled to the ground.

"Shit," Trent breathed.

"In the car," Vera hissed, trying not to talk too loudly. She unplugged the car and got behind the wheel.

Electric cars make about as much noise as an electric can opener. Vera pressed the anachronistically named "gas pedal" and the car backed out of the driveway. As usual, it scraped the pavement as it pulled into the street.

Palmer turned to see the old electric swing around and start down the road. He hit Freeman on the arm. "Hey, look!"

Freeman saw the escaping Chevy. "Damn," he spat. He ran for their car. The electric was going around the corner by the time they got into the Fiat and started the engine.

"All units," Palmer was saying to his label, "suspects are escaping in a distressed, gray Chevy Erg."

"Roger," the woman replied. There was no answer from the man watching the side door.

"Skwodovska," Palmer said, "there's no reply from Ligon. Check it out."

"Roger," the woman said.

Palmer then used the car's computer. "Patch me into the Alexandria police."

Freeman put the transmission in gear and slammed on the accelerator. The motor screamed as it burned hydrogen and oxygen into water. Freeman threw the car round the corner, ignoring protests from the tires. He glimpsed the taillights of the electric turning another corner. He couldn't see around the turn because of trees and bushes. The Fiat accelerated until Freeman braked just before the next intersection. Again the tires squealed as Freeman put the car around the corner. Then he slammed on the brakes. The electric had stopped in the middle of the street and its lights were off.

The Fiat whacked the back of the electric, propelling it forward a few feet. The air bags blew in the Fiat and the belts tightened momentarily and then loosened.

Freeman and Palmer jumped out and ran to the electric. Trent and the other woman were sitting in the front seat, dazed and bruised but, as far as Freeman could tell, unharmed.

Deflated air bags hung from the steering wheel hub and the dashboard and into the women's laps. The side airbags hadn't blown. Freeman pulled open the door and wrenched Trent's rotund form out and against the car. She offered no resistance. He heard Vera say, "Don't touch me, damnit," and saw that Palmer was pulling her out the passenger side. Freeman brought Trent's hands around to her back and clapped on handcuffs.

Palmer looked at Freeman while holding a struggling Vera by the handcuffs around her wrists. "Why'd they stop?" he asked.

Freeman looked down into the car. A red light blinked on the instrument panel. Freeman started laughing.

"What?" Palmer asked.

"They ran out of juice."

The next morning he finished up his paperwork. He kept smiling. The electric car ran out of juice. Explaining the damage to the Fiat, government property, was going to be interesting.

The computer beeped and he hit the answer button and turned to the screen. It was Chaikin.

"Freeman," she said, "I've been looking for you. McConnell's missing. His wife says she doesn't know where he is. Airline records show that he bought a ticket to Seattle."

"You called the Seattle office?"

"Yes and they met the plane. He wasn't on it. He bought a ticket in Whaltham's name to L.A. but he wasn't on that flight either."

"Damn," Freeman said. "What happened to him?"

Chaikin shrugged. "He disappeared into thin air."

***

McConnell tried not to think about how thin the air was outside the tiny window. The shuttle took off just like a spaceplane but continued to accelerate into low Earth orbit. It docked with the intra-lunar shuttle and the passengers and equipment were transferred. Using Masuka drives manufactured by Space Resources Inc., the stubby, cylindrical shuttle proceeded to the Moon.

McConnell hated free-fall and lost his last meal into a little bag. He was happy when the Masuka drives kicked in. He looked for Trent and half expected her to be on the shuttle. She did have eight hours to catch up.

He watched the news from his seat and learned Trent had been arrested. The FBI was being closed-mouthed about the charges but there were reports it had to do with terrorism. *Oh, well,* McConnell thought. He never liked that old dyke anyway.

There was a lot of news on the continuing drama of the asteroid and some on the Los Angeles shoot-out. Beatty, it seemed, had found that SRI spy in the hospital but she'd killed him. And they weren't charging her. In fact, she was being treated like a hero by the right-wing, establishment media. He turned off the news program in disgust.

Then he smiled at the memory of his last night in L.A.

***

Charlie's doctor released her, reluctantly, on the evening of the second day after she'd been admitted. With Williams in the lead, two local cops, and a nurse, Charlie was led to a room marked "Checkout." A tired looking clerk sat behind a computer.

"Name?" he asked.

"Charlie Jones," a cop said. "Admitted under Jane Doe in the ER."

The clerk spoke softly to the computer for a moment, then said, "Uh-oh. We have a problem. You must not be a U.S. citizen. You're not covered under MediSecurity. You'll have to pay for your treatment or apply for government assistance."

"Space Resources Incorporated Medical Services will be paying the bill," Williams said, handing her SRI ID.

"What's this?" the clerk asked.

"Treat it like a MediSecurity card."

He put the card in the slot on the computer and watched the screen, occasionally raising an eyebrow. He spoke to the computer a couple of times, then looked surprised.

"Okay," he said, "paid in full. You're free to go." He handed back the ID.

With her entourage, Charlie left the room. In the lobby, police were watching everything and everybody. They wheeled Charlie out the door into the cool night air, where even more police and an ambulance waited. Behind it was an empty van. The nurse and Williams helped Charlie into the ambulance and the nurse made her lie down on the stretcher. Williams knelt beside her.

Just before the door of the ambulance was closed, Charlie saw men and women that she assumed were just passersby run to the van and start to get in. The ambulance drove away and the van followed.

At the airport, after passing through a gate, the ambulance drove out on the tarmac. The world's only business-sized spaceplane, built for SRI by Mitsubishi-Sukhoi, was sitting on the concrete, bathed in light that was beating back the darkness. With its curved fuselage and delta wings, it looked like a living thing, a lovely, powerful bird ready to spring into space.

SRI Security personnel exited the van and fanned out around the ambulance. Charlie saw their weapons glisten in the harsh, artificial light. Charlie wondered briefly how many laws were being broken.

Cathy Williams looked out the window in the van's rear door.

"Looks secure," she said. "Let's go."

The door to the ambulance opened and Charlie's stretcher was gently pulled out and taken to the door of the spaceplane.

Charlie gingerly stood and, with Williams's help, moved to the door.

Mitchel came out of the plane.

"Mitch!" Charlie exclaimed and held out her arms. "You old son of a bitch, I'm glad to see you."

Mitchel came down the stairs to meet her and gave her a gentle embrace. "Hi, Charlie. Ready to go home?"

"Home?" she asked as he released her.

"I can have you on the Moon in two days if you feel up to it and the doctors approve."

"You mean off this dirt-ball?"

"Yes, ma'am."

"Let's go!" she said moving too quickly. "Ow, damn it."

In the descent phase of the SRI spaceplane's parabolic arch over the Pacific, Mitchel looked at Charlie and said, "What are you going to do now, Charlie?"

"I don't know," she answered. "I still have to recover from this."

"Yes, but after that?"

"I don't know. I really don't."

"There's still asteroid positions available for 2062. That'll be a rush job because of what happened to 1961. It'll be a challenge, but after this I think you can do anything you put your mind to."

Charlie shrugged. "I don't know, Mitch. I don't know if I can do it. If it hadn't been for your help I'd still be stuck in Esmeraldas. And Frank helped me a lot on the Moon."

"I don't understand, Charlie."

"I mean, on the Moon, Smitty had to save me when my suit blew. The police rescued me from the GA. I've never been able to succeed without help from you, or Frank, or someone else."

"What about Beatty?" Mitchel asked. "He killed three cops to get to you and you, practically unarmed, stopped him."

"I got lucky and he was stupid."

Mitchel looked out the window for a second. Then he turned to look at her. "Well, think about it Charlie. You did a hell of a job and I can get you anything you want. Even a safe job on the Moon, if that's what you want."

"Thanks, Mitch."

The spaceplane landed at Narita and Mitchel and Charlie moved to a helicopter. It rose into the morning sky and headed south.

The SRI archology rose out of Suruga Bay like a monolithic monument to technological hubris. The rising sun made its glass and metal curtain wall glitter against the backdrop of Mount Fuji.

Flying in on the helicopter, Charlie didn't realize the scale of the structure until it grew bigger and bigger and still bigger. The first hundred or so floors were finished but the next hundred were only a lattice framework. The last hundred hadn't even been started. The archology was six hexagons surrounding a central, hexagonal core. Each hexagon was, when the building was finished, to be a different length than the others and no length an integer multiple of any other. This was to prevent standing waves from forming on any of the sections in case of an earthquake. Suruga Bay's entrance was delineated by a major fault line.

"Where are we going to land?" Charlie asked Mitchel.

He pointed to a ledge hanging about 70 stories above the water. It looked big enough for, maybe, a large bird.

"There?" Charlie asked.

Mitchel nodded. "There."

The balcony grew to remarkable size by the time the helicopter set down on it. Two doctors and three nurses met them. Charlie was put in a robotic wheelchair that had multiple control options including voice command. Mitchel said good-bye.

"Where you going, Mitch?"

"It's morning, time for me to go to work," he said. "Give me a call when you reach the Moon, Charlie."

"I will, Mitch."

"And take care of yourself."

"I will. Good-bye."

"Bye, Charlie."

He boarded the helicopter that lifted and headed north toward Tokyo.

Charlie was wheeled into the hospital and thoroughly examined.

They filtered some of the perfluorodecaline artificial blood, that which had been replaced by Charlie's own, from her circulatory system. Only then did they approve her to go to the Moon if, and only if, once she got there she checked into the NESA hospital for a check-up and to have more PFD removed. They spent a few minutes teaching the chair to recognize Charlie's voice, although she was sure that she'd only be using it a short time and the joystick control was fine. But they insisted, saying it was a useful function to move the chair near your bed when you wanted to get up, for example. Also, a young Japanese man accompanied her, checking her blood pressure and temperature like a worried mother with a sick child. Charlie at first resented the nursemaid but then decided to enjoy the trip despite him.

They wheeled her back to the helipad and another helicopter was waiting for her. The helicopter rose from the balcony and flew directly over the archology. The nurse looked down and said, "Reminds me of coronene."

Charlie didn't ask and leaned back in her seat. The aircraft took her and her nurse back to Narita. The spaceplane was ready to go again. She was flown to Esmeraldas where the SRI spaceport was located, and the shuttle to the Low Earth Orbit Facility was waiting for her. Charlie gave up adding up what this must be costing SRI. The delay of the shuttle meant it had to expend more fuel and spend more time maneuvering in space, at a cost of maybe millions of dollars, or billions of yen. Charlie tried practicing her Japanese with the nurse, but he wanted to practice his English.

At the LEOF they transferred to another shuttle. Some passengers looked at her with a mixture of curiosity and anger; apparently they knew she had been the cause of their delay.

The new shuttle used its Masuka Drives to accelerate toward the Moon.

"Damn," Charlie said as she watched the LEOF grow smaller against the blue and white Earth.

"What?" the nurse asked.

"I forgot bubble bath."

Her nurse shook his head and continued looking out the window.

***

In the hours since the attack, Bente Naguchi had felt pretty useless. Her main drives were gone and, after spinning the asteroid a quarter rad per second, she had no job. She had her two subordinates in their quarters or the galley and strapped down. Chun was rotating one of the control room crew on watch alone. There was really nothing to do. She monitored various systems, but the crews in charge of them were doing the same. Occasional messages passed through the control room from one section to another, but all she had to do was listen in to see if there was anything she needed to know. There wasn't.

So, she had nothing to do; nothing to do but think and worry about her father. She'd used her message to assure her family she was well. She was hoping for a return message but wasn't sure her family would try. They knew how critical communications were. She doubted they'd send a message even if her father died.

She'd left so much unsaid to her father, and now she had plenty of time for regrets.

Maybe I should have gone into research, she thought. She missed the academic environment at the NESA University where she'd earned her B.S. in Astronomy. She could have gotten her master's and doctorate tuition free since she was a resident.

She'd known she would study a science as long as she could remember. It was tacitly assumed in the Naguchi home that the children's education would be science or, at worst, engineering. Bente remembered when she realized what she wanted to study. When she was about ten, her mother took her to the farside observatory during a school vacation. Astronomy had lost most of its romance since computers and automated electromagnetic radiation sensors did most of the work. Also, because the visible part of the spectrum held only a minuscule part of the information available throughout the entire EMR spectrum, astronomers rarely put their eye to a lens to view the heavens.

But at farside there was one small, 700 millimeter, Keplerian telescope. It was made of highly polished brass and rested on an oak tripod. Its lenses were Crysteel. Because the Moon rotates so slowly there was little need for a clock mechanism on the telescope.

Saturn was at opposition and Bente's mother (while an automated telescope did her work) helped Bente find the ringed giant. Although she'd seen the rings in pictures taken from the numerous robotic craft that had visited Saturn, there was an almost mystical sensation in seeing the rings for herself: having the actual light reflected and refracted by the rings impinge on her retina. It was then she decided to study astronomy. She had no idea that she'd later decide to join SRI instead of continuing her education and going into research. But the exploration of space fascinated her. She'd studied its history from Sputnik to NESA. When she learned she could go into space (she didn't consider the Moon "space") by working for SRI, she took her knowledge of the heavens and sent a resume to Tokyo. When she was hired, her father, normally restrained almost to a fault, threw a fit. And since then the rift had grown so much that the hundreds of millions of kilometers between them now seemed the shorter of the two gulfs that separated father and daughter.

Bente stared at her computer's monotonous display. *I wonder,* she thought, *why my father isn't more like Director Chun.* Chun reminded her of what her father was like when she was a child. They were both about the same build and height and Chun was about the age now her father was then. The biggest difference was that Alex was half Korean, half Caucasian, and her father was Japanese. But Alex seemed to accept people for what they were. She'd never seen him become angry with anyone without good reason. She imagined he'd make a good father.

***

Griffin was dozing in the acceleration couch in the center of the *Rock Killer*'s bridge. He was barely aware of Knecht as she came and went from the engine compartment to the bridge and back again. He heard her say, "Goddamn fiber optics," but wasn't sure if it was a dream or not. He was almost positive that he dreamed she leaned over him and said, "I love you."

A beeping awakened him. He opened his eyes and Cole was staring at Trudeau's undamaged radar equipment.

"That just started beeping," she said.

Griffin unstrapped himself and pushed himself over to it. The screen displayed:

RADAR SOURCE X:136.5, Y:026.3, D:???.?
CORRELATING FREQUENCY, MODULATION, AND POLARIZATION
WITH USES. PLEASE WAIT ONE MOMENT...

"What the hell is this," Griffin wondered out loud.

AN/APN-453(A) U.S. AIRBORNE NAVIGATION RADAR, the display continued.

SRI/XPQ-34(V)   SPACE   RESOURCE   INC
NAVIGATION/DF RADAR
RUSSIAN   FEDERATION   TINCAN   AIRBORNE
NAVIGATION RADAR

"What's going on?" Knecht asked, pulling off her helmet as she entered the bridge.

"This thing," Cole said, "is displaying something."

Knecht pushed over and looked at the growing list.

AN/DPS-002(X) DRONE RANGE BEARING RADAR, it added as she watched.

"Shit," she yelled. "How could I be so stupid?" *And why,* she thought, *am I the only one who has to think of these things?*

"What?" Griffin demanded.

"The XPQ-34 victor is the primary navigation radar for SRI. That must be the asteroid tender."

"So?" Griffin asked.

She rolled her eyes. "So, they can find us. This is a radar receiver. I just hope we're not reflecting enough yet for them to pick us up. Strap down, now!"

She jumped to her navigation controls. "Everyone down?" she asked, and before anyone could answer yawed the *Rock Killer* violently.

Griffin wasn't buckled in and was thrown from his chair. He hung onto the seat belt with the hand on his good arm and was swinging around the air on its end.

Knecht started the ship rolling and then pitched the ship. She heard Griffin slap against the floor and mutter a few obscenities. She watched while he painfully pulled himself into the chair and buckled the seat belt. Pain contorted his face as he was forced to use his broken arm in the process.

"I'm turning the lights off," Knecht said.

The bridge became unearthly dark. Out the windows, the stars spun as if God was shaking the universe in a dice cup. Occasionally the Sun passed before a window and burned a streak on the retina.

"How long have we got to stay like this?" Griffin asked angrily.

"Until they pass us."

Chapter Sixteen

"Warm up those missiles."

Griffin carefully pulled on an emergency pressure suit just enough to get the helmet over his head without it cutting into his shoulders. He was worried about his arm. The pain was slowly and inexorably growing. Bagalos, who died on the lunar plain, was the medical expert. The splints helped, but the arm was turning shades no human skin should be.

Knecht had been in and out of the engine compartment. After the asteroid tender passed, as evidenced by the radar receiver's silence, she gave the ship a stable attitude. Then, she'd slept a few hours before returning to her task. She had completely ignored him for the past day since the attack. He was tired of it and decided to do something about it.

Griffin took a minute or two to figure out the radio in the suit helmet and the controls on the arm. "Barbara?" he asked over the radio.

"What?" she snapped. She sounded breathless.

"What's wrong?"

"There are some damaged connectors I need to fix. I just hope I can do it," she said accusingly.

"No," Griffin pleaded, uselessly shaking his head. "Are you mad at me?"

There was a long pause. Griffin was about to ask if she'd heard when the radio crackled. "Listen," Knecht said. "I'm a little too busy now to deal with your adolescent, hormonal problems. Get off the damn radio."

"Okay," Griffin said flatly. He turned off the radio and pulled off the suit.

Cole looked at him. She was smiling enigmatically.

***

Alex was, for the first time in his life, thankful for the relative free fall he experienced in his quarters. As a mental exercise, he had calculated that the 2.4 rpm spin of the asteroid resulted in about five one-hundredths of a gee acceleration here; just enough that if he let go of anything, it eventually ended up on the outside wall.

His chronic space sickness had dulled to being merely excruciatingly uncomfortable. But, if he'd been in any greater acceleration, he knew his body would be killing him. He'd been strapped down on the bed in his quarters for 25 hours. Almost half the time was gone until the *Kyushu* would rendezvous and take them off.

The intercom system gave him regular reports. Communications Chief Manna relayed a report from the *Kyushu* that it had found the *Rock Skipper*. It was tumbling and apparently lifeless. Alex wondered if there would be an attempt to salvage it.

The mass driver was being repaired but they were having trouble with the superconductors. They didn't work in vacuum so some miners were building conduits they could pressurize around the vital, ceramic fibers. They said they'd be finished soon. He hoped so. Even the mass driver's small acceleration of a tenth of a gee would speed rendezvous if Naguchi turned the rock and used the mass driver to accelerate opposite to the *Kyushu*'s acceleration vector.

As if she'd heard him think of her, the navigator descended into his quarters.

"Bente," Chun said, "you shouldn't be moving."

"I wanted to see you," she replied sheepishly. "I'm sorry."

"Well, you're here. What can I do for you?" He looked at her. Her long body floated in front of him. She was a stunning beauty because of her mixed heritage alone. But she was raised on the Moon where her body grew long and svelte, exotically enhancing her loveliness. Again he wondered why she seemed so lonely.

"Do you think we'll make it?" she asked.

"I don't know. Taylor in life support says there's a good chance."

"What if we don't?"

Chun unstrapped himself and sat up, except he wasn't actually sitting because he was hanging onto the bed to keep from floating off the mattress. "I try not to think about it," he said with a smile.

"Could you," she asked haltingly, "hold me?"

Alex considered a moment. Then he pushed off the bed gently and bumped into her. He clumsily put his arms around her. Their combined masses slowly bumped into the wall pressing them together for an instant before they bounced back into the middle of the room.

She snaked her long arms around his back. Alex had to admit it felt good to hold her despite the layers of their two pressure suits separating them. He tried not think about the fact his feet reached to about her knees. He was also ignoring the signals he was getting from other parts of his body.

She moved to kiss him. He let go of her with a small push and they separated.

"No," he said simply.

"I'm scared," she whispered.

"So am I," Alex replied. "But we need to limit movement."

He cringed at his excuse. She looked hurt at the brush off.

"I'm married," he added.

"We could die," she said, almost whining.

Alex looked over her. "I know. But we could, probably will, come out of this alive. And even if we didn't, I don't believe that makes it all right."

She looked at him. Tears were building on her eyes. She shook her head and the tears floated free as blobs. "I'm sorry," she finally said, emotion hanging in the air like her tears.

Alex shook his head. "Don't be. A hug feels good sometimes."

She nodded and turned to push out of his office.

"Bente," he called after her.

She used the metal doorframe to turn around. "Yes?"

"Is everything okay? I mean, other than the obvious."

She nodded. "Yes," she said. Her voice quivered slightly.

Alex smiled at her. "Really? You got an emergency message on the *Kyushu*."

She started crying softly. He moved to her and pulled her into the room, closing the door. It was most comfortable just hanging in the air, slowly drifting toward the outside wall. Slowly she calmed.

"I'm sorry," she whispered. She shook her head. "I'm being real professional." She wiped her tears away.

"What's wrong, Bente?"

"My father had a heart attack. I don't know how he is and I'm afraid if he hears the news of the terrorist attack it could make him worse."

"Did you send a message letting him know you're all right?"

"Yes."

"Do you want to send another? I'll approve it."

She shook her head. "No. I've nothing to say."

"Okay," Alex said. "Let me know if there's anything I can do for you, okay?"

"Sure," she replied. "I apologize for crying."

"That's okay. Are you close to your father?"

"No," Bente said. "We haven't gotten along for years."

"Really? Why?"

"He thought I should do research for NESA instead of working for SRI."

"That's funny," Alex said.

Bente stared at him.

"No, no," Alex corrected. "That's funny because I had almost the same exact problem with my father. I call it the Asian/Confucius guilt syndrome."

Bente laughed quietly. "He wanted you to do research?"

"No. He wanted me to take over his store on Olympic Boulevard in Los Angeles. Obviously I didn't."

"Did you have a brother or sister who did as your father wished?"

"No," Alex said. "I was an only child. That's too bad because it might have been better if I had."

"Don't count on that," Bente grumbled. "My father is always holding up my younger brother, Akio, as the perfect child. Does your father do anything like that?"

"No," Alex said. "He died a few years ago." His complexion darkened and his black eyes grew angry. "Some piece of garbage gang killed him in a robbery."

"I'm sorry," Bente said softly not knowing what else to say.

Alex shrugged. "It's okay. I'm used to it now," he said with a sadness that proved he was lying, if only to himself. "They never found them; never prosecuted. He was just one more Korean storeowner killed by the gangs. My mother didn't live long after that."

Bente stared at him with empathetic eyes.

"Bente," Alex asked, "could you do something for me?"

"Yes?"

"First, don't lose your father. It's not worth it. If he's alive when you get home, reconcile your differences."

"Okay, I will."

"And second," Alex said, "would you hold me?"

Bente smiled slightly. "Sure." She pushed off the wall. They met in the middle of the room and held each other for a few long, friendly minutes. Despite differences in age and status Alex knew they were now friends.

One cannot share hidden pain with another without some kind of bond forming.

"I've got to get back to the control room; it's my watch soon," Bente said when they separated by mutual, albeit tacit, consent.

"I should go up there myself," Alex said. "I'll go with you."

***

Knecht, still wearing the suit but with the bubble helmet removed, was standing over the navigation computer. "Here goes nothing," she said more to herself. She punched a power button.

Griffin was surprised. He expected to hear or feel something. Instead, the only indication was green lights on Knecht's read-out.

"Full power available," Knecht crowed happily. "That's it," she continued, working the computer. She heaved a large sigh. "It's a good thing the reactor wasn't damaged. Prepare for acceleration...now!"

The *Rock Killer*'s acceleration quickly built up to one and a half times the acceleration of Earth's gravity.

Griffin smiled–smiled despite the pain. The pseudo-gravity was killing his broken arm. "How long to rendezvous with the asteroid?"

Knecht worked on her computer. "At full acceleration, 12 ½ hours, assuming the asteroid didn't accelerate."

"How you gonna find it?" Griffin asked.

"Look." She typed on her computer. Her holographic display showed a nebulous trail.

"What is that?" Griffin asked.

"Helium, or more accurately, alpha particles. Their reactor releases minute amounts of it. It's the ash of the fusion reaction."

"It's not dangerous, is it?" Griffin asked.

Knecht looked at him. His face showed his fear. She wondered why she never noticed before how stupid he was. "No, it's just ionized helium. Harmless."

"Oh," he said, trying to sound as if he understood.

"It's a lot hotter than the space around it and shows up in the infrared sensor," she continued. "We'll just follow it to them."

"Then we've got them," Griffin said. He smiled and moved to put an arm around her.

She shrugged it off her shoulder and glared silently at him.

***

Alex was alone in the control room. It was his turn at lone watch. Alex checked the computer; twelve and a half hours, about, until the *Kyushu* rendezvous–and safety.

Thorne entered the room. He pushed over to Alex's chair and hung on to it.

"How's it going?" Alex asked.

Thorne smiled weakly. "I've got an itch I can't scratch in this suit. This is the longest I've ever worn it. It's gonna stink when I get out of it."

"I know what you mean," Alex said, unconsciously trying to scratch his leg. "Any problems?"

"Well, some mining tunnels collapsed because they weren't re-supported for spin."

"Who cares?" Alex mumbled tiredly, immediately regretting it.

"We had one minor injury when a storage locker worked loose and 'fell' on someone's leg."

Chun was immediately attentive. "Why wasn't I told? How badly were they hurt?"

"They were bruised, that's all, Alex."

Chun relaxed visibly. He'd already lost too many people on this trip. "Any other problems?"

"No. Everyone is being cooperative."

"Good," Alex said. Not surprising, he thought. They know the risks and the fact they're in space in the first place indicates their level of intelligence was higher than the average.

"How are you?" Alex asked.

"Okay," Thorne replied casually.

Liar, Alex thought. "I heard they recovered Diana's body," he prodded.

Thorne's face hardened. "Yes," he said simply.

"I'm sorry," Alex said sympathetically.

Thorne simply acknowledged with a small nod.

"Sometimes I think about Diane," Alex continued, "and I get so angry I..." He stopped, knowing clichés weren't adequate for the composite of anger and sadness he was experiencing. Alex had first felt the concoction of rage and grief when Joey Hernandez was killed. He experienced the amalgamation of emotion again when Theresa Gold died. Every time Alex lost a friend, he would wonder if it would hurt less the next time. So far it hadn't. He was glad Kirsten refused to leave the Earth, but there were dangers there, also. Alex's father was on Earth when he was killed. "It's just like Theresa," he said softly.

Thorne looked at him. "What about Theresa? I know you were there. That Chinese spy killed her."

Alex shrugged. "When we caught Woo trying to steal trade secrets, he killed her." Alex's voice became unsteady. "Used his shotgun. She died, while I held her, a few minutes later. I was never so angry. I chased him onto the surface of the asteroid and down by the mass driver. That was back when they only had about a twentieth of a gee acceleration and you could still climb on the outside."

"I know," Thorne remarked.

"We were making long traverses over the surface. I don't know where he was trying to go. I kept telling him over the radio there was no escape. Right after he'd planted a piton he fired at me, missed, but it propelled him up. When his rope went taut he started swinging back toward the surface of the rock."

Alex stopped.

Thorne waited while Alex regained his composure.

"I undid his snap link," Alex said.

"What?"

"I reached down and undid his snap link. He continued on a tangential trajectory. He went into the mass driver exhaust. I told everyone his piton came loose."

"Why, Alex?"

"I wanted to kill him."

"Why? Theresa was a friend, but—"

"We were having an affair," Alex said softly.

Thorne just looked ahead.

"Yeah, it was after that that I decided you were okay. After all, I'd made the same mistake you did. It started on Europa. We were there for three years while the facility was being built and she and I just got along really well. We fell in love and let that cloud our judgment."

"What about Kirsten? Does she know?"

"She figured it out," Alex said. "And we don't talk about it anymore. Old baggage, she calls it. It's been seven years."

Alex paused. "But you know, Bill, it's funny. I loved Theresa and still loved Kirsten just as much, just differently."

"But why did you kill Woo?"

"I guess I was angry—wanted revenge."

"I'm angry, too," Thorne said, his voice tense. "God damn it, Alex. I think we were in love. Those damned...I just hope they died in great pain trying to breath vacuum."

Alex nodded in agreement and was angry with the terrorists for making him feel good about human suffering.

***

"How long will you be staying at the Nippon/European Space Agency Facility, Mr. Oaks?" the customs inspector asked.

"A few weeks," McConnell said.

"You realize it's very expensive to stay here on the Moon."

"Oh, yes," McConnell said. But he had access to a network of bank and SRI accounts full of GA money that even Beatty didn't know about and therefore weren't in that damned computer.

"Fine," the inspector said, putting McConnell's visa in the computer slot.

Here goes, McConnell thought. *We'll find out if that was worth what we paid for it.*

Apparently it worked. The inspector read the screen and then handed the visa back. "Thank you, Mr. Oaks."

McConnell had visited the Moon once before using his own name and money. He knew the way to the opulent Selene Hotel.

Checking in was not a problem; his visa opened his room and he went in. There were two rooms, one a bathroom. A large bed dominated the main chamber. Most of the furniture was wood and cloth and the floor was covered in carpet. A window, about half a meter wide by one meter tall, looked out over the gray moonscape and the black, starry sky.

McConnell also knew the computer in his room could connect him to almost any service imaginable. Last time he couldn't afford to sample those services. But on GA money it was no problem.

After all, he deserved a little extra service at the GA's expense considering what he'd sacrificed for the alliance.

About an hour later the door buzzer rang. He pulled it open. The two girls smiled and walked in. And he'd only started on the first page of the "Personal Services" menu.

***

Mitchel turned off the communications program on his computer after talking to Freeman. His friend was at a loss.

"I can't see any way to find McConnell," Freeman had said.

But, Mitchel had resources not available to the FBI. He spent a good hour writing a search program. It took less than five minutes to run. SRI had access to most banks' credit card databases through a long standing but expensive contract.

Mitchel's program sifted through the billions of credit card transactions for the past two days for those at Denver's two airports within four hours either side of McConnell's ticket purchase.

Next it eliminated all seats bought in pairs and all tickets that were reserved in advance (this required correlating airline data also), leaving a large amount to filter through. Anyone who bought a ticket for the places Mitchel thought McConnell would run to or bought a second ticket at their destination for one of those places was selected. This left a few less.

Finally, the credit reports of all those people were checked for activity. Any with very little activity before the ticket purchases were chosen. These were displayed on Mitchel's computer. There were about a hundred but he noticed two in particular. He had the computer display only them. One was a female going to Damascus via London. The other was a "Oaks, Rodger J." who was going to New York and then Cayenne. That one had zero credit card activity before that ticket was purchased. While McConnell might run to Damascus, Mitchel didn't think he would be traveling in drag from what Charlie told him about McConnell.

Cayenne is in French Guiana, Mitchel thought, *and NESA's spaceport is there.* SRI and NESA shared information in an agreement that went back to the original privatization of Space

Resources. Mitchel wondered if NESA knew how much SRI held back and wondered how much NESA kept from SRI.

NESA's database included information on travelers to the Moon. Roger J. Oaks had bought one ticket to the Moon. The price of the ticket was determined by the mass of the person and their luggage. Charlie said McConnell was more than a little pudgy.

Roger Oaks massed 120 kilograms. His single bag, less than ten. Oaks arrived on the Moon and checked into the Selene Hotel. Very expensive, but Oaks had the credit rating. Which, come to think of it, was very unusual for someone with no activity on their credit account–unless it was a bogus account and a bogus credit rating.

Mitchel switched to the communications program and got a visual link to the Moon.

After talking to Rodriguez, Mitchel got a secure line to Mr. Kijoto's office. Mitchel briefed the CEO on the situation on the Moon and in Syria. Kijoto approved Mitchel's plan. Mitchel then contacted Yamauchi, the intra-lunar tug fleet commander at the LEOF, by secure signal.

***

Knecht was rubbing her eyes. She had to manually follow the spoor of hot helium left by the asteroid. Except for a short catnap while repairing the *Rock Killer*, she hadn't slept since hours before the attack almost 50 hours ago.

The asteroid hadn't changed direction and a second trail of alpha particles was paralleling the first. The speed at which the helium in the second trail moved, which indicated the speed of the source as the atoms left it, was slowing by 44.3 meters per second per kilometer. That corresponded to a negative acceleration of the source of one tenth of a gee. That would be the asteroid tender, she decided. It must be trying to reach the asteroid. From the speed of the rock and the speed and acceleration of the asteroid tender, she was able to predict when they would rendezvous. It was so close to the time the *Rock Killer* would reach the asteroid that she couldn't predict which would catch up first.

She'd also found a parallel cloud of diatomic hydrogen molecules. It was much cooler than the helium from the fusion reactors. It had the speed of the asteroid, so she knew the rock was its source. She calculated from its heat that when it left the asteroid it was about room temperature. She wondered what the hell that meant.

Griffin came up behind her as she bent over her navigation computer. She stiffened at his approach.

"You need to get some sleep," he said. "How long?"

"About three hours," she said simply.

"You could take a nap," he suggested. "Cole is."

"I'm okay," she snapped.

He hesitated a moment. "I'm just worried about you."

She turned to look at him. He didn't look well; it was obvious he was in a lot of pain. She'd watched him try to sleep but the pain was too much and his sleep was restless. He refused the pain medicine available.

"I'm okay," she restated.

He reached his good arm out to her.

"Don't," she ordered, shying away.

He pulled back. "What's wrong?" he asked with the hurt evident in his voice.

"What's wrong?" she asked incredulously. "You're just like all the rest."

"The rest of what?"

"You treated me like a thing just like all the rest."

"What do you mean, Barb?"

"I mean you said you loved me but you just used me and then you didn't care."

"I don't understand."

"I let you have me," she said, her voice getting shrill. "But then you didn't consider me worthy of normal consideration. You wouldn't listen to me and Trudeau is dead and we almost all got killed and almost ended our mission."

"You mean the mass driver? I didn't understand the danger. You saved us, Barb. I appreciate that."

She looked at him for a moment. He thought he might have dented her shield of anger.

"No," she barked. "You still thought of me as a thing. Otherwise you would have taken my word for it. Leave me alone," she said with a finality that indicated the conversation was over.

Griffin walked away not without pain to his arm in the high gravity. And that wasn't the only pain he felt. He turned to look at Knecht. Already she was absorbed in her work. He couldn't see the tears on her face.

***

The intra-lunar tug fleet commander, Masatoshi Yamauchi, contacted Director Nakajima of SRI-1960 on a secure communication. Nakajima agreed to arrange to provide what Yamauchi required.

Trusting no one else to complete the job, Yamauchi personally piloted the tug. This also reduced the number of employees that knew about the strange mission Mitchel had given him. He left the LEOF and moved toward the Lagrange point where SRI-1960 was being dismantled. The tailings were about all that was left. That would be sold cheap to NESA for radiation shielding. But one hunk of rock, about the size of car, was separated from the rest. Yamauchi picked up the boulder with the tug's mechanical and magnetic grapples. Yamauchi then dropped the tug's Earth orbit to about 950 kilometers.

***

The time was soon, Faruq knew. Timing was everything. General Zuabi was in Damascus on official business and could control the army; the Baath party was so angry about the inaction of the president against the Zionist state that it could soon explode; the leaders of the other United Baath Arab States were distancing themselves from him. There was hardly a member of the Party who did not know that Faruq had been instrumental in the brilliant attack on Space Resources Inc. Faruq could almost feel the party's support swinging toward him. The time was ripe to move.

Two of the nine rotating presidential bodyguards would be on duty at the same time tomorrow. Those two had sworn loyalty to Faruq.

In less than 24 hours Faruq would rule Syria. In less than 48 hours the Zionist state would no longer exist.

* * *

Charlie watched out the window as the shuttle descended to the Moon. She was on the wrong side to see the SRI observation lounge. She was thankful for that. The tube extended and they walked in the shuttleport; except Charlie, she rolled.

Rodriguez met her and her escort.

"We think Whaltham, a.k.a. McConnell, a.k.a. Roger Oaks is here."

Charlie's eyes grew wide. "Here? Where? I want him."

"He arrived on the last NESA shuttle."

"Let me at him."

"That's a problem. He's staying in a hotel and as far as anyone can tell he hasn't left his room. He's been sending out for food, entertainment, clothes."

"Entertainment?"

"Yes," Rodriguez said. "He's patronized almost every 'personal service' in the computer bank."

"That sounds like Whaltham," Charlie said. Her hand moved to her cheek.

"I've got us a meeting with a NESA Security official," Rodriguez said. "Feel up to it?"

"Damn straight," Charlie growled angrily.

"Excuse me, Ms. Jones," the nurse said. "But you were to check into the NESA hospital for an examination. You're still very weak."

"I'll tell you how weak I am," Charlie chided him. "You just make sure my b.p. doesn't get too low."

"But, Ms. Jones—" he started.

"No," Charlie said. "I want Whaltham. Let's go, Rodriguez." She shoved the joystick on the chair forward as far as it could go. The chair lurched down the corridor with surprising speed.

The Japanese man shook his head but followed Charlie's chair.

***

In Boulder, Colorado, Kirsten looked at her wrist computer's time display. She had it set to Universal Mean Time, which Mitchel called "Zulu" time. It was a half hour from the time Mitchel had told her the *Kyushu* would rendezvous with Alex's asteroid. She moved to the front window and looked out on the lawn. A reporter was standing in front of a camera. Kirsten turned back to look at the large computer screen. She just caught a glimpse of her face looking out the window of her house behind a reporter and then her face on the screen turned to look inside the house.

She moved quickly away from the window. On the screen, she moved quickly away from the window.

***

Alex returned to the control room from his quarters as the control room crew assembled for the rendezvous. He'd actually gotten in a catnap. Bente was watching her computer. She saw him enter and they exchanged small smiles.

"About half an hour, sir," Banda reported.

Alex nodded and hit the intercom. "Taylor, how's it going?"

"We just ran out of water except a tiny bubble that keeps breaking up. I think we should shut it down now."

"Understood. Can we last half an hour?"

"Yes, easily, if nothing unforeseen happens."

"Great," Alex said. "Bente, stop the spin."

***

Knecht looked at the monitor that showed the view though the rear-facing telescope. She could see the asteroid. She smiled and looked at her computer. Less than 15 minutes.

"Cole," she said. "Warm up those missiles."

CHAPTER SEVENTEEN

"...can't take another hit in the rear."

Mastoshi Yamachi, commander of the intra-lunar tug fleet, was sweating like a first year trainee as he worked his calculations on the tug's computer. He had to release the piece of rock at just the right velocity at just the right moment in just the right place. His task was complicated by the necessity of avoiding the powerful military radars of the U.S., China, Russia, Japan and the EU.

Yamachi worked it out on his computer repeatedly and had it calculated to the fifteenth significant digit. Unfortunately, his equipment only gave him five-digit accuracy. And the common-sense-defying reality of orbital mechanics, where one speeds up to slow down and slows down to speed up, made the task formidable. Yamachi wished more than once he could have delegated this responsibility.

And, even with all his careful calculation, Earth's unpredictable atmosphere would do as it wished to his plans. Even the best supercomputers couldn't model a chaotic system like Earth's sheath of air.

Yamachi checked his numbers and released the rock. He turned his tug around and did a retroburn (although the word "burn" was an anachronism left over from the chemical rockets) with the main Masuka drive to bring him into a lower orbit where he could rendezvous with the Low Earth Orbit Facility. That, and he didn't want to be anywhere in the vicinity when the rock hit its target.

At LEOF, he had some computer work to do to cover his trip. Officially, it never happened.

***

We're going to make it, Chun thought. The air was stuffy and Alex noticed he found exertion becoming difficult. *The partial pressure must be dropping,* he thought. But they were going to make it. "How long until the *Kyushu* can match orbit?"

Naguchi said, "Fifteen minutes."

Chun smiled. "We're going to make it," he said.

"We're going to make it," Banda repeated.

***

Both the *Rock Killer* and the *Kyushu* were traveling ass-backwards, slowing to match velocities with SRI-1961 after racing to catch-up.

The *Kyushu* was closer to the asteroid, between the *Rock Killer* and her target. The *Rock Killer* was moving faster.

On the bridge of the asteroid tender the forward-looking window in the ceiling of the bridge was actually looking behind.

"Do you see that?" the navigator said.

"What's that, mister?" Captain Takashara asked.

"It's a ship, negative accelerating."

"Radar?" the Captain barked.

The radar man released a pulse. His computer matched the return signal with stored profiles and displayed its conclusion.

"It's the *Rock Skipper*," the radar man said, incredulous. Last he'd seen that ship it was tumbling.

"Damn," Takashara spat. "Communications, get me 1961."

***

"What about the other ship?" Knecht asked.

"Ignore it. Are we close enough?" Griffin asked.

"Yes, no mistake this time," Knecht replied. "But I still think the other ship—"

Griffin ignored her. If she wanted to think he didn't consider her opinion worthwhile, he wouldn't. "Cole, turn on your radar."

"I have missile lock."

"Launch missile," Griffin ordered through clenched teeth.

***

Chun changed the intercom from "Communications" to the recently repaired line to the mass driver. "Is the driver working?"

"Soon, sir," a voice said. It was female. Alex wondered why it bothered him more to risk a woman's life.

"We need the mass driver in 20 seconds or we're all dead."

"We'll—" The rock shuddered with the same motion as two days before when a missile hit. The intercom went dead.

"Control room, this is Perez. I'm at the new emergency doors. We just took another hit in the mass driver. The first door was breached slightly but we've got it controlled."

"Survivors?"

"I doubt it, sir," Perez said softly.

Alex spat, "Damn it!" and wanted to wallow in his anger, but Takashara cut him off.

"Nineteen sixty-one, this is the *Kyushu*, you've been hit and your mass driver is gone. I don't know what you can do."

***

Griffin smiled as he watched the mass driver tumble away from the asteroid. "Launch again."

A missile shot forward, yawed 180 degrees around its center and, after slowing to a stop, flew at the rock.

***

Chun grimaced. "Bente, put our side to that ship. We can't take another hit in the rear."

"Control room, communications, they launched again."

Damn it, Chun thought, *we need a weapon, missiles, a laser, anything. The miners have some small lasers,* he thought. *But by the time they get them to the surface... should have thought of that before,* Alex chided himself.

"Nineteen sixty-one, this is *Kyushu*. They just passed us."

The Kyushu has that laser to drill through rocks, Chun thought. *Damn, I am getting stupid.*

"*Kyushu*, use your laser, kill that ship!"

The control room bounced.

"Stabilizing attitude," Bente said, her voice betraying her own emotion.

***

Captain Takashara hesitated. "Can we do it?" she asked no one in particular.

"I can yaw the ship," the navigator reported, "and then I can aim the laser using pitch, yaw and roll controls."

"Do it," Takashara ordered. "And do it fast."

***

Griffin stopped smiling. "Is there any way to aim the missiles? We're just blowing out sections of rock."

"I told you," Cole said, "that it hits the center of the facing profile. I can't do a damn thing about it."

"The other ship," Knecht said, "is turning."

"So what?" Griffin barked. The pain in his arm was creeping up to his shoulder and down his side.

"Damn it," Knecht barked angrily. "Last time you ignored me we almost got killed! Cole, launch a missile at that ship!"

Griffin opened his mouth but Cole cut him off.

"I have to get missile lock; it will take time."

"Do it now!" Knecht screamed.

***

The navigator on the *Kyushu* yawed the ship as fast as he could. He slowed the turn just as the *Rock Skipper* was straight ahead between his ship and the asteroid. But both ships were accelerating.

"dV/dt equals acceleration," he mumbled working with his skilled fingers on the computer. In school he never thought he'd do differential equations on a three-space vector problem that was a life or death situation. He solved for a time five seconds later. The computer displayed a coordinate prediction of where the *Rock Skipper* would be at that time and the Euler angle to be pointed in that direction. He placed the laser-aiming reticle on those coordinates. Three seconds.

"Fire the laser," he said.

The laser fired its arm-thick beam. It missed the *Rock Skipper* and sliced harmlessly into the stone surface of the asteroid. Two seconds. The stolen ship was getting closer.

***

"I've got missile lock," Cole reported loudly.

"Launch," Knecht yelled. "They're firing a laser!"

Cole reached for the panel.

She never made it. The ship passed through the waiting beam of the laser. It burned through the hull of the *Rock Killer* in the bridge, showering the interior with melted metal in a cone of blazing heat that burned everything flammable in the room: paper, plastic, cloth, flesh. The air expanded explosively, ripping the ship apart. In the airless drive section, the buckling of the deck tore open the fusion reactor and lithium plasma coolant exploded into the vacuum, damaging the reactor controls. The magnetic bottle failed, and the hot hydrogen plasma fuel, much, much too cool to fuse but still inconceivably hot, became a massive blow torch shooting the missile compartment. That ignited fuel and warheads. The *Rock Killer* became two convergent spheres of expanding, rapidly cooling debris.

Metal and plastic flotsam rained harmlessly upon the surface of the asteroid. Some wreckage hit the *Kyushu* causing minor breaches that were quickly and efficiently plugged by damage control teams that she'd left in place even after finding the *Rock Skipper* apparently dead. *Just in case,* Takashara had told herself.

***

"Nineteen sixty-one," Takashara's voice said via the intercom, "this is the *Kyushu*. The *Rock Skipper* is dead. We'll have matched velocities in just a few minutes."

Chun let out a long breath and then breathed in the thin air in the asteroid. "Tsuji."

"Yes?" the miner asked.

"Unseal one of the tunnels to the surface, install an airlock, and get a miner on the outside. The *Kyushu* will match velocity soon. They'll be sending over a telegraph line."

"Roger."

***

Helga Moeller regarded Charlie after greeting her politely. Moeller then greeted Rodriguez like an old friend.

"What can I do for you?" she asked, the pleasantries finished.

"You have in the Selene," Rodriguez began, "a Roger Oaks, American. We have reason to believe he is Whaltham, a leader in the Gaia Alliance."

"What reason?" Moeller asked.

"That's the problem, Helga. We have nothing firm now. But Charlie knows Whaltham. If she can get a look at him..."

Moeller frowned. "Then go look. What's the problem?"

"He hasn't come out of his hotel room. He's ordered out a lot but that's it. About the only way we could get Charlie to see him is to put her in a pressure suit and lower down to the window."

"That would break our privacy laws," Moeller said, either not noticing or caring that it was a joke. "It's obvious you have his room under surveillance that, without due cause, is also a violation of our laws and the agreement between SRI and NESA."

"I know," Rodriguez said. "May we present our evidence to see if it is enough that NESA will ask him out of his room?"

"Yes," Moeller said.

It took about a half an hour for Rodriguez to go over the data Mitchel had sent him. At the end Moeller shook her head.

"No, this is not enough."

"But he could be—" Rodriguez started.

"I know," Moeller said interrupting him. "But we have very strict privacy laws here. We have to; this is too small and closed-in a society for it to be otherwise. The danger of despotism is greatest in such a place. We could, like the Russians on Mars, place cameras in strategic places and easily control the population. Especially since we control the air. But we don't and we do pay a price for it. It is one reason why the 'personal service' section of the data bank has the most records. But, otherwise, we'd risk an oxygen dictatorship."

"I understand, Helga," Rodriguez said. "Is there nothing we can do?"

"No," she said. "But I will overlook your surveillance of his room. If anyone else catches you, I know nothing about it."

Rodriguez looked at the floor. "Well, thank you anyway."

He stood.

"What about," a voice said, "his visa?"

Everyone turned to the Japanese man that seemed so much part of Charlie's chair no one paid any attention to him.

"Excuse me?" Moeller said.

"His visa," the nurse said. "Was it legal?"

"Yes," Charlie said. "Can you give his visa more than just a routine check with the evidence we've given you?"

"No," Moeller said, smiling. "But we do give random visas thorough investigations. I think Mr. Oaks' will be one."

She turned to her computer and typed while narrating. "Okay, his number is not a duplicate, but that would have been checked on Earth. It was purchased at the Japanese consulate in San Francisco on May third of last year. Hum, that's interesting."

"What?" Charlie and Rodriguez asked simultaneously.

"Your data indicate that Mr. Oaks first used his credit account to purchase an airline ticket?"

"Yes."

"Well, as you know, for a visa we require either a credit check or a large cash deposit. Enough to get you back to Earth if you go broke."

"Right," Rodriguez said.

"Well, according to this they did a credit check in San Francisco and it came up good. But if he's never used credit (hard to believe in itself)... hang on. Let's call up a credit check on Mr. Oaks. I can get his credit account number from the hotel and..."

There was a wait while the data were transmitted from Earth.

Moeller frowned. "It seems the credit services have never heard of our Mr. Oaks. So either the Japanese screwed up, which I find incredulous, or it's a fake visa. Plus, he's probably using an invalid credit account." She looked at Rodriguez. "I have to investigate this. If you and Ms. Jones want to tag along, I can't stop you."

269

"All right," Charlie said. "Let me at 'im."

"In your condition?" Moeller asked.

"I don't care," Charlie replied indignantly. She was tired of the invalid routine. She'd stand up and walk if it didn't hurt so badly.

"Listen," Rodriguez said to the women. "We just want her to finger him."

"Lead me to him," Charlie said.

In front of the Selene, Charlie recognized Smitty although he was in civilian clothes. He moved up to her and grabbed her hand.

"Charlie," he exclaimed. "You look great."

"You lie like a dog, Smitty," Charlie said. They both laughed. Charlie laughed even though seeing him reminded her of when she and Smitty found Frank's body.

"Has he come out?" Rodriguez asked Smitty.

"No. A lot of girls have gone in, though."

"He's not alone?" Moeller asked.

"I think now he is," Smitty reported. "A bunch just left. They didn't look too happy."

"I can understand why," Charlie said softly.

There was a short silence.

"Listen," Moeller said. "I'm going to ring the bell and when he comes to the door ask him some question and then take his visa for authenticity tests."

"You're not going to arrest him?" Charlie asked.

"I can't until I have proof it's a fake visa. Besides, where would he go?"

"What if I finger him as Waltham?"

"Then I'll arrest him on the spot."

"Okay," Charlie said. "Let's go."

Moeller looked perplexed for a moment. "Okay. You may come to the door with me." She tapped the Glock nine millimeter at her hip. "If it's not him I want you out of there fast, understand?"

"Yes, ma'am."

Moeller pressed the button for the bell. Charlie was beside her in the wheelchair. The nurse was across the hall.

"What is it?" a male voice called.

The hair on the back of Charlie's neck came to attention.

She looked up at Moeller and nodded. Moeller unsnapped the strap holding her weapon in its holster and spoke softly into the radio on her cheek, "This is Moeller at the Selene. I need backup at room 3872."

"I said who is it?" the voice said again, somewhat irritated.

"NESA Security, Mr. Oaks," she said.

There was a long pause.

Finally: "Can you come back later?"

"No, sir. I can't. Would you please open the door?"

Again there was a long wait. "Okay, just a minute. I'm getting dressed."

More waiting. "He has ten seconds," Moeller said, "then I'm going in."

The door opened inward.

"Hi, Whaltham," Charlie said to the familiar, corpulent form.

McConnell looked down at her and then at Moeller who was drawing her pistol.

McConnell hit the panic button.

It was located near the door. This automatically closed the emergency door that was flush with the wall of the corridor. It swung shut with unbelievable speed. Moeller jumped out of the way but the door slammed into the back of Charlie's chair and propelled both into the room.

"Damn," Rodriguez yelled and ran to the emergency door. "Open it," he demanded.

"You know I can't," Moeller said.

"Oh, shit," Rodriguez said softly. He knew the door was on a fail-safe. When McConnell hit the panic button, the room was sealed. All the ventilation was sealed and the central life-support computer had to make sure the pressure wasn't dropping before its programming allowed the room to be opened. And that took time.

"How long?" Rodriguez asked.

"Minutes, as many as ten."

***

Mitchel had a constant connection from his computer to the one in the Chun home. On the Boulder end a security man from the school monitored it.

Mitchel's face appeared on the screen. "Let me speak to Mrs. Chun," he said.

"Yes, sir," the security man said. He walked to the front room where Kirsten was still holding vigil in front of the large screen showing news. She'd only slept occasionally and for a few minutes.

"Mrs. Chun, it's Mr. Mitchel," he called out.

"Computer, window on the large screen."

Mitchel appeared in a box in the corner of the screen.

"Yes, Mitch?"

"The *Kyushu* should have rendezvoused with the asteroid 20 minutes ago. We should have word pretty soon. The radio travel time is making it difficult. But everyone should be safe."

Kirsten sat. "Thanks, Mitch." She let out a long sigh as if she'd been holding her breath for the past 44 hours.

***

Perez used the two emergency doors as an airlock. He entered the mass driver section. He could see the two holes punched in the shell of the asteroid. The equipment was a jumbled mess.

He shined his light around the room looking for survivors. "Anybody hear me?" he asked over the emergency frequency. He flashed his beam into every nook and cranny.

"Help," he heard. It was so soft he couldn't tell if it was a man or a woman.

"Where are you?" Perez asked.

"Help. I'm hurt." It was sounding more feminine.

"Okay," Perez said. "Stay calm. Where are you?"

"I don't know."

"Do you see my light?" Perez asked, sweeping it back and forth.

"Yeah, I see it."

Perez stopped moving his light. "Is the light near you?"

"No."

"Tell me when it's close." He began moving the white spot slowly around the chamber.

"There," the voice said as it passed over a jumble of smashed equipment.

Perez pushed himself over while changing frequency.

"Control room, I've got a survivor in the mass driver section."

Alex, Thorne, and Tsuji went through the surrogate airlock formed by the two emergency doors. Because there was no pump to remove the air each trip through lost them the volume of air trapped between the two doors. Air they could ill afford to lose.

Dr. Ibrahim Jubair was shaking his head while bending over the wreckage. He saw the director coming and signaled he wanted to change frequencies.

Alex said, "How's it look?" when he had switched.

"Not good, sir," the doctor said. "She is pinned between massive pieces of equipment."

Alex realized the problem wasn't the weight of the wreckage but the mass and the entanglements.

Tsuji had been looking over the mess. "It'll take a while to cut through all this."

"Yes," Jubair said. "You must be very careful. But there is a complication."

"What?" Alex asked.

"Her leg was crushed between a beam and the stone of the asteroid. It amputated it. But the pressure of the beam is keeping her suit sealed. If we move that beam her suit will decompress and she'll die."

Alex let out a long breath. "Okay," he said. "Get everyone off the rock to the *Kyushu* except—oh, hell, who do you think we'll need?" Alex was tired of making decisions that could have fatal consequences.

"I do not know, sir," Jubair said.

"Everyone go to command freq," Alex said. He switched. "Banda, you in the net?"

"Yes, sir," the AD reported.

"Good," Alex said. "Tsuji?"

"Yes, sir."

"Get who you need in here and get the rest off this rock. Thorne, I want two security in here to help look for other survivors; get everyone else off. Banda?"

"Yes, sir?"

"You're in charge of getting everyone off the rock to the *Kyushu*."

"Yes, sir."

"Sir?" Jubair said.

"Yes?"

"I'll need two of my assistants."

"Okay, get them down here. Taylor?"

"Yes?"

"How's the air?"

"Getting thin."

"How's everyone's suits?"

Everyone was fine.

Perez chimed in, "She's only got half an hour." No one had to ask who "she" was.

"Then I guess we'll have to hurry," Alex said. "Anybody got any ideas how to get her out of there alive?"

The net was silent.

***

McConnell looked over Charlie's prone figure and laughed.

Charlie looked up at him then looked for her chair. It was about a meter away on its side.

"Well, Shari," McConnell said. "Nice to see you again."

"Fuck you," Charlie replied, still lying on the carpet.

"No thanks. Already did."

"What's your problem, Whaltham?"

"I don't have a problem."

"Yes, you do," Charlie said trying to move to sit up. If she could get him talking, defending his position, it might buy her enough time for Moeller and Rod to get in the room and save her.

McConnell pushed her over with his foot.

"Do you hate people in general," she continued from the floor, "or do you just want power for yourself?"

"I want to save the—"

"Bull shit," Charlie cut him off. "If you cared about the environment more than you care about political power you'd support technology, not attack it."

"Technology is the enemy of all living things. If SRI is allowed to continue to take asteroids from the belt it could destabilize the entire system, causing asteroids to rain down on the Earth."

Charlie looked at him. "Do you believe that?" she asked incredulously. "Or can one get a psychology degree in the United States without studying freshman physics, Dr. McConnell?"

"I don't see what that has to do with—"

Charlie cut him off again. If she kept him off balance, maybe she'd get a chance to do something, anything. "Then you'd know that Jupiter affects the asteroids more than anything humans can do; you'd know how to calculate the forces involved. You'd know enough not to accept the theories of every so-called scientist promoting grandiose theories to compete for grant money." She'd slowly sat up. He was watching her but if she got him mad enough he might lower his physical guard to erect a mental barrier.

"There's more to this than the asteroids. SRI is raping space for profit," he said.

"SRI is providing natural resources from space so they don't have to be taken from the Earth. Resources needed—"

"Needed for what?" he yelled at her. "Faster cars, bigger houses. Humankind must live a simpler lifestyle."

"Why, when the resources are there to live as we wish?"

"Because technology is de-humanizing and life destroying."

"So we have to become subsistence farmers to be human?" Charlie asked. She scooted toward him. If she could pull his legs out from underneath him. "Or is the plow too much technology for you? Do we have to be hunters and gatherers?"

275

She was almost close enough. "Or maybe we should abandon the club, and fire. We can sit in caves shivering and huddling and hoping nature doesn't kill us. Then, living like animals, we'll be human?" She poised, ready for him to make a mistake.

"Maybe so," he said. "It's better than choking in our own wastes."

"Oh, like the unprocessed human waste that polluted rivers alongside cities before technology cured that problem? Like the fossil fuel waste that polluted the air before technology made it practical to use hydrogen? Like the nuclear waste that was dangerous for 20,000 years until technology made it possible to transmute it to short-lived forms?"

"All those problems were caused by technology. You expect technology to fix them. Technological 'solutions' are only temporary and leave us worse off in the end."

"Do you believe that lie or just parrot it for political gain?"

"I don't have to listen to this," McConnell stated. He turned away from her.

"Truth hurts?" Charlie grabbed his ankle and yanked. Since his weight was low she easily pulled him off balance. His mass flopped to the floor. Charlie jumped at him but he moved surprisingly fast and had turned around to meet her assault. He used his massive arms to push her aside and she landed on the floor. Hot pain grabbed at her back and stunned her for a moment. McConnell's fist pounded her face until he picked her up and threw her across the room.

"Fuck you," McConnell said.

"No thanks," she said, grimacing with pain. "I already have and frankly, I'd rather die."

"That can be arranged." Silently McConnell went to the emergency closet and pulled out an emergency suit. He pulled it on as if he'd practiced just as the notice on the door suggested.

Charlie tried to get up but every time he'd push her over. She noticed her back was sticky-wet. It wasn't sweat.

When McConnell had the suit on and sealed he picked up a small wooden table. The use of wood indicated the luxury of the

Selene Hotel. And, since it was a hard wood such as oak, it made an excellent, albeit small, battering ram. McConnell moved to the window and began pounding on the edge of the Crysteel.

Charlie knew he'd never break the high-tech, transparent material, but he could loosen it in its frame enough to depressurize the room. And there was no way he'd let her get into a suit. Rod, she screamed mentally, get in here and save me!

CHAPTER EIGHTEEN

"I will not risk the wrath of such an adversary."

Faruq looked up in surprise when the presidential bodyguards burst into his office with their pistols in their hands.

One was loyal to him; or had been.

"What is the meaning of this?" Faruq demanded. "When the president—"

"The president orders you to appear before him," the guard that had been his accomplice said.

Faruq gave the man a questioning look but his face was carefully neutral. Faruq stood and walked out of his office.

The guards followed.

What had gone wrong? Faruq wondered. Who talked?

In the president's massive office General Zuabi was sitting in a chair. All eyes were on the large computer screen but it was blank. Faruq tried to get a clue from the soldier but he averted his eyes.

"Ah, Faruq, *sadiqi,*" the president said sardonically. "Please sit." He indicated a chair facing the screen.

"What is this about, *aqid?*" Faruq asked trying to sound calm despite the sirocco blowing through his guts.

"This," the president said, "was on the Western news media about half an hour ago."

One of the guards spoke English to the computer. The screen lit up with a display of a typical high-tech newsroom.

The female anchor (immodestly dressed as usual) said, "The growing problem of 'space junk' became all too apparent today when Space Resources Incorporated announced that a collision between the jettisoned reactor of an old Soviet spy satellite and a discarded booster rocket resulted in the reactor debris entering a decaying orbit.

"For details we go to SRI headquarters in Tokyo."

A reporter was standing in the SRI auditorium that had been seen so much in the news recently.

"An SRI spokesperson just briefed the press," the reporter said. "We have a recording of that briefing."

The scene was the same but a woman was standing at the podium.

"From 1970 to 1988," the woman said, "the Soviet Union deployed 31 spy satellites that were nuclear powered. When the satellites' orbits decayed the reactors were boosted into a 'parking orbit.'

"The orbit," she continued, "was meant to keep the reactors in space for several hundred years. By the time one entered the atmosphere its radioactivity was to have decayed significantly. Unfortunately, a discarded booster rocket of unidentified origin collided with one of the 28 reactors still in orbit. Our information indicates the reactor, mostly intact, and its radioactive nuclear fuel will impact the Earth somewhere in the Middle East, Syria probably."

The image froze. Faruq needed to take a long breath but couldn't because of the tightening of his chest.

"I personally," the president said, "contacted SRI. A man named Mitchel told me it will impact in or near the Omar oil field. This is the same kind of reactor that impacted Canada in 1978. But, Mr. Mitchel said that, unlike that incident, the debris would be spread over only a few square miles, contaminating our oil fields. Do you realize what this will do to our oil production?"

"No," Faruq said.

"No one will buy our oil unless we spend billions of pounds and years decontaminating."

"It is a tragic accident, *habibi*," Faruq said.

"No," the president bellowed. "It is not."

"It isn't?" Faruq asked.

"No," the president yelled, hitting his desk with a fist. "Mr. Mitchel told me that this is revenge for Syria's role in the asteroid incident. Our entanglement with that Gaia Alliance was your doing! This is your responsibility, Faruq!"

Faruq gaped like a man in vacuum.

"Now SRI is taking revenge and there is nothing we can do about it," the president concluded.

Faruq saw a last chance. "Nothing? We can put a bomb in their headquarters or in the archology they are building. We can arrange an explosive decompression in their Low Earth Orbit Facility or on the Moon. There are groups that would help us."

"And next time they drop a small asteroid on Damascus?" the president asked. "This, Mr. Mitchel said, was their other option. No. I will not risk the wrath of such an adversary. Such a power we should make our friend, not our enemy."

Silence was long and thick.

"Take him away," the president said with a dismissive wave of the hand.

"But," Faruq started as the guards lifted him from the chair.

"*Ma'salamah*," the president said without feeling. God be with you.

Faruq pulled his arms from the guards and walked out the door. The president was glad his friend would die with dignity.

General Zuabi looked at the president. "I must be getting on with my duties, sir."

The president dismissed him with a grunt.

"*Ma'salamah*," the general said. "I will report to you from Tyre."

"*In sha'allah*," the president said. If God is willing.

The general's replacement was already in Tyre. Zuabi would never again see the site of Alexander the Great's victory over Darius.

***

McConnell was concentrating on the window, still pounding on its edge with the table. The table was scratched and dented and the wood was splitting but McConnell kept hammering with the incredibly expensive furnishing. *For the money paid to lift the wood from Earth to make that table, one probably could feed and clothe a family for a year,* Charlie thought.

She also realized Rodriguez was not going to rescue her; she'd have to save herself. On the dresser was an ovoid glass objet d'art of glass about the size of a cantaloupe. Charlie dragged herself to the dresser and used it to pull herself up. She hefted the egg, heavy even on the Moon–and therefore very massive–and, using the long dresser for support, shuffled up behind McConnell.

A shrill whistle indicated he was making progress separating the window from the frame. Charlie raised her make-shift weapon above his head and let it drop, putting all her strength into speeding its descent.

McConnell saw her reflection in the Crysteel and turned, but too late. The spheroid's momentum smashed it through the bubble helmet and into McConnell's skull that cracked with the sound of a twig being snapped.

Charlie lost control and the egg dropped, making a red stain on the carpet. McConnell slumped slowly to the floor. Blood pumped out of the gash on his skull.

Charlie let herself fall to the carpet and crawled to the wheelchair. She righted it with some effort and painfully climbed in.

She drove it to the closet with the emergency suits on the other side of the large bed. She pulled one on, continuing to ignore the torturous pain in her back that was trying to conquer her brain in a physiological war of attrition. Her defenses against it were being slowly ground down.

***

"If we put a tourniquet on it before moving the beam," Alex suggested.

"No," Dr. Jubair said. "She'd bleed to death long before we get her out of vacuum because of the pressure gradient."

Alex watched the three miners work. Once, in Boulder, he was taken to a trauma center because of a rock climbing accident. He had been conscious enough to admire the skill, speed, and efficiency of those that worked on him. Tsuji and her helpers reminded him of those doctors as they worked their way quickly but carefully to the injured woman. She was, mercifully, unconscious.

Thorne and his two helpers returned from searching the cavernous chamber. "There's three more bodies in various locations. We got their ID's. That accounts for all but two."

"Before she passed out," Perez stated, "she said that there were two working on the base of the mass driver when the missile hit."

"We'll have the *Kyushu* use its radar to look for their bodies," Alex said. "Good job, Thorne. I don't think I need you here. You can go."

"Listen," Thorne said. "I read a book once. It was about space combat. The book's almost a hundred years old but I remember that to deal with trauma the suits would close off an injury and breach with a thing that would snap closed like a, a..." he made a circular opening and closing motion with his fingers.

"An iris?" the doctor asked.

"Yes," Thorne exclaimed. "It would close off the wound, stopping the depressurization of the suit. It also amputated the limb but it saved the life."

"Yes?" Alex prodded.

"I was wondering," Throne continued, "if we cut a piece of plate steel and sharpened one end. Then if we shove it into her leg just above the beam and seal the whole thing with DC foam we could save her. Her leg's gone anyway."

"Doctor?" Alex asked.

"It might work. If the bone is intact we'll never get a plate through it, though. But if the bone is shattered, and I think it is, it could work. The steel would have to be sterilized."

"I don't think so," Alex said. "What's going to survive this vacuum?

"Tsuji, you been listening?"

"Yes, I'll get right on it."

"No," Thorne said. "I've used a laser. I'll cut the metal so they can keep working. You other two," he said to his security personnel, "Go on and get off this rock."

They nodded and wished Thorne and Perez luck.

"Good," Alex said. "Perez, how's her air?"

"Ten minutes."

"Okay," he said and switched frequencies. "Banda, Chun. How's it going?"

"Slow but steady," the deep voice came back. "Another 15 or so minutes and we'll be done."

"How's the air?"

"Getting worse."

"Listen, in about ten minutes we may need to get this injury across that rope immediately. Be prepared to clear the corridor to the airlock." They were evacuating through an airlock at the end of a tunnel drilled radially from the central tunnel. Under acceleration the tunnel would have been level.

"Yes, sir."

The room lit up with sparks as Thorne started cutting metal with a miner's lasers. The flickering light made the rock interior of the asteroid, filled with metal smashed into bizarre and grotesque shapes, look like a scene from hell.

***

Moeller used her authority to enter the room next to McConnell's and get to the computer. The guest was perturbed but Moeller said she could complain to NESA authorities and that seemed to make her happy.

Moeller accessed the NESA Security net using her ID in the slot and thumb on the plate.

"Damn," she said as Rodriguez watched over her shoulder.

"What?"

"It's got a leak. It's slow but eventually the room will be uninhabitable."

"What about the door?" Rodriguez demanded.

Moeller shook her head. "It won't open now for my access code."

"Then for whose?"

"A Level One executive. The head of NESA Lunar Security, Mr. Takayanagi, could do it."

"Then get him to open it."

"Wait a moment. I have to locate him first."

***

Thorne returned with a crudely cut circle of metal. One side was somewhat beveled to a sharp edge. Tsuji took it and worked her laser against the sharp edge.

"That should be sharp enough to cut through her suit," she said.

She handed it to the doctor who looked at it disparagingly.

"I said I could handle a laser; I didn't say I was good at it," Thorne remarked.

"You'll have to put it in," Jubair said.

"What?" Thorne exclaimed.

"I must keep a tourniquet around her leg to slow the bleeding. You must put the plate in and do it in one clean stroke. Tsuji reports she can move the beam any time now. We are ready."

"I can't do this," Thorne pleaded.

Alex's gloved hand touched Thorne's suited shoulder.

"Perez, how much longer?"

"Three minutes," Perez replied. He looked at Thorne in a tacit plea.

"You can do it," Alex said. "Don't let another one die."

Thorne took a deep breath. "Okay."

Thorne put the sharp end against the woman's thigh just above where the beam pinched the leg down to nothing. Thorne braced himself and Alex put his mass against Thorne's back while trying to jamb his legs between two metal beams. Alex hoped Thorne wouldn't move and the plate would.

Jubair used a miner's rope to tie a tourniquet. He pulled it tighter and tighter; so tight that Alex thought he was going to breach the suit.

"Now," Jubair said unexpectedly.

Thorne shoved with all his muscles. The plate sliced cleanly into the suit and through the flesh and only hesitated at the bone. Thorne stopped when he felt the metal bump against solid rock behind the leg.

Perez quickly sprayed DC foam around the plate. Some white foam turned gray as it mixed with blood that was slowly boiling out. They waited interminable seconds while the foam hardened.

"She's out of air," Perez said. It wouldn't take her long to expend the oxygen in her suit."

"Okay," Jubair said. "Now, Tsuji."

The three miners pushed their combined masses against the beam. It moved and Perez and Thorne lifted the woman up.

"To the emergency door, fast," Alex said redundantly. The two security men moved quickly and skillfully. Jubair followed and Alex stayed out of the way. He watched them go in the first emergency door.

Alex let out a long sigh that his helmet mic amplified. "At least there's one that won't die," he breathed.

Tsuji placed a hand on his shoulder. "You saved a lot of lives, Director."

Alex turned to look at her. "What? Ten people died because—"

She cut him off. "Because some fools decided to use violence to make their idiotic point. You saved 120 lives. And those who died are the responsibility of those that started the violence."

Alex turned away from the miners. "Let's go," he said angrily. "Let's get the hell out of here."

***

Charlie sealed the helmet. The damn emergency suit for civilians didn't have a transmitter, just a receiver for getting instructions. It did have a loud speaker on the chest (she'd heard it called a "bitcher" somewhere). At least she could communicate with the chair until the air ran out. *Oh, well,* she thought, *I can wait.* She felt blood and perfluorodecalin from the wounds reopened on her back pooling in her boots. She just didn't know

286

how long she could wait. She used her gloved hand to push the joystick to the side, turning the chair around to face into the room.

McConnell was running toward her with the bloody glass egg in his hands. Fragments of his broken helmet were lodged in his cranium.

Charlie tried to stand to run but managed only to fall out of the chair.

McConnell stood over her and grinned. She saw him say something. He raised the art above his head.

"Chair, voice command mode, forward, fast," Charlie yelled superfluously as the speaker amplified her voice. The chair slammed into McConnell throwing him off balance in the unfamiliar gravity.

He dropped the egg, grabbed the chair and heaved it away from him. It bounced over the bed and serendipitously landed on its wheels.

Meanwhile Charlie was crawling away from him. He scooped up the sphere and again towered over her prone figure.

Charlie tried to crawl away but it was no use, he'd trapped her in a corner.

Charlie could see the wheelchair between McConnell's legs. It was near the Crysteel window facing away from it–the window that was already loose.

"Chair, backwards, fast," Charlie yelled again.

The chair's back crashed into the window's bottom edge.

"Chair, forwards, fast, backwards, fast, repeat," Charlie said.

McConnell smiled at her, ignoring the chair and her commands. He mouthed, exaggeratedly, "Fuck you," and—

And the chair hit the bottom of the window and the Crysteel plate popped out. There was enough air left in the room that decompression was explosive. McConnell fell back on the floor dropping the egg. It shattered. Everything was dragged to the window. Charlie landed on top of McConnell, who flopped like a landed fish. It was over soon and he was dead.

Charlie rolled off him and looked at his face. It was a portrait of absolute terror, frozen forever like that.

***

Director Chun hung from the rope between the rock and the *Kyushu*. He was just at the airlock in the side of the ship when he paused to look back at SRI-1961. Because he was the last off, his asteroid was now an empty shell falling through space carrying only the three bodies they'd been forced to leave behind. He wondered as to its fate. If its velocity were sufficient it could escape the solar system. Or it might be captured by the sun again and go on in some other orbit as if indifferent to the human conflict and death that had occurred because of it.

"Director Chun," Takashara's voice came over Chun's suit radio. "Are you okay? Do you require assistance?"

"Negative," Chun replied crisply and he moved clumsily into the airlock. When it had cycled he pulled off his helmet and wiped tears from his eyes.

Takashara floated in front of him. Her hair was constrained in an intricate braid.

"Captain," Alex said. "You've never looked so good to me."

"Your doctor," Takashara said, "reports the injured woman will be all right."

"Well," Alex qualified, "as all right as one can be after losing a leg."

***

Charlie was getting tired of waking up in hospitals. The first thing she saw was that damn nursemaid shaking his head.

She half expected him to shake a finger at her.

Rodriguez's face was the next thing they let her see.

"We got an emergency airlock in to take you out," he said. "You lost a lot of blood."

"That's okay," Charlie said softly. "Most of it wasn't real anyway."

Rodriguez laughed softly. "When you're released and feel up to it I'd like you to be the Assistant Security Chief here."

"I don't know," Charlie said. "I've been thinking about getting off the Moon. Maybe I should move into asteroids or go to Jupiter or Ceres."

"Whatever you like," Rodriguez said.

"Yeah," Charlie said, "maybe I'll go to Mars. I'll think about it."

"You do that," Rodriguez said. "You could probably get whatever you want from SRI, at least until Chun gets back."

"Who?"

"Alexander Chun. He was the director on the asteroid the GA attacked. They say he saved many lives."

"Hum," Charlie said. And all she did was end a few.

Rodriguez stood and said farewell. Charlie ignored the nursemaid.

She wondered why she didn't feel better about killing McConnell.

***

Caroline Zalesky wondered why McKenna had called her into the chief's office. Caroline had finally gotten to sleep after hours spent worrying about David on the asteroid that had been attacked. When McKenna called her, she had to get dressed and downed some coffee to wake up.

"Chief?" she asked poking her head through the open door to McKenna's office.

McKenna looked up. She was strapped in her chair working at her computer. She looked as if she hadn't slept in days. Her blue eyes had dark rings about them and her usually lustrous red hair was stringy and uncharacteristically slovenly.

"Caroline," she said. "Come in; close the door, please."

Pulling the hatch shut, Caroline asked, "What is it?" She held on to a handhold in the air.

"There was a second attack on the asteroid," McKenna said softly.

"Yes?"

"David, your husband, was killed."

Silence coagulated in the compartment.

"Caroline?" McKenna asked.

She didn't respond but, letting go of her grip, she started floating in the air, staring straight ahead.

***

The *Kyushu* was too slow a ship for just about everyone on board. For the most part the asteroid crew spent the trip back in a somber, bitter mood that was the antithesis of the trip to the belt. It was better when the ship was close enough to Earth to make conversation practical, but Captain Takashara limited everyone to one ten minute call to Earth or the Moon. That gave Alex just enough time to tell Kirsten he loved her and was all right.

There was time spent in the saloon, but most of it was spent in gloomy reflections on lost friends. Alex saw Thorne very little and when he did see his friend, Thorne was surly at best and enmeshed in grief to the point of almost being comatose. Alex hoped he'd pull out of it.

He met Bente in the corridor one day as they approached the Moon.

"Did you call home?"Alex asked.

"Yes," she replied.

"How's your father?"

"He's alive, at least," she breathed. "The doctors say it's still indefinite if he'll be all right."

"I'm sorry," Alex said. "I hope he's okay."

"Thanks, Alex."

Eventually the old, balky ship entered lunar orbit. Since this was unusual, the intra-lunar shuttle had to be used to take everyone off and down to the Moon. The extra passengers meant it had to make two runs, taking it off its profitable LEOF-Moon run for twice as long.

Alex suspected that with the asteroid loss and the shuttle losses, SRI's profit would be exceptionally low this year. SRI was self-insured, meaning all the loss came straight off the bottom line. That meant the stock wouldn't increase in value, or might even decrease. A lot of normal folks' retirement accounts would take a hit.

On the lunar surface the head of SRI's Lunar Facility, Mr. Takeda, the new security head Rodriguez, and just about every SRI employee on the Moon was there to greet them. There was no media, thankfully.

Alex was surprised to be greeted as a hero. The crowd actually cheered when he entered the shuttleport. Takeda enthused at length about Alex's actions. Alex's own opinion of his actions that, in his mind, cost ten people their lives, contrasted directly with the proclamation that he was a hero.

Alex quickly paid his respects to Takeda and then, to the disappointment of the gathered throng, went to a hotel where SRI had rented rooms for the crew of the asteroid. There he began writing letters, actual hand-written on paper letters. He had to write ten of them.

***

Bente passed through the gauntlet of well-wishers and finally broke out into an open corridor. Akio was there. Bente ran to him and grabbed her brother, giving him an embrace.

"Akio, I'm sorry," she said.

"Sorry?" he asked a little embarrassed by her display of affection. "For what?"

She looked at him. "I don't know–for being away and not being here."

"Don't worry. And Father will be fine. He needs to slow down, that's all."

"Can I see him?"

"Of course," Akio said. "And he wants to see you."

They took the subway to the hospital.

Mrs. Naguchi was inside the room with her husband. She came out and greeted her daughter. "I'm so glad you're all right," she exclaimed happily.

Bente entered the room alone. She took in a breath—her father looked so fragile. He had more wires and tubes hooked up to him than most computers she'd seen.

"Hello, Bente," he said. She was surprised how soft his voice was.

"Hello, Father." She moved to his bed and carefully took his hand that had no tubes in it. She gently held it.

"I'm glad to see you're all right," he said.

"I'm glad you're okay, too," she answered.

Father and daughter looked at each other.

"Father?"

"Yes?"

"I love you."

"I know," he said. "I love you, too."

There didn't seem much more to say. Father and daughter sat holding hands for a long time.

Finally he said, "There were news reports that you helped stop the attack by the terrorists."

"I didn't do much," she responded.

"You did your job well," her father said. "That is something. I'm proud of you, Bente."

"I'm proud of you, Father."

CHAPTER NINETEEN

"It was a group effort."

Mitchel entered his office in the morning. The crisis was over and it was back to work as usual. Sure, in a few days he'd board the corporate spaceplane for Esmeraldas to greet his friend Chun as he returned to Earth. In the meantime, he had a lot to catch up on; first the reports from the information gathering departments and the news services.

From Pyongyang, Republic of Korea: there was a report that a group called the *Yuk'ee-oh yo'don*, or June Twenty-fifth Brigade, was making threats against SRI interests on the peninsula. The name, according to the report, referred to the date when imperial American and South Korean armies invaded the peace-loving People's Democratic Republic of Korea in the first Korean War.

He wrote a memo to remind himself to have someone look to see if the Chinese, the last bastion of Marxism outside academia, were succoring the Brigade.

Mitchel shook his head. Hard to believe there were still idiots in the world trying to rewrite history.

From Tel Aviv: United Baathist Radio announced the murder of hero of the Socialist/Arab Revolution General Zuabi and a presidential aide by Israeli death squads operating in what used to be southern Lebanon. A protest to the UN was expected.

From San Francisco: the governor of California named Green party member Mike Winston to fill Linda Trent's seat in the House of Representatives as the "alleged" terrorist had resigned. Also, the governor planned to protest to the World Trade Organization on the unfair trade practices of Japanese Space Resources Incorporated's move to pull all their business out of his state.

And from Suruga Bay, Japan: Greenpeace was still flying helicopters dangerously close to the archology. So far they'd just tried to hamper construction and thrown some paint balloons—organically degradable paint, no doubt. But once they flew too low over some workers and the down wash of the rotors almost blew a worker off where she was standing. They still insisted the archology was an environmental travesty despite SRI spending trillions of yen to appease them and those like them. Mitchel wished the structure was in international waters. He'd mount some anti-aircraft artillery and discourage low over-flights. He could buy them from Philippe Thorez, the arms dealer. Mitchel understood the Frenchman was having problems since his SRI account, containing billions of euros, was accidentally credited to the account of a charity that helped refugees from the parts of the former Soviet Union that the Chinese had conquered.

And so it went in the office on the hundred and thirtieth floor of the SRI headquarters building, where one man tried to keep his company safe from the zealous, jealous, evil, and just plain stupid ones humanity seemed never to stop breeding.

***

Caroline Zalesky held a printout of the letter in her hand. It had been transmitted from the Moon. Chun had described how David had died trying to repair the mass driver. His body wasn't recovered.

Caroline decided she was becoming numb because the letter didn't affect her at all. She did briefly consider finding Mouret, being held in security, and killing him. But she dismissed that fantasy. The miner's ship had been confiscated and he would be sent back to Earth on the next shuttle. She didn't wish a similar fate for herself.

She read the letter again. Below Chun's scrawled signature was a hand-written message, barely readable because of his

294

illegible penmanship and the low quality of the fax. It said, "I can't tell you how sorry I am David was killed. I would have prevented it if I could."

She almost laughed bitterly at that. The only way to stop David's death was to stop the terrorists before they got a chance to kill. She decided the next time she had a chance, she'd shoot a terrorist on sight.

***

Thorne called Diana's family from the Moon. He didn't know them other than an address in Iowa. He talked to her mother. "Are you planning a memorial service?" Thorne asked.

"Yes," the woman replied on the screen. "But someone else from SRI called and asked that and I told them when it was."

Thorne nodded exaggeratedly to indicate he understood that. "Yes, that would be someone official. Someone from her division will attend any memorial service you have. I was a friend of Diana's."

The woman studied Thorne through the computer. He could see some of Diana in her mother. It was disturbing.

"We're you and my daughter close?" the woman asked.

"Yes," Thorne said. "I also want to explain to you, to her family, how and why she died."

"Why?"

"I think it's important. I want you to know she didn't die needlessly. She was doing her part to save lives."

"Why is that important to you?" she asked.

"I want to do the right thing for Diana. God knows I didn't get a chance to do much else for her."

Thorne saw Diana's mother assess him again. "The memorial service," she said finally, "will be in three days; Saturday at ten a.m. Can you get here by then?"

"Yes," Thorne said. "I'll be there." He made another call.

"Pa, I'll be home in about a week. Can you pick me up at the airport in Idaho Falls again?"

"Sure, son."

***

295

Perez walked into the NESA hospital room. She looked at him.

"Excuse me," she said. "Who are you?"

"Perez," he replied. "I was in the mass driver. I found you."

"Oh," she replied. "Thank you. I guess I owe you my life."

"No," he said. "I just helped. It was a group effort."

"Well, thank you anyway."

"You're welcome, uhm...I'm sorry. I don't know your name."

"Sharyl Svensen."

"Miguel Perez."

"Well, thank you, Miguel."

"You're welcome, Sharyl."

Neither spoke as the sound of the medical equipment droned on.

"How do you feel?" Perez asked.

"As well as could be expected."

"That's good," Miguel said. "I mean, I'm glad you're doing good."

"Thank you."

"You're welcome."

More silence.

"Listen, Sharyl," he said. "When you feel up to it, do you want to go out for a drink or something?"

She looked at him and smiled. "I think I owe you at least one. Sure. Doctor says it won't be long and I can try my prosthesis."

"Good," Miguel said. "I'm not going to Earth so I'll be here."

"Okay, Miguel," she said smiling.

***

While Charlie detested the thought of her grandmother's body being in a concrete box in the ground, she did find some comfort in a physical thing, the grave and marker, that remained as a memorial to that remarkable woman.

With Frank there was only a plaque. It was in the briefing room that Frank had lectured in and been eulogized in. It listed the names of SRI Security personnel killed, either by accident or violence, in the line of duty on the Moon. Frank's name was under

Prince and Nakamura's at the bottom of about 20 other names. The three names were in bigger type, as were all that died by violence.

Charlie stared at the nickel plate. The metal had come from an asteroid, of course.

Anger, denial, then either bargaining or depression, then finally acceptance. Charlie had first read about Kubler-Ross after her grandmother died. The stages of grief were the same as for dying, they said. She didn't remember going through all the stages before acceptance—probably too busy. But, looking at the engraved letters of Frank DeWite's memorial, she could remember Frank and rejoice in their relationship instead of only mourning his loss. She took one last look at the deep, dark script and said good-bye.

She flicked the joystick on her wheelchair and headed for the door. As she reached out to open it, the door swung aside. There was a short, Asian man coming in the room. He was wearing a blue command uniform and director insignia.

"Excuse me," he said and stepped out of her way.

"Thank you," Charlie replied as her chair passed by. *Not too bad looking,* she thought, *if he wasn't so damn short.*

***

Alex Chun sat in the employee lounge, sipping water. He hoped he'd keep that down. His space sickness was unusually acute. He tried to distract himself by looking out the window at the Mediterranean 400 kilometers below. He could see Italy, the Adriatic, and the Greek islands, where Odysseus had labored to return home for–what was it, ten years? *How many of his crew did he lose on that trip?* Alex wondered.

The shuttle to Earth was leaving soon and Alex would return home to his wife. Yet, ten of his crew would never go home again.

"Director Chun," a familiar voice called out.

Alex looked away from the window. Tsuji was pushing her compact, muscular body toward him.

"Chun," she said, coming closer and pulling herself into a chair. "Going back to Earth?"

"Yes."

"Good," she replied. "Have a nice time."

"Thanks."

"I hope we can work together again, soon."

Alex looked at the miner. For a rock-cutter, that was almost a marriage proposal.

"I do too, Tsuji."

"Chun," she continued. "You did one great job out there. Using the laser on the *Kyushu* probably saved all our lives."

Alex looked at her. "I wish I could have saved all the lives."

"Well, you're not God. You did the best you could and that was enough. You should be proud of what you did."

Alex smiled wryly. "I don't know. Maybe someday I'll be able to feel good about my actions. Right now, they don't seem to have been enough."

"Why?"

"Because ten people died."

Tsuji pushed out of her chair. "Director," she said, "I'll be glad to work with you anytime."

"You, too, Tsuji," Chun replied. "Where you going now?"

"Home."

"Where's that?"

"SRI-2062. A rush job. Good-bye, Director."

"Bye, Chief."

Tsuji moved away and Alex watched her go. In his memory he couldn't think of a time a miner said three words to any non-miner that didn't have to do with work.

Well, if Tsuji thought he did a good job, maybe he did.

He looked back out the window. The Black Sea and the Crimea were visible through broken clouds.

If only he didn't feel so bad.

***

A Lexus coupe stopped in front of the Catholic Relief Society's shelter. Cathy Williams walked inside and talked to the volunteer in the foyer.

"Yes," the woman said, "she is here."

"Could you ask her if she'd come with me, please?"

298

"Okay," the volunteer said. "If you'll wait here." The woman went into the large room behind the entrance. As the door swung open, Williams could see the floor was covered wall to wall with small cots.

The volunteer returned with a small, elderly woman. "Ms. Williams, this is Mrs. Cortez."

"Mrs. Cortez," Williams said. "I'm from Space Resources Incorporated. You helped one of our employees."

"Yes?" Mrs. Cortez said tentatively.

"Ma'am, could you come with me, please?"

The old lady looked at the volunteer.

"I'm sure it will be okay," the volunteer said.

"Okay," Mrs. Cortez said.

Williams led her to her car and they drove toward the Pacific. Eventually, they were following the coast out of the city heading north. "Mrs. Cortez," Williams said as she drove, "We talked to your friends in your church, and learned you wanted to live near the ocean."

"Yes."

"You helped Charlie Jones and it cost you everything you had. We can't replace what you lost, but we hope this helps."

Williams drove the car off the road and down a driveway to a small house just off the beach.

"*Por Dios*," the lady cried.

Williams got out and ran around the car to help Mrs. Cortez out. "It's yours, if you want it. It's a good area, too expensive to have terrorists live next door. I don't think there's a smash house within 20 miles."

"But it's too big, I can't take care of it."

"Don't worry," Williams said. "Come on, let's look inside."

Williams showed the woman how to put her hand on the sensor plate to open the door. The interior was furnished. A young woman was waiting inside.

"Mrs. Cortez," the young woman said, "I'm Julie Lide. I'm your housekeeper."

"I can't afford a housekeeper," Mrs. Cortez protested.

"SRI's paying my salary," Julie said.

"And if she doesn't work out, or leaves, just call our San Francisco office and we'll find someone else."

"Why are you doing all this?" Mrs. Cortez asked incredulously.

"Because you saved the life of one of our employees; SRI repays its debts."

Mrs. Cortex looked around the house. "Thank you," she said. "*Gracias.*"

"You're welcome," Williams replied. "I'd better be going. If you have any problems, just call me in San Francisco. The number's in the house computer."

"I will."

Williams walked out. *The rent on the house and the housekeeper's salary for a year are probably less than a small fraction of what SRI spends every day,* she thought to herself as she got into her car. And Mrs. Cortez was going to be surprised when Julie charged all household expenditures to SRI. Sure, there was no profit involved in helping the old lady who helped them. At least, not the kind that showed up on a balance sheet.

Williams entered the highway and drove north.

***

Esmeraldas is barely 80 miles north of the equator on Ecuador's coast. SRI had located its spaceport there for the boost the spin of the Earth gave departing ships, not for the weather; it was unbearably hot and humid. But, as she stood on the runway at SRI's facility there, feeling the sweat run down her back, Kirsten didn't mind. SRI had decided to hold this whole greeting and celebration outside to accommodate the horde of media.

"How long?" she asked Mitchel.

"A few more minutes."

Kirsten looked around her. Mr. Kijoto was a silent statue in the bustle and excitement of other SRI employees. The press, blocked off a few meters behind the SRI people, had even caught the carnival atmosphere. Then the double clap of a sonic boom vibrated everyone to their feet. All looked up. The shuttle was a black dot against the blue sky. Kirsten smiled: Alex was on that shuttle.

The shuttle eventually landed almost exactly like the first reusable shuttles did decades ago. Then, using its jet engines, it taxied like a plane to where the crowd waited.

Kirsten waited with what she thought was infinite patience for the door to open. Finally, about a century later, it did. Out came a man too tall to be Alex. *Damn*, Kirsten thought. Then Alex's small frame was in the door in front of a massive black man. *That would be Banda*, Kirsten thought. Both men walked down the stairs. Mr. Kijoto, for the first time in many years, moved to greet someone first.

Then Alex had to talk to each SRI officer, followed by the black man. Alex finally reached Mitchel and the two men pounded each other on the back like the old friends they were.

Then, Alex turned to his wife. Ignoring Mitchel, Banda, Kijoto and the other SRI officers, the other employees, and the press who blatantly beamed the live pictures around the world, husband and wife wrapped themselves together into their own, safe universe.

ABOUT THE AUTHOR

S. Evan Townsend is a writer living in central Washington State. After spending four years in the U.S. Army in the Military Intelligence branch, he returned to civilian life and college to earn a B.S. in Forest Resources from the University of Washington. In his spare time he enjoys reading, driving (sometimes on a racetrack), meeting people, and talking with friends. He is in a 12-step program for Starbucks addiction. Evan lives with his wife and two teenage sons and has a son attending the University of Washington in biology. He enjoys science fiction, fantasy, history, politics, cars, and travel.

Be sure to check out his other published works:

www.ingramcontent.com/pod-product-compliance
Lightning Source LLC
Chambersburg PA
CBHW020915200626
46814CB00001BA/344